DOUBLE Abduction

Chris Beakey

New York

1230 Park Avenue
New York, New York 10128
Tel: 212-427-7139 • Fax: 212-860-8852
bricktower@aol.com • www.BrickTowerPress.com

Library of Congress Cataloging-in-Publication Data

Beakey, Chris
Double Abduction
ISBN-13: 978-1-59687-379-7
ISBN-10: 1-59687-379-5
Library of Congress Control Number: 2007937275
Adult/General, Fiction/Suspense, Mystery

First Edition
October 2007

Author photo by Pamela Lepold Photography

Printed in the United States

10 9 8 7 6 5 4 3 2 1

Dedication

This book is dedicated to
the National Law Enforcement Officers Memorial Fund
and the National Center for Missing and Exploited Children.

Acknowledgements

The most suspenseful stories are driven by visceral fears. I mined mine deeply in writing this book, but I always knew that the light would shine through. This would not have been possible without all of the wonderful people around me. Special thanks to Adam Shapiro, Joe Clayton, Margaret Dunning, Phyllis Blaunstein, Scott Widmeyer, Lee Jenkins, Lynne Leigh and the rest of my colleagues and good friends at Widmeyer Communications. Thanks also to Thom Racina and Genny Ostertag, two gentle souls and very fine people, who served as my first ambassadors into the world of publishing, and to John Colby at ibooks for his heroic rescue and all of the thoughtful support and kindness along the way. And of course an extra special acknowledgement is due to my amazing agent, Bob Diforio, a great man who keeps me as sane as anyone in this business can be, and who made it all happen – twice!

Thanks also to all of the early readers for their praise, insight and support, especially Lisa Manley, who encouraged me to keep the fire burning, and always helped me manage the art and the business of my writing life.

And to my parents, Dan and Lee Beakey, for a lifetime of love, encouragement and good times. And to Lisa, who has always had a special place in my heart – even more so thanks to Johnny and those spectacular girls – I love you all like crazy. And to my closest friends, David Whitten, Charlene Duline, Katherine Harker, John Mini, Robert Perri, Michael Mancuso and Jim Friesen. You are the best people I know, and I'm hugely grateful for all of the goofiness that keeps us together. I'm pretty sure you're all getting into heaven, after putting up with me all of these years.

And finally, most of all, thank you to Michael, for two decades of the best kind of happiness, and a great adventure that gets better every day.

One

Stealing a child in broad daylight could be tricky, but the shopping mall almost made it simple. Blending easily with the crowd, the abductor followed Mary Bennett and her brother, Michael, from a distance of 30 feet, feeling a restrained sense of excitement as Mary's son, five-year-old Justin Bennett, took advantage of a moment of inattention and slipped away.

Eyes trained like a laser at the top of Justin's head, the abductor followed. There was a moment of hesitation when the child stood among a large, slow-moving group of shoppers, looking back at his mother and his uncle to see if they had turned around and noticed his absence. Seeing their backs, Justin followed through, heading quickly and more deeply into the crowd.

The abductor moved swiftly, following the child back toward the direction from which Michael, Mary, and Justin had come earlier. Spotting the boy's likely destination long before Justin could see the store sign above the adult bodies in the crowd, the abductor walked ahead, passing within four feet of him. Justin Bennett had a dark red-wine stain on his right cheek. It was a birthmark that would have brought him misery in adolescence. As a five-year-old it made him easy to identify, which made taking him riskier still.

Moving ahead, but glancing occasionally back to ensure Justin was making progress, the abductor made quick notice of two exits, one on each side of the mall, and both within a 30 second walk of the store where Justin Bennett was surely headed. Once the grab was made, it would be easy to get to the van on the second level of the garage. Once inside, his little body would be laid down on the backseat floor and covered with a blanket, unnoticeable to the attendant as the van exited the lot.

After that the task would be simple—nothing to do but get Justin Bennett to the relay point one hour away. Shortly afterwards, the boy would be dead.

The store that drew Justin away from his mother and uncle sold discount shoes from shelves that went up nearly six feet, with narrow aisles in between. The aisles were crowded with stray samples and half-empty shoeboxes, and the single clerk on duty was flustered by a long line of customers at the counter.

The child was apparently drawn back to the store by a double life-sized standup cutout of Captain Steel, a Saturday morning cartoon character that was now branded to a line of children's shoes. Today for Justin Bennett the character was like a Pied Piper, a bright burst of color from 20 feet away. For marketing purposes, the cutout had been placed in the middle of the store, to draw customers deeper into the midst of the merchandise.

Hidden by the tall shelving, the abductor stood four feet behind the display—a perch that was just a little over an arm's length away from the Captain. The abductor was fairly certain that the child wouldn't have time to protest, but it was important to plan ahead just in case. With a quick but careful movement, the prick of the needle would feel like nothing more than a light scratch on the boy's arm. Within 30 seconds the liquid Valium shot into his bloodstream would render him semiconscious. He would be carried silently away, the wine-stained cheek hidden by the abductor's shoulder, looking like an anonymous child headed for an afternoon nap.

A muscular little boy in denim coveralls, Justin approached the display with a grin. His eyes were wide as he stared open-mouthed, then quietly uttered "cool."

"Justin!"

The abductor jumped back at the woman's voice, retreating behind the tall shelves an instant before Mary Bennett rushed down the aisle and grabbed her son. Mary was shaking, holding Justin as if protecting him from an attack of pit bulls. Attracted by the commotion, the other shoppers had left their own aisles and were gathering around her now.

Still concealed, the abductor watched through a narrow opening in the shelves as Michael Bennett came through the crowd. Apparently brother and sister had split up for the panicked search. Michael's face was pale, his breathing labored. He looked as if he'd run two miles.

Stopping a few steps away from Mary, who still held the boy tightly, Michael leaned forward, his hands on his knees, and waited until his sister met his eyes.

"He okay?" Michael asked her.

She nodded, and looked back down at her son.

"We were worried, little buddy." Michael reached over and touched Justin's shoulder. "We got scared when you ran off like that–"

"You were supposed to be holding his hand."

The coldness in Mary Bennett's voice made Michael visibly tense.

"I'm sorry," he said.

"I know you're *sorry,* Michael. But that wouldn't have helped us."

Even through the narrow space between the shelves it was easy to see the sag of Michael Bennett's shoulders. At 25, Michael was in peak condition and he had obviously been working out with heavy weights, trying to look like the bodyguard he no doubt imagined himself to be. From the tone in his sister's voice, the moment of inattention would cost him dearly.

And it would hurt her trust in him even more.

The abductor felt a small sense of satisfaction, something to counter the frustration of losing a perfect opportunity. Michael and his sister were standing near the front now, chatting with the clerk, who was offering Justin a lollipop. Mary was shaking her head, saying *no.* Her light brown, shoulder-length hair had the texture of silk, and during the search several strands had loosened from a barrette and drifted forward across her high, narrow cheeks. She was 5'8 and a good 10 pounds thinner than she should have been, one of those wiry women who always seemed harried and nervous.

But beautiful still.

It hurt to see her so close to being happy. After five years she seemed to be healing, but the blow that was coming would take her down hard. It might even push her over the edge. Loveless, childless, *empty*, she would be reduced to a shell of her former self.

The abductor thought about that for just a moment, acknowledging that the horror ahead was far worse than she deserved.

But there was no other choice. Tomorrow, or the next day—whenever the chance arose—Justin Bennett had to be *eliminated*, his voice silenced long before the inevitable questions could be asked.

Michael and Mary Bennett were walking out of the store and back into the mall now. Between them, holding their hands, Justin Bennett was a tiny, beloved, flesh-and-blood link.

A bond about to be broken.

Two

Steps away from the dance floor, near the front of a swelling crowd, Harland Till watched as Bobby Freed spun and swayed to the thumping beat.

A white male in his mid-20s, Freed was dressed to lure in a sleeveless white t-shirt and tight, tattered jeans. His hair was shorn military-style above broad cheekbones and a heavy jaw. His skin was leathery from years of sun. Blue-gray tattoos on his biceps shined with sweat.

Looking past him, Till had a spectacular view of Club Night and its crowd. Up to the mezzanine where the couples—male-female, female-female, male-male—kissed and groped. Back toward the long, curving bar, tended by men and women moving in swift, easy rhythm as they tilted the bottles to fill glass after glass. Toward the two mirrored walls at the corner of the dance floor, where he watched a reflection of Bobby Freed's pumping fists, the swaying of his muscled arms, the gyrations of his hips.

Watched and waited, knowing that Freed's eyes would eventually meet his own.

Till glanced away when it happened. But he glanced back a moment later, wearing the hint of a smile as he moved closer, his shoulders rolling with the beat as the hip-hop music video morphed into soft-core gay pornography on a screen rising two stories high.

As if on cue, the light around the dancers became a rapid-fire strobe, capturing Freed in hypnotic poses. Poses that tempted and provoked as Till held his gaze, then nodded toward the bar at the rear of the room.

The rendezvous happened exactly as Till had hoped it would, free of small talk and any other diversion as he pressed Freed's back against the bar, slipping his leg between the other man's thighs and speaking directly into his ear.

Minutes later they were in the nightclub's back parking lot, agreeing to the specifics about what would happen next. With only the slightest bit of indecision Freed consented, giving Till the address and room number of a hotel just a few minutes away from the club.

Till watched as Freed got into a beat-up pickup truck, but felt a twinge of anxiety at the sight of the truck's burned-out taillight and out-of-state license plate. Mounting his Harley, giving the man a bit of a head start, he made sure he followed at a safe distance, from which it would be easy to simply speed away if Freed happened to be pulled over. Till had already been back to Club Night too many times since the last incident, and he wanted to minimize the chances of having a D.C. cop doing a check of his own license.

The hotel was what Till expected—and hoped for—a rundown low-rise on New York Avenue. He watched Freed park the truck, then drove the bike around the block twice to plan his exit. Interstate 95 was nearby and it cut right through the center of the city. He knew that he could be on it and heading north or south in less than two minutes.

He parked several car lengths behind the truck, in the darkness under a burned-out streetlight. The Harley had a small, locked compartment behind the seat, inside of which Till kept the knapsack with all of his traveling gear. The bag was heavy and there was a distinct clinking sound as Till brought it out and set it down. He kept a baseball cap with a large bill in one side compartment and a roll of duct tape, two thin towels, some sturdy twine, and several pairs of sheer rubber gloves in the other. The condoms he had bought earlier in the evening were in the pocket of his jeans.

Wearing the cap with the bill pointing slightly downward, he slung the knapsack onto his back and walked into the lobby. The clerk was reading a magazine behind the counter. Till headed straight to the bank of elevators, hoping to look like a guest accustomed to coming and going. It didn't matter. With a stroke of luck, a phone underneath the counter rang as he walked by. The clerk answered it, and turned around to face the boxes that held the room keys as Till moved swiftly across the lobby.

He pushed the button for the elevator but thought better about it as he listened to its slow, groaning approach. It was already past 2 A.M. but the hotel looked like a place accustomed to all-night traffic. People who might remember him. The stairs were a better option, and he was relieved to find the heavy stairwell door unlocked.

He exited at the third floor. The hallway was brightly lit, the carpeting tattered. The sweet, fruity scent of cleaning fluid filled his lungs as he moved toward Bobby Freed's room.

He knocked lightly, stepping inside immediately as Freed came to the door. With only a hushed "hello" Till clasped him by the belt and pulled him close, halting any possible conversation with a long, open-mouthed kiss, pausing only to turn the deadlock and slip the chain into place.

He was pleased to see the drugs that had been laid out before his arrival: Several lines of cocaine on a pocket mirror, a fat marijuana cigarette in the ceramic ashtray, a bottle of amyl nitrate on the table next to the bed. Stripping down to white cotton briefs, Freed did three lines and took two long hits of the joint as Till set the knapsack next to the bed and slowly undressed in front of him. Freed did not seem to notice as Till then pushed both his clothes and his shoes far underneath the bed.

Reggae music from the radio was low and rhythmic as Bobby Freed slipped out of his briefs and reclined back on the bed, stretching his arms and catching his breath as Till bound his wrists. For a long moment Till's mind skipped back to the dozens of photographs of Bobby Freed that he had committed to memory. Under the light of the bedside lamp, Freed's long body bore several more tattoos. As Till had expected, Freed's nipples and navel were pierced with several small silver rings. The skin at the underside of his penis was pierced with a ring of gold.

Freed moaned with pleasure as Till put on a condom and climbed on top of him; Till's arousal apparent as his hands slid up to grasp Freed's wrists and his weight held him down.

The rest happened quickly, in seconds of gasps and moans over the creaking bed and the pulsing music and the flurry of images racing through Till's mind; Till forcing himself *not* to cry out loud with the sudden, final *release ...*

For several seconds afterward Freed appeared to be completely relaxed, his eyes fluttering shut. He was already beginning to doze as Till rolled over and reached down to the knapsack next to the bed.

Slipped his hand into the center pocket and gripped the leather handle above the long, narrow steel blade.

Turned his face back toward Bobby Freed, who was breathing calmly, wearing a subtle, contented smile. Till felt his own desire dissolving completely as he ran the fingers of his left hand down the man's torso, tracing the sign of a cross over his abdomen, his heart racing as Freed opened his eyes.

"You wanna untie me now?"

Freed's voice was an unexpected interruption to the reverie. Till had hoped he would simply drift off to sleep. But if he was talking he could soon be screaming...

"Yeah," Till said. "Let me get somethin' to cut it with."

The roll of black duct tape was between the two thin towels. Till glanced back and saw Bobby Freed's eyes fluttering shut again as he let go of the knife and leaned down just a bit lower. He cleared his throat to cover the sound as he pulled off a long piece of tape and bit the edge to tear it off the roll. Then, with a quick but careful movement, he pushed the whole bag underneath the bed so that it sat next to his clothes and shoes.

Holding both ends of the tape, he slowly rose, keeping the tape out of sight as he climbed back on top of Freed. Till used his weight to hold him down as Freed opened his eyes again.

Till let Bobby Freed look into his eyes for a long moment, and felt the angry smile coming to his own face.

"Get ready..." Till whispered. "Cause here it comes–"

Till brought the tape down quickly, slapping it over Freed's half-open mouth, pressing with both hands to secure it as Freed reared up, eyes wide with panic, his bound hands slapping Till's chest as Till reached down to the floor, Till still managing, just barely, to hold him down as he grabbed the knife again, Freed's eyes going even wider as Till raised it high above his chest, holding the handle with both hands in a tight double fist, holding it as if he were about to perform a ritual as he whispered...

"Fucker..." and thrust the knife down, the blade plunging between Bobby Freed's ribs; Freed bucking and lurching as Till pulled it free... and brought it back down again, and again; out and down and out and down in a spastic flurry, the blood shooting up like a bright red geyser with Bobby Freed's last silent scream.

* * *

The *afterward* feeling came on quickly, sweeping over him in peaceful waves as he slid off the body and stood next to the bed. The blood had drenched both of them and the stink of it filled the room. There were splatters on the lamps, the tables, and virtually every other surface that Till could see. Taking a long, deep breath, he turned in a slow circle to survey the scene that surrounded him.

The scene like so many others in hotel rooms and apartments and distant houses in several different states. Some of the victims, like this one, wore familiar faces on familiar bodies. Others were simply anonymous; men who had made themselves available for quick, furtive thrills with virtually no questions or worries about what could happen.

Till looked back at the victim, remembering the first time he had seen him on a Web site, his slim, muscled body naked and tense with arousal, eyes looking straight into the camera. Till had felt the victim's stare calling him, luring him.

You got what you deserved, Till thought. *Yessir ... got it in spades.*

The clock next to the bed read 2:20. Time to get moving. Till's mind cleared quickly as he began the steps for a secure exit.

He went first to the bathroom, ran warm water in the sink, rinsed the blood from his hands, and wiped them dry. Slipped the condom from his wilted penis and wrapped it in a washcloth that would be carried away in his bag and discarded later. He then went back into the room and carefully reached underneath the bed, putting one hand below the knapsack and the other above it to keep it off the carpet as he brought it out.

He took it straight to the bathroom, which was still clean and white, and laid it down on the back of the toilet. Went back and repeated the same motion with his clothes and shoes, keeping them away from the blood, clean and dry.

The shower came next—hot, soapy and not too long—Till becoming more aware of the time and everything he still needed to do. He gave the knife a good washing as well, even though it would need to be fully soaked and cleaned of all residue later, when he was safely away. When he was dry he put on most of his clothes, leaving his socks and shoes on a clean spot of carpeting just inside the hotel room door and rolling up the legs of his pants.

Back in the bathroom, he pulled a pair of rubber gloves from the knapsack and grabbed a clean towel. At the bathroom doorway he paused, remembering every surface that he had touched. He had little reason to worry. He had never been arrested, or fingerprinted, so there was no evidence that he knew of to link him to any of his crimes. But he was never sloppy or overly confident, and the steps that he took next were crucial to the ritual.

He started at the doorway, wiped the deadbolt and the chain, moved to the bedside table and headboard, finished with the shiny metal and porcelain surfaces in the bathroom. Went back to the entrance to the room and mentally traced his actions to make sure there was no place he had missed.

It was nearly 3 A.M. now. Time to get out. But the last step of the ritual beckoned as Till went to the pile of clothes that the victim had left next to the bed. They were splattered with blood, but with his fingertips he was able to lift the wallet out of the back pocket of the victim's jeans. The plastic sleeves inside revealed a driver's license from West Virginia and a membership card to a health club. There was another rolled up condom alongside the cash in the main fold. Till carefully took out the cash: two $50 bills and three 20s. Not a lot, but a nice addition to his own stash. Slipping the money into his pocket, he glanced over at the shoulder bag that the victim had placed in the corner of the room. If the victim had traveled here from West Virginia without credit cards he probably had more cash, which he probably would have left back at his hotel room to avoid carrying it around.

Still wearing the gloves, Till carefully lifted the bag and reached inside.

On top of the victim's clothing was a camera, in a leather case, along with a snap-on telephoto lens. It looked expensive and would probably be worth at least $100 if he could fence it, Till thought, although he had never been stupid enough to take anything that could connect him to a victim. Tilting the bag toward the light, he fished around some more, then turned the bag around to check the pockets on the other side.

He felt two envelopes as he reached in; one large and thin and another smaller one from the PhotoExpress store he had seen just down the block.

He glanced at the clock again, knowing he needed to get moving as he opened the larger envelope. It contained an issue of the *Washington Blade*, a gay newspaper, and what looked like transcripts from an Internet chat room. Till had always had trouble reading but he usually managed by going through passages several times and finding familiar words. The type on the transcripts was small and nearly illegible but there were several words that *did* stand out ... words that made him feel lightheaded as his eyes went back and forth over the first two pages.

"Damnation," he whispered.

His hands were shaking, his thoughts racing through a prism of memory as he opened the second envelope and reached inside ... panic fluttering in his chest as he flipped through the photographs of the little boy playing in a yard ... a beautiful little boy laughing and running and jumping into the arms of a grown man ...

A beautiful little boy turned nearly *ugly* by the dark red-wine stain on the side of his face.

* * *

Officer Gloria Towson took the call at 9:45 A.M., cutting quickly through the alleys even through she knew the call about a "disturbance" at the Capitol Hotel would probably amount to nothing more than a fight to oust one of the homeless white guys who occasionally tried to sleep in the lobby. But she quickened her pace at the sight of the maid who looked as if she had collapsed in the lobby chair and the shock on the face of the clerk who simply said "room 305" as she came through the revolving door... took the stairs two at a time to reach the third floor... felt the muscles tensing between her broad shoulders as she saw the wide-open door near the end of the hall ...

And gasped as she reached the threshold.

"Oh God." Her hand went to her gun as the images and smells assaulted her mind... the naked man who had been savaged on the bed... the odor of stale marijuana lingering in the air... the blood splattered into every corner of the room.

She stepped back, wondering if she had already screwed up by getting too close to the scene. Glancing down at the dry, clean carpeting under her feet, she realized she had stopped just in time. She heard the *ding* of the elevator door and turned to see the clerk getting off, his eyes wide with curiosity as he said something about the floor being "nearly empty" and the only other "guests" running straight down to the lobby after glimpsing the sight that had caused the maid to scream.

"Good, that's good." She held her arm out, motioning him back. "I need to ask you to go back downstairs now. Please. And don't let anyone leave. Keep that lady—the maid—who saw this in the lobby till we can interview her. Please. *Jesus*."

"Are you okay ma'am—"

"*Yes.*" She paused, took a deep, calming breath. "You'll need to stay down there for a while too, until we can get a statement."

She turned away, back toward the room. Priority-one at a scene was "officer safety." She did not believe she was in danger; the killer was surely long gone.

Priority-two was the "health and welfare of the victim," and under most circumstances she would be expected to check for life signs but... *no, not here.*

Priority three was "protection of the scene." She pulled the radio from her belt, a surreal chill radiating through her whole body as she called it in, blurting out that the victim's wrists were bound even though it was a detail the dispatcher did not need to know. She stayed just outside the doorway to make sure that no one—from curious guests to the first wave of patrol officers who would soon be filling the hallway—contaminated the crime scene.

She realized then what she had forgotten. The hotel room was small and from the doorway she could see every corner, but the bathroom was only partly visible through the open door. Procedure dictated that she check for any other victims without damaging the scene.

Gloria took out her gun. "Police. Is anyone here? We're coming in."

There was a narrow perimeter of carpeting that appeared to be free of bloodstains and she walked sideways along it toward the bathroom. She crouched and peered around the doorway and was relieved to see that she could do a visual sweep of the inside without entering. The curtain in the tub was open; the tub was empty. There was no other victim.

She retraced her steps as she moved back to the hall, eyes sweeping side to side and taking in more details. In the far corner, the victim's traveling bag appeared to have been emptied; a pile of clothes left on the floor. The radio was on, tuned to a station where the newscaster spoke with a lilting Caribbean accent. There were marks in the bloodstained carpet that looked like they had been made by bare feet. And there was a photograph lying in blood near the foot of the bed.

A little boy. Gloria squinted, but the photograph was partially obscured by the tousled bedspread and it was difficult to pick out the details from five feet away. There was a strange shadow on the child's face and he appeared to be looking sideways, not at the camera.

The sound of an approaching siren took her attention back to the doorway and the crime scene that had to be protected. Less than a minute later there were four other patrol officers in the hallway. Gloria stayed at the door to stop anyone from entering and pulled the notebook from her back pocket to begin her log, writing down the names and badge numbers of the other officers as they arrived and assuring herself that she had done everything *right* as Louis D'Amecourt stepped out of the elevator and met her eyes.

D'Amecourt, the Fifth District Commander, coming down the hall with surprising speed and already looking as if he had something to say.

D'Amecourt grilling her but not looking at her as he stood at the threshold, staring into the room, every question putting her more on edge. What time did she get the call? Who discovered the victim? Had she trampled on, touched, or done anything else to damage the crime scene?

Her heart was pounding but she was confident that all of her answers measured up. Yet she was still on edge as homicide detective Tommy Payne came through the stairwell door. Payne looked warily at D'Amecourt as he approached the scene, and gave Gloria a little wave when he met her eyes.

"Hey Glo."

D'Amecourt flinched at Payne's greeting, the use of her first name.

"Hey Tommy." Her voice croaked. "Thanks for—"

"Okay, Towson, we'll take it from here," D'Amecourt said.

"I have witnesses to interview," Gloria told him. "The maid downstairs and some people who were staying in the rooms on this floor—"

"Just make sure they don't go anywhere. We'll talk to them in a minute," D'Amecourt said sharply.

"I was the first on the scene. I'd like to get their statements."

"You heard me, Towson. You're done."

Well goddamn you, too. Her jaw was locked and it was impossible to keep the anger out of her eyes as she stared back at D'Amecourt, waiting for him to look away.

"I'm sure you've taken good care of everything so far," Payne came to her rescue, which only made her feel worse. But the chirping of her cell phone cut through the air before she could respond.

"You can take that down in the lobby," D'Amecourt said dismissively.

"We'll do a debrief in a little while," Payne said, his gentle gaze promising her that they would.

"Okay," she said quietly, unable to resist another harsh look at D'Amecourt as she turned away. She answered the phone while walking down the hall and was relieved to hear the voice of Booker, her husband of four months, who was also a police officer but off-duty for the day.

She gave him the details in the stairwell, telling him what a bastard D'Amecourt was, as if Booker didn't already know.

"He came in here like a freight train," she told him. "Like he was desperate to run me out."

"What about Tommy Payne?"

"Payne was okay, but he knows I am *pissed off.*"

"D'Amecourt's always been hands-on, Glo."

"Well he's freakier than usual today. I think there's something going on."

"What do you mean?"

Gloria paused, thinking about the possibility that D'Amecourt was reacting not to her but to the crime scene itself. "Something about the way he acted. Like maybe he was scared of something."

"Yeah right." Booker's laugh was short and hollow. "Only thing that man's scared of is an empty bottle."

Gloria looked back through the narrow glass window in the heavy stairwell door. There were two new officers guarding the scene now, and apparently D'Amecourt and Payne were both inside the room. As the Commander of the Fifth District, it made sense that D'Amecourt might have come to the scene, and that he would keep an eye on the processing carried out by a homicide detective under his watch. But it still surprised her that he was among the first to arrive.

She told Booker that she would call him later, that she needed to go down to the lobby to make sure that anyone who might have seen anything stayed put. But curiosity kept her rooted to the spot as she hung up, and moments later she was heading back down the hall, her mind racing for an excuse to go back to the scene.

Both of the officers at the doorway, Rutherford and Sanchez, nodded stiffly as she approached, and neither man looked as if he would move an inch. But the door was still open and she had a clear view of D'Amecourt, stooping down alongside the pile of clothing on the floor.

With his back to her, she scanned the room again, her eyes coming back to the victim, the blood-soaked sheets, the *empty* space under the bed where she had seen the child's photograph just moments before.

Three

Refusing to be paranoid about premonitions, Michael Bennett sat on the edge of the bed as Justin hugged his stuffed spaniel dog and whispered:

"Momma was *scarwed*, Uncle Mike."

Justin had a froggy, elfin voice, and he had always had trouble with Ws, Ls, and Rs.

"She made me scarwed, too."

The sadness in Justin's eyes brought a small ache to the back of Michael's throat as he pulled the covers up under the boy's chin, then patted them down to create the snugness that Justin craved. Then he sat down on the bed and placed his palms on both sides of Justin's face.

"Your mom loves you very much," he said. "And it's true, she *does* get upset when she turns around and you're not right there."

Justin blinked, and Michael knew he was ashamed that he had violated one of his mother's "most important rules." Michael decided to speak matter-of-factly, to take the opportunity to make a point.

"You have to remember, when you're out with your mom, or with me, it's very important that you stay close by. You have to hold our hands like you were *supposed* to today. Do you understand?"

Justin frowned for a moment, then nodded. Relaxing, finally, Michael sat next to him and listened to the child's gentle breathing.

"But what about on the *wides*?"

"What do you mean?"

"Uncle *Michael*," Justin chastised him now. "When you wide the ponies you have to hold on with *both* hands."

"Oh yeah, right," Michael smiled at the earnestness in Justin's eyes.

"And also when you *dwive* the little cars," Justin told him. "*Both* hands on the wheel. That's what you said last time, remember, Uncle Mike?"

"Yeah I remember," Michael said. His sister's ever-present apprehension had made last month's trip to the AdventureWorld amusement park tense at first, but she had eventually relaxed. Pestered to submission, Mary had agreed to let Justin go again. This time, tomorrow, with his Uncle Michael alone.

Michael gave Justin a serious look. "I'll tell you what. Because you're getting to be a *big boy* now ... when you're on the rides, you *do* have to keep a grip on the reigns or the wheel. And when you're with your mom or me, you have to hold her hand or mine. But guess what else?"

"What, Uncle Mike?"

"Tomorrow you get to on a couple of the rides by *yourself*. We'll start with the merry-go-round, and then move onto the cars. You think you're up for that?"

Justin nodded and grinned, then frowned again.

"But where will *you* be, Uncle Mike?"

Michael thought about it a moment, knowing he had to balance his own fears with Justin's need for independence. Then with what Justin called his "crazy face," he leaned closer.

"I'll be right here. *Grrrrrrr*," Michael growled and giggled and tickled him. "All *right*, little boy?"

"All *wight* Uncle MIKE!" Justin let out a peal of laughter, kicking his legs under the covers as Michael tickled and squeezed him again and again.

* * *

Later he would regret the tickling and the squeezing, and he would have nightmares about what happened next.

"Michael, what are you doing?"

Mary's voice startled him. He was in the basement, at the workbench. He hadn't heard her come down the stairs.

"I've got Justin's ID bracelet. I'm working on the clasp."

Mary came closer. She was wearing a light blue nightgown and a frumpy white terry cloth robe. Under the harsh light Michael saw new lines around her eyes and wondered if the scare at the mall had aged her.

"Are you fixing it, or taking it apart?" Mary joked.

"I'm bending it so it won't come loose again."

"It came *loose?*"

Michael rolled his eyes. "No, Miss Overreact to Everything. I was wrestling with Justin and realized that it was about to, which is why I'm fixing it."

Michael felt her watching as he closed the rings on either side of the clasp. Justin had been complaining about the tightness of the bracelet, and about a taunt he'd gotten from another little boy at kindergarten who told him jewelry was for girls. There was no possibility of his nephew going without the bracelet, which listed his name, address, and telephone number, but Michael had decided earlier today that the least he could do was make it more comfortable. The bracelet was designed to be lengthened as Justin grew, but when he had started working on it the clasp had jammed, and it had almost slipped off when he tickled Justin in bed. Michael felt responsible; the late-night repair at the workbench wouldn't have been necessary if he hadn't fiddled with the bracelet in the first place.

"I didn't *overreact*, Michael. And I don't appreciate you joking about it either."

The tone of Mary's voice made it clear she was still thinking about the morning's incident. The rest of the day had gone by without any discussion of it. Michael had hoped she wouldn't mention it again.

He sighed, knowing now that she would have to talk it through. "You mean at the mall."

"Of course that's what I mean."

"I feel awful about it." He lowered the bracelet and looked at her. "But it's *okay*. Justin was fine."

"Well it scared the hell out of me," she said harshly. "Michael, we have to be careful with him."

She said "we," he thought, with some relief. "I know."

"I'm not saying it was *completely* your fault."

"And I'm not saying it wasn't," he offered. "It was just for a few seconds that I wasn't holding on to him, but that's what you were counting on me to do."

"Then we'll share the blame." Mary made an attempt to smile, and gave his forearm a squeeze. "Okay?"

"Yeah." The look in her eyes bothered him. *She still believes you're a screw-up*, he thought.

He went back to the bracelet. The clasp felt secure now. "Okay, it's done. See?"

He handed it to her and she held it under the light, squinting slightly as she checked it. After a moment she shuddered.

"What's wrong?"

She looked at him, blinked quickly, then shook her head dismissively. "I just had a strange feeling."

"What kind of feeling?"

"I don't know. Just sort of ... *sad*."

Michael found himself nodding slightly. He had had similar feelings off and on all day. Feelings that intensified as Mary met his eyes.

"Oh never mind." Mary tried to smile. "I'm sure it's just my imagination turnin' me into an old hag."

Michael laughed. His sister was 31 now, the same age their parents had been when they died. The rest of their childhoods, and the past five years in particular, had been a battleground of risk and redemption, stemming from the tragedy that could have made them enemies but had brought them far closer instead.

"You don't have time to be a hag." He put his arm around her shoulder. "You're too busy bein' my big sissy."

"I thought *you* were the sissy, Michael."

"Then you ain't seen me pumpin' iron, darlin'."

"Yeah well I also ain't seen you *working* the iron either, *darlin'*." She elbowed his stomach and handed the bracelet back. "It's your turn this week, and since I happen to work in a *legitimate* dining establishment I prefer it when my fine polyester aprons look nice."

"Yikes, I fail again," he moaned.

"Yes, that's you, Michael." Abruptly, she kissed him on the cheek. "Failure Boy extraordinaire."

The words hung in the air as he watched her go up the narrow stairs and into the kitchen, feeling a rush of gratitude that, after everything, she didn't really believe it. The bracelet felt delicate in his hand as he switched off the light.

And saw the flash in the window.

It had come at him in an instant, a beam of white light that hit him directly in the face. The basement windows were at eye level, and when he moved closer he realized the flash had come from headlights belonging to a car that had pulled up to the curb. The three-level townhouse Michael, Mary, and Justin lived in was on a corner in the woodsiest section of Northwest Washington, on a short side street that backed up to parkland. There were only four other houses on the block. Michael continued to stare at the car at the curb, anxious to see who got out.

For several seconds nothing happened. As his eyes adjusted to the light he was able to see the outline of the car, something out of the late 1960s, he thought. A muscle car, maybe. He felt a catch in his breath, the mere shape of the car bringing back a memory that he instantly tried to push out of his mind.

With a revving of the engine, the car backed up, paused, and pulled away.

Probably just someone turning around. The incident at the mall had jangled his nerves, but he had to stop thinking about disaster at every turn.

Just put it out of your mind, he thought, and headed up the stairs.

* * *

The feeling of being *watched* struck him again as he stepped out of the shower. He had stayed under the hot water for a long time. The windows were steamy but it wasn't hard to imagine that under the bright overhead light someone could see him from the dark woods at the back of the house. With a swipe of the towel on the glass he looked out and saw nothing but old trees and the passing headlights of traffic on the Rock Creek Parkway 100 yards away.

He shut the blinds and wrapped the towel around his middle, then stepped into the attic bedroom that comprised the third floor of the house. The feeling of unease faded away as the thumping beat of club music filled the room. The beat was catchy, and he tapped a rhythm against his thigh as he moved toward the dresser.

He caught sight of himself in the full-length mirror and was pleased.

"So it's working," he said out loud as he thought of the harder-than-usual workout the day before. He flexed his right arm, then twisted to the left, a semi-serious attempt at a muscle-boy pose, which he held for no more than five seconds before he laughed and turned it into a parody. Sometimes it amazed him that despite everything, he had done more than just survive. Somehow between the faith of his sister and the support of his very *un*traditional family he had found it possible to look forward to the common joys of everyday life. Health. Success. A future of open doors. The last few years had taught him to relish it all.

Thanks to Justin, he thought. *And a second chance a hundred times better than you deserve.*

The music was reaching a fever pitch. It heightened his anticipation for the night ahead as he ran his fingers through his towel-dried hair and slipped into a pair of baggy jeans and a bright white t-shirt. It was already the first week of October, but several warm days in a long Indian summer had only deepened his tan, giving his confidence another boost as he stood in front of the mirror again.

You look happy.

His mind flashed on the face of someone he had met a week before. The name and phone number that had been scrawled on the matchbook. The smile meeting his across the bar.

Ready to try again.

He was ready to slip out into the night when he accidentally kicked over the stack of magazines and papers he'd been collecting. He remembered Mary's comment about the ironing. She was right; he hadn't paid as much attention to his own household chores as he should have recently. Knowing it would take just a minute to make some headway, he decided to sift through the pile and toss everything he didn't need to save.

At the bottom of the stack was an article Mary had written weeks earlier for the *Washington Blade*. Michael picked it up and felt a familiar clenching in his gut as he thumbed through the article, which began with a harrowing description of the abduction and death of her first son, Benjamin, five years before. He was still anxious about the many details his sister had chosen to reveal, but comforted by the way the story evolved into a description of her "deep appreciation" for his role as a father figure to Justin, and the happiness of "our odd little family" at present.

As if we've moved right on, he thought. *No more worries. No more questions—*

The attic room had storage built under the eaves. It was a good hiding place for the box that contained items that he hoped neither his sister nor anyone else would ever see. Knowing that this issue of the *Blade* was something he would keep forever, Michael slipped it into the box.

With one more look in the mirror and a dash of cologne at the back of his neck, he headed back downstairs. On the second floor were two bedrooms, one for Justin and a larger one at the front of the house for Mary. Her door was partially open as he walked by and he could hear the television turned to low volume. When he opened the door a little wider he saw that she had dozed off. He stepped into the room and was just reaching over to turn the television off when he saw what she was holding.

His breath came up short, his mood plunging as he gazed at the light brown teddy bear in Mary's arms. *Benjamin's bear*. Michael had noticed that it was missing from Justin's room earlier in the afternoon and had carefully *not* asked his sister where it was.

Feeling suddenly like a trespasser, he stepped back. A creak in the floor sent a shiver up his back and made him step even more quickly out of the room.

In the hallway he felt his heart pounding.

Calm down, think of something else.

Justin was afraid of the dark, and he liked to keep his door open to let in light from the hallway. Standing in the doorway, Michael could tell he was now sleeping soundly with the stuffed cocker spaniel in his arms. He stood there for nearly a minute, reminding himself that the windows were locked. The house was alarmed. Justin and Mary were completely safe.

It was a mental checklist he went through three more times as he stepped outside and slipped behind the wheel of the Jeep. He was at the end of the block before he realized he hadn't turned on his lights. Doing so sent his mind moving forward as he headed more deeply into the city, toward the noise and distraction of Club Night, where thoughts of Mary and Justin and the incident at the mall would quickly fade away.

Down the block, forgotten by now, the muscle car pulled up to the curb again.

* * *

Mary heard the door shut: nothing more than a *click* that for some reason sounded louder, like a punctuation mark to all of the conflicts of the day.

She had dozed off in front of the television with her arms wrapped snugly around the teddy bear that now belonged in Justin's room. The stress had worn her down and brought tears to her eyes as she drifted into the netherworld between consciousness and sleep. It was in that state that the memories were most difficult to manage. She had already been awake when Michael had stepped into the room, but had kept her eyes closed. She just hadn't been up to conversation.

Now that he was gone, she suddenly wished that he wasn't.

"Sorry, little brother," she muttered into the darkness. She still felt badly about snapping at him in the shoe store, but she almost wanted to *hit* him, to call him stupid for letting his attention wander. And yet for the rest of the afternoon she had been haunted by the look on his face at the moment they realized Justin was gone.

You can't keep doing this, she told herself. *You have to move on.* Knowing how difficult it could be to get back to sleep, she decided to head downstairs to study. She brought Benjamin's bear with her and propped it up on the breakfast table. She eyed the scotch bottle in the glass-fronted cabinet but opted for the more sensible choice of a club soda instead. Within minutes the words from the textbook on libel laws were blurred by tears. After reading the same page three times with little comprehension, she was ready to give up.

But still wide-awake. At 10:15 she needed to be winding down, getting ready for the day that would follow. She was working a lunch shift at O'Malley's, the popular restaurant and pub owned but no longer managed by her Uncle Martin. She would be serving her regular tables and a special gathering, hosted by Martin, of his political supporters. *It'll be good money and an easy time*, he had joked. *If any one of those blowhards gives you trouble, I'll be right there.*

The recollection cheered her. Uncle Martin and Aunt Joan were the lifeblood of the recovery that her shrink had tried to convince her she had reached. In her darkest periods she prayed they would never be farther than a phone call away.

Even now, she thought as she looked at the clock, knowing that Joan usually stayed up until 11, and then "wound down" by reading crime novels for half an hour or so before going to bed. Picking up the phone, she was ready to excuse herself immediately if the woman was too immersed in one to chat, although she couldn't think of a minute in her whole life that her cherished aunt hadn't given her full attention.

"Hello?" Joan's voice was upbeat, as expected.

"Are you busy?" Mary pictured her sitting in the comfortable wing chair alongside the big carved mantel in her historic Cleveland Park home, drinking a glass of sherry. It had been three weeks since the two of them had seen each other. Joan had busy gearing up for Martin's city council reelection campaign and Mary missed her more than ever. "Can you talk?"

"Of course I can, baby. How are ya?"

"Crappy," Mary answered with her usual honesty, and then described the scare at the mall and the sense of fear that had stayed with her for the rest of the day.

"I can only imagine what it must have been like." Joan's voice was comforting as always. Mary could feel her gentle smile. "It's so easy to overreact when something like that happens."

"I know, but—"

"Besides, how can you compete with Captain Steel?" Joan chuckled. "Defender of the Universe."

"And 'Protector of the World.'" Mary laughed. Over the past month the Saturday morning cartoon character had become Justin's absolute favorite. But she was still anxious at how easily the 12-foot tall cardboard statue had lured her son away.

She decided to change the subject. "So anyway, how are you? Did you get some shopping done today too?"

"Are you *kidding*?" Joan had recently retired from a long, successful career as an Assistant District Attorney, a difficult job given her constant anger over the inability of the system to protect innocent victims. Working as a campaign aide to her husband, a city councilman, had proven to be only slightly less draining.

"I've been pinned to the desk all day. This event of Martin's is going to be the death of me," Joan said. "I think I was at it for seven hours without a break before being chained to the phone for a conference call that took another two."

"It's going to be great." *But sad*, Mary thought. She had helped her aunt write a portion of Martin's speech for the event, which would dedicate a new pediatric AIDS wing at George Washington Hospital, where Martin would share the podium with the mayor, the university president, and probably a celebrity or two.

Mary heard the call-waiting beep and looked at the clock. "God, who could be calling so late?"

"You have to go?"

"I guess so," she sighed wearily. "There's never enough time to just relax anymore."

"I feel the same way," Joan said. "Especially with the pressure we're starting to get from the Moral Minority."

Mary recognized the reference to Martin's most significant opposition, a Republican running on a law and order platform, who continuously bolstered his position by citing the high homicide rate in the city's tougher neighborhoods, an implicit criticism of Joan's previous effectiveness as a prosecutor. After an impassioned public debate two nights earlier, Louis D'Amecourt, one of the best-known police officials in the city, had been interviewed by a local newscaster. D'Amecourt had put up an appearance of neutrality, but his support of Martin's opposition was pretty clear. Mary had had a distinct feeling that D'Amecourt was still motivated by personal animosity, and that he would have done anything to see her uncle defeated.

"So you're pretty sure they'll be back?" she said.

"Oh yeah, marching on that same old bandwagon—"

The call-waiting click came again.

"Ugh!" Mary snapped. "It's probably a damn telephone solicitor."

"Probably. You take care, honey."

"You, too." She felt another pang of regret at having to say good-bye, a renewed uneasiness as she disconnected.

With another click she was on the new line.

"Hello?"

"Mary. It's me. Scott."

Scott. The voice knocked her breathless as she pressed her back against the wall, looked at the locked door. The kitchen window. The darkness outside.

"I'm home," Scott said. "In D.C. I need to see you."

She gripped the phone tighter, and thought of the last time she had seen him, five years earlier, on his way to prison. Thought of the letters, the phone calls, the lurking *presence* of him every day since.

"I'll beg you if I have to. Come on Mary, *please* ..."

Four

The Club Night sound system boomed dance music in time with a spectacular light show, but Harland Till focused on Michael Bennett like a hunter stalking a deer in the woods.

Bennett the child molester.

The thought sharpened Till's concentration as he watched Bennett at the other end of the bar, where for much of the night he had been surrounded by admirers. Bennett's brown hair was shiny and full, his skin healthy and clear. When he moved it was with the ease of a natural athlete, a boy-man who looked more like a popular college kid than the perverted monster that he was.

Fooling everybody. Walking free—

Till clenched his jaw, felt the grinding pressure on his molars, looked toward the mirrored wall behind the bar where his surveillance of Bennett would be less obvious. Dry ice below and above the dance floor sent white clouds tumbling around the room. Till saw them momentarily as familiar ghosts, the spirits of butchered men. The sight crystallized in memories of the killing the night before. The chat room transcripts. The pictures of the little boy. The article in the gay newspaper that tied it all together.

Standing barefoot in the room full of blood, he had struggled to breathe; hot, angry tears stinging his eyes as he tried to jam everything back into the large envelope; his hands shaking; the photographs falling and scattering across the wet carpet. Quickly, recklessly, he had stooped down to pick them up, the photos becoming slippery with blood, the blood soiling the envelope and the papers and the knapsack as he shoved it all inside.

Getting out had suddenly become dangerous with the blood so clearly visible. Willing himself to stay calm, he had stepped back toward a clean spot on the carpeting, wiped his feet, put on his socks and shoes, wrapped the gloves in a washcloth, and put it inside the knapsack to discard later. Loud voices of two women who sounded like drunks in the hallway had forced him to wait for the sound of a closing door. But seconds afterward he made it to the stairwell, the knapsack under his arm and shielded by his jacket on the brisk walk through the lobby and out to the bike.

An hour later he was safe inside his own hotel room outside the city. But thoughts of the little boy had kept him up all night, and his face was pale and tear-stained when the morning sun cut through the blinds. Later, when he went through everything in the envelope again, he realized that he only had four of the five photographs, which meant that he had left one in the room. He was not worried—he had been wearing gloves, so there would be no prints. But he was intensely curious about how the police would react when they found the photo, and whether they would somehow be able to identify the child and connect him to Michael Bennett. At several points during the day he had logged onto the Internet and scanned the local newspaper and television Web sites looking for news of the killing. He was surprised to see no mention of it at all.

But there would surely be news tomorrow, Till thought. News about the murder of Michael Bennett. Till wanted it to be quick but painful, and he wanted to be sure that Bennett knew he had been *exposed*.

Michael was finishing a tall, clear-colored cocktail now. Till watched as he set the empty glass on the bar and headed toward the restrooms. Moving closer to where Michael had been standing, Till waved a five-dollar bill and motioned for the bartender.

"Give that guy another drink, on me," he said. "Just set it down where he was standin' before."

The bartender took the money, pouring and delivering the drink with a few, quick automatic movements before moving on to the next customer. Reaching into the right-hand pocket of his tight-fitting carpenter pants, Till pulled out a capsule of Rohypnol. When the bartender was looking away he emptied the powder from the capsule into the drink and gave it a quick stir.

He was standing next to the drink when Bennett returned. Obviously used to the attention, Bennett gave him a small smile and an acknowledging nod, and took a long sip.

With a glance in the bar mirror—a glimpse at his pale complexion, his tired, bloodshot eyes—Till smoothed back his hair and tapped Bennett's shoulder.

"You didn't say thank you," he said.

There was a small twitch in Bennett's cheek. "Oh. Sorry. Thanks."

"You're welcome." Till tried to smile, already knowing the expression would fail. Under low lights, in clothes that accentuated his muscled arms and narrow waist, Till usually found it easy to attract the attention of men out for a night of rough, anonymous sex, but most people tended to get uneasy after a few moments of talking with him. He had become acutely aware of the signs when they pretended *not* to be. Bennett had already moved back a step and looked like he was calculating an excuse to slip away.

"You like kids, don't you?"

The phrase brought a look of confusion to Bennett's face.

"I saw the story in the *Blade* about you," Till said. "The one that said you worked here."

Bennett stiffened slightly and raised the cocktail again. His Adam's apple bobbed as he drank most of the rest down. Till remembered a photograph that went with the story, a picture of Michael at a daycare center for homeless children, where he was a "volunteer."

"I read about how you want to be around 'em all the time."

"Yeah when I'm not here," Bennett tried to smile. "Working, making money—"

"I know what you been doin' to that little boy."

"What?" Bennett frowned.

Till gave him a threatening glare. "I *know*."

"What's that supposed to mean?" Bennett pretended to be dumbfounded.

Till stood up a little straighter and squared his shoulders without looking away. "What d'ya think it means?"

"I'm asking you. What are you talking about?"

Till nodded toward the hallway that led to Club Night's backroom bar, where the music was lower and it would be easier to talk. Then, before Bennett could speak again, he turned and began walking.

He went no more than 10 feet before Michael Bennett grabbed his shoulder and spun him around.

"You want to tell me what the hell is going on?"

Bennett's grip sent a pleasant pain radiating throughout Till's upper body. Till realized he had moved too soon. He should have waited longer before speaking the words he had practiced all day. With ten more minutes of small talk the drug would have made Michael weak and wobbly, and it would have been much easier to lure him into a nearby alley, where a quick move with the knife would have slashed right through the tender skin of his neck.

But you can still mess with his head, Till thought. *Scare him good.*

Till looked past him to make certain they weren't being watched. "I think you better let go."

"Who *are* you?"

"I'm gonna' count to three." Till shifted his weight slightly, his right hand already moving into a fist. "One..."

"*Tell* me."

"Two..."

"Why did you think—"

Till punched him hard, his fist going deep into Bennett's gut. Bennett's eyes bulged, but before his knees could buckle Till pressed him close to the wall, and held his body there in what looked like an intimate embrace. Bennett's head started to roll forward and Till stopped it with a kiss to Bennett's mouth. He felt the sudden, urgent throbbing in his groin as Bennett drew his head back, gasping for air.

"*God...*" Bennett's eyes reddened. The anger had turned to fear.

Till stepped back, and with a glance in both directions saw no sign that the 10-second altercation had been noticed above the loud music. Bennett had both hands on his abdomen and he looked like he was about to slide down the wall.

"You perverts oughtta be cut up." His lips brushed the side of Bennett's ear as he whispered. "And people who hurt little boys deserve to have it hurt *real* bad."

Without thinking he had laid his palm flat against Bennett's left pectoral muscle. He felt the rapid, panicky beating of Bennett's heart. The sensation sent another pleasant surge through Till's groin, a tingling in his testicles as he whispered again.

"Think about that next time you get that urge." This time his smile felt real, and he knew it would scare Bennett even more. "Think about what's gonna' happen to you."

He kept his hands on Michael Bennett's chest for several seconds. When he was certain that he was too weak, and too scared, to make a scene, he moved easily back into the crowd, unaware and unconcerned as Michael turned into the restroom and vomited into the sink.

* * *

The muscle car pulled away from the curb just two minutes before Michael turned onto the block. Terrified of being stopped for drunk driving, he had made his way back home like an old man, five miles below the speed limit, both hands clenching the wheel. He was still expecting to see revolving lights in the rearview mirror as he eased into the narrow driveway behind the house.

The moment he turned off the ignition he opened the driver side door and looked toward the second-floor windows at the back of the house, the windows to Justin's room. From the driveway they looked undisturbed; each one bearing the stickers that notified would-be intruders that the house was alarmed. His stomach was still tender as he went to the back door and pressed the security code on the keypad to let himself in. He took his shoes off to minimize the noise as he climbed the stairs. At the second floor landing he noticed his sister's door was halfway open.

A bad sign. It happened once in a while, when Mary was seized by the sudden, irrational fear that Justin would disappear. She would insist on being able to see into the hall as she drifted off to sleep, and again as she awoke off and on during the night.

He wondered if she had somehow found out about the incident at Club Night. If there were some kind of connection—

Of course not, he thought. *She was here, safe.*

On the final flight of stairs to his third-floor room he thought of the article Mary had written for the *Blade*, the photographs of Benjamin and Justin at the center of the page. The article had revealed so much information about their lives.

Maybe too much.

His whole body went limp as he sat on his bed. His head was clearing but his temples throbbed as the stranger's words rang in his ears again.

"You perverts oughtta' be cut up."

A jolt of terror made him sit up straight. His heart was pounding hard, his eyes wide open but seeing nothing as he stared toward the dark window. In an instant his memory took him back two years earlier, to the sight of a body, the wrists cuffed to an iron headboard, the blood-soaked, tangled sheets.

"Think about that next time you get that urge."

The stranger's voice came at him again, taunting, knowing.

"Think about what's gonna' happen to you."

Weak and fully dressed, he curled into a fetal position, hands clasped over his stomach, the edge of a knife cutting into his dreams.

* * *

The headache was brutal. Michael's eyelids felt as if they were coated with sandpaper as he sat up.

The room was already flooded with sunlight. It was almost 8:30. He had planned on going for a run through the park and being on the road with Justin by 10. Still seated on the edge of the bed, he massaged the side of his head as memories of the night came back. The stranger. The punch to his gut. A nightmare in which he looked down at his own naked body, seeing stab wounds from his neck to his thighs.

The nightmare had stayed with him all night. There had been several moments when he had opened his eyes to see the stranger in front of him. The body in his bed, *next* to him—

At some point it had become too much, and he vaguely remembered picking up the phone, calling Louis D'Amecourt, leaving a message on D'Amecourt's private line, telling him "*something happened—*"

His mind felt as if it was wrapped in cobwebs, his reflexes dulled as he gargled mouthwash, brushed his teeth, scrubbed color into his cheeks, and tried to convince himself that the fight with the stranger had been nothing more than a coincidence.

No, you know better.

The feeling was too strong to ignore as he made his way downstairs and found Mary sitting at the kitchen table, her face drawn and her eyes reddened by lack of sleep. His customary *"hey girl"* greeting was cut short.

"They let Scott out of prison."

Michael looked at his sister, who was staring despondently at the top of the table, and felt a fluttering in his chest. Determined not to overreact, he reached for one of the coffee cups that hung on wall hooks next to the stove. The cup was shaking in his hand as he set it on the counter.

"I found out last night," she told him. "After you left."

"You were asleep when I left, weren't you?"

"I woke up later."

"How did you find—"

"He *called* me, Michael. He wants to see me."

Me, too, probably. Michael thought of Scott's letters. Nearly five years worth, all stored in a desk drawer in his room. Letters loaded with threats to "get even" for the betrayal that sent him to prison. Letters that stated over and over again that Scott *would* stay involved in Justin's life, despite the continuing efforts of the lawyers to cut him off.

"This wasn't supposed to happen," he told her. "His sentence was for 10 years."

"His *sentence* was for selling drugs, Michael."

"But surely they know about... I mean what he *really* did."

"Either they do or they don't—what does it matter. They let him *out!*"

Michael wanted to believe her anger was directed at Scott Brown alone, but the unspoken truth made it impossible to meet her eyes.

"We shouldn't jump to conclusions," he said. "In fact, if you've told him how you really feel, he'll probably stay as far away from us as possible."

"Michael, do you *really* think that?" Mary's voice had an edge of ridicule.

"No," was his honest answer. Leaning against the counter, he remembered the stranger's warning the night before. His thoughts skipped quickly, looking for connections. *Scott kidnapped Benjamin but never got convicted of the crime... A weirdo who read Mary's story has convinced himself that you had something to do with it, and that you're about to do something to Justin... He's threatened to* cut *you—*

"What's *wong,* momma?"

Mary flinched at the voice of Justin in the doorway. She looked extraordinarily weary as she reached over and put her arm around his waist.

"Momma's fine honey." She drew him close. "Just a little tired is all."

Justin let his mother hug him tightly for a moment, then looked up. "Hi, Uncle Mike."

"Hey you." Michael's voice quivered.

"Are you ready to *go,* Uncle Mike?"

Over Justin's shoulder, Mary met his eyes.

"I will be in a little while." Michael turned away from her and poured the coffee. "Just need to get revved up here."

"Justin, you feel like you've got a little fever honey. You okay?"

Michael turned around, saw his sister frowning at Justin with concern.

"I'm fine, momma. Uncle Mike and me are going to Adventure-World!"

"We sure are," Michael said firmly.

Mary looked at him again. He thought of the stranger's odd insinuation, and wondered if he should cancel the outing.

No, fear should never lead your life. Step out in front of it. Beat it and step away.

"You better go get dressed, kiddo," Michael said.

"Okay." Justin was suddenly cheerful, oblivious to the tension. "I can do it *myself!*"

The silence was loaded as they watched him leave the kitchen. Michael listened to the sound of his footsteps reaching the top of the stairs before meeting his sister's eyes again.

"We've been planning this for weeks, Mary."

"I know that."

"I can't let him down."

"And I can't help it that I'm nervous. He's only *five.*"

"Which is plenty old enough to be in the company of an adult who knows how to take care of him. You can't lock the kid up forever for Christ's sake."

Michael watched her closely as the meaning set in, knowing that his sister would ultimately put her phobia aside to protect the feelings of her son.

"Please don't make me go up there and tell him it's off," he added. "Just trust me, okay?"

She nodded, but her eyes were suddenly filled with tears. Michael instantly felt guilty. Maintaining that the day-trip *would* take place had been like winning an argument. But the sight of his sister crying made him regret that he had.

He kneeled down behind her, put his arms around her thin shoulders. "Come on, you know it's going to be all right. I'll have the cell phone with me all day. I can check in every hour."

"Yeah, well you better." Mary yielded to the embrace for just a moment before straightening up. Forcing a smile, she turned halfway around and gave him a light, playful punch. "If you let him out of your sight for one minute, Michael, I'll kill you myself."

"Ouch," he rubbed the spot on his chest where she had hit him, managing to meet her eyes as he thought once again about the incident at the bar.

Tell her?

No. It would only lead to more questions about D'Amecourt, and about the secret that he still kept from her.

But you can't just do nothing. He thought of his first face-to-face meeting with D'Amecourt, five years earlier, during the interrogations around the disappearance of Benjamin. Thought, too, of the last exchange, two years ago, when he stood in front of D'Amecourt with blood soaking through his clothes ...

It was one of the most horrifying experiences of Michael's life. The grief and guilt were always with him, a shadow at the edge of his vision. Today the shadow felt closer, an ominous weight still lingering from a whole night of bad dreams.

He wondered again if now was the time to tell Mary about the secret he shared with D'Amecourt, and if his sister's full acceptance of him would be greater than her uneasiness over what he had done.

"I'm WEDDY!"

Justin's voice stopped the thought. Michael turned around to see the boy back in the kitchen doorway, a fistful of dollar bills in his hand, dark kiddie-style sunglasses slipping down over his nose.

"God help us," Michael joked.

The cargo shorts from the Gap had been bought on sale for Justin to wear to school when he grew into them the following year. But now they came down three inches below his knees.

The boy's favorite polo-style shirt was at least two sizes too big, and had been worn earlier in the week. Justin had evidently fished it out of the hamper.

"The shoes were my idea." Michael sheepishly remembered laying the brand new red Converse sneakers out next to the bed the night before.

Mary shook her head. "You're a real piece of work."

"Justin, or me?" Michael grinned.

"The both of *ya*. That shirt is *lime-green*."

"Bright, huh?"

"It'd probably glow in the dark. Justin, are you *sure* you want to run off with your crazy Uncle Michael?"

"Yup!" Justin was beaming. He raised the hand with the dollar bills higher. "I got my whole *awowance*."

"Your allowance." Mary worked to keep a straight face. "And how did you earn an *allowance*?"

"For all those days he drove me to the store," Michael deadpanned. "Also those shifts he picked up for me at the bar."

"You're incorrigible, little brother."

"I know."

"And an absolutely *terrible* influence."

"I know," Michael grinned and gave Justin a hug as he made his way out of the kitchen. Upstairs he went into his room, shut the door, and dialed Louis D'Amecourt's cell phone number again. D'Amecourt evidently still had the phone turned off. Michael left a recorded message, reiterating some of the details of the night before. He finished by telling D'Amecourt they were going to spend the day at AdventureWorld, a long-planned outing that he did not want to cancel. Knowing that D'Amecourt would want to question him about the conversation with the stranger, Michael offered to meet him, later.

But it's hours from now, he told himself. *Too far away to ruin your time with Justin.*

Michael finished the mug of coffee and took a long, hot shower, scrubbing his skin briskly and feeling just a bit better 30 minutes later when he came back downstairs.

Mary was noticeably more relaxed, due in part to another conversation with Joan, who had probably reminded her of the importance of making her son's childhood as normal as possible.

Which meant being able to let him out of her sight, Michael thought. *Letting him go—*

"We'll be getting there about 10:30," he said. "We'll give you a call at O'Malley's at about 2:30 when the lunch rush is over. We'll be home by 4, okay?"

Mary was barely listening as she reached out and brought Justin into a tight, confining hug. Her eyes were dreamily closed, her lips pressed against Justin's forehead.

"Mary?"

"Got it." Abruptly she stood up, as if it was suddenly imperative to put distance between herself and her son. The gesture was obviously difficult.

"All right, Michael." She smiled at him with a sense of trust that felt both subtle and profound. "He's all yours."

There was an awkward silence as he reached for Justin's hand. "Okay little boy, AdventureWorld, here we come."

"Okay!" Justin grabbed his finger and squeezed it, leading him to the door. Michael paused to check for his wallet, keys, and sunglasses. The two extra Tylenol he had put in his shirt pocket brought back a flash of the night before, a shiver at the back of his neck as he looked down at his nephew's sleep-tousled hair.

You can still call it off, he thought. *Postpone it. Give yourself a day to calm down.*

"Don't worry, momma." Justin smiled brightly at his mother. "Me 'n Uncle Mike will be okay."

"Of course we will." Michael told her as he stepped out to the front porch. Then without looking back he took Justin by the hand and headed to the car.

Five

Timing is everything. The thought was at the top of the abductor's mind as Michael and Justin Bennett moved through the swelling crowd less than 30 feet away.

The disguise had come together perfectly. A dull gray baseball cap with no logo. Dark sunglasses that subtly altered the shape of the face. A non-streak Mennen bronzer that in two hours had done the work of an entire summer in the Caribbean sun.

The cool temperatures were also beneficial. The nondescript khaki windbreaker was about two sizes too big, leaving plenty of room in the shoulders and around the waist for padding that added the appearance of 40 pounds.

The abductor was pleased to see that Michael looked distracted, his normally bright eyes and handsome faced dulled by a fatigue that slowed his step and occasionally made him cringe from the childish screams and clanging carnival music that accompanied most of the rides.

It's going to be so easy. On a busy day like today AdventureWorld accommodated upwards of 10,000 visitors. The sheer size of the crowd would be a thick barrier between Michael and Justin once they were separated. From there the getaway would be a cinch. No chance for Mary to swoop in for the last-minute save.

No way out for Michael, a prime suspect once again.

* * *

Justin had gotten frightened and teary-eyed on the Mini Jack-Rabbit, a kid's version of the park's rollercoaster. But after the first short plunge the terror faded. Almost immediately he wanted to ride it again.

"This time by *myself!*" he announced bravely.

Michael told him no twice before Justin let it pass. The child was excited to the point of sensory overload and he had wandered out of Michael's sight for over a minute as they scouted through the crowd for an empty lunch table.

Which made the disappearance of the bracelet even more disturbing.

"It *bwoke* again." Justin's eyes widened in fear over the edge in Michael's voice when he noticed that it was gone.

"When?"

"When you went to get more napkins."

In line now at the Sidewinder, Michael looked back 300 yards to the food stands where they had eaten lunch 20 minutes earlier.

"I put it on the picnic table," Justin said. "The *red* one."

"Why didn't you tell me?"

"I forgot."

"Justin..."

"And I just *wemembered*, right now."

Michael felt a grinding cramp in his stomach. He had made the mistake of eating a hot dog topped with melted cheese. A bad move considering the lingering nausea from the night before. He was certain now that the stranger who had approached him had put some kind of drug in his drink. It was the only way to explain the knifing pains in his gut and the headache that simply would not go away.

"Okay, line 'er up!" the attendant for the Sidewinder called out. Michael watched as the train emptied and children began crowding into the seats. There were at least a dozen kids ahead of them, most of them in a crowd of rowdy pre-teen boys wearing church group t-shirts that Michael had noticed at several points during the day.

"Come *on,* Uncle Michael!"

"I don't know..." Michael hesitated. The Sidewinder was a long, low-slung train ride. They had already waited in line for 20 minutes. Going back for the bracelet meant losing their place.

"Come *on*, Uncle Michael." Justin pulled insistently on his hand. Two of the boys who had gotten in the middle seat changed their minds and stepped out. Seeing plenty of extra room, Justin jumped up and down with anticipation.

"*Aaaallll* aboard," the attendant called out.

Michael looked back at the picnic tables. He thought of Mary standing next to him at the work bench the night before, remembered the worry on her face as she held the bracelet in her hand.

"Sorry, little buddy." Michael leaned down to eye level with Justin. "But we're gonna' have to go back to the hot dog stand for a few minutes. Your mom would go crazy if she knew we lost that bracelet."

"*Noooo.*" Justin looked forlornly at the ride, his eyes welling up in tears.

"Come on, we'll make it a quick trip, okay?"

Justin pushed out his lower lip in a pout.

"Hey." Michael said. Then with a playful growl he picked the boy up, squeezing and tickling him about the waist. Justin couldn't help but giggle as he hefted him over his right shoulder and started back toward the picnic tables.

He took no more than five steps before the pain hit him again.

"What's *wong,* Uncle Mike?"

He had stopped in mid-stride. It felt as if someone were scraping the inside of his stomach with a serrated knife. He set Justin down with a groan, and leaned against a lamppost.

"Your Uncle Mike's got a tummy ache." Nausea rolled up in a wave, making him gag. "A bad one."

He looked toward the hot dog stands again. The lines were long. The picnic tables were crowded. He took Justin's hand. "Come on, little guy."

Despite the relatively cool temperatures, he was sweating heavily. Stopping at a water fountain, he took the two Tylenol he had in his pocket, remembered hearing somewhere that too much of it would make his stomach bleed, then shuttled the thought away as he moved toward the picnic table where they had eaten lunch. The table was crowded with a large family speaking Spanish now. Michael approached the table and asked, in English, if they had seen the bracelet. The adults and older children gave him blank looks but Michael noticed a twitch of recognition on the face of a younger boy.

"A silver-colored bracelet," he kept eye contact with the child, speaking this time in Spanish.

"I found here." The boy told him, pointing under the table.

Michael sighed with relief and looked at the bare ground.

"But I already take to the cook," the boy said.

"Where?" Michael stood up.

The boy pointed back toward the hot dog stand.

"*Gracias*," Michael told him. He smiled down at Justin, but felt another bolt of nausea, a dizziness that made him lean against the picnic table for balance.

You're about to get sick. He looked around to get his bearings. The restrooms were a good 200 yards away. At the hot dog stand there were at least a dozen people in line, and one harried teenage clerk taking orders.

Beside him, Justin looked anxiously toward the Sidewinder as the train let out a long, mournful whistle. He took a deep breath, taking Justin by the hand and intentionally tightening the muscles in his abdomen as he moved toward the hot dog vendor.

"Excuse me," Michael said.

"You gotta' get in line," the clerk answered.

"I'm not ordering anything. I just want to check and see if someone turned in—"

"Back of the line," the clerk snapped.

Michael felt his face flushing under the glaring looks of the people in line. His throat was tight as he leaned closer to the counter, speaking both to the woman who had been giving her order and to the clerk. "Look, my nephew lost his ID bracelet at the picnic tables over there. A kid told me he brought it up here. Can you please help me?"

The woman at the front of the line nodded slightly, as if agreeing to stop her order so the clerk could respond. The clerk gave her a look of betrayal and glared back at Michael. "I haven't seen it."

"Can you check—"

"Hold on." The clerk set his order pad and pencil down and went back into the tiny kitchen, where Michael glimpsed a large-bellied woman in a white apron doing the cooking. After a full minute of retrieving keys and unlocking drawers the clerk returned wearing an annoying smirk.

"You were wrong. We don't have it."

"Are you sure? The kid over there said he brought it up to the counter."

The clerk looked toward the picnic tables and frowned. Michael turned around to see the Hispanic family had gone. Behind the clerk another cook opened the door to the glass-fronted hot dog roaster. The sweet-burnt smell of the meat hit his nostrils with a force that made him gag.

Michael stepped back, holding Justin's hand tightly, and gasped for fresh air.

"Uncle Mike you look *sick*!"

He pressed his fist against his lips and nodded as he picked up Justin, and started jogging toward the restrooms. He was 20 yards away from the men's room door when the vomit reached the back of his throat. Breathing through his nose he managed, just barely, to hold it in.

Stepping inside, he found the men's room swarming with boys from the church group crowding around the sinks. He looked in a panic toward the stalls, all occupied but one.

He set Justin down and moved quickly toward the stall door. There was an "out-of-order" sign on the toilet. Michael ignored it as he leaned over and violently threw up.

His undigested lunch came up in chunks, the smell making him gag again. Outside the stall the restroom filled with more raucous noise as the boys were joined by several more.

Still leaning over the toilet, he tilted his head toward the doorway. "Justin, you okay?"

"Yes, Uncle Michael."

He turned his head just in time to throw up again. Behind the sound of his retching he heard two boys laughing hysterically, and the sound of several toilets flushing at once.

Suddenly the boys were yelling. Michael stepped back and pushed the stall door open to see water spreading across the tile floor. The door swung back on loose hinges as he let go, and turned around toward the toilet again.

"*Ooh*, Uncle Mike—look!"

Justin's voice was followed by a wave of laughter.

"There's pee pee all over the floor!"

Justin's announcement brought the sound of a stampede as the flowing toilet water spread across the room. Michael opened the door and looked down to see it heading toward his own stall. The sight and the lingering smell of his own vomit made him retch again. Outside the door the children were starting to scatter.

Both of his palms were pressed to the tile wall and his head was spinning when the voice of the stranger came back to him.

"I know what yer doin' to that little boy."

He gagged again, dryly this time. When he blinked there were white flashes in front of his eyes, a memory's snapshot of blood-soaked sheets, blood on the ceiling, the walls—

"Justin—." He reached back to the stall door, swung it open, turned around ...

And stepped out of the stall. The tile floor was covered with water and urine from the overflowing toilet. The restroom was half-empty and the few boys who remained were rushing to get out the door.

He looked in both directions for Justin. For the lime-green shirt and red shoes ...

He must have gone outside with the crowd.

Michael leaned forward, both hands on his knees, feeling as if his insides had been emptied out. The filthy water from the choked toilets was still spreading across the floor as he made his way toward the sinks. He took just a moment to splash cold water on his face and grab a paper towel to dry off, the lingering sensation of vomit in his throat and the sight of the overflowing toilets making him almost certain he was going to throw-up again.

Somewhere else, not here, he thought. He went to the door, the bright sun stabbing at his eyes as he stepped outside.

"Justin?" His voice was hoarse and weak as he turned around.

The group of children had begun to disperse, and he was struck again by the sheer size of the crowd in the park beyond.

"Justin...?"

His eyes were wide, searching, searching ...

"JUSTIN!"

His heart slamming against his ribs as he called out again.

Six

The victim in the Capitol Hotel killing had a driver's license and registration that belonged to a man who had died in an auto accident years earlier. He had paid for his room in cash, signing the register with the name that matched the license: Bobby Freed. He had a green stamp on his hand that indicated he had been at a nearby gay bar shortly before he was murdered.

"A place called Club Night," Tommy Payne was telling her. "I'll probably go in there at some point to see what I can find out."

Gloria doubted it would be Payne's first visit. She had already figured out why he never talked about a girlfriend, and why he had chosen to live in a pricey one-bedroom condo in Dupont Circle instead of the much cheaper apartments in the nearby suburbs. Seated across from her now, in a secluded booth at the back of the Trio restaurant, he was wearing a faded denim jean jacket that set off his bright blue eyes and a white turtleneck shirt that showed off his well-built chest. He had arrived after a workout at Results, a U street gym a block from the Third District police station, where he would have fit in well with the pretty-boy crowd.

"Those are the basics of what I got after running around for a few hours." Payne tilted his head forward, his sun-streaked hair catching the late afternoon light streaming through the window. "Before D'Amecourt gave me my walking papers."

For a moment she thought she heard him wrong.

"I started to tell you as soon as I got here but I wanted you to know what I found out so far." Payne's face was tight as he sat back and crossed his arms. "He claimed I'm already working on too many open investigations. He wants me to spend my time shoring up the loose ends on those. He wants someone more senior handling this."

It was a strange justification, Gloria thought. Payne was only in his early 30s, but he was very well regarded for his abilities.

"Is that the only reason?" she asked him.

"Officially, I don't know." Payne stared down at his coffee. "Personally, I can take a guess."

"Personally."

"D'Amecourt's never liked me much."

She waited for Payne to continue. But instead of elaborating, he turned and reached into the gym bag on the seat next to him and pulled out a manila envelope.

"I want to show you something. I hope you don't get squeamish easily."

"No," she lied. She had eaten almost nothing in the last 24 hours, and images from the crime scene had flashed through her mind all night.

Payne kept his hands folded over the envelope. "Yesterday at the scene I started thinking about Sylvia Barshak. You know who she is, right?"

Gloria nodded. Barshak was a former D.C. homicide detective who had closed a number of high-profile cases before moving on to the FBI.

"One of the last murders she handled before her big move was really similar to this one. It was about two years ago." Payne pulled out a stack of 8 x 10 photos from the envelope and put them face down on the table, and studied her for a moment. "I should warn you—."

"I'm sure I can handle it," she cut him off. "Whatever it is."

She picked up the photos and lowered them below the edge of the table ... her heart quickening as she took in the details in every shot.

A male victim, naked, wrists tied to an iron headboard.

The eyes, half-open, glazed.

The wounds to the abdomen and legs, the chest—

The cloth over the mouth ... the large open wound in the neck.

She turned the pictures back upside down and set them on top of the table. "Where did this...?"

"It happened at The Larchmont, that swanky apartment building on Connecticut Avenue. The victim was leasing under the name Tom Handler, but his wallet was missing when the place was searched. The murder was almost identical to the case we're talking about now, from the multiple stab wounds to the circumstances that might have brought the victim and his killer together."

"They met in a bar?"

Payne nodded. "Club Night. At least that's what it looks like, since this victim was also seen there just a couple of hours before he was killed."

"So both victims might have met their killer in the same place."

"It looks that way."

"Did you tell D'Amecourt about the similarity?"

"Oh yeah, I told him. And was immediately *corrected*."

Gloria frowned. Payne leaned slightly forward and lowered his voice.

"He insisted I was wrong. He made a big deal of the fact that in the Larchmont murder the front door to the apartment had been jimmied and forced open, meaning the killer broke his way in. He also pointed to the fact that there wasn't any evidence of drug use in the first case. I told him those characteristics were peripheral and we'd have to be stupid not to see the similarities. We got into an argument. It was tense."

"So you think that had something to do with you getting reassigned?"

"I'm sure it didn't help, especially not with our history."

"Your history?"

"We'd argued a lot about this earlier case, too. D'Amecourt got ticked off when he found out I was pushing Barshak for more information on it. Plus, there were some other factors that really made me question..."

Payne looked past her, as if he were summoning the nerve to continue.

"Question what, Tommy?"

"This earlier case never made the papers. And I'd be willing to bet I'd be talking to a brick wall if I asked Barshak about it now."

It took a moment to process what he was telling her.

"You mean it's been buried."

Payne nodded. "You want to take a guess about why?"

Gloria looked back at him without answering.

"I found out the victim had been in several pornographic magazines and Web sites." Payne blushed. "All gay."

"*You* found out?"

Payne nodded.

Gloria cleared her throat, felt the heat coming to her face. "Did D'Amecourt ask you how?"

"No, but I didn't really need to spell it out, Gloria."

Payne's embarrassment was palpable, a sharp contrast to his normally confident, almost macho bearing. Gloria knew where it was coming from. D'Amecourt's demeanor had always made it clear that he found it difficult to relate to women officers, and his reckless comments about the "numerous problems" that came from the Metropolitan Police Department's aggressive recruiting of Blacks and Hispanics had made it into the papers more than once. Having a gay homicide detective on his watch was probably pushing him to the edge.

"So he's got a problem with your lifestyle," she tried to sound casual. "Join the club."

"Right," Payne said. "But it could be more than that. You know what a blowhard he is about all of that 'cleaning up the streets' crap."

Gloria nodded. In the early 1990s, D'Amecourt had developed a reputation as a law and order cop who had forced numerous crackdowns on massage parlors, bathhouses. and stores that had sold pornography. Several busts had drawn the attention of television cameras and made headlines. and there had been plenty of grandstanding in D'Amecourt's public statements.

Gloria wondered what the commander would find more objectionable—the fact that the victim was gay, or that he posed for dirty pictures. Both factors could have led to his compulsion to take over—or conceal—the investigations of both crimes.

And you still don't know what happened to the picture of the little boy.

The question had been at the front of her mind all morning. She was about to ask about it as Payne leaned forward and pulled a piece of paper out of his back pocket. "There's something else I want to show you."

Payne put the paper on the table and turned it around. It was a print-out of an email message. Gloria felt Payne watching her intently as she read it through.

From: quietriot22
To: hotboy2@SENTRY
Subject: Re: What you owe
Received your message but will not deal through this email address. Contact me at 512-3211 when you arrive.

"Where did this come from?" she asked him.

"The original was in an inside pocket in the duffel bag in the Capitol Hotel victim's hotel room," Payne said. "I found it when I took the victim's property to the evidence locker. I missed it when I first went through the stuff at the scene."

"What have you done to check it out—did you call the number?"

"It's been disconnected. It was a number for a cell phone that was probably stolen. They're pretty easy to pick up on the black market."

"So it's untraceable."

"As far as I know."

Gloria looked at the message again. Over the past year her husband had developed an interest in the use of computers in criminal investigations. She had picked up enough information from their conversations to know that email addresses could be tracked—something Payne should have already done.

"The victim didn't have a computer in his hotel room." Payne looked as if he had read her mind. "But there was a receipt from a cyber-café around the corner in his wallet. He'd obviously used those computers to go online. He probably printed the email out so he'd have the number on hand."

"Do you know anything at all about who sent it?"

Payne looked frustrated. "No. I've used search engines for reverse email look-up, Web directories, everything I can find. I've gotten nothing. I was expecting to send it up to a computer expert at the FBI but then I got kicked off the case."

"After you showed this to D'Amecourt?"

"No."

She crossed her arms over her chest as the implication became clear. "So he doesn't know about it?"

Payne shook his head. "Like I said, I'd planned on getting it analyzed. But then he booted me off. I got suspicious—a little pissed off, too, I guess—and held it back. Now I'm sort of past the point of no return. If I add it to the report now D'Amecourt will see it, and ask me why I didn't tell him about it."

Gloria gave him a wary look. "You're playing with fire, Tommy."

"I know that. But I also know if I turn this over to D'Amecourt I'll never get the story behind it. I've gotta' see what I can find out on my own."

"You mean giving it to an expert," she said. "Someone on the outside."

"Yeah. Someone like your man, Booker."

"Whoa..." Gloria sat back.

"I know he's gone to two seminars on computer crime, and that he likes to tinker around." He gave her a self-deprecating look. "I'm sure he's eons ahead of me when it comes to the technology."

Payne was right about her husband's computer skills. Over the past few years he'd learned enough to start a second career. Not that he ever would. Right now all that mattered was working his way up through the ranks, making detective, although in this case it would be Payne who benefited most from his efforts.

"So what if we find out where it came from?" she asked.

"Then I'll take it to D'Amecourt. I assume he'll give it to whomever he's assigned to take my place."

"You could get in a lot of trouble for messing with the chain of evidence."

"I know that. But I've got every intention of sharing what I know, *when* I know it. Why should I just turn it over before I get a chance to find out what's behind it?"

Gloria looked at the note again. It was an intriguing clue, and she was anxious to see what Booker could learn. But Payne was leading both she and her husband into dangerous territory. In an instant she re-calculated the stakes. Demotion. Firing. Humiliation. Even if she kept her job D'Amecourt would hold a grudge forever.

"I need to ask you something before I decide," she said.

"All right."

"I saw something while I was waiting for you at the scene. A photograph on the floor, just barely under the bed." She watched Payne closely. "I went down the hall to answer a phone call, and when I came back it was gone."

"Gone?" Payne frowned.

"Yes. And this was long *before* the guys from the mobile lab got there, before the scene could be photographed or processed. There's no way it should have been taken away so fast."

Payne looked past her. His expression was difficult to read.

"Did you see it, Tommy?"

He made eye contact again. "No."

"And D'Amecourt didn't say anything about it either?"

Payne shook his head, and there was a new spark of interest in his eyes. "What else can you tell me?"

Gloria paused, fervently wishing that she had been able to get a closer look. "It was a picture of a little kid, a boy. From the shoulders up. It was practically covered by the bedspread and I couldn't see much. But I think there was a mark or something on his face."

Payne frowned again. For a moment he looked as if he was about to speak, but he stayed quiet.

"It felt strange to come back there and see it gone, Tommy, and I'm almost certain D'Amecourt took it."

Payne cleared his throat. "But you didn't *see* him—"

The ring of her cell phone cut him off. She glanced at the incoming number, and saw that it was from Booker, who was on duty today.

"No, I didn't see him, but I know it disappeared just a couple of minutes after he got there. Do you mind if I get this?"

Payne shook his head. There was a faraway look in his eyes.

The connection was filled with static, but she picked up the stress in Booker's voice right away.

"A little boy got kidnapped today. It's all over the news."

For several seconds she was unable to speak.

"It happened this afternoon at AdventureWorld," Booker said. "They're showing his picture on TV right now. It looks like it could be the kid you saw. He was with his uncle when it happened."

Gloria looked down at the email and the envelope with the crime scene photos, a feeling of dread sweeping through her.

"Where are you now?" she asked him.

"I'm at the lounge at the Fifth District. Standing 10 feet from D'Amecourt's office."

D'Amecourt, again.

"He's been out all day but he came rushin' in just a few minutes ago. I caught him in the john. I made the mistake of askin' him what was wrong."

"What do you mean?"

"He told me to mind my own goddamn business," Booker paused. "Then he started to cry."

❧

Seven

I left him alone.

Michael gripped the edge of the table and fought the urge to scream.

Knowing something wasn't right.

He had known the instant he stepped out of the restroom that Justin would be gone. Had felt his *absence* as he spun around, his eyes frantically searching, his voice going hoarse as he shouted Justin's name.

It had taken at least 15 minutes for one of the security guards to radio a physical description of Justin to the rest of the patrolling force. And by the time the Montgomery County police arrived Michael was in shock, his entire body seized by an uncontrollable shaking. Seated now at the conference room table in the AdventureWorld administrative office, Michael watched as one of the officers stood by the door in the hallway, chatting with a secretary.

Talking about you. The tilt of the cop's head and the woman's occasional glance into the room made it obvious. Michael shut his eyes and covered his face with his hands. *As if you're a suspect. Again.*

At the sound of footsteps he looked up to see Mary coming down the long hallway toward the room. Martin had his arm around her, his free hand at her elbow, halfway supporting her as they approached.

Michael sat up as she came to the door. For several seconds she simply stared at him, wide eyed, gaunt.

Justin is gone?

He saw the question in her eyes and knew that regardless of what she had been told, she had been desperately hoping it wasn't true. But now she knew that it was. Michael felt a troubling buzz at the back of his brain, a sensation that signaled the onset of one of the now-familiar moments in which he and Mary would communicate without speaking. The buzz became a roar as the words he could not bring himself to say raced through his mind.

Mary, Mary. I'm so sorry. One minute he was there. The next he just wasn't.

"Noooo! "she screamed, jerking away from Martin, her whole body tilting forward, both hands palm down on the conference room table.

Go to her, now. Michael was aching to hold her, to beg forgiveness, to tell her *anything* to give her hope. He was conscious of his chair falling backwards as he stepped away from the table... of the surreal stillness of the room as he moved toward her ...

Of another anguished wail as she collapsed to the floor.

* * *

"I think you need to go through this again," the Montgomery County police official, a big, black, sharply dressed man named Bender, was saying. "'Cause I'm still havin' trouble understandin'."

"I've told you the whole story." Michael's voice cracked. "Twice."

"Yeah I know, but it all still sounds *funny* to me; you know?"

"*No.*" Michael summoned the courage to glare back at him. His eyes were burning. "I *don't* know."

"You said he had a bracelet with his *identification*," Bender frowned and pretended to be more confused than he really was, "but you took it off when you went to get your lunch."

"I didn't take it off. It broke."

"Why? 'Cause you loosened it?"

Michael knew exactly where the questions were going. Immediately after Mary had collapsed she had been led into another room. Obviously, she'd been questioned. *So they could check her version against yours.*

"I didn't loosen it." He swallowed, tried to keep his voice even. "Yesterday it came loose on its own. Last night I tried to fix it."

"But it came off again?"

"Yes."

"Without you knowin' it."

"I told you. As soon as I realized it was missing we went back to the hot dog stand to find it. You can ask the clerk—"

"I already got somebody to do that. He said they never saw it."

"He's wrong. Another little boy found it and put it on the counter. Someone either took it... or maybe it just got lost."

"But somehow you *knew* that was where it got lost?"

"That's where Justin said he thought he dropped it."

Bender squinted, looking more doubtful. "And what happened then?"

"I got sick so I ran to the restroom. I was inside the stall, throwing up when a bunch of kids backed up the toilets and everybody rushed out." Michael pressed his fingertips against his forehead as the images rushed back. "There was piss in the water, covering the floor. The kids all ran from it, including Justin."

He sat back and met Bender's eyes. "By the time I got out, he was gone."

"Just like that," Bender said.

"Yes."

"And what time was that, did you say?"

Michael looked at the wall clock. "A little after one, I think."

Right in the midst of the lunch rush. He shut his eyes, saw Mary serving her customers, imagined her laughing with the bartender, winking at Martin at the head of his table. He knew that she, too, would have been keeping an eye on the clock, anxious for the call at 2 o'clock, when he had promised to check in.

"What did you do then?" Bender asked.

"I told you. I reported him missing and went looking for him." Michael felt a fresh surge of panic. "We should both be out there still—"

"Security already put out an all-points," Bender was scribbling notes in a pocket-sized tablet, not bothering to look up. "We got people goin' over the park... checkin' the rides... all the places where he could be hidin' out."

"But I need to be out there, too." He stood up. "*Please*—"

"No." Bender held up a hand. "We need you here to claim him when they figure out where he ran off to and bring him back."

Michael looked toward the hallway that Mary had disappeared into a few minutes earlier. He felt an odd sense of unease over what she might be revealing as her own questioning continued. He thought of the altercation the night before. The stranger at Club Night had talked about cutting people up, and had clearly known about his life with Justin. All through the night he had focused on his own fears, thinking mostly in terms of D'Amecourt, the murder from two years earlier, the insinuation that he might be next.

"I know what you been doin' to that little boy."

The voice of the stranger came at him again.

"I know—"

"I don't think he ran off," Michael said.

Bender frowned.

"I think he was *taken*."

Bender squinted slightly, eyeing him even more suspiciously. "What makes you say that?"

"Something happened to me last night... at a bar." Michael's jaw twitched uncontrollably as he struggled to say the words. "At Club Night."

Bender tilted his head as he listened to a description of the conversation and the assault. Michael watched him closely, looking for any sign of belief that *someone else* might have managed to lead Justin away from the restrooms, into the crowd, into a void—

"So what do you think he meant?" Bender said as he finished.

"I don't know."

"You're saying at the time you thought he was just threatening you, but now you think he knew something about your nephew?"

"Yes," Michael answered. "It sounded like he had information that something was about to happen."

"And you're tellin' me *now* that you were scared."

"Yes."

"But not enough to call the police."

Michael looked at him, and considered admitting that he *had* called the police. He had left Louis D'Amecourt a voice mail revealing everything he remembered about the altercation.

But he knew that D'Amecourt would have wanted him to keep quiet about the incident. D'Amecourt would be worried that Bender knew about it now. Worried about another cop picking up a trail that D'Amecourt wanted hidden at all costs.

"No, not at the time," he answered. "I didn't find out until this morning that Scott Brown was out of prison."

"Who?"

"Scott Brown." Michael felt the muscles in his face twitching as Bender continued staring at him. Bender was obviously unaware of who Scott was, or what he had done.

But then another young cop stepped into the room. Michael remembered Bender had sent him off to "verify" the conversation with the hot dog vendor. The cop was carrying a folder now.

"Did you find anything?" Michael asked.

The cop gave him a sour look and motioned for Bender to step into the hallway. Michael heard the murmur of their voices, and then Bender, saying "Well I'll be goddamned."

He knew what had transpired even before Bender stepped back into the room and opened the folder. Bender's eyes gleamed as he took out the *Washington Blade* with Mary's article and laid it down like a winning poker hand on the table.

"So what do you think?" Bender asked. "You gonna' try and get away with it again?"

Michael glanced down at the article and the photos, saw the old shot of Benjamin, playing in the backyard. A recent photo of Justin, dressed up on Easter Sunday. A five-year-old picture of Scott Brown after the trial, his face twisted into a snarl, hands cuffed behind his back as the FBI led him away.

He shut his eyes, saw himself back in the kitchen, Mary's eyes shining with tears of worry.

"If you let him out of your sight for one minute, Michael, I'll kill you myself."

Beneath him the floor began to spin. The walls tilted and closed in around him. He grabbed the side of the table with both hands. "You have to believe me. *Please..."*

Bender shook his head, his disgust apparent as he looked down at the article again.

Eight

The disappearance of Justin Bennett made news within hours, thanks to an Associated Press reporter who had heard the scanner call to the Montgomery County police and had gotten to AdventureWorld in time to capture a photograph of Michael Bennett being questioned by the officers on the scene.

By the next morning, the *Washington Post* had a front-page story topped by a headline "For Second Time, Family Faces Tragedy, Suspicions." Gloria read it in the online edition at 5 A.M., after hours at Booker's side, surfing the web for as much information as possible about the abduction of Benjamin Bennett five years before. While much was being made out of the fact that Scott Brown, the lead suspect in the first kidnapping, was out on parole and nowhere to be found, the reporter also noted that, again, Michael Bennett was only a few yards away when the child disappeared.

And yet for the second time he claimed to have seen nothing.

"That's what he said, huh?" Booker turned his heavy body in the swivel computer chair and gave her a dubious look.

"It's a story he apparently stuck with," Gloria said, "even though it made him look guiltier."

Gloria glanced again at the first item that had come up in the Google search of Michael's name, a recent article in *The Washington Blade.* The article was written by Michael's sister, with a raised quote on the first page: *"My brother lives for his nephew. He loves Justin as if he were his own son."*

Underneath the quote was a picture of Michael holding Justin Bennett on his shoulders at the child's fifth birthday party, Justin playfully pulling at Michael's hair with one hand and trying to cover his uncle's eyes with the other.

Alongside it was a photo of Michael Bennett from St. Albans, an expensive preparatory high school, where he had played tennis and lacrosse.

Next to that was a photo of Bennett just a year later at the city's annual Gay Pride parade, shirtless and laughing as another muscular man, apparently in his early 20s, planted a kiss on his cheek.

On the following page was a series of photos: Bennett sitting with Justin in an inflatable pool in the backyard of the house that he shared with his sister. Another shot of Bennett looking sleepy-eyed in front of a computer screen. The article went into some detail about how Bennett had begun college as an early elementary education major, and that he had planned to spend his life as a teacher. And even though he had never been charged with the abduction of his nephew, the steady stream of damning information about his personal life made it extremely unlikely that he would ever work in the teaching field. So he had changed his major to computer science, "trading in a life around children for a life around machines," as Mary Bennett wrote in the article.

Gloria turned the page, gazed for a long time at another older photo of Michael Bennett seated on a beanbag chair, his arm around a little boy's shoulder as the two of them read aloud from a book. Both she and Booker recognized the chair and the room around it, in the Happy Haven daycare center. Happy Haven was annexed to a shelter for homeless families on the 7th Street corridor. The parents of children who stayed there during the day were part of a subsidized job training program, and generally powerless to have much of a say as to how the Center was run. Michael Bennett had been a longtime volunteer there.

She realized that regardless of his tarnished name, Michael Bennett *still* aspired to spend his life around children. His sister was probably correct in saying that he would never get a job as a teacher, or be hired to work around children of middle-class parents. But he had probably never even been questioned at Happy Haven. The staff at the center was thrilled with any help it could get.

Weary from lack of sleep, her mind swimming with questions, Gloria glanced again at all the photos of Michael Bennett, juxtaposed them with her memory of the Capitol Hotel murder victim.

You could have stopped this. She was almost certain of it as she remembered the anxious look on D'Amecourt's face as he came to the murder scene. *If you had asked him about that picture right away.*

The guilt was sudden and intense as she looked again at the folders containing the documents that Payne had given her. She and Booker had reviewed them all at length hours earlier. She had been dozing off on the couch when Booker had said something about one of the photographs of the Capitol Hotel killing, which Payne had emailed her shortly after they had left the restaurant. The photos came from the digital camera that Payne now carried with him to all crime scenes, to ensure that he would always have back-up shots.

She clicked until she found the photo Booker had referred to.

"I want to look at the tattoo again," she said.

Booker clicked into a close-up of the photo, which had been taken to show the wounds on the victim's thighs and calves. The bed sheets underneath were soaked in blood. The victim's legs were hairless. The left ankle had a tattooed illustration of a thick cross that came to a sharp point at the bottom. The point impaled a snake that had wrapped itself around the cross. The snake was baring its fangs in an expression that all-at-once blended anger, evil and pain.

"John Lee Ferguson had one like it," Booker said.

John Lee Ferguson was a white man who had run one of the largest cocaine and heroin rings in the city, one that had supplied countless addicts in and around the once solidly middle class neighborhood that Booker had grown up in. Booker had played a major role in the raid that had taken down half a dozen of the neighborhood's crack houses, and had counted it as one of the greatest successes of his young career. The circumstantial evidence tying Ferguson to the ring had been substantial, but on the basis of a technicality the entire case had been dismissed. Ferguson had gone free.

But he had not gone unexposed. During the trial, investigators had also turned up clues that linked Ferguson to several other enterprises, including a prostitution ring and several pornographic Web sites that included material geared toward pedophiles.

Gloria thought of the photo at the foot of the bed, her stomach knotting at the possibility that Justin was in Ferguson's hands.

"Ferguson is a freak, but because he's a skinhead there are guys all over the country who are trying to emulate him," Booker said. "Having the tattoo is like wearing the colors of a gang. A statement. But you know there's so many guys that got 'em, there's no way to be sure this victim had any connection to the cult. He could have been just another wannabe."

"According to the driver's license, he's from West Virginia," Gloria said. "I know it's fake but—"

"It could mean something," Booker said. "Remember that's where Ferguson went—or supposedly went—after the trial."

Gloria remembered one final article done by the *Afro-American*, a weekly that had covered the trial. Ferguson reportedly lived at a compound in a West Virginia county "that had often been hostile to outside law enforcement." A place where the local police had also refused to cooperate in providing any information to journalists who continued to follow the story.

But how is it connected to Justin Bennett? She pushed her thoughts back to the circumstances around the kidnapping itself. Returning to the *Blade* article, she focused on the paragraphs that discussed Scott Brown, Mary Bennett's former boyfriend, who was still the lead suspect in Benjamin Bennett's kidnapping. The evidence against Brown had been substantial, but had fallen just short of what had been needed to bring the case to trial. In a completely separate case, Brown had been tried and convicted on drug distribution charges, and sentenced to prison.

Separate but not unrelated, Gloria thought. At the top of the stack of articles was a five-year-old *Washington Post* story about the circumstances of Scott Brown's arrest. The article that accompanied the picture described the friendship between Michael Bennett and Scott Brown, going into detail about what Brown's friends and family called "an act of betrayal" by Michael that resulted in the charges that sent Brown to prison.

But the article also described Brown's background, his hobbies—

And his "genius." Gloria read through an interview with one of Brown's former college professors. Like Michael Bennett, Scott Brown was a computer whiz. He had been sentenced in 2001 and—thanks to his family's connections—sent to a minimum-security facility in eastern Pennsylvania, no more than a three-hour drive from Washington.

Gloria was virtually certain that he would have had access to a computer there. *Plus the freedom to practice what he knew*, she thought. Suddenly it was easy to picture Scott Brown in the "library" of a country club prison, hunched over a keyboard, arranging the abduction online—.

She looked at the print-out of the email message Payne had given her. "We need to talk about this. It sounded like it would be impossible to trace—"

"I already got a head start."

She frowned in surprise. It had been just a few hours earlier that she had shown it to him for the first time. "When?"

"When you were dozin' on the couch."

There was a gleam in his eyes. She knew at once that she no longer needed to convince him to get involved. The tattoo, the email, and the thought of John Lee Ferguson had gotten him hooked.

"What did you find out, Booker?"

"Not a lot, but—"

"But *what?*"

Booker turned the swivel chair to face the desk, tapped the keyboard, and brought the computer screen to life. "Enough to make me wonder what Michael Bennett's really trying to hide."

Nine

Ten blocks east of North Capitol Street, in the back room of a derelict row house, Harland Till shifted the broken floorboards and hid his tools.

The compartment underneath the boards was large enough to hold everything: the gun, the electrical tape, the eight-inch hunting knife. The compartment was located in a room at the back of the house rented to an old man Till had murdered two hours earlier, a man who lived alone and faithfully paid his rent in money orders to a landlord who lived two states away. Till had met the man in a rundown gay bar on Capitol Hill months before, had followed him home, and allowed the man to fondle and kiss him for several minutes for the $50 that the man had pulled out of a kitchen drawer. Knowing that he might have a need for more money in the near future, Till had watched him for several more days to determine that he was a recluse, and earlier this afternoon Till had met up with him again, submitting to just a few moments of grappling—the man visibly salivating as he ran his hands along the muscles of Till's thighs—before swinging around with a punch that had taken him down hard.

Strangling him had been easy. And with a short trip in the man's ancient but remarkably well-preserved Buick, dumping him in the landfill in rural Howard County had been easy, too. There was no real jolt, no real *release*, in the killing. It was merely a convenience. He knew the man wouldn't be easily missed, and his house would offer as much shelter and seclusion as Till needed to put the plan in place.

Till felt restless as he watched the stories over and over on the evening news, his anger intensifying as Michael Bennett stared straight into the camera, proclaiming his innocence, asking for the *"public's help!"*

"Liar," Till said out loud as he sealed the compartment. "Liar..."

Till lowered his voice, whispering vows of vengeance with a plea to God. The same God that had allowed the innocence of Harland Till as a young child to be stolen by the Reverend William Willow. But as he closed his eyes and said the words and tried to *think* about God, the visions brought him the image of Willow instead.

Willow soaking wet, with his long, black hair plastered wildly down across his long, pale face as he appeared at the front door, seeking shelter from the rain. Willow letting himself in, finding Till's mother passed out in her easy chair, a near-empty bottle of vodka at her feet. Willow stooping down, whispering something in her ear, pulling a knife from his pocket...

Slitting her throat ...

As a five-year-old Harland Till had watched it all from the crack of a partially open closet door. Had cried out loud at the sight of her waking, standing, falling back on the chair. Had cowered in the closet as Willow reached in, grabbed him by the neck and pulled him out into the slick, blood-soaked floor...

Willow had held him tightly under one arm as he carried him—wriggling and crying—out to the waiting car. Then he had shoved him in the back seat and held the bloody knife just inches above his face, keeping it there until he promised to sit still. Yet just seconds after he had nodded in terrified agreement Willow had swung around with a cloth soaked in a smell that Harland as an adult knew as chloroform; had shoved it against his nose and stared at him until the world went black.

It felt like days later when he awakened, halfway across the country. Reverend Willow no longer had a long black beard. His face was clean-shaven and the hair that had hung in a long ponytail was cropped close to his skull.

"You're mine now little boy," Willow had told him. *"It's God's will and it's my will. And if you ever defy either of us you'll be sacrificed like your mother and all of the whores who came before her."*

Willow had begun molesting him immediately, had made it a nightly occurrence for nearly 12 years as the two of them traveled across the country. Willow's preaching on the revival circuit never made a lot of money, but it was enough to keep the two of them in good cars and roadside motels; places on the edges of the towns where Willow worked, but always distant from the houses and schools and families of normal children. As Till's body began to change Willow became more gentle, and by the time he was in his middle teens the Reverend no longer dominated him. Instead he became almost docile.

"I always knew you'd grow to love me," Willow's last words were said in a breathy, fervent whisper. *"I always believed you'd be grateful for the everlasting redemption—"*

The underhanded thrust of the knife had stopped him, the blade going up and deep into Willow's ribcage. The shock delaying Willow's reaction just long enough for a 17-year-old Harland to wrench the knife free and bring it quickly back down; the next blow glancing off Willow's cheek but twisting right into his neck and sending a spray of bright arterial blood onto the walls, the ceiling, the linens of the motel bed. The blood covering both of their naked bodies and pooling beneath Till's feet as he stepped back to look from a distance at what he had done.

Later, after a long hot shower in the motel bathroom and a cross-country bus ride that took him to a new life, he realized that the killing had taken less than a minute. But the peaceful, almost tranquilizing feeling of *relief* had stayed with him for weeks. And it was nearly six months later, in another bedroom where he had allowed himself to be taken, and *touched*, that the rage had slammed into him again.

It was hard to remember how many men he had killed since then, but the first, Reverend Willow, was fresh on his mind as he thought about Michael Bennett. Bennett, a homosexual who had obviously been involved, for the second time, with the disappearance of his own sister's child.

"Open your eyes to God. Confess—"

The phrase floated like scripture in Till's mind. He imagined speaking it as a commandment as Michael Bennett hung by his wrists. Imagined himself cutting Bennett in as many places and for as long as it took to find out *where* Justin Bennett could be found. He felt a sense of angry exhilaration as he made his way back to the house's front parlor, which was filled with a mismatch of second- hand furniture and piles of yellowing newspapers. The small TV cast a greenish glow on Till's face as he watched another round of news coverage of Justin Bennett's disappearance at the park.

The camera panning the crowd, the delighted faces of so many innocent children.

Cutting to an image of Michael Bennett rushing to an awaiting car, his head tilted down, his face caught in a scowl as someone off-camera gripped him by the elbow, spinning him around.

The next shots were the same as those that had been used on the earlier broadcasts. Still photos of the first child that Michael Bennett had stolen five years earlier. Old news footage of Michael Bennett in handcuffs, cutting to Bennett leaving a courthouse, wearing a dark suit.

Cutting to an image of Bennett walking free.

Not this time. Till sat back as the news story ended. *Not now.*

Till looked up at the overhead beams that ran across the back room ceiling. Hours earlier he had knocked out the ceiling drywall so that rope could be tied around them... *so that Michael Bennett could be hung from them...* with the heavy twine binding his wrists and ankles. Remembering the photographs he had found in the dead man's bag, the transcripts from the Internet chat room, the article in the gay newspaper, Till began thinking about the call he would soon make to Michael Bennett—a call that would use the threat of blackmail to lure Bennett into the trap.

Within hours Michael Bennett would have no choice but to follow his directions. This time tomorrow he would be captured, bound, compelled to tell the truth about what he had done.

Then, after *another* session with the knife, Harland Till the killer would become Harland Till the avenger. He himself would guide the child home.

On the television the newscaster was promising "more details" on the story during the 11 o'clock broadcast as the camera zeroed in on a picture of Justin Bennett taken at kindergarten. The homely wine stain made him look even more vulnerable with his shy smile and wide, alert eyes.

"God loves you boy." In the bank of memory, Till heard the voice of Reverend Willow as he recited the words. "God's gonna help you find your way soon."

* * *

In the front parlor of a spacious Victorian house at the edge of Frederick, Maryland, less than an hour's drive from the amusement park where the boy had been snatched, Zachary Alan Taylor took a long sip of Jameson's Irish Whiskey and tried to summon the nerve to do the job.

The booze burned as it slid down his throat. It turned his complexion bright pink in his mirrored reflection over the little bar. And it made it him feel even more anxious as the minutes ticked by.

"*Make it painless but quick*," the kidnapper had told him. "*Put the body in a box and weight it down so it sinks to the bottom immediately. You'll get paid in a week, after I'm absolutely sure there are no loose ends.*"

Hesitation had been his first mistake. Hesitation driven by surprise at the sight of the birthmark on the side of the child's face. Hesitation, surprise, and then anger at the realization that killing a little kid was still damn difficult, regardless of how much money was at stake.

It was already after 5 P.M. The cell phone on the table was going to ring any minute. In the basement, the little boy might already be awakening, and crying, his voice echoing between the thick cement walls...

Taylor drained the glass, sighing as his nerves began to calm. On the kitchen table was a pillow that he could use to cover the boy's face, making it possible to suffocate him without ever looking into his eyes. It would be quick, but if his experience with adult victims was any indication, the boy would struggle even with the sedative in his system, the body fighting reflexively against the sudden assault of death.

"*It's more money than you've ever made, Zachary.*"

The kidnapper's voice was a tinny memory in his mind.

"*Enough to let you get away for good.*"

He sighed again, envisioning the emerald waters and the sprawling cottage on the Belizean beach where he would soon be living, retired and rich. The beach and the cottage were like a mirage in his mind as he headed toward the kitchen and the basement stairs.

The heavy chime of the doorbell stopped him. Taylor turned to see his neighbor waving at him through the window alongside the porch. He had no choice but to answer.

"Hello, Zachary." The woman who lived in the pink house directly across the street was named Charlotte. She had apricot-colored hair swept up and sprayed into a stiff bob and a wide, round face with cream-colored skin that she sheltered from the sun. She was wearing a fresh coat of lipstick and a powdery perfume that instantly made Taylor's eyes water.

Taylor said hello, his body blocking the doorway. He wanted this over with quickly. With a ceremonial flourish, the woman swung a plate of brownies around from behind her back.

"*Voila.*"

Taylor offered his often-practiced shy smile. "You shouldn't have," he said, for want of anything better. He reached out to take the plate, his mind racing for an excuse for not inviting her in.

"You need to find a little classier place to hang out in, Zachary."

Taylor felt a catch in his breath. When he didn't answer she put both hands on her wide hips and shook her head. "The Mountain View Pub?" She was smirking now. "*Really*. I couldn't believe it when I saw you pulling out of that parking lot today."

Taylor affected a look of innocent confusion as his heart quickened. The Mountain View Pub was an abandoned restaurant on the least populated end of town. The exchange of the child had taken place behind an old dumpster in the secluded parking lot.

"You were there?"

"My brothers want to go into business together, partially with a loan from *moi*, of course. They sent me out to take a look at that dump. I drove up right when you were pulling out of the parking lot."

Taylor felt slightly relieved. The child had been unconscious on the floor of the backseat and covered in a blanket. Charlotte couldn't have seen him then.

"I did what they wanted—took a five-minute look and immediately decided I didn't have any interest at all in turning *their* dream investment into *my* financial nightmare." Charlotte waved her hand dismissively. "But I did think it was ironic that you'd be passing through there right as I arrived."

"I was out running errands," he told her. "I think I pulled into that parking lot to turn around."

"I figured it was something like that, which is what I told my cousin."

"Your cousin?"

"Jimmy. He's a Frederick County cop. The guy used to *live* at the Mountain View. I told him I'd seen you there when he asked me about you today. He's heard me complaining about how many times I've wished you'd finally get off the dime and take me out to dinner. He's as worried as I am that I'm never gonna get a fella." She smiled, as if she found her forwardness amusing. "He thinks I'm barkin' up the wrong tree. But he's always been suspicious any way."

"Suspicious." Taylor involuntarily repeated the word.

"Says any 50-year-old man workin' in a public library probably decided long ago what he wants in life and what he doesn't."

She was looking at him appraisingly now. Taylor was wiry and deceivingly strong. But to her eyes, and to anyone else in the small, sometimes claustrophobic little town, he knew he came across as bookish and sedentary. A quiet lifetime bachelor who drove a seven-year-old car. A man who was unfailingly polite to his neighbors but who apparently valued his solitude behind the curtained windows of his home.

Remembering the real reason Charlotte Johnson was standing in his doorway, he knew exactly what to do.

"Well if your cousin Jimmy *has* to know," he said, "I'm finally tying the old knot."

Fat Charlotte's smile faded.

"It happened quickly. On a trip to D.C. for the bookseller's convention. Went lookin' at books and met a girl." He affected the Maryland backcountry accent that he expected *cousin Jimmy* held dear. "So, finally, I guess I'm not one of those confirmed bachelors anymore."

Charlotte shifted her ample weight from one foot to the next. Her little eyes turned glassy. "Well, I'll be sure to let him know. When are you, uh..."

Taylor had the answer ready. "Three months."

She nodded, looked down at the plate of brownies and tried to reconstruct the smile. "Congratulations, Zachary. I'm really happy for you."

"Well I'm happy for me, too." He gave her a big grin. "You take care of yourself, Charlotte."

He had the door almost shut when she spoke again.

"Did you see who was in the van?"

Taylor froze. "What are you talking about?"

"In the parking lot, behind you?" She frowned when he didn't answer. Through the narrow space between the door and the frame he felt her eyes appraising him again. "You must have seen it. It was the only other car there."

Taylor's mind raced. The van had held the child. He had been parked alongside it for an exchange that had taken no more than 30 seconds. The driver had intended to exit out the opposite end of the lot.

She said she saw you pulling back out onto the street. She didn't see you in the lot.

"I really didn't notice. As I said I was really just turning around—"

"Well *I* noticed. The driver came out of there like a bat out of hell, nearly ran me down."

Taylor stayed calm.

"I'm sorry about that, Charlotte."

"Yeah, me, too. Where was Jimmy my tough guy cop when I needed him? Any way, Zachary, I hope you enjoy the brownies."

Taylor quickly shut the door, his mind skipping through all the possible implications of what she had seen. The van had been in and out of the lot in a matter of seconds. Charlotte had obviously had neither the time nor inclination to get a plate number, and probably remembered next to nothing about the make or model.

Still he worried, feeling suddenly fragile, exposed, as he moved back to the bright yellow kitchen. Still dazed, he dumped the brownies into the sink, flicked on the disposal, grimaced as the complications addled his mind.

He realized the story about the fiancée could easily backfire. Charlotte Johnson had been pining away for him for years. She would still be watching him closely, never more than an idle chat away from the "suspicions" of her redneck cop cousin.

Next to the sink was a framed photograph, a vista of red and orange fall foliage and the deep green Catoctin River. The boy's body was supposed to be at the bottom of the river by an hour after dusk; the kidnapper notified by midnight that it had been done. Taylor gazed at the image for a long moment before grabbing the pillow and opening the basement door, then moved quickly down the steep stairs toward the room's darkest corner, where the air was rank with mildew.

It took several seconds for Zachary's eyes to adjust to the absence of light, and when they did, he flung the pillow to the floor, spun around—

"Boy!"

His voice echoed off the cement walls and shot another dose of adrenaline through his veins.

"Boy YOU CAN'T HIDE—"

A sudden movement at the corner of his eye made him turn toward the workbench. He caught a glimpse of a lime-green shirt and red tennis shoes as Justin Bennett tried to push himself farther underneath.

Taylor felt the sweat trickling down from his armpits as Justin Bennett put his hands over his face, as if it would somehow hide him. But after a moment, when he didn't charge forward, the boy spread his fingers and peeked through them.

In the half-light of the basement, their eyes met.

"Heee ...ll ... p." The boy stammered and tried to push himself deeper into the tiny space under the bench.

With no need to hurry, Taylor stooped down, his hands against his knees. He had a mind's-eye image of himself as a snake peering at a hatchling, trapped in a nest. He imagined himself reaching in, squeezing the child's tender neck. He had no choice.

Especially now that he's seen you.

The boy began to cry as Taylor gazed at the wine stain. An ugly defect that made Justin Bennett stand out in a crowd.

All the more reason to cut your losses.

The boy whimpered like a wounded dog as Taylor reached for him.

All the more reason to just kill him, right now.

Ten

"*Get the hell away from me!*" Michael yelled at a reporter who literally cornered him as he tried to sprint from the side of the yard to the front door. He felt the hot lights on his face and knew immediately that the cameraman had gotten the outburst on tape. Martin grabbed his arm and pulled him inside before the reporter could question him again.

Michael slammed the door behind them and flinched at the *whoop whoop* siren of an approaching cop car, which had probably been summoned to calm the crowd.

"Where's Mary?" he asked.

"Upstairs," Martin told him. "In her room, by the phone."

The moment Michael started after her Martin had grabbed his arm and held him back.

"She needs to be alone," Martin said.

You mean away from me.

"She needs to stay *by the phone*," Martin clarified, putting both hands on Michael's shoulders, looking into his eyes as if striving to keep him calm. "So if Justin calls, from wherever he is, she'll be there to get it. In the meantime..."

The rest of what his uncle said was lost as Michael leaned against the foyer wall, fighting tears as he thought of Justin coming down the stairs hours earlier. Yet the message was clear. Mary wanted him out of the house, out of her sight. For now Martin just wanted him to pack a few sets of clothes, things to wear while he took shelter at his uncle and aunt's house.

Martin stayed with him as he went upstairs. At the second floor Michael was surprised to see a D.C. cop posted outside Mary's bedroom door. He knew that his uncle had arranged it, that by now Martin and Joan were probably already working with the police and the FBI to have taps on the phones in case they got some kind of ransom call.

In the car Martin had told him that the police were looking for Scott Brown, and that when they found him the interrogation would push all of the limits to reveal any connection Scott might have.

They would also be looking for the stranger who had assaulted him at Club Night. Martin assured him of this after hearing a full description of the conversation, the wrinkles in his forehead deepening with worry. Martin had been a father to him for more than twenty years, and Michael had always felt a calm comfort in being able to speak openly and honestly about *almost* anything that troubled him. But he did not feel comforted now. Martin had still been at the restaurant when the police arrived, and he had been at Mary's side as she heard the news. He couldn't help but wonder if Martin blamed him, and if that blame would intensify over the next few hours as more details of his relationship with D'Amecourt inevitably came to light.

Michael told himself that protecting the secret of that relationship no longer mattered, that he would betray D'Amecourt and reveal everything in the quest to determine how the stranger knew something was going to happen. And with the attention now being paid to Justin's disappearance, he knew that he might not have any choice. For at least the next 72 hours there would be a D.C. police cruiser in front of the house. And the FBI had already put Justin's photograph into its national database. With luck, Martin told him, at least one of the national news networks would run a full segment on the abduction, beaming Justin's instantly memorable, wine-stained face to millions of homes across the country.

They're doing everything they can. Michael tried to be encouraged by the thought. But the image of Bender—with his glaring, accusing expression—stayed on his mind. For a moment he wondered if the attention would come at a terrible price; if it would ultimately push Scott over the edge. Turning a kidnapping into murder.

Just like before—

He willed the thought out of his mind as he packed jeans, t-shirts, underwear, and extra shoes into his overnight bag. He thought of Benjamin's abduction and his previous lawyer's advice to cut off his long brown hair. To wear a tie, a button-down shirt, and a suit to the deposition that would eventually "clear" him as a suspect. The fear of going through the experience again almost made him throw up as he finished zipping the bag and turned toward the desk, where his computer rested, his email unchecked for the past several hours.

His whole body quivered as he sat down and logged on, his mind racing through the files that had been saved on his hard drive, the deep well of love, lust, and memories that he still could *not* manage to get rid of.

Incriminating evidence, he knew. *Enough to doom you forever if it ever got out*. For a moment he considered deleting the files, throwing out the software, destroying the memories. Obliterating the last vestiges of the secret that had given him fresh nightmares after his encounter with the stranger at Club Night.

He shut his eyes and saw the stranger standing in front of him again.

"I know what you're doin' to that little boy."

His fingers moved quickly, automatically, across the keyboard as he called up the menu of files on the hard drive. There were pictures, audio recordings, streaming video. In the box alongside the desk, and in the hiding place under the eaves, there were CD roms, printed photographs, backup files saved on discs. His breath was shallow as he saw himself getting rid of all of it, destroying it forever.

Because you're a suspect now, which means they'll probably stop at nothing to get to the truth.

"No," he said out loud. He stared at the file menu, his eyes stinging as he dropped his hands to his sides, away from the keys. Then, as if to force himself *not* to change his mind, he quickly logged off. He was uncomfortable leaving the computer in his room, but it would take too long and be too difficult to pack up and take with him to Martin and Joan's. And yet he still wanted to have easy access to his email, to the Internet, to every information resource he might use on his own to figure out what might be happening. Fortunately the laptop he often used to take notes in class was fully charged. It was also small and would be easy to conceal as he slipped away.

He was just about to leave when he looked toward the bedside table. There was a picture of Justin next to the alarm clock, a picture that for months had been the last thing he looked at before dozing off to sleep. It showed Justin riding on his back, holding on to the collar of his shirt, as if it were the reins of a horse, as he walked on hands and knees around the backyard. It was one of the boy's crazy habits, pulling on his t-shirt collars, stretching them out whenever he was carried. Justin had always been a physical kid, had always relished hugging him, climbing on him, kissing him. From the time he was a toddler the boy had gone to him the instant he walked into a room. From his first uncertain steps, until just this morning, Justin had automatically reached for his hand whenever they walked side by side.

"Oh baby," Michael whispered as he sank to his knees beside the bed and began to cry. He was still crying when Martin came into the room. Martin's skin normally had the ruddy glow of someone who spent a lot of time outdoors. Now his tie was loose and he looked far more haggard, and even sadder, than just 10 minutes before.

Martin's touch was gentle but firm as he laid his hand on Michael's shoulder and reiterated that the two of them needed to leave.

"We'll go out through the basement and walk down the alley toward the end of the block," Martin told him. "Joan's waiting for us in our neighbor's Volvo. If we do it right we'll be halfway across town before they ever know you're gone."

Like I'm escaping, Michael thought. *Running. Hiding—*

"Martin, what's happening?" Michael gazed through the haze of his tears. "Why Justin... and why *me*, again?"

"I don't know. Michael, is there anything else that you remember?"

Martin met his eyes, and for an instant Michael felt as if his uncle knew that he was holding something back.

"No, I've told you everything."

He thought again of the stranger's accusation the night before, looked away as images of knife wounds, blood-soaked bed sheets, and Louis D'Amecourt rose up in his mind.

Everything but that, he thought as he picked up his overnight bag and slipped out of the house and into the backyard, the darkness saving him from looking his uncle in the eye.

* * *

"Get the hell away from me!"

Michael's outburst in front of a TV reporter had sounded like a shriek as Mary stood at Justin's second-floor window. For an instant—as Martin grabbed him by the shoulders and pulled him away from the cameras—Michael had met her eyes. *He looked psychotic*, she thought. *Out of control.*

As soon as Michael and Martin had come into the house she'd gone into her room, told the cop on the porch that her brother was *not* to be allowed in, and pulled herself into a fetal position on the bed. That's what she had looked like when Martin had come to the door, his voice gravely updating her with information that she already knew.

Justin had disappeared into a crowd right outside a public restroom, where he'd been left alone as Michael vomited inside a stall.

He had vanished into the crowd of children, and no one had reported seeing anything that even remotely resembled a kidnapping.

He had vanished shortly after Michael had tried to retrieve the bracelet that he had fiddled with the night before, after *surprising* her with the news that it had been loosened.

Which meant that he *wasn't* wearing it now—

In the rapids of the river.

"No..." she whispered.

His body slipping toward the falls.

"NO!" She sat up, stared at her face in the dresser mirror.

"Miss Bennett?" the cop knocked on the door.

Benjamin, not Justin. She fought to clear her mind. *It was Benjamin who died. Justin is still out there. Justin is still alive—*

"Miss Bennett?" When she didn't answer for the second time the cop turned the doorknob.

"It's okay; I'm fine," she lied. She was glad she had locked the door when Martin left. Glad that Officer Troy Hernandez couldn't see her as she turned toward the closet where she kept the gun hidden in a locked box on the top shelf.

"Can I get you something?" The officer had a slight Hispanic accent and the manners of a Navy cadet.

She told him no again, her forehead pressed against the wall, her mind still contaminated with the images of the ditch. The rain. Benjamin's body.

She wondered if she was going crazy. If she was *continuing* to be crazy. If the last five years since her last child had been kidnapped and killed had been a purgatory *at the edge of CRAZY* and now, like Benjamin, she, too, was slipping over the falls—

Get a grip girl. It was the jarring, humored voice of her brother that she heard now, coupled with a memory of yesterday morning. Michael leading Justin by the hand. Out the door. Out of sight.

She touched the locked box but kept it up high on the shelf. Handguns were illegal in the District of Columbia and she was taking no chances of having Officer Hernandez find out she had one; that she was willing to *use* one if the time came.

But for what? She thought again of her brother, begging her to agree to the trip to AdventureWorld. Thought of Scott, out on parole. She wondered if she could shoot either one of them to get her son back.

Scott YES, but Michael?

She sat on the hard floor, put her face in her hands, and listened to the clock ticking away at the other end of the room. It had been almost 10 hours since Justin had disappeared. She had already been distraught when she got to AdventureWorld, after begging the Montgomery County police officers who had come to the restaurant to tell her about Justin's disappearance to take her there. The sight of Michael being interrogated had been too much for her to handle.

So you did exactly what they wanted. Her own questioning in the next room had been gentle, the police bending over backwards to treat her kindly as they asked for her version of the day's events. But in their eyes she had seen a strange gleam, an intrigue fueled as much by her reaction to Michael as by the fact that he had been so close when Justin disappeared. She had known without a doubt then that he was a suspect. That they felt as if he had gotten away with the earlier crime and he would *not* get away with it now.

They're wrong. She pressed a fist to her lips. *"My brother loves Justin as if he were his own son."* Her own words in the *Washington Blade* article haunted her now. *"He's so good with them. It's like he's got this gift..."*

Michael's whole life was about children. Taking care of them. Teaching them. This was the most important point of the article, which had begun as an assignment from her magazine class, a response to the professor's suggestion that she write *"a story only you can tell, something that sheds new light on what you were feeling at the time, and how you've recovered now."*

Reticent at first, she had begun slowly, with an objective listing of all of the facts that surrounded the abduction. A straightforward explanation about why Scott Brown, now in prison on drug charges, had been driven to commit the crime. She had also written, with complete honesty, of her conflicting emotions during the months that followed. She had been two months pregnant with Justin when Benjamin disappeared, and had carried the child in the midst of a fierce legal battle that had given Scott once-a-month visiting rights—in prison—simply because he was Justin's biological father. Five years later, the memories still bothered her, but the tone of the article focused on the much happier times of the present, describing in glowing detail why it was her brother, Michael, whom she valued most as a father figure in Justin's life.

It was a brave assertion in light of the questions that still surrounded Benjamin's disappearance. Questions that still fueled speculation among strangers that Michael himself had been involved. Believing that her own opinions—her own *certainty*—could halt the rumors once and for all, she had made it clear that she believed her brother was innocent. But she could only go on so long before the driving current of emotion pulled her into a long stretch of narrative that emerged, almost subconsciously, from the well of memories. Honest words about how difficult it had been to reconcile the fact that Benjamin disappeared while under Michael's care. Candid truths about her own unanswered questions. Revelations about how truly *complicated* her relationship with her brother had become.

Months earlier she had made a confession to the shrink. In her worst moments—a sudden change of mood as the daylight dimmed; a wide-awake spell hours before dawn—she imagined that God had given her some kind of terrible choice. That by giving up the life of her brother she could have Benjamin returned. Wracked with guilt, she had listened to the psychologist's explanation that it was perfectly understandable and nothing to be ashamed of. *So there are chinks in your armor*, she had been told, *but your conscious mind is stronger than ever. In reality you're well on your way to recovery.*

Except for the problem. Mary climbed back onto the bed and pulled Benjamin's bear to her chest, remembering the last time she had done a thorough cleaning of the house, entering her brother's third-floor sanctuary to dust the blinds and clean out the attic. She thought of the box he kept under the eaves, never expecting her to search.

She had been fascinated, and repulsed, and even more curious about the strange chemistry that had made her brother who he was. At one point a few years earlier she and her psychiatrist had talked about the "origins" of his homosexuality, the shrink giving her a long and ultimately confusing explanation about "nature and nurture" and "id and ego," and a bunch of other crap that made her wish she'd never even brought it up.

"I think he's just special," she had said in the end. She had doted on Michael from his earliest years, and after the death of their parents she had become a confidant and protector. It was she who had walked him to school

on the first day of first grade, she who had cheered him when he made the varsity lacrosse and tennis teams at high school, she who had been the first to learn why none of the relationships with girls he had dated in high school had lasted any longer than a few weeks.

Yeah, he's special all right. Again she thought of the box in Michael's attic eaves, wishing she had spent more time looking through it, as if for some crazy reason it might have a connection to what was happening now.

She thought about going upstairs to look at it again, but quickly reconsidered. The phone in Michael's room was on a separate line, with a separate number. One of the two numbers Justin had memorized was for her own phone, on the bedside table. She wanted—needed—to be next to it when and if it rang.

But it's not going to. The voice in her mind was insistent. *It's going to be like last time, with no sign of him until it's too late—*

Benjamin's bear was soft and tattered in her arms as she sobbed her way into a twilight zone at the edge of sleep, a place where Benjamin became Justin and Justin became Michael, who became Benjamin again. In her mind she saw Justin and Benjamin standing side by side in a crowd of anonymous children, saw herself running with open arms toward them, saw them fading, and disappearing, just inches away from her grasp.

"NO!" Her eyes shot open to the sight of the police officer, his hands at her shoulders.

"Miss Bennett, I'm sorry. Are you all right?"

For several seconds she simply gazed at him. *Hernandez*, she remembered. *Guarding the door.*

She looked at the clock. The dream had seemed to last a moment but had gone on much, much longer. It was nearly 5 A.M. She'd been asleep—or close to it—for over an hour.

"Miss Bennett, you need to get up now."

A bolt of panic hit her in the chest. "Oh God did they find him?"

"No, not yet." Hernandez shook his head as footsteps filled the hallway. At the door were two heavy men in bulky clothes, with badges on their chests. The one in front had a rolled-up piece of paper in his hand.

The cop's voice was quiet, filled with regret when he spoke again: "They're from the FBI."

Above them came the sound of more footsteps, on the floor of Michael's bedroom.

"They've got a warrant to search your house."

* * *

The phone call came at the edge of dawn, just moments after Michael had drifted into a half-sleep on Martin and Joan's guest room bed.

Without thinking he'd picked it up at the same moment as his uncle downstairs, and had heard Mary hysterically telling Martin to go to her house *now*.

He'd dressed quickly, haphazardly grabbing clothes from the suitcase, slipping into shoes without tying the laces, racing down the stairs, and reaching the garage even before Martin and Joan.

"Why are they doing this?" Michael asked them. Somehow in the back of his mind he'd convinced himself that Martin's status as a city councilman and Joan's intricate knowledge of the legal system gave him the inside track to any new turns the investigation might take.

"I don't know," Martin answered. "I can only guess—."

"They did it because they're bastards," Joan interrupted him, her eyes sharp behind her wire-rim glasses, her grayish hair matted after a short, restless sleep on the couch next to the phone. Her anger over the FBI's strong-arm tactics five years earlier had never weakened. Michael had no doubt that she'd get the story behind the search warrant even if Martin could not.

Martin drove quickly, barely slowing for the stop signs on the nearly deserted streets. It took no more than five minutes to get back to the house. But the street was so crowded with cop cars and satellite vans from the local TV news stations that they could get no closer than half a block away.

Joan spoke through clenched teeth as Martin pulled to a stop. "Looks like every Fed in town is here."

Michael noticed two gunmetal gray vans with men wearing bulky sweaters standing at the open doors. And there were two silver sedans that obviously belonged to white-shirted federal agents.

Joan was out of the car immediately, moving quickly up the walkway. Michael followed, ducking his head as two television reporters stepped out of their trucks and headed toward him, with cameramen running behind.

A uniformed officer stopped them at the front door.

"I'm sorry ma'am." The cop gave him a sullen look. "And sir. You can't enter the premises right now—"

"The hell we can't." Joan pushed forward but the cop held out his hand and blocked her at the waist. For a moment Michael was certain she was going to fight him off, but then Mary appeared in the doorway.

"It's okay, Joan." Mary's eyes were red and puffy. "I'll come outside. I need some air."

They followed her back to the side porch, which was inaccessible from the front yard, and blocked by tall bushes from the cameras on the street. Over Joan's shoulder, Mary met Michael's eyes.

"It could be worse, I guess," Mary said quietly. "They could be taking the entire house apart, destroying everything. But it looks like they're just going after certain things."

"What kind of things?" Joan stepped back, but kept her hands on Mary's arms.

"Things in Justin's room," Mary paused, gave him an uncertain look. "And Michael's room."

Michael's heart lurched as a woman agent in plainclothes came out of the house with his computer. On her heels was a uniformed officer, carrying a plastic bag containing the back-up discs.

Mary looked at him again, her expression noticeably sad. "They've also been in the attic, Michael."

Oh God, she knows. He was certain of it as he pressed his hands against his temples, his face burning with embarrassment at the thought of his sister looking through the box under the eaves. He thought of the police finding it now, rifling its contents, analyzing them for clues.

His fear was confirmed a moment later as another cop stepped through the open door with the box in his hands.

Now they're going to know too.

The cop with the box gave him a brief sideways glare as he walked toward the gunmetal gray van at the curb, his expression making it clear that he had already looked inside.

And they're going tell everyone. His vision blurred as he scanned the crowd and began backing away. He was tempted to run, fighting the urge to cry out loud as he turned around and quickened his pace.

Just get to the car, he told himself. *Get inside, lock the doors.*

The ring of his cell phone stopped him. Before leaving the house, he had forwarded all calls that went to the phone in his bedroom to the cell.

Michael lowered his head and kept his back to the crowd as he answered.

"Hello."

He heard a sharp intake of breath, a man's voice. "You... sick *devil*."

His breath stopped at the base of his throat and his knees were shaking. "Who is this?"

"I know *everthin'*."

Michael recognized the slight twang of the voice. It was the stranger who had hit him at Club Night.

"And I'm gonna *tell*."

Michael felt a staggering dizziness as the stranger continued speaking, and threatening, every word hitting him like another punch to the gut as he looked back at the police, the federal agents, the new wave of reporters and camera crews setting up on the front lawn.

Eleven

The sender of the email found in the Capitol Hotel victim's property was someone who knew how to avoid being found. His secrecy had kept Booker awake for hours, ferreting through the jungles of the Internet on hundreds of twisting paths that led nowhere...

"Until I remembered the hacker's riddle." Booker leaned back and reached for the mug of strong coffee she had brought him. His big body looked cramped by the small chair. "From the mouth of Benedict Arnold himself."

Gloria remembered that one of the FBI seminars that Booker had attended featured a notorious computer hacker who had avoided jail time by agreeing to work for the government, revealing trade secrets to law enforcement. The man had introduced himself as "Arnold Benedict," with a smirk that made it clear to everyone in the room that he saw no illusions of honor in what he was doing.

"The hacker talked for hours about how no system was as good as its security people hoped it would be—that there was no such thing as a fortress," Booker said. "That goes for SentryMail, too."

SentryMail was the name of the email service the Capitol Hotel murder victim used to receive the email that had been found hidden in his bag. But because the email was printed out in hard copy, with the sender identified only by a screen name—quietriot22—none of the identifying information that would have been revealed in the electronic codes behind the screen name was visible.

"I worked half the night trying the same stuff our friend Payne did—reverse lookup search engines, online directories—and got the same result. Nothing." Booker said. "I was sitting there at 3 A.M. ready to give up, when I started thinking about the other way to find out about him, which would be by finding a way into the recipient's SentryMail account."

"Booker leaned back in the chair and gave her a sideways smile. "Without a password it's supposed to be impossible—"

"But now you're saying otherwise." Gloria's fatigue practically vanished as she sat down next to him. "You're saying you got in?"

Booker didn't immediately respond, but his fingers were tapping quickly across the keyboard.

"One of the selling points of SentryMail is that it's free, and anyone can set up an account that can be accessed anywhere," he said. "The company line is that the accounts are secure as long as you protect your password and they talk about how it's impossible for any kind of hacker to get into your personal business, which is what most people use these kinds of addresses for. When you want to send personal email from work, talk to your mistress, confide in someone about your gambling debts—"

"Or whatever," Gloria cut him off with an impatient look.

"I'm just saying that they're wrong. Hackers have gotten in. The guy who spoke at the seminar was a mastermind of an attack that exposed the accounts of something like two million users just a few weeks before he was busted. For a 24-hour period it was possible for any reasonably good hacker to get into the email accounts of SentryMail customers and read everything that had been received or sent."

"Which is exactly what we need to do."

Booker continued at his own pace. "What makes Sentry and Hotmail and other services like it so great is that they're free and easy to access—all you need is your password. But with this flaw, you could break into an account and rewrite the user's password. It was like having an open window to a locked room. All you had to do was climb in."

"But you said that was last year."

"Right. Some geeks in Europe found out what the script was and circulated it to hacker sites all over the world, and Sentry claimed they had it fixed within a day. But the hacker at the seminar hinted otherwise."

"He *told* you how to do it?"

"No, not at all—that would have been way too easy," Booker smiled slightly. "He just went on and on about how there would always be open windows and there would always be hackers to exploit 'em. Sentry was one of the few services that he went into detail about, and I remembered he said the code was still in the wild."

Gloria frowned at the last sentence. "You have to translate that."

"In the wild—a term the hackers use to describe a code that can be used to create a virus or break into a secure system, something that's still circulating throughout the hacker's world. Generally it refers to information that hackers know but don't necessarily choose to exploit, at least not until they're pushed."

Booker tapped the keyboard again, revealing on the left side of the screen a long list of Web sites.

"I spent hours going to all of the sites that I knew were geared to hackers and I combed through the newsgroups looking for any clues about how to get into Sentry again." Booker exhaled wearily as he typed in a new address in the browser. "It wasn't easy..."

After a few seconds the screen flashed white and then black and then white again. Text rolled across the screen, a message telling them they were being shuttled to a new Web site.

"Hackers Realm." Booker read the name of the site, which was written in a gothic script over an illustration of a stone arch that reminded Gloria of the entrance to a Victorian era cemetery. After another moment several lines of text appeared, in bright red against a background of white.

> **If you are part of America Online staff, FBI, IRS, CIA, Scotland Yard, INTERPOL or any other law enforcement organization—LEAVE NOW. If you choose not to leave, you are fully responsible for what you access. It is your responsibility to check the applicable laws in your state and country. The primary interest of this Web site is to provide information necessary for studying reverse engineering techniques. Hacking tools available on this site are created by the top hackers, including password cracks, Trojan Horse wrappers, UNIX and LINUX scripts ...**

The text ran out at the bottom of the screen. "You get the picture?" Booker asked.

Gloria shook her head.

"The site promises a step-by-step tutorial, which is false advertising, since I still had to go on a scavenger hunt that took at least an hour.

Benedict Arnold or whatever the hell his real name is has got some sense of humor."

With a few more keystrokes he took the screen to another page. "When Sentry created its site, the programmers wrote a login program to enable users to easily access their email from any machine. What made it vulnerable during the hack last year were a few lines of HTML code that served as a skeleton key to get into the site. All you need to do is go into the web page's source code and replace the username with the SentryMail user name—which in this case we have: HotBoy2. This enables you to get into the account without a password. The flaw is that the system thinks you're coming in through a secure URL when you're not. A hole big enough for a freight train..."

Booker typed in the username, and after a moment got a screen listing the emails received in the Capitol Hotel victim's account. There were only a handful, and Gloria saw immediately that most were spam mail advertisements for more SentryMail services.

Except for one. From "quietriot22."

"God," she said. "I can't believe we're actually here."

Booker nodded, and moved the cursor over to the "sent" items.

"You already have the email he received—the printed-out version that Payne gave you. Here's the email that someone, probably the victim, sent before it."

Don't try to deny it. We have proof.

Gloria gazed at the message, felt an eerie sense of unease as she thought of the victim sitting in front of the keyboard, typing it in.

"And you already know what he got back." Booker switched to the inbox, and clicked on the message that the both had memorized.

> **Received your message but will not deal through this email address. Contact me at 512-3211 when you arrive.**
>
> The email appeared exactly as it would have in the Capitol Hotel victim's SentryMail account, and with a few clicks of the mouse she knew that Booker would be able to reveal the codes behind the sender's email address. She wanted to feel triumphant, but her husband's demeanor told her she was about to be disappointed.

"So where does this take us, Booker?"

He paused, leaned back, and gave her an apologetic look. "A long way—to a brick wall."

"But you said you could trace it, if you could look at the email header."

"I did. Whoever sent the email to your victim uses Stonewall as his Internet service provider. It's a company that was set up about 15 years ago when the Internet was young. For the most part it was like AOL or any other provider except that it made a big point of the fact that it guarded every user's privacy more zealously than any other service."

Gloria frowned. "Are you saying you don't think they'll cooperate?"

"I don't know."

"Even though the person who sent this is probably connected to a murder?"

"Probably, but we don't know for sure. And you'd still have to get a court order before you even talked to them, which means going back to D'Amecourt—"

"I know that."

"All right." Booker paused. His eyes were bloodshot from exhaustion.

Gloria rubbed the back of his neck, felt the tension in his muscles barely yielding to her touch. "A few minutes ago you said you were wondering what Michael Bennett is really trying to hide," she said. "What did you mean?"

Booker turned back to the screen. "One of the areas of the Internet that's hardest for law enforcement to patrol are the newsgroups and chat rooms," he said. "They're like a back alley, where you can find just about anything. Each ISP can decide what will be allowed to be on its system. Some, like Stonewall, refuse to block any newsgroups or chat rooms whatsoever. Each newsgroup can be found by typing in keywords that are tied to its subject matter."

She watched as he tapped the keyboard again, and in a few seconds she was staring at a screen for DejaNews, a search engine. He moved to a box marked "forum" and began typing in a number of terms:

Sex boys preschool

"What the hell are you doing?"

"Searching," he replied. "Showing you what's out there."

After a moment she was staring at a screen filled with four columns. Under the column marked "forum" were keywords that corresponded to the terms that Booker had typed in.

Gloria stayed quiet as he moved the cursor up to the line marked "next." He hit it again, and again, and again.

"There are 25 postings on each page," he said. "And I was able to call up more than 500 in the last two months alone. All of the newsgroups are hosted by Stonewall."

She gazed at the screen, at the "subject" column, where there were short taglines hinting at the messages.

Looking for cute boys
Street kids for sex
Young hustlers

She stared for a few moments longer, feeling dizzy as she thought of the anonymous faces behind the sickening queries. She looked at Booker again, and felt like she had missed something.

"You're saying the guy who sent the email to the victim is one of these people?"

"I don't know that yet. All we know is that the person who sent the email to the murder victim used Stonewall. Stonewall hosts these newsgroups. And given Bennett's background—"

"You mean because he's gay."

The muscles in Booker's shoulders tensed. In two years she had never heard him say anything outright homophobic, but he clearly felt Bennett's past was incriminating.

"I don't know, at least not yet," he said. "And chances are most of the guys posting on the newsgroup are doing it anonymously. The only sure way to connect him would be to find an incriminating newsgroup posting and trace it to the same email address."

Gloria looked at the list again, wondering how long it would take to go through 500 messages.

"Newsgroups are for people with similar interests," Booker said. "In this case people who trade child pornography. If Michael Bennett or Scott Brown have done anything really incriminating—sending pictures, saying something that could be connected with the kidnapping of the kid—I've got a hunch they did it on that network."

"So how would we find evidence of that?"

"We could go a couple of different routes. We could go through every one of these messages, looking for anything that might already tie one of them to the murder or the kidnapping. Or we could create a bogus nickname and join the newsgroup, find a way to lure him into a discussion."

So we'd have to pretend to have something they want, she realized. *Pictures of children—*

"Gloria, you're shaking."

"I can't help it. I just don't know if I can do this."

"Then don't." The serious expression on his face worried her. "Call Payne and tell him you want him to go through the right channels—and to leave you out of it. You've already taken a risk by going this far."

"Do you *want* me to back off?" she asked him.

"No, not if you feel like it's something you have to do. But you could still go past Payne. Take this straight to D'Amecourt himself."

She thought about it for a moment. "But what if D'Amecourt's the one we're looking for?"

Booker gave her a dubious look.

"Think about it," she said. "If D'Amecourt were 'quietriot22' then he would have had a definite connection to the victim found at the Capitol Hotel, and a reason to get there and check out the crime scene. He would have wanted to get rid any evidence that might have incriminated him. If that really was a picture of Justin Bennett in the room, it would mean that the kidnapping is tied to this murder."

"And, D'Amecourt surely knows what Justin Bennett looks like."

"Yes, he'd have to." Gloria thought about the five-year-old *Washington Post* articles they had pulled from the Web. D'Amecourt had been the lead D.C. investigator in the kidnapping of Benjamin Bennett, and he had gone on the record stating his belief that Michael was involved. The fact that there wasn't enough evidence to formally charge either Michael or Scott Brown probably infuriated D'Amecourt. Gloria knew that he wouldn't have just walked away, particularly when Michael's sister had another child.

"We need to call Tommy Payne and tell him what we found out," she said.

"You already talked to him."

"I asked him if he saw the picture before it was taken away. I didn't tell him anything more because at that point I wasn't sure."

"You're sure now?"

"Yes." She quickly thought it through again. "I'm sure that it was a picture of Justin Bennett and I'm sure that D'Amecourt took it from the scene. I'm also sure that the murder at the Capitol Hotel and the murder two years ago were committed by the same guy. And the fact that

D'Amecourt wants to keep both crimes under wraps makes me even more certain he's afraid of being implicated."

Booker nodded. But she saw worry in his expression. Going any farther to investigate D'Amecourt or to help Payne continue his own investigation after being told to move on would put both of them in danger.

But you can't walk away. It had been nearly 24 hours since Justin Bennett had disappeared. Mary Bennett's first child had died just two days after being abducted.

She turned to Booker, who had been watching her, waiting for the go-ahead. "Let's keep looking," she said.

"You're sure." He still looked concerned, and worried about crossing D'Amecourt, she suspected. "'Cause if you want to play it safe we can still go back to Payne and—"

"No." She glanced at a newspaper photo of Benjamin Bennett as she cut him off. Next to it was a picture of the ravine where his body had been briefly spotted, before disappearing beneath whitewater falls.

"Let's just do it, Booker."

There was a knot in her throat as she thought of little Justin Bennett suffering, terrified, meeting the same fate.

"Let's see if we can track him down."

Twelve

"I know what you were doin' to that little boy."

The stranger's words echoed through Michael's mind as he drove through the residential streets of Louis D'Amecourt's D.C. neighborhood with $10,000 in cash stashed in the knapsack on the front seat.

"And I know why you took him away."

The stranger's accusations had rendered him speechless, but he had anxiously listened to every word, willing himself to remember any details that D'Amecourt would grill him for later. The stranger made it clear that he knew something was going to happen to Justin at least a day before he actually disappeared.

But how?

According to what Scott had told Mary on the phone the night before, Scott had been on parole for two days before the kidnapping. Certainly long enough to create a plan for snatching Justin away, but the stranger's accusations made it sound as if he had hard evidence of something more.

As if Scott had help. Someone on the outside—

Michael gripped the wheel tightly, his mind racing back to one of the many unanswered questions relating to Benjamin's disappearance. When D'Amecourt first interrogated him, his theory had been that Benjamin had been kidnapped by either Scott or himself, but an accomplice had been involved as well. The rain-swollen stream where Ben had been spotted, crying and dazed and clinging to a fallen branch, had been in the foothills just beyond Martinsburg, West Virginia. Benjamin had been seen just before dusk, at a time when both he and Scott had been under interrogation in Washington, which made it apparent that someone else had been watching the child in the place where he'd been held captive. In the hour that it took for the EMTs to arrive Benjamin had gotten swept away.

But he almost made it. Michael seized on the tiny hope that if Benjamin had been able to escape from his captors that somehow Justin would, too. But he doubted that Scott or his accomplices would take any chances this time. According to Martin, Scott's parents were claiming they had no idea where he was, but Michael had the distinct feeling that he was nearby.

The same feeling you had two nights ago, he thought. *In the basement. The headlights in the window.*

The car that had pulled up to the curb had had a retro shape, the bulky lines of an early 70s Mustang or Camaro. Michael remembered Scott's father had liked old cars, that he had an expensive hobby in restoring them.

If he was watching the house he could have followed you to AdventureWorld, waiting until he had the chance to get Justin alone.

Michael thought back to the conversation at Justin's bedside the night before, Justin's promise to stay by his side. Justin's once-a-month visits with Scott and his parents were brief, but Justin had clearly come to like Scott, and he probably would have been happy to see Scott at the amusement park.

Happy enough to let Scott to lead him away.

Michael felt his heart beating faster. In a matter of minutes he would be standing in Louis D'Amecourt's living room, revealing the stranger's assertion that he arranged the kidnapping. He would also relay the stranger's demand for money and the threat to make an anonymous call to the police if he didn't comply.

Forget D'Amecourt. You need to go to the FBI right now.

Again he hesitated. Bender, the police official who had interviewed him right after Justin's disappearance, had acted as if he had made up the story about the stranger assaulting him at Club Night. Michael knew that the man would immediately pass the information on to the task force that was now working the case. It was difficult to imagine anyone believing that the stranger had somehow found out the inside details of the kidnapping, but that he was "blackmailing" the wrong person.

But he isn't really a stranger. Michael's memory flashed on the image from two years before. The body on the bed. The blood-soaked sheets. D'Amecourt's plea to pretend the murder had never happened.

You have to find out what he knows.

Michael winced and laid a palm across his stomach.

You have to talk to him again.

For $10,000 the stranger claimed to be willing to withhold the information from the police. For the same amount of money he *had* to be willing to sell the information, to give up every clue that might bring Justin back alive.

But 8:15, the stranger's designated meeting time, was nearly four hours away. Michael remembered a detective speaking about Benjamin's case on television, insisting that leads in the first 24 hours after a disappearance were the most crucial. And yet the thought of going to Bender, who wanted nothing more than to charge him with the crime ...

Especially now, with the search warrant, the box in the attic.

His resolve was firm as he turned onto the tree-lined street on the eastern end of Chevy Chase, where Louis D'Amecourt had lived alone for many years. D'Amecourt's colonial house was made of ugly red brick and every window was covered by heavy drapes. It was a dark, sad place.

"A house of horrors."

Long buried in his memory, the phrase was at the front of his mind as he pulled up to the curb, taking a deep breath and whispering a quick prayer as his cell phone rang again.

Thirteen

From a distance, with his darkened brown hair, mirrored sunglasses, and muscles toned hard and sleek after five years of daily workouts in a prison gym, Scott Brown bore a much stronger resemblance to the models in the "Landscape Artistry" advertisements than the laborers who did the real work. He felt well-disguised as he piloted one of the company's signature green vans into the leafy old-money neighborhood where Martin and Joan Raines made their home.

He was no more than 50 yards away when Michael Bennett slipped out the side door and headed toward the alley, where his jeep was parked. Michael's face looked thin, drained of color.

Scott wondered what he was up to now.

Running from the police? Going into hiding?

Either scenario was possible, but it was a third possibility—that Michael had remembered something crucial from before—that almost made him follow the Jeep as Michael pulled out onto the street and drove away.

Scott grappled with a moment of uncertainty. Three days without sleep and a night of hard drinking had left him looking even worse than Michael. He felt stupid, clumsy, and addled by the rage that spiked intensely as he pulled over to the curb in front of Martin and Joan Raines's house.

The clock on the dashboard read 4:30. He wondered what Martin, always a man of action, had been doing all day. Sitting at home and waiting for the phone to ring wasn't like him.

Or her. Joan Raines was standing near the second-floor window. She'd obviously heard the sound of the Jeep starting and had watched Bennett drive away. Little Joanie looked worried, and angry, like a dog ready to bare her teeth at anyone who threatened her territory. Joan Raines had been an athletic, pretty woman in her younger years, but in her late 40s she was a plain-faced political wife who could alternately charm or chastise with her bluntness and sense of humor. The press had always loved her, viewing her as a champion for her attempts to get a restraining order to keep him away from Mary. And her efforts to fight the court order that allowed the once-a-month visits between himself and Justin at Groveton Prison had made her downright heroic.

Fortunately, his family had legal resources of their own. When the prosecutors were unable to come up with enough evidence to formally charge him in Benjamin's kidnapping, his father's staff of well-paid lawyers had immediately argued masterfully and successfully for his rights as Justin's biological father. One of those lawyers, the one his father truly trusted, was well aware of his activities now. "Landscape Artistry" had been maintaining the Raines's yard and many others in the neighborhood for years. It was also one of the many businesses the Brown family had a little-known, never-publicized, stake in, and the van and uniform had already been ready for him a week earlier when he came home from the prison. Landscape Artistry vans were commonplace in the tonier sections of Cleveland Park, where established professionals were too busy being doctors and lawyers and politicians to trifle with yard work. It made a perfect hiding place on a balmy evening as he waited for Martin and Joan Raines to leave the house.

Scott hoped it would happen soon. His picture had been in today's *Washington Post* story and was shown repeatedly on the local TV newscasts. Despite the disguise, he couldn't afford any more time than was absolutely necessary within sight of Michael, Mary, or anyone else in the Bennett family. Grateful again for the van's dark, tinted windows, he turned his attention to the laptop, which was connected to the Internet via the cable in his cell phone, linking him immediately back into the cyberworld that had been a staple of his life virtually every day of captivity. Pedophile chat rooms. FBI databases. Kiddie porn. He'd seen it all... gotten immersed in it all... stayed up countless nights looking for the *truth* behind it all.

Focus. He rubbed his temples, forced himself back to a rundown of the plan he had worked so hard to put into place. Two months earlier, on the same day that he had learned that he would indeed be paroled, he had begun sending incriminating, taunting messages into the newsgroups and chat rooms where his alter-ego had been living for more than a year. The responses had made him more determined than ever to carry the plan through. With the laptop on his knees it took just a few moments to log on again. Seconds later he was scrolling down, his thighs tensing and his mouth going dry when he found what he was looking for. With only a brief hesitation he typed a very quick response.

He clicked "send" the moment Joan and Martin Raines walked out the door. Joan scanned the yard. The skin on her lean face was paled by fatigue. Even with the distance he could see her thin shoulders quivering as Martin wrapped one arm around them. The sight transported him back to the steps in front of the courtroom where he had been tried on the drug charges. The jury had been instructed to ignore all of the evidence that he had taken Benjamin, and there was never enough to lead to kidnapping charges against him, but none of that had stopped either Martin or Joan from making their "true feelings" known. For several hours after the abduction they had tearfully pleaded in front of the television cameras for him to simply "bring Benjamin back." Confronted with the news of Benjamin's death, their faces had turned to stone, both of them vowing that the case would never be closed.

"To hell with both of you," Scott whispered, absently slipping his hand inside his jacket, his fingers tracing the shape of the black market Glock pistol. For one long moment he fantasized about lowering the window and gunning both of them down.

He took a deep breath as the moment passed. Joan leaned against her husband as they made their way toward the garage at the back of their property. Moments after they drove away he folded up the laptop, reached for the "Landscape Artistry" signature cap, and got to work.

* * *

The houses on Newark Street had deep backyards accessed by a wide, clean alley. Scott approached the gate leading to the Raines's backyard with the nonchalance of a contract gardener on his weekly rounds. He carried an edger and a metal toolbox with the "Landscape Artistry" insignia on the side. The gate had a lock that took only seconds to pick, and with his back to the alley he was certain that anyone peering down from a second-floor window from any of the houses backing up to the alley would think he had a key.

Once he was in the backyard, he moved quickly toward the kitchen door. For obvious reasons Martin and Joan Raines had a security system; a "state-of-the-art" wireless model that was nearly identical to the version he had installed at Mary and Michael's house years earlier. It took less than 30 seconds to disarm.

Inside, the home had a hushed, clean elegance that reminded him of the upscale digs of his own childhood. There were Shaker and Mission antiques on inlaid oak and mahogany floors. Old oils in gilded frames in the formal rooms and watercolors on Joan's sunroom porch. A Steinway in the parlor.

And in the guestroom, just as he'd hoped, Michael's laptop sat atop the simple pine desk. Two days ago, when he had broken into Mary's house to steal a glance at Justin as he napped, Michael had been at school, and had evidently taken the laptop with him. It made sense that without access to his main computer he would have the laptop with him now.

Scott popped it open and while he waited for it to boot up went into his own toolbox. He took out the network packet "sniffer" software that would enable him to track every keystroke on the computers. He had already installed it on Michael's home computer, and had been able to trace all of Michael's Web site and email traffic. The process had also given him a look at the passwords used for Michael's online purchases and "members-only" sites. According to the traffic on Michael's computer, he still had an intense fascination with the technology, still kept up with all of the latest developments.

The installation went more quickly than he had expected, even after the practice he had gotten by installing the same software in Martin and Joan's computers the day before. For a moment his mind wandered, drawing him toward the upstairs rooms. His knees felt shaky as he stepped into the back bedroom that Martin and Joan still kept for Mary. Throughout the room were mementos of her childhood, her adolescence, the summers home from college. Here were her trophies from the debate team, the scrapbook of articles written for her high school and college newspapers, a photo of Mary in a tank top and shorts, her long legs deeply tanned, with Justin cuddling up next to her on a bench.

The clash of attraction and anger intensified as he sat down on the queen-sized bed with its lavender-blue comforter and lace and looked closer at the framed photo of Mary and Justin on the nightstand.

"Five years," he whispered as he held the picture in his hands. He just barely fought the urge to slip it into his pocket as he smoothed down the comforter and backed away.

Downstairs the rest of his computer work was completed in less than a minute. The security system was restored, the back gate re-locked. Still cognizant of the need to look like nothing more than a day laborer on the job while homeowners were away, he barely glanced around the alley as he made his way back to the van.

His vision was clouded with hot tears as he drove toward the rented garage where the van would be temporarily stored and where the Mustang Mach 1 was waiting. The muscle car was a comforting, cheering presence after a long morning in the clunky truck. He barely resisted the urge to gun it as he headed out of the city, to the green, rolling foothills around Frederick, Maryland, probably the last place where Justin Bennett could be glimpsed before vanishing for good.

Fourteen

Gloria spent several hours on the computer, reading hundreds of archived postings in the pedophile newsgroups. The technology and the depravity were new to her and she was still struggling to understand both when Booker told her it was time to get ready for work. Roll call for the evening shift began at 3:30 P.M. They both needed coffee and a decent meal to be up for the night ahead.

Two hours later they sat at opposite ends of the Fifth District assembly room alongside two dozen fellow officers as D'Amecourt passed out photographs of Scott Brown and Justin Bennett, saying that he wanted to be notified immediately if they were spotted. Gloria was surprised. The abduction had taken place in Maryland and D'Amecourt's watch extended only as far as the boundaries of the city. It seemed unlikely that whomever took Justin would be holding him close to home.

She filed that thought away as D'Amecourt finished and as the officers began shuffling out of the room. But then she overheard two rookies, Blanton and Nickerson, whispering about Michael Bennett. She followed them outside and stopped to talk before they got into their car to begin patrol. She asked point-blank what they had heard. Blanton volunteered that his roommate had worked an earlier shift, and had been asked to help secure the scene while FBI agents searched the house where Michael and Mary Bennett lived. Blanton was cagey, reluctant to give her any details other than "they found somethin' in a brown cardboard box. We was close by when they carried it out."

Blanton then told her that moments later a cursory search of the box in the back of an FBI van had revealed something that had prompted an immediate visit from D'Amecourt. His face was flushed when he returned, and for the rest of the afternoon he had been shut up in his office, on his own computer, his expression through the glass-paneled door making it clear he didn't want company.

Married for four months, Gloria and Booker no longer patrolled in the same car, but she did manage to spend two minutes at the curb alone with her husband before he headed out.

"I think it's a setup," she told him. "I think Michael Bennett's taking the fall for something he didn't do."

Booker was clearly surprised. "Since when?"

"Since this morning, when we got on the Internet and I started reading the kinds of things people were saying in that newsgroup. It got me angry, and scared I guess, but none of it sounded like anything Michael would write."

"How do you know that, Gloria? You've never even *met* him."

"That's true, but think about it. For five years he's been dogged with rumors that he had something to do with the earlier kidnapping. He lives his life knowing that half the people he comes across, regardless of what they say to his face, probably trust him even less because he's gay. He knows he's pushing the envelope in all kinds of directions helping his sister raise her child, working in a daycare center, working in a place like Club Night. Why would he blow it all by incriminating himself on the Internet?"

"He probably assumes it's all anonymous."

"But if he's as smart as he seems he'd know that eventually he could be tracked down. If someone pushed it. If they had a reason—"

"Like the kidnapping of his nephew."

"Exactly. He already lives under this cloud of suspicion. He would have known that the second that boy disappeared his whole life would be an open book again. I just don't see it."

"Then what *do* you see?"

She glanced toward the side door of the police station. Any second Booker's partner would be on his way out, ready to begin patrol. She knew she was about to commit herself to breaking protocol again and she wanted to have her say quickly, without worrying that she'd be overheard.

"I see D'Amecourt standing at the front of the room, telling all of us that he wants to gain as much control as possible over the investigation into Justin Bennett's kidnapping. And I think it's because he wants to control the flow of information—to get a chance to talk to Scott Brown before he's interviewed by the FBI. I think he wants to do whatever he can to cover up any connection the kidnapping has to the murder that he's also trying to keep quiet."

Booker leaned against the car, his arms folded. "You sure you're not seein' too much?"

"His face was *twitching,* Booker. The man was about to snap up there."

"So what do you think is going on?"

"I think he's worried about what's going to happen if Scott Brown or Michael Bennett *are* charged with something. In other words he's worried about *himself.*"

She told him what Blanton had said about the search of Michael and Mary Bennett's house, the discovery of the box that brought D'Amecourt rushing to the scene. Around them officers were getting into their cars. Gloria turned and saw Booker's partner, a rookie named Cuevas, heading toward them.

"You should talk to Tommy Payne," Booker said quietly. "Tell him what you're thinking."

"Maybe I will, at some point." She avoided his eyes as she answered, and was already turning away as Cuevas came within earshot. "But there's someone else I'd like to talk to first."

* * *

Two hours later she got the chance. The Petworth neighborhood where she and her own partner were patrolling was just north of the Fifth District police station. As soon as she heard the radio call that another unit was bringing Michael into the station for questioning, the plan kicked into gear.

"I'm afraid I've got to cut it short tonight, John," she moaned as she pulled into an alley, and before he could respond she opened the driver's side door, leaned out, and made retching noises. After half a minute of pretending to have the dry heaves, she slipped back in. "Damn flu," she moaned again.

She radioed to the shift supervisor, and was instructed, as expected, to go back to the Fifth District, where her partner would get reassigned for the rest of the shift and where she could change into her street clothes and sign out for sick leave. She positioned herself behind the counter and pretended to be shuffling for the right forms to get a good look at Michael Bennett when they brought him in.

His ragged appearance was a sharp contrast to the photos that had appeared in the *Blade* and the *Post*. Michael's eyes were bloodshot and dazed, his hair matted on one side of his head, as if it had been pushed there during a fitful sleep and never combed back. Two days without shaving had made him look so seedy he could have passed for a drunk or even an addict picked up for a petty crime. He was carrying a knapsack, holding it close to his chest.

She watched as he was led to one of the interview rooms. She knew D'Amecourt was in the building and she guessed she had no more than two minutes before he joined Michael.

Michael was sitting at the scarred wooden table when she stepped in. She immediately shut the door and they stared at each other for several seconds before she broke the silence.

"My name is Gloria Towson." She showed him her badge. "I've only got a couple minutes to talk to you before you get grilled by someone I don't think you really want to see."

He continued staring at her, as if he had no idea how to respond. The knapsack was on the table, resting under his right arm.

"You know who I'm talking about, don't you, Michael?"

"No," he answered.

"I think you probably do, and even though I believe you're innocent, I'm clearly in the minority, judging by what I've read, which is probably because I know so much more than I'm supposed to."

"Do you know something about Justin?" Bennett leaned forward anxiously.

"I'm not sure." She met his eyes and held them. "The FBI took your computer today, didn't they?"

His face reddened, and she saw a flash of anger in his eyes. "Yes."

"Why? What do you think they were looking to find?"

"I don't know."

"Well there must have been *something* that sent Commander D'Amecourt to your house."

Bennett tensed at the mention of D'Amecourt's name.

"What about the box, Michael? Was it that?"

Bennett stared down at the table. She was wondering if she'd lost him when he answered, "Yes." He looked up at her again. "But now there's something else."

"What?" she said too quickly.

"I can't talk about it."

"Why?"

"Because I can't. Is Lou—Commander D'Amecourt here?"

Gloria registered the use of his first name. She paused, knowing what she was about to say could doom her.

"Yes, he's upstairs. Probably on his way down right now. It's up to you to decide it you really want to talk to him—or *trust* him."

He gave her a look that she couldn't quite read.

"Five years ago, when Benjamin was abducted, D'Amecourt was the lead investigator. That meant he spent a lot of time talking to you, right?"

Michael met her eyes, and nodded slightly.

"Which meant he knew where you lived, and about how close you were with Benjamin."

"Yes," he said quietly.

Gloria thought back to everything she had read about the first abduction, and about D'Amecourt's repeated insinuations in the media that Michael was involved.

"Michael, is there anything else you can tell me about what's going on?"

He sat up a bit straighter. She knew that her bluntness and assertion about his innocence had won him over. To a point.

"No," he said. "All I want is to get Justin back."

She reached into her pocket for one of her cards. "My cell phone and home phone number are listed here. Put it in your pocket—quick, and don't let D'Amecourt see it. Can you call me tonight?"

"Why?"

"I think you're being railroaded, and I want to find out what's really going on."

"I shouldn't be talking to you about this."

"Yes. You *should*. I want to help you. You have to believe that." Her card was still lying on the table. She pushed it forward. Any second D'Amecourt was going to walk in the door. "Please, put this in your pocket, *now*. Call me as soon as you get out of here or as soon as you possibly can."

He took the card, but when he looked at her again there was a wariness that worried her.

She decided to take a chance, before reason could stop her. "I know about the murders—the two guys who were stabbed to death. I know D'Amecourt is trying to cover up both crimes, and that the second one has a definite connection to Justin's kidnapping."

"The *second* one?" Michael's eyes widened.

"Yes. At the Capitol Hotel, two days ago." She watched him carefully for a reaction. "Do you know anything about that?"

"No."

Michael nervously bit his lower lip. She wasn't sure if he was telling the truth.

"The victim's wrists were bound and he was stabbed God knows how many times. He had a fresh stamp on his hand that showed he'd been at Club Night shortly before. We think he picked up someone there and brought him back to his hotel room for sex."

"Oh God..." Michael moaned, leaning forward, both hands coming up crosswise over his neck.

As if he knew exactly what the guy in that hotel room looked like. Gloria thought. She also realized that even if Michael Bennett was being truthful about being unaware of the Capitol Hotel murder, he *did* know about the murder two years earlier, at the Larchmont.

She heard voices in the hallway, and glanced at the door. "Michael, I promise you I'll do anything to help you get Justin back," she said. "But in the meantime you have to keep quiet about me being in here and talking to you. If I get the slightest indication you've said something to D'Amecourt I'll deny it up and down, which will just make you look crazier, and you don't want that, okay?"

He nodded as more voices filled the hall. The conference room had a second door that led to a corridor on the opposite side. She moved toward it quickly and her hand was on the knob when she looked at him again.

"Don't trust him, Michael. Trust *me*."

The nod of his head gratified her but there was a chill at the back of her neck as she slipped out and moved toward the exit door to the street. The exit door had a pane of glass that gave her a mirrored reflection of the corridor behind her, an image of D'Amecourt coming around the corner, an instant away from seeing her as she walked away.

Fifteen

Michael felt a clash of dark emotions pulling him down like a drowning man as Louis D'Amecourt came into the cinderblock room. He started to speak but his anger made it hard to even breathe as Louis apologized for having him "escorted" into the police station. It had happened just seconds after he had pulled up to the curb in front of D'Amecourt's house. It had been D'Amecourt on the phone, calling from his office at the police station, suddenly sounding very determined to talk with him. Michael had agreed, but had driven no more than two blocks before a police car pulled out of a side street behind him with the lights flashing. The officer had taken a look at his license and then followed him. The officer had then gripped him on the shoulder and led him in as if he were a suspect.

"That was unnecessary," Michael said. "And stupid. It made me look like I'm guilty of something."

"I told you I'm sorry." D'Amecourt bristled. Michael knew he wasn't used to being challenged, and that he spent most of his day barking orders and keeping everyone around him on edge. "I wanted to make sure you got here."

"You waited a whole day before calling me back. Why?"

D'Amecourt blinked nervously, scratching the stubble on his cheek. He looked thin and drawn in his navy blue uniform and during the past two years his thinning hair had turned white. His nose and cheeks had the red, mottled look Michael had seen on alcoholics.

"I was looking into what you told me."

"That's bullshit, Louis. All I told you was that some freak came up to me at the bar and said he knew I was hurting Justin, and implied that he was going to do something to me. The only way you could have *looked into it* was by calling me back. But you didn't—not even after Justin was kidnapped."

Michael realized D'Amecourt's hands were shaking.

"Did you get drunk again? Is that it?"

D'Amecourt crossed his arms. And when he looked down at the floor without answering Michael knew he was right. He felt a tightening in his chest as he thought of what the woman cop had told him just seconds before leaving the room.

There was another murder two days ago. D'Amecourt's trying to cover it up. He probably started drinking right after he found out, reliving everything all over again.

"I'm sorry, Michael." D'Amecourt's voice was quiet, regretful. "I'm just kind of... overwhelmed right now."

"Right. So overwhelmed you didn't do anything, even though I *told* you he was in danger."

"That's not true."

"Sure it is—"

"*No it's not!*" D'Amecourt snapped. His face was bright red. Michael waited for the man to regain his composure. The wall clock ticked a full 30 seconds before D'Amecourt spoke again.

"Tell me exactly what he said."

"So *now* you want to know."

"Michael—"

"I told you everything in the voice mail I left you right after it happened. He implied that I was hurting Justin in some way."

"Molesting him?"

"I don't know." *Not true*. Michael paused, feeling the heat on his face. "Or at least I didn't know *then*. He just implied I was doing something bad. Then he called me a pervert, and said I deserved to be *cut up*."

Michael's hand went involuntarily to his neck. He felt the beat of his jugular vein under his fingertips.

"He said he wanted it to *hurt*."

D'Amecourt stared back at him. There was a slight tightness around his mouth. But otherwise there was almost no change in his expression.

"I *know* it's the same guy, Louis, and I'm sure he's killed other people."

It was the perfect opening, a prompt for D'Amecourt to tell him about the new murder. Michael waited.

After a long moment, D'Amecourt looked past him, his eyes glazed and distant.

Michael felt his anger rupturing. "You really are a *prick.*"

D'Amecourt flinched at the sharpness of his voice.

"You really *don't* want him to get caught—"

"That's not true, Michael."

"Good. Because I already told the first cop who questioned me after Justin disappeared that this guy approached me the night before."

D'Amecourt's eyes flashed with alarm. "You *told* him—"

"Of course I told him, Louis. So the information is out there, and there's nothing you can do to squelch it."

"Fuck..." D'Amecourt exhaled, lowering his head and massaging his temples, looking as if he had just heard the worse news of his life. Michael wondered how long he would go before he got drunk again. It was easy to imagine the man pushing himself into two or three days of oblivion. He knew D'Amecourt had done it many times before.

"What else do you know about the investigation?" Michael asked. "What is the FBI doing now?"

D'Amecourt looked past him, toward the door. Michael remembered he had locked it from the inside when he had come into the room. He realized the woman cop had been right. D'Amecourt had wanted him to be sealed off, unable to talk to anyone else.

"They're working with the Maryland State Police," D'Amecourt said. "They've gone to the area where Benjamin was held before he died. They've scoured the trails and ravines around the stream and haven't found any sign of Justin. But it's a huge area, and Brown's family owns half of a mountain up there. There are other caves, cabins, plenty of places where he could be hidden."

"What about Scott. Any sign?"

D'Amecourt shook his head.

"You're going to have to tell them everything I just told you, Louis."

D'Amecourt met his eyes but did not answer. "You said he called you, after Justin was taken."

"Yes. This morning. My number's listed, so it would have been easy to find. He told me he *knows* I'm a pedophile."

D'Amecourt blinked quickly, anxiously. "What did you say?"

"I denied it. But he said he has proof. And he's going to make an anonymous call to the police and tell them everything he— quote— *knows* if I don't pay him $10,000. Today. He wants me to meet him at a vacant lot on Central Avenue off Bladensburg Road in Northeast."

D'Amecourt scribbled the address on his notepad.

"It's a rough neighborhood," Michael said. "I drove over and took a look at it right after I got the call. There's a rundown park with benches that face the street. He wants me to meet him there. With the money. I took it from my savings account right after he called me. It's in this bag."

D'Amecourt stopped writing. "You're going to *pay* it?"

"*Yes*. If he really does have proof of something then he might know what really happened to Justin." Michael heard the desperation in his own voice. "I have to confront him."

"Which is basically going to convince him that he was right. That you've got something to hide."

D'Amecourt's words hung in the air, reminding Michael of the box that the FBI agents had taken from the attic. He knew it wouldn't be long before the contents were made public, and that they would cause tremendous damage to his claim of innocence.

But they're going to bring suspicion to you, too. Michael looked at D'Amecourt. *Pulling the lid off the biggest goddamn secret of your life.*

"You know what the FBI agents took out of my house," Michael said. "What they found in my room—"

"I know." D'Amecourt's voice was suddenly hoarse.

"I'm sorry." Michael looked at him. "I never would have wanted that to happen, for your sake—"

"But now it has." D'Amecourt rubbed his eyes. Michael felt a twinge at the base of his throat. A minute earlier the man had filled him with rage, but now he felt pity creeping back.

The shrill, short ring of a cell phone filled the air. D'Amecourt pulled it from his belt, and clenched his jaw as he read the number on the display window.

"I have to take this down the hall," D'Amecourt said.

"Why, who is it?" Michael asked.

"No one... nothing to do with you."

Michael knew he was lying. He thought about the woman cop, Gloria Towson, as D'Amecourt moved quickly toward the door.

"Don't trust him Michael. Trust me."

"I need to get some air," he said to D'Amecourt. "I'm going outside."

"Don't go too far."

Michael was annoyed at his tone. He did not like the idea of D'Amecourt giving him orders. "Don't worry. I'll be right out front and I'm only leaving for a couple of minutes." He gave D'Amecourt a pointed look. "It'll give you time to figure out how to help me."

D'Amecourt looked like he wanted to argue, but the phone rang again, quickening his departure.

Michael went out the door on the opposite side of the room. He thought about the woman cop again as he headed down the exit stairs. Their conversation had been short and strange. But it had also been encouraging to know that someone in law enforcement believed in his innocence. And yet he wondered what she could really do. Towson was a young patrol officer, and right now staying *out* of D'Amecourt's sight was clearly important to her. To really help him she'd probably need to know everything about his relationship with D'Amecourt, and he felt a certain wariness about telling her.

But he had to trust someone.

He stepped outside. The Fifth District police station was in a residential neighborhood of townhouses and apartment buildings. Across the street, on the front porch of a faded but tidy home, an elderly black woman sat in a rocking chair. Michael saw a flash of recognition on her face, and was suddenly curious about what might have been shown on the afternoon news programs. D'Amecourt knew what was in the box, but had said nothing about the contents being made public.

At least not yet.

Michael took Gloria Towson's card from his pocket and dialed her number on his cell phone. He got her voice mail, and left a message saying that he wanted to meet with her again. He set the time and the place and hoped that he would indeed be there.

He hung up and clipped the phone to his belt. The late afternoon sun was warm on his face as he looked back at the woman. He was reminded of the older black staffers at the Happy Haven day care center, none of whom knew, or admitted to knowing, that he had been fired from his last teaching job. He had begun as a volunteer in the kitchen that prepared meals for the homeless, and had later offered to be a chaperone for a children's outing to a museum. When no one had objected, he had signed up to be a once-a-week tutor in the after-school program. The experience brought back the simple joy—the absolute rightness—he had felt in his previous days of teaching.

But behind it there was the ever-present fear of exposure, the knowledge that he might one day walk in to find he was no longer welcome. He had been on edge for several days after the publication of the story in *The Washington Blade*, knowing that the fact that he had never volunteered information about his past would only make it worse, as if he really did have something to hide. Up until now, nothing had been said. But with all of the publicity around Justin's disappearance, he knew it was only a matter of time before the children were questioned about any contact they might have had with him.

His throat was tight and dry as he headed back into the police station. He went up the stairs without stopping at the desk and simply scowled at a secretary who tried to stop him from walking through the administrative wing.

D'Amecourt's door was closed. He gave it a perfunctory knock and turned the knob.

D'Amecourt was on the phone, hunched over as if trying to keep his conversation quiet. His mouth dropped in mid-sentence and he was obviously angry at the interruption.

"It's getting late," Michael said.

D'Amecourt covered the receiver with his hand. "You can wait in the hallway."

Michael stepped back but did not close the door. D'Amecourt lowered his voice and it was impossible to hear what he was saying. Moments later, he hung up, and Michael opened the door wider.

"So are you going to help me or not?"

"Yeah, Michael, I'll help you." D'Amecourt stood up and opened a desk drawer without meeting his eyes. He took a gun out of his desk and slipped it into the holster on his waist, reached back in the drawer and pulled out another gun, a small revolver, and fastened it to a holster around his ankle.

The sight of the guns made Michael even more anxious as he thought of D'Amecourt finding an excuse to gun the stranger down, *silencing* him...

"So how are we going to do this?" he asked.

"I sent an officer to take a look at the site where he told you to take the money," D'Amecourt said. "There's a bus shelter about 50 feet from the bench where he told you to wait. An undercover officer will be stationed there. There's a liquor store across the street and another guy will be positioned there. You'll put the bag on the bench. Then you're going to walk back to your car and—"

"No," Michael interrupted. "The only reason I got the money was so I'd have the chance to confront him, to find out how he knew Justin was in danger."

"You *will* find out. When we take him into custody."

"But what if you don't? What if he sees your people, gets spooked—"

"He won't see them Michael."

"But what if he gets away?"

D'Amecourt's lips tightened. "He's not going to get away."

"You don't know that for sure, and I'm not going to take the chance."

"No, Michael."

"Yes, *Louis*."

"*No.* You know what we're dealing with. You know what he's capable of."

D'Amecourt's hands were trembling. For the first time he actually looked frightened. *Like he's worried something is going to happen to you*, Michael thought.

It was a surprise. For years he had believed that Louis D'Amecourt hated him, and that the history between them brought nothing more than shame. And yet he was still haunted by the memory of the one time he had seen D'Amecourt break down, his fists pressed against his forehead, tears streaming down his cheeks.

Michael wondered if D'Amecourt would ever cry like that again. He thought of the way the stranger—the killer—had punched him and then held him against the wall, felt the muscles in his abdomen clenching at the thought of a knife cutting through his gut.

But you don't have any choice.

Michael rested his head back against the wall and wearily exhaled.

"I know what you're afraid of," he said. "But his instructions were clear. I have to take him the money, in person. He obviously wants to talk to me too. And if I can convince him he's wrong about me, then—"

"You're not going to convince him." D'Amecourt said.

"Well I have to try."

Michael looked at the clock on the wall. In two hours he needed to be at the bench, money in hand.

"I have to find out what he knows."

Sixteen

Looking down from a second-floor window, Harland Till waited for Michael Bennett to walk into the trap.

Below him, across the street, the bench where Bennett had been instructed to sit with the money was illuminated by a harsh streetlight that cast long shadows underneath the dead trees. Occasionally a street person would shuffle along. In another life Till imagined himself moving among the crowd of vagrants with an open bible, quoting the scriptures with the fervent force of a true believer.

No—Reverend Willow saved souls. Tonight you're going to save a little boy.

The rowhouse across the street from the tiny park was long-abandoned, occupied off and on by neighborhood drunks and mental cases who had pulled the plywood off a rear alley window. Hours earlier he had approached one of the "tenants" with a proposition that to someone less inebriated might have seemed too good to be true. But to "Mookie," a homosexual crackhead who had taken to turning $10 tricks in the alley, the promise of easy money was too good to be denied.

Right now "Mookie" was at the end of the block, as instructed, sitting on a milk crate and watching as a Jeep pulled up to the curb. After a moment the driver's side door opened and Michael Bennett got out. Bennett was carrying a knapsack and he was right on time. But Till felt a twinge of apprehension as Bennett looked side to side and then upwards, toward the abandoned building where Till was hiding. Till doubted that Bennett would have involved the police, not when his own actions were so clearly incriminating.

But something ain't right. From the second-floor window Till watched as Bennett sat down on the bench, both hands holding the bag on his lap. For obvious reasons, Bennett looked disheveled and nervous but he also looked highly alert and possibly ready for a fight.

But he's paying for me to keep quiet, he thought. *Like I knew he would.*

Bending at the knees, Till lowered himself so that his eyes were barely above the windowsill, watching intently as Mookie got up from his crate and headed toward the bench.

* * *

Michael told himself that he wasn't alone, and that he had no reason to believe Louis D'Amecourt would not live up to his word. Among the homeless people camped out at the bus shelter or sleeping in the abandoned buildings across the street there were allies, watching him.

But he was beginning to feel otherwise as the bum who had been staring at him made his approach. The man was black, with grayish stubble on his cheeks, and a twitch that Michael could see from several yards away. Michael looked again toward the bus shelter and the liquor store across the street and saw no indication that any of the people camped out in front of either spot had even noticed the man's approach.

The man had moved quickly and stood directly in front of him, licking his lips, staring at the bag. "Yo, you got to come wit me, all right?"

Michael tightened his grip. "Why?"

"To get what you want."

Michael detected an effeminate edge to the man's voice. His fingernails were long and had chips of polish. "And what is that?"

"You know. Come on, it's just a little way." He nodded toward an alley filled with garbage. The alley had been blocked off with a high, chain-link fence topped with barbed wire, but at some point someone had cut a hole in the fence that was big enough to pass through.

"You want me to go back there," Michael gave him a wary look. "With you."

"*Thass* right. I'll take you to the dude you got to see."

The possibility that the stranger would send someone else to get the money hadn't even occurred to him, and he doubted that D'Amecourt or the undercover officers would be able to follow them without revealing themselves.

You can always give them some kind of signal right now. Call out, bring them running. Take him into custody—

No. He instantly reconsidered. *Find out as much as you can. Do whatever you have to lure him out.*

Michael straightened his spine, and glanced toward the bus shelter again. "Who sent you?"

"Your friend, I guess. White man—"

"What's his name?"

"Don't know. He got marks on his face."

Michael remembered the stranger had pale skin, scarred by acne.

"What has he told you?" Michael asked. "About me?"

"Nothin." The man put both hands on his hips. "I just know you got to come with me, all right?"

Michael glanced past him again, noticed for the first time that a woman, heavily bundled in ragged clothing, with a shopping cart full of cans, was looking in his direction. Their eyes met for an instant, and when she gave him a small nod Michael knew what he had to do.

"Tell your friend to fuck off."

The bum flinched in surprise.

"Tell him we had a deal. I'm not leaving this bench. If he wants it, he's got to come out here, *now*."

The bum was frowning, obviously confused about how to react. Michael was encouraged that he didn't instantly say no. He glanced down the block toward a vacant lot and looked again at the derelict rowhouses across the street.

"You can also let him know him he's wrong. I didn't have anything to do with what happened to my nephew." Michael's voice was suddenly shaky. "I just want him back. If he knows something—anything—he has to tell me. I'll give him this money and more. I'll give him everything I have."

The bum was frowning, confused now. Michael guessed he had been told very little. But he was certain that whatever message he gave the man would be delivered.

And yet the man was stepping back, shaking his head.

Michael tensed, realizing he had probably said too much. The man turned away and Michael felt a flurry of panic in his chest.

"Hey—"

Without thinking he had started to stand up. His weight was on one foot when the man spun around and punched him in the face. The blow knocked him back against the bench, the top of the seatback smacking into his spine. The next punch landed just under his ribs and knocked the air out of his lungs. He tried to get up and the man kicked his knee.

The pain shot from his head to his legs, clouding his vision and causing him to double over on the bench as the man went for the bag.

"D'AMECOURT!" Michael screamed. The bum had a firm grip on the bag. Michael tried to pull it back and the man hit him squarely in the nose. He tasted his own warm blood and saw it on the front of his shirt as he tried to get up. His leg buckled and he fell forward, both hands smacking the pavement as the bum broke away and headed toward the torn chain-link fence.

"No! NO!" He screamed as he tried to get up. Daggers of pain pierced his temples and his blood fell in fat droplets to the pavement.

"STOP!" His voice went hoarse. "GOD SOMEONE GET HIM TO STOP!"

He managed to get up for just a moment before the pain buckled his leg and he fell backwards again, the pavement smacking the back of his head.

He imagined that he opened his eyes, but he saw nothing but blackness. He struggled to get up but couldn't get his arms or legs to move.

"Michael..." The sound of his own name brought the world back into focus. Above him the homeless woman with the shopping cart looked worriedly into his eyes.

He managed to say "Who—" before his mouth filled with blood.

"I'm Sylvia Barshak. With the FBI. Just please, Michael, calm the hell down."

* * *

The scene played out over and over in Michael's mind as the unmarked police car raced through the city streets, the woman FBI agent staying silent behind the wheel. Michael's tongue was swollen and he was barely able to talk, but still he persisted, begging her to tell him what the hell had happened. Where were the other cops? Where was Louis D'Amecourt? Why had they let the man who grabbed the money run away?

"We didn't," Agent Barshak told him finally.

Michael straightened up, met her eyes in the rear view mirror.

"Lou—Commander D'Amecourt—went after the guy who took your money, but not directly—"

"What do you mean, not directly?"

"He doubled around the block, tried to catch him at the other end of the alley."

"But you let the guy get away," Michael punched the back of the seat.

"Michael, please—"

"You know D'Amecourt's *secret*, don't you?"

There was a sudden rush of color at the back of her neck. "I don't know what you're talking about."

"Of course you do. You're helping him hide it."

Barshak said nothing, but he knew he was right.

She pulled into the hospital driveway, stopped the car, and turned around. "Come on, you need to see a doctor."

"No, I don't."

"You do, Michael. You've already passed out twice."

Michael looked at the dashboard clock. It was 9:30. He had a vague recollection of getting up off of the ground and being led unsteadily toward the unmarked car before the drive across the city. And now the woman was suddenly at his side, her hand on his arm as she urged him to step out.

He was dizzy again when he stood up, and she only walked him a few feet before putting him in a wheelchair and pushing him down a long corridor.

At the end, in a small room, D'Amecourt was waiting.

"I'm sorry, Michael."

"Fuck you, Louis."

"We did everything we could."

"You did shit. And now he's gone. He got away."

D'Amecourt and Barshak looked at each other from across the room. Michael remembered now why she looked familiar. She and D'Amecourt were former partners. D'Amecourt had done the bulk of the interrogation after the murder two years earlier but Michael remembered seeing a picture of her in the den of D'Amecourt's house, which was where D'Amecourt had taken him secretly to be questioned.

"You sold me out," he said without thinking. "Both of you."

"No, Michael," D'Amecourt shook his head.

"The FBI and the D.C. police weren't even told what was going to happen tonight. It was the two of you alone, hoping you could bring him in yourself."

Michael looked at Barshak, who had taken off the scarf and shed the ragged coat. Her hair was auburn, and streaked with gray. Her eyes were a faded blue.

"How did he talk you into it?" he asked her. "Did he make you feel sorry for him? Tell you his career would be over?"

Barshak stared back at him as if she was unsure how to respond.

"You're reading this wrong, Michael," D'Amecourt said. "We were as surprised that he sent someone else to get the money as you were. Agent Barshak was wearing an earpiece and I was talking with her the whole time."

"Where the hell were you?"

"Watching. From a place where I couldn't be seen. I was the one who told her not to go after the guy when he ran away. I saw him go through the hole in the fence and tried to intercept him when he came out of the other end of the alley so I could track him."

"What do you mean, *track* him?"

"We wanted to see where he was going, if he would lead us to the man who called you."

"But that didn't happen, did it?"

D'Amecourt gave a slow shake of his head. Michael noticed that his thin white hair was hanging in strands over his forehead, and there were spots of dirt on his knees. Perhaps the story of a running chase was true.

"What *did* happen?"

"I lost him."

"What about the money?"

"It's gone."

All your money. Gone. With the only link to the man who might know where Justin is.

Michael winced at a sharp pain in his temples. He looked at D'Amecourt again. "So what are you going to do now?"

D'Amecourt leaned against the tile wall. "I've got several officers looking through the area for anyone who fits the physical description of the man who beat you up at the bar. And as you can see we've got the FBI involved, too."

"Oh, right, the *FBI*," Michael glared at Barshak. "It was the FBI that *searched my house*."

"That was a precaution Michael," Barshak looked embarrassed. "At the time we didn't feel like we had any choice."

"You honestly thought I had something to do with Justin's disappearance?" Michael felt a sickening sense of déjà vu. "What possible reason?"

"Michael there's something Commander D'Amecourt didn't tell you earlier."

"Sylvia, *please*." D'Amecourt hissed.

"He needs to know." Barshak gave D'Amecourt a regretful look. "You should have told him when it happened and you *certainly* should have told me."

"Told you what?" Michael glared at both of them. "What are you talking about?"

"There was a murder two nights ago, at the Capitol Hotel," Barshak said.

Michael almost nodded, but was stopped by the memory of Gloria Towson's warning. He stayed quiet, waiting to see how much they would tell him.

"It was just like the last one," Barshak said.

"The *last* one?" Michael looked at D'Amecourt. "Is that the way you refer to—"

"Yes, Michael." D'Amecourt cut him off.

"There have been others, out of the area," Barshak said. "All of the victims were involved in pornography. They appeared in magazines, movies, and on Web sites."

Michael felt a tingling in his cheeks, a rush of embarrassment so intense he had to look at the floor.

"There was also some evidence that either the killer or the victim knew Justin."

"What kind of *evidence?*"

"Evidence that shouldn't have been ignored," Barshak said. "But unfortunately it was, and when everything unfolded yesterday we had to look at you as a suspect. We didn't have any choice."

"*We?*" Michael glared at D'Amecourt. The accusation was stupid. Louis D'Amecourt never would have believed him guilty of anything when it came to Justin's safety.

"So you *knew* Justin was in danger," Michael said. "You knew it two days ago..."

"He clearly made a mistake," Barshak spoke before D'Amecourt could answer. "Yesterday, when Justin got kidnapped he immediately called me. I was one of the investigators on the first murder."

"Yeah, but it was *D'Amecourt* who questioned me." Michael gave her a pointed look. "And we all know why that was."

"Michael." D'Amecourt's voice had a warning tone.

"He wanted to take me on himself." Michael glared back at him. "He already believed I was some kind of pervert who had kidnapped Benjamin three years earlier and he wanted to believe I was a murderer too. But the most important thing was keeping it quiet, not letting anyone know about his own *connection*. "

Michael felt short of breath and suddenly pitiless toward D'Amecourt, who looked as if he was about to collapse.

"So when he found out about a second murder he wanted to keep a lid on that, too. He didn't want me to be questioned by someone else because he was afraid I'd reveal what I knew about the *first* one."

D'Amecourt shook his head. His cheeks were burning red.

"That's why you never told me about the threat to Justin. You knew if I found out he was in danger I'd do anything to protect him, even if it meant going past you and demanding that *both* murders were fully investigated. You knew your *secret* would come out."

D'Amecourt lowered his head, and covered his face with his hands.

Michael turned to Barshak again. "What else do you know about the guy who killed them?"

Barshak was watching D'Amecourt, her eyes looked weary with sadness. "We don't know much. None of the investigations have ever uncovered prints or witnesses. We think he travels up and down the East Coast, since that's where the murders have occurred. The victims all lived within short driving distance of Miami, Washington, or New York, which is where they were murdered. Some of the victims were prostitutes who arranged to meet customers via links to their Web sites. We think the killer offers to pay some of them for sex and then kills them."

Michael looked at D'Amecourt. "But they aren't *all* prostitutes."

"No," Barshak said. "Not all."

Michael kept his eyes on D'Amecourt. "Why do you think he's so sure I've been hurting Justin?"

"We honestly don't know," D'Amecourt answered.

"Well what about this evidence? What makes you think the killing has something to do with Justin's kidnapping?"

"We can't really say," Barshak spoke before D'Amecourt could respond. "It would compromise the investigation."

"The *investigation*? God, I can't *believe* I'm hearing this." Michael made an abrupt move to stand up. The room spun and the pain inside his mouth intensified.

"You can't leave," Barshak said.

"The hell I can't."

"A doctor has to look at you."

"No." Despite the dizziness he was already moving toward the door. "The last thing I want to do is hang around here."

D'Amecourt stepped away from the wall and stood in his way. "Michael if you hear anything else from him you have to promise—"

"Right, *Louis*. I promise to call you right away," Michael sarcastically cut him off. The pain inside his mouth had dulled a bit, but he still tasted blood.

The sensation stoked his anger as he looked at Sylvia Barshak again. "So are you happy with what you found when you ransacked my room?"

"We weren't looking for what we found—"

"No, but now you have it. What good is it going to do?"

"Michael, I can't change any of the mistakes that have been made." The woman's voice had an earnest, pleading tone. "But you have to believe I want to get your nephew back."

"Why?" He smirked toward D'Amecourt. "To save your friend here?"

"Yes." Barshak folded her arms over her chest. "And you, too."

Michael glared back at her for a long moment before stepping back toward the exit. Behind him D'Amecourt called his name twice as he moved toward the emergency room's automatic doors and stepped out into the night. Tears were streaming down his face as D'Amecourt's admission ran again and again through his mind.

He knew. Hours before it happened, he knew.

In seconds Michael was running, away from the hospital, away from D'Amecourt, a cry coming from deep within his lungs as he thought of how different it would have been if D'Amecourt had come forward, warning him, warning Mary…

Moments later he was weeping, leaning against a brick wall on Wisconsin Avenue, losing control completely as the voice of Officer Towson came back to him.

"Don't trust him, Michael. Trust me."

He wondered what she could possibly do for him if he did. His heart was still pounding as he went to the curb and hailed a cab. Five minutes later he was back at Martin and Joan's house.

He was feeling guilty and foolish as he paid the driver and stepped out. And he was so distracted that he almost missed the blue Toyota parked at the curb.

Gloria Towson flashed her headlights and motioned for him to get in.

Seventeen

Late at night, after closing, the upstairs backroom of O'Malley's pub smelled of lemon polish and Pine-sol, but underneath it were 60 years of cooking and wood smoke permanently burned into the rafters from the fireplace that took up half of the back wall. Gloria found the mix of scents comforting as she watched Michael Bennett slip into the bus station, where he poured her a big mug of coffee and himself a mug of water before leading her to a back booth.

"My sister Mary works lunches here and my uncle Martin is part-owner, so they sort of give me the run of the place." Michael's voice was thick and subdued. "They were here when it happened."

Michael set both mugs down on the table, then lowered his head and pressed a fist against his lips. Gloria knew that he was doing his best to hold back his sorrow. Sensing his embarrassment, she pretended not to notice, focusing instead on what she had learned immediately after Michael had gotten into her car, telling her *"all right, let's go somewhere we can talk."*

During the drive, he had told her that a stranger had approached him at Club Night and insinuated that Justin Bennett was in danger. He then explained that D'Amecourt had been tracking the stranger for some time, enough to know that he had killed half a dozen men. The revelation surprised and confused her as she thought about D'Amecourt's intense desire to cover up the crime. She understood why D'Amecourt might be territorial, why he might have remained obsessed with the murders even though he was no longer a homicide detective.

But if he was that anxious to bring him in, why not look for more help?

The question gnawed at her as she remembered the look on Michael's face when she had first told him she knew about *both* of the murders that had taken place in Washington. She was now certain that Michael had been aware of the first, but was surprised to hear about the second. And she was still curious about his strange allegiance to D'Amecourt, and the guarded way he spoke about the man even now.

When he calmed down, she asked him why.

"It's history," he told her. "And I really don't think it has anything to do with Justin's kidnapping."

"Are you sure?"

Michael paused. "I don't know. Not now."

"Not *now*?"

Michael ran his hands through his hair, and held it in his fists as he stared down at the table. "He said he found some kind of evidence in the guy's room that made him think something might happen to Justin."

Gloria leaned slightly forward, waiting to see how much D'Amecourt had revealed.

"He wouldn't tell me what it was," Michael said. "He said it would 'compromise the investigation,' whatever the hell that means."

It means he's not coming clean, Gloria thought. *And you're not pushing him hard enough to find out what he's hiding.*

"Look, can we talk about Justin now?" Michael gave her an anxious look. "You said you think you think you can help me find him. How?"

Gloria watched him carefully for a reaction to what she was about to say. "I have access to information that D'Amecourt doesn't have. I think the man who was murdered at the Capitol Hotel knew Justin was about to be kidnapped. He might have even been involved in planning it."

Michael sat very still, and by the look on his face she could see that he was not surprised. D'Amecourt had at least told him that much.

"How do you know this?" Michael asked.

"I have some sources I can't reveal right now," Gloria said. "But I was also the first responder, so I saw the victim."

She mentally debated again the danger of telling Michael even more.

"I also know a little bit about that evidence that he told you about. There was a picture of a little boy on the floor of the room. I'm pretty sure it was a picture of Justin, and that D'Amecourt took it without telling the detective in charge of the case."

"A picture..." Michael stared back at her. His hands began to tremble around the mug. "That you saw him take?"

"No. I just know the picture was on the floor one minute and gone the next. There was a detective on the scene and I don't believe he took it."

"What did you do?"

"Nothing, at least not right away. Commander D'Amecourt is a senior police official. I wasn't ready to go up against him. But I did start my own investigation, through back channels."

"But you didn't say *anything*?"

"No," she said. "But at the time I didn't realize it was a picture of Justin. I saw it from five feet away, and it was partially under the bed. And the next day I *did* have a conversation with the detective, who's a friend."

Michael was frowning at her, his broad shoulders tight against his neck. His expression made her feel even more guilty about not confronting D'Amecourt at the scene.

She sat back slightly, knowing she had to regain control of the conversation. "Do you want to hear what I know, Michael?"

"Yes," he said. "Tell me."

"I might have a way of tracking the kidnapper through computer traffic. I think it's possible that there's a connection between the abduction and a pedophile chat room."

Michael sat very still, his eyes flat as he stared back at her. He did not look surprised. She thought again about the FBI search of his house, and his longtime interest in computers, and watched him carefully as she continued.

"I think Louis D'Amecourt knows something about this—and that's why he took the picture."

"You think Benjamin's being molested."

"Benjamin..."

"Justin, I mean." Michael blinked quickly, nervously.

Gloria paused. "You said Benjamin."

"I meant Justin."

She watched him shift uncomfortably in his seat. "It was Benjamin who was at the top of your mind. Why?"

"I was confused."

"Confused or *accused*?"

Michael broke eye contact. His silence sent her mind spinning back to everything she had read about the first kidnapping.

"Michael?"

He looked down at the table. "I was never formally accused."

"Was it implied at some point?"

"Once." Michael pressed the mug with both hands, looking as if he was about to crush it. "Maybe twice."

"By who?"

"An employee at Benjie's day care center. A real bitch." He met her eyes again. "But I know it didn't have anything to do with—"

"What did she say, Michael?"

"I don't want to talk about it."

"You have to," Gloria said. "I can only help you if you're completely honest with me. Please tell me, what happened?"

"She said there were signs of abuse."

"Sexual abuse?"

"Well, maybe. She said he had told her something about having his picture taken, when he was naked."

"Did you ever—"

"*No*, of course not."

"How did you deal with it, the accusation?"

"We didn't. The woman was a bible thumper who had always given me the cold shoulder when I picked Benjie up from day care. We assumed she was paranoid, or lying."

"Were you the only person who picked Benjamin up from day care?"

"No. Sometimes it was Mary. Sometimes Scott."

"But she never accused Scott."

"She probably wouldn't have. She knew he was Mary's boyfriend."

"You mean she knew he was *straight*."

"Yes."

"What did you do when this happened?"

"Nothing, really."

"Nothing?"

"It was too late." Michael nearly choked out the words, and shut his eyes to block more tears. "Benjamin was already gone."

"So she came forward *after* he had been kidnapped, and accused you?"

Michael nodded.

"And you knew she was talking about Scott. Who did you tell?"

"We told Louis D'Amecourt, who at the time was a detective. He was leading the investigation by the D.C. police and working with the FBI."

"D'Amecourt." Gloria felt a chill between her shoulder blades. "Anyone else?"

"No." Michael shook his head. "It didn't seem like there was anything we could do about it at that point. Scott wasn't officially charged with the kidnapping. Benjamin was dead."

"And you also knew that it would put the scrutiny back on you too."

"*I* didn't do it!" he said sharply.

"I know." Gloria regretted the insinuation, even if it was probably based in truth. By the time Benjamin's death was confirmed Michael was already as much of a suspect as Scott, and going public with the day care worker's accusation would not have helped him.

"Look, I believe you, Michael. But I still have a lot of questions. Like what really happened the day Benjamin disappeared. Why Scott Brown was never charged with the crime. Why D'Amecourt apparently still didn't rule you out as a suspect."

"Surely you've read the papers, Officer Towson."

"You can call me Gloria. And I did read about it, but not until last night. I want to hear it from your point of view, so I know what the media may have left out."

"About Scott?"

"About all of it. Your friendship. The drug bust. The night Benjamin disappeared."

"Do *you* think Scott is a pedophile?"

"I don't know. Do you think he really loved your sister?"

"That's one way of putting it. You could also say he lived and breathed just to be with her. The man was obsessed with her, and really possessive. Mary didn't think she loved him any more and was already starting to pull away. But she was reluctant to break it off completely because she knew he would fall apart. And she was afraid of what might happen if he did."

"She was afraid of him?"

"A little, I think. She knew he had a temper."

"And then he went to prison."

Michael nodded. "And that was because of me."

"Because of the drug bust on the boat."

"It was a *yacht*. Scott's second love. The place where we had some of the best times of our life. Until everything fell apart."

"Tell me what happened."

Michael set the mug aside and rubbed his eyes. "Scott had been away for two weeks, on his own down in the Florida keys. The day he came back he took me out on the Chesapeake Bay. I knew he had cocaine—we were both using it that day. I just didn't know how much he had on the boat."

"A million dollars worth, in street value." She remembered the story from the *Washington Post* archives. "At least that's what came up at the trial."

"That's right. One minute we're out on the bay, lying in the sun, the next we're surrounded by the Coast Guard, helicopters, the whole deal. The drugs were found in a compartment underneath the cabinets in the galley. Scott had loaned the boat to friends the day before and he tried to claim he didn't know about it."

"But you testified otherwise."

Michael nodded. "I had to. I was facing charges. My Uncle Martin and Aunt Joan were devastated. I was offered a deal."

"And the deal was what made Scott so angry?"

"We think so. At first we both stuck to the same story—which was that Scott had loaned the boat to a friend. He picked it up, docked it in Annapolis. His friend was supposed to take it to Baltimore the next day. We just happened to be on it for a few hours in between."

"But he found out you had changed your story."

"Yes."

"And then he took Benjamin."

Michael nodded.

"Can you tell me about that?" She prodded him. "How did it happen?"

"I was at home. It was a hot afternoon and I was really, really depressed. I'd spent the morning giving a deposition, admitting that I saw Scott going below and bringing up the cocaine that both of us were using. I was going to get immunity for testifying and my testimony was going to get the prosecutors everything they wanted. A conviction against Scott. Seizure of his boat. A clean case.

"I was there alone. Mary was at work and Benjamin was taking a nap in his room. Scott showed up. Evidently he'd already heard a rumor about what I had done. He asked me point-blank."

"And you told him."

"Yes."

"How did he react?"

"He freaked. Told me I was ruining his life—Mary and I together, actually. He told me we were both going to suffer."

"And then?"

"And then he left. At least that's what I thought. I watched him get in his car and drive away. Then I went inside, up to my room on the third floor. I sort of collapsed on the bed. I was so worn out."

"I remember reading... you said you were asleep when it happened."

"I think I was. The stress and exhaustion finally caught up with me. I slept for about an hour or more." Michael paused and met her eyes. "That's why I never heard him come back inside."

"So you didn't lock the door?"

"No. I don't think so. We think he pulled his car around to the back of the house, parked it there, came back in the front, took Benjamin, and then went out the back door. We're 30 seconds from the Rock Creek Parkway, and only a minute from Connecticut Avenue. From there it's a straight shot out of the city."

"You really believe that's how it happened?"

Michael thought about it a moment, then nodded. "The back door was always kept locked, but when we saw that Ben was gone we realized it was open."

"Is it possible he got up and wandered out?"

"No. We found his favorite stuffed animal right by the door. A bear. It was on the floor, as if it had been dropped. Ben and his bear were inseparable and there's no way he would have walked away and left it. Mary still sleeps with it at night."

Michael's eyes reddened with the last statement, as if merely saying it deepened his sorrow. Gloria thought about easing up and giving him time to compose himself but quickly changed her mind. There was too much she needed to know.

"I'm sorry everyone believed it was you, Michael."

"Me, too." He looked at her again. "Especially since there was so much evidence that I *didn't* do it."

Gloria had to agree. The rapids where Benjamin Bennett was briefly spotted before being swept away were only a mile from a cabin that had been owned by Scott Brown's father. It was virtually a given that that's where the boy had been held before getting away. According to newspaper accounts a local sheriff and deputy ransacked the cabin and combed the whole area, but

Brown was too fast for them. Nothing was found to definitively connect him to the crime.

Except for the witness, she remembered. A local drug dealer named Gerry Gray, who claimed to have seen Benjamin Bennett with his captors. A man who had made a call to a local lawyer who then asked the police to come get his statement, but who was shot in the face and left for dead inside his burning house by the time the police arrived.

Gloria looked at Michael again. "So neither you or Scott had an alibi for the time Benjamin actually disappeared, right?"

"No. I was asleep when it happened. Scott claimed that he was just aimlessly driving. But we all knew he did it."

"He hated you that much?"

"He knew he'd be in prison for a long time, and that Mary would never stay by him. He always had a hot temper. Always acted on his emotions first. He wanted to get even with us in the worst possible way. It was a snap decision."

Gloria thought again of everything Mary had written in her *Washington Blade* story about Scott Brown. The next question that came to her mind was an enduring mystery in the abduction of Benjamin. The answer was perhaps the most important clue to the abduction of Justin.

"What do you think Scott had intended to do with Benjamin when he took him?"

"I don't know." Michael answered.

"Is it possible that he never intended for Benjamin to die? That maybe he wanted to kidnap him and take him somewhere instead?"

"What are you saying?" Michael stared at her.

"What kind of relationship did Scott have with Benjamin, Michael?"

"They got along great."

"Like father and son, almost, right?"

"Yes. Ben's biological father was killed in a motorcycle accident right after he was born. Scott and I both spent as much time as possible with him to make up for that absence."

"What kind of relationship *would* Scott have had with Justin, if he hadn't gone to prison?"

Michael blinked and looked away. "I really don't know. Mary was two months pregnant with Justin when Benjamin was kidnapped. Scott was already in prison when Justin was born."

"But he still insisted on having some type of relationship with Justin."

"Yes. And there wasn't anything we could do to stop it. Scott's father is a powerful man. He got his lawyers to force Mary to allow Justin to spend time with that side of the family. Scott's parents took Justin to Groveton to see Scott every month."

"So Scott and Justin have spent quite a bit of time together."

"*Yes*," he groaned, as if the mere idea made him feel sick.

Gloria thought back to a pivotal moment in both kidnappings. Benjamin Bennett and Justin Bennett were both taken during the middle of the day, quietly and without protest. Which would have been easy for Scott if he were close to the boys. She thought of the child in the visiting room of the prison, felt a wave of unease as she thought of Scott and the child, spending even a few minutes alone. Scott Brown at the amusement park, taking the boy's hand, urging him to come along...

"What do you know about Scott's family, Michael?"

"Well they're the complete opposite of ours," he answered. "His father's about as right wing as they come. He hates gays, and hates the fact that I've always been so involved with Ben and Justin's lives. They thought it proved we were immoral, or something, which is especially weird with the way Scott's turned out."

"But if someone pressed you, you'd have to say that Scott still feels a connection with Justin, just like he did with Benjamin."

Michael nodded. "Yes. I'd have to say that he does."

Then maybe he's still alive. She wanted to be certain of it, wanted to believe that whether or not Scott Brown was a pedophile, he would never kill his own son. But the tattoo on the Capitol Hotel victim's leg and the connection to John Lee Ferguson the pornographer still frightened her. And she still couldn't reconcile why D'Amecourt had taken the photo, covering up the murder even though it was obvious that Justin was in danger.

You need to push him, she looked into Michael's eyes. *You have to find out what D'Amecourt's really hiding*.

Under the table, Gloria placed both palms on her knees and squeezed as hard as she could. It was a familiar gesture, used often to release tension just prior to making a high-risk arrest or confronting an uncomfortable situation. Her faith that Justin Bennett was still alive was shaky, and she was determined not to let it show on her face.

"You said the guy who roughed you up at the bar called you this morning. Can you tell me exactly what he said?"

"He didn't say that much— just that he knows I arranged for Justin to be kidnapped."

"What else?"

Michael frowned.

"What else did he say, Michael? Tell me exactly."

He looked past her, toward the darkened dining room as he repeated the entire conversation. Gloria listened intently, and there was an involuntary gasp from the base of her throat as the truth hit her.

"Oh no," she whispered, unintentionally, as she met Michael Bennett's eyes across the table.

"What?" Michael's face reflected the shock he read in hers.

Between them the air felt electrically charged, buzzing with tension.

"What?" Across the table Michael looked as if he was afraid of what she had discovered. "What are you thinking?"

That I know exactly how those little boys were kidnapped, and why.

The theory was pure conjecture. Difficult to investigate, and probably impossible to prove.

But dead on. She was even more certain of it as the messages from the Internet newsgroup rose up again in her mind.

Eighteen

Scott watched the girl carefully, alert to any sign of fear. The tips of her hair were frosted orange and a tiny earring pierced her eyebrow, but the careful application of silver lipstick and brown eye shadow told him she had primped a bit, wanting to look her best for her "date" with an older man.

Tiffany Potter had claimed in her emails to be 18 years old, but his own careful research told him she was barely 17. Ten years ago, finding her would have been a miracle. But with the Internet it was fairly simple to line up the clues: a five-year-old *Washington Post* item reporting a rumor that a young girl had seen a man running from the home rented by Gerry Gray. A Google search that turned up the girl's name and photo on a Web site called "LoveMatch." And then the back-and-forth emails, which had begun with Scott's craftily worded "message from a friend of Gerry's" and led up to today's meeting, which had all of the intrigue of a highly anticipated romantic rendezvous.

Before meeting in person they had both insisted on trading pictures, and in real life she looked younger, sweeter, and far more innocent than the semi-naked photographs she sent him had suggested. Gazing at her across the table, smiling slightly as she poured sugar into her coffee and fired up her third clove-scented cigarette, he found himself wondering how she had managed to survive. Why hadn't someone just taken poor Tiffany away from her self-described "bogus" existence with her "asinine" parents and simply eliminated her? It was obvious that she still had vivid memories of the night, five years earlier, when the identical brick house across the street from her own burned to the ground. The house that had been occupied by the man who had claimed to know the identity of Benjamin Bennett's captor, but who was shot in the face just minutes before the local police arrived to take his statement.

"Gerry Gray," Tiffany said the name with a relish. "Purveyor of the best weed known to man or beast. He grew it, you know, in a greenhouse set up in his backyard."

"Oh?" Scott replied.

"He used to take me out there. He had it set up like a party house. We made love on an old couch there a few times."

When you were 12, Scott thought. *Young and fresh and so naïve to the ways of the—*

"I matured early," she caught his glance at her ample breasts and smiled. "Physically, I mean. It wasn't really any big deal." The smile became sly as she leaned back against the banquette. "I've always liked older men."

"Well Gerry was definitely a good person," Scott said. "And I know he really liked you."

Her brown eyes widened. "He *did*?"

"Oh yeah. He talked about you a lot."

"Wow." She said quietly. "That's kind of a surprise. I never knew he really cared that much."

"Well it's true." Scott's mind moved quickly, scanning his memory of the email stream. The discussions had gotten intimate fairly quickly, and by the time he arranged the meeting he knew he could convince her to give him everything he needed.

"He said you were sweet," Scott told her. "And that he really liked your poems. He said they were..." He looked past her and squinted, as if trying to remember the exact word. "*Prescient.*"

"Wow," she said again. "That's like, psychic, right?"

"Yes, that's right. He really cared for you Tiffany."

"I'm kind of awed." Her eyes turned glassy, vulnerable.

It was the perfect opening. "Well I'd really like to get the animal who took him out," he said.

"So would *I*," she replied.

"So what all did you see?"

She gave him a blank look. "What do you mean?"

"You told the police that you saw the guy who shot Gerry."

"Yeah, for a few seconds."

"So what did he look like?"

She thought for a moment. Scott remembered her assertion that she still smoked pot virtually every day and wondered about its impact on a five-year-old memory.

"He had short brown hair and he was wearing dark clothes," she said finally.

"Was he young, middle-aged?"

"I'm not sure."

"Tall? Short?"

"Average." She looked at him. "About like you."

Scott held her gaze without flinching. "What else?"

"He moved fast." Her eyes took on the faraway look again. "Came out the side door where the garage is. I remember wondering why he didn't shut it. Why was he running? That was what I was thinking right then. I guess it was about a minute later that the whole place exploded."

Scott felt a chill of trepidation. Gerry Gray's house had gone down very quickly. He thought about how easy it would be to do the same to hers.

"I'm really sorry you had to see that." Scott reached across the table and put his hand over hers. "It must have been really terrifying to see someone you cared about get killed that way."

"Well you, too."

"What do you mean?"

"I mean, he was your friend, too. That's what you said."

"Oh. Right." Scott paused, and managed a look of pained but controlled sadness.

"So did you guys go to school together, or what?"

His mind skipped back to the stream of emails, remembering the story he had come up with. "Nah, we just hung out. My old man's got a cabin not too far from where Gerry lived, near Camp David."

"That's back where the president has his retreat."

"Yes," he nodded. Tiffany now lived with her family in Laurel, Maryland, a mere 10 minutes from the city's northeast boundary and a long way from Frederick, where they had lived at the time of Benjamin's abduction. But between the dope and the sleeping around, he remembered her telling him that her grades in high school had been good and that she was headed for the University of Maryland in the fall.

So she's more credible than you realized, he thought.

The next question had kept him up countless nights in prison. "Where were you when all this happened?"

She took a drag of the clove cigarette, blew smoke toward the ceiling. "Up on the roof."

"The roof?"

"Of my parents' house. That's where I always was back then. I'd go up there to get away after we'd been fighting. It was shaded by a big oak tree, so I could smoke up there—reefer, cigarettes, whatever—without getting scammed."

Scott thought for a moment, spoke carefully. "So that's why *the guy* didn't see you as he ran out the side of the house."

"Yeah I guess."

Which is why you're still alive.

Tiffany Potter's eyes glazed over as she stubbed out the cigarette. She wrapped both hands around the coffee mug as she leaned back against the banquette. "It's so sad," she said after a moment. "'Cause Gerry was finally getting his life together."

Scott gave her a quizzical look.

"Didn't he tell you?" she asked. "He'd been something like three months behind in his rent and finally, that afternoon, he'd come up with what he owed. He'd gone over to his landlord's house and paid it in full, in cash."

"His landlord." Scott felt a twitch in his cheek.

"Yup. Finally no worries about a bounced check or an eviction. We were going to go out later and celebrate."

Scott counted to three before the next question, and tried to make it sound casual. "Do you remember his name, the landlord's?"

She looked toward the ceiling, where the sweet-scented smoke still hovered. "Taylor. That was his last name."

"Taylor." His throat tightened as he repeated it.

"His first name was Zachary. *Zach the crack*, as Gerry called him. He was a real creep, from what Gerry said."

Scott paused, his mind working through the possibilities, realizing just how much Tiffany Potter really knew, and what she could reveal if someone pushed her.

"Do you know where Taylor lived?"

"In an older subdivision near Frederick I think. I never saw the guy in person."

Which is the other reason you're still alive. Scott leaned forward slightly, thinking again of what he needed from her. "Listen, Tiffany, I was wondering... how would you feel about going away?"

The blank look came back again, this time with a glimmer of fear. "Away?"

"With me, for a day trip. Like I said I've got this cabin."

"In the woods."

"In the woods." Scott nodded. "There's a big room with a fireplace, a bedroom with a double bed. A Jacuzzi. A full bar with great wine and the kind of dope that used to shoot Gerry to the moon."

"Gerry." Her eyes glazed over as he laced his fingers with her own. "I never really forgot the way he treated me."

"Well you have to look to the future, Tiffany. You can't shut yourself off forever, you know?"

"Yes." Something in his voice brought her back to earth. She gave him a small smile across the table. "I know."

Scott watched her for a long moment, trusting his instincts enough to lean across the table and lightly brush her lips with his own. Her eyes were closed. His were open but unseeing anything but the image of her on the gently sloping roof of her family's house.

Still a witness.

The explosion lighting up the night.

Still remembering enough to make the ID, even now.

Scott's mind moved quickly. To the cot he had set up at the back of the Landscape Artistry van. To the drugs he had stashed at another one of his father's hunting cabins, deeded in a second cousin's name and completely unknown to the police or FBI agents who were searching for him now. To the ruse of seduction that would lure Tiffany Potter away.

"Come with me Tiffany, just for a day or two."

Her smile broadened, and for a one shining moment she looked like a young girl.

"I'll show you a whole new world."

Nineteen

Mookie Byrd knew he was going to die.

Naked and shivering in the back room of the rowhouse, his wrists raised high over his head and bound to the exposed joists in the ceiling, he had already begun to beg for mercy. There was a gash on the side of his face from the blow that had first knocked him unconscious. Several loose teeth slurred his speech. But after a while Harland Till found him easy to understand.

"I said I was sorry," Byrd groaned. "I took the money but it was only for you."

Till was only half listening as he turned his back, reached into the knapsack, and picked up one of the long knives. It had been more than an hour since Byrd had shown up at the old rowhouse with*out* Michael Bennett at his side. Till had let him in and listened for half a minute to the made-up story about Bennett arriving without the money before wheeling around with a brick and ramming it into Byrd's teeth.

Byrd was already strung up when he came to, his ankles wrapped in a rope secured to a cinderblock on the floor to keep him from kicking once the torture began. He pissed all over himself when he looked down and saw his naked body. The sour, rancid smell of urine still hung heavy in the air.

"You're lyin'," Till told him. "I known it since you walked in 'cause I was watchin' the whole thing. Now you gotta' pay..."

"I still got it, man," Byrd began trying to talk his way out. "By my bed. At my house."

Till met his eyes, tried to determine if Byrd was telling the truth. For a moment he considered cutting him down, getting him dressed, prodding him at gunpoint to take him to the money. If Bennett had come through as directed it would have been a lot of cash, enough to live on for the next six months.

But he knew it would never work. Byrd was probably living in either a shelter or squatting in one of the neighborhood's other vacant properties. Following him was too risky.

Besides it don't matter now. All that matters is getting Bennett here. Getting to the truth about the boy.

Up until now all of the homosexuals Till had killed had died quickly. But Byrd was going to be tortured, slowly. Byrd was practice for what he would do to Michael Bennett. An opportunity to see how many times, and how many places, a man could be cut before he either confessed his deepest secret, or died. Child molestation and kidnapping were serious crimes, and the fate of the first child, Benjamin Bennett, added murder as well. He expected Bennett would go quite a while before revealing what he had done.

But Till knew he would. Knew it with the deepest certainty as he slowly walked around Byrd, looking at his naked body from every angle. Byrd's addictions had left him almost emaciated. Till knew he would only be able to cut so deeply before hitting sinew and bone. But Michael Bennett would probably last quite a while.

Because he was young, strong, beautiful...

Till gasped at the sudden jolt in his groin, the erection so powerful it made him lean dizzily back against the wall. In moments the image of Mookie Byrd became Michael Bennett, his muscular arms over his head, his trim torso quivering at the first prick of the blade.

Till was only half-aware of Byrd watching as he transferred the knife to his left hand, reached down and freed himself, *touched* himself. The sensation swept up over him, through him, the muscles in his arms and legs stiffened into veined marble, his vision blurring as his eyes rolled back.

He came quickly, violently, shooting semen into the air, shuddering with the *release.*

For several seconds he rested, his back against the wall. The *afterward* sensation was always the worst. A deep sadness fell over him, making him feel as if he were looking up from the bottom of a dark well. Like always, he felt Reverend Willow slipping into his bed, his breath reeking with the sweet and sour smell of booze, Willow's whiskers scraping against his own tender skin. The *afterward* was the time when Hell came up and grabbed him, *seized* him with the feeling of Willow's hands, moist and heavy, as they moved across his little boy's body.

An involuntary gasp pushed the vision away. Across the room Byrd was muttering a prayer. Till realized his fingers were still covered with semen. He wiped them on the side of his pants, but kept his zipper down as he transferred the knife back to his right hand.

The room was dark except for the light of one overhead bulb. Till raised the knife up under it so Byrd would catch the glint from across the room.

"*Please...*" Byrd begged again.

Till drew his arm back as he approached, focused on Byrd's scrawny belly as he thought about the first upward thrust. "You're wastin' your breath," Till said. "'Cause it really don't matter now."

"Nooo..." Byrd wailed.

"Yes..." Till smiled into his eyes. *Oh, God yes...*

Twenty

Gloria Towson's blue Toyota backfired several times as she drove through the late-night Connecticut Avenue traffic, but the silence inside the car was intense.

"Something happened a few minutes ago," Michael said. "Upstairs, in the bar."

"I don't know what you're talking about," Gloria said.

"Yes you do. I saw it in your eyes. When I told you about that phone call. You figured something out."

Gloria leaned back slightly in her seat, and gave him a look he couldn't read. "I don't know what I've *figured out*. But I did make a connection."

"What kind of connection?"

"We have to trust each other, Michael. It's the only way I'm going to be able to help you. You *want* me to help you, don't you?"

"Of course I do. I can't believe you'd even ask that."

"Then you have to be completely honest with me. From everything you've said, it sounds like Benjamin was kidnapped on the spur of the moment, and you think Scott did it because he was angry with you and Mary."

Michael nodded.

"But the kidnapping of Justin is obviously very different. Something that was planned for over a period of time. The kidnapper probably had help."

"Yes," he agreed. "Probably."

"Well, in a few hours I'm going to have to come forward with everything I know, and when I do, a lot of people are going to automatically think that that *help* came from you."

"That's ridiculous. I would never—"

"I know that. But you're still going to be a suspect. And for that I'm sorry. "

Something in Gloria's voice struck him, made him turn to her again.

"I know what it's like to be judged," she said. "Because you're gay."

"Why, because you're black?" he spoke without thinking. Words that might have been awkward but somehow, between the two of them, were not.

"Yes," she kept her eyes on the road. The admission clearly made her uncomfortable, and for a moment Michael actually found it difficult to believe. His first impression of Gloria Towson in the interrogation room of the police station had been made under duress, but even then the woman had had a *presence*. Her skin was dark and smooth. Her coarse, shoulder-length hair was swept back and it accentuated the broad, strikingly attractive angles of her face. Her gaze was direct but disarming, and when their eyes met it felt as if he could have—even *should* have—told her everything she wanted to know. Dressed now in a ribbed navy blue turtleneck and tan jeans, with traces of red polish on her short fingernails, she looked feminine but athletic, and radiated strength and intelligence that seemed far more powerful than the racism she might have encountered.

But she does know what it's like to be different. Michael thought back to the first meeting, hours earlier at the police station, when Gloria Towson had assured him that she really did believe in his innocence, regardless of the mounting evidence against him. He wondered now if there was something in her own past, her own life, that compelled her to reach out to him, regardless of the cost.

"Okay," he said, "so we both have something to overcome."

"Yes, although there's a different dynamic when you're talking about race. I can't hide the color of my skin, so there's nothing I can do to stop people from automatically making judgments about me. But a lot of people *wouldn't* look at you and know about what makes you different, right up front."

Her tone made him feel defensive. "I've never tried to hide anything. When Mary wrote that article in the *Washington Blade* I was totally fine with everything being out and in the open."

"Yes, I read that article, Michael. I know you've always been honest about who you are. But on the street, to people who don't know you, your handicap is invisible, at least until you decide to display it, or until word gets around. But what you're doing is testing people's tolerance. Working in a day care center, being completely *out* even though you're around little kids."

"There's never seemed to be any choice," he said. "It's what I always wanted to do."

"Really?"

"Yes." Michael felt uncomfortable with the challenging look in her eyes. He turned his head toward the dark night and city streets beyond the windows, remembering the weeks after Benjamin's disappearance. At 20 years old, he had been just a year away from his degree in elementary education and loving every moment of his part-time job at the Bright Start Academy, with its colorful playrooms and storybooks, its lush playing fields, its classrooms filled to capacity with children yearning to learn. But they were also the children of well-heeled parents who paid thousands of dollars a year for tuition. The notice that he was being put on unpaid leave came just one day after Benjamin disappeared, and the back of his neck had burned with humiliation from the stares of his co-workers when he returned to clean out his desk. He knew then that it would be absolutely impossible to have a career as a teacher. With the exception of the few hours a week of tutoring at the shelter, any parent who came into contact with him would always wonder about the safety of a child in his care.

"But you also like computers," Gloria said. "You always looked at that as your second choice, right?"

"I switched my major in school after Benjie was kidnapped and got into the tech stuff full time. I knew I'd never get a job as a regular teacher. I knew I'd always live under that cloud."

"Well, I think that cloud's about to get a lot darker. Because even if you do get Justin back you'll be suspected of being a pedophile for the rest of your life, unless you can prove your innocence for good."

"I don't know how I'm going to do that."

"Is there anything else you want to tell me, Michael?"

"What do you mean?"

"Anything else that's happened to you at some point? Anything else that could be connected to all of this?"

He stared back at her, his mind feeling blank and crowded at the same time. She was grilling him as if she didn't trust him, but speaking to him as a friend.

"No. I can't think of anything."

"What about D'Amecourt?"

"What *about* him?"

Gloria gave him a hard look as she stopped for a red light, the engine sputtering until she shifted into neutral and gave it extra gas.

"I think D'Amecourt had a role in the kidnapping, Michael. Or he purposely decided not to stop it. In fact I'm sure of it."

"That's not true," he said.

"Are you sure?"

"*Yes*," he said, trying to sound completely certain. "I admit he has problems, but I know he didn't have anything to do with—"

"What was in the box that got taken out of your house?"

Suddenly the car felt very small. Michael touched the handle of the door. He needed to get out.

"I can't tell you that," he said.

"Was it something to do with Justin?"

"No."

"Was it connected to the murder? At the Capitol Hotel?"

"No." He glanced at his watch. By now the FBI had probably taken apart his hard drive and done a thorough search of everything else in the box. "The other one... two years ago."

"At the Larchmont apartments."

Michael felt a twinge in his groin. "Yes."

"Could you tell me why D'Amecourt is so obsessed with that murder, or why he seems determined to keep the investigation from becoming public?"

No, not yet. "I'm sorry, I can't," he shook his head. "But you have to believe that I would, if there was any chance that it would get Justin back."

"Well, you might not have any choice." Gloria's voice was suddenly quite cool. "There's no way D'Amecourt will still be able to *control* this once the FBI gets fully involved."

"They already are," he said. "There was an agent working with him tonight."

"Working *with* him?"

"Yes. Someone he's close to. Agent Barshak."

"Barshak... Sylvia," she said. "Who used to be a D.C. cop. She was also an investigator on the first murder, at the Larchmont."

He nodded.

"So they're in it together."

"In what?"

Gloria's expression was impossible to read, but he sensed her mind working, making more connections, putting more pieces of the puzzle together. Her face was tight as she pulled up in front of Martin and Joan's house, the engine rumbling as she put the car in neutral.

"What are you going to do now?" he asked her.

"I'm not sure, Michael."

There was an edge to her voice. Michael knew she was angry with him for holding information back. She wanted to show him that she could do the same. His anxiety deepened as he realized the connection between them had frayed, realized too that he wanted Gloria Towson on his side, *believing* in him.

You have to tell her about what D'Amecourt's really worried about. Tell her about the box—

"Go on Michael, but call me later if you decide to come clean."

Gloria Towson gave him another cool look, revving the engine to keep the little car from stalling again.

"No matter what, I think you're in for a *very* long day."

Twenty-one

Sylvia Barshak had managed her rage remarkably well. Despite her fear that Michael Bennett knew way too much about what Louis D'Amecourt had done. Despite her certainty that it was only a matter of hours before the whole debacle came to light. It was only when Bennett walked away, knowing that they couldn't hold him back, that she had snapped.

"You bastard." Both of her hands were balled in to fists and she barely resisted the urge to break Louis D'Amecourt's jaw as he stammered through yet another pitiful, half-assed defense of his actions.

His hands were covering his face when she left him. He looked as if he'd finally been *broken*, that he would no longer able to maintain the ex-marine, *über*-masculine persona that still seemed so important to him. The moment she stepped out into the parking lot she had a vision of him driving to a secluded spot somewhere in the woods and swallowing his gun. But neither her own fear nor complicity was enough to make her turn around when he called her name, sounding as if he suddenly expected *her* to come up with a solution for the problems he had created.

The beat-up Ford Taurus with the broken headlight that she had borrowed for her "undercover" assignment was still parked by the Emergency Room entrance. There were two tickets on the windshield. She told herself it was a good sign. If the hospital's rent-a-cop didn't recognize the Taurus as a police vehicle then the killer probably hadn't noticed it parked near the spot he had chosen for the blackmail payment either. *Because you know he was watching*. She was virtually certain of it as she thought about how the failed exchange had gone down. The thought of being so close rankled her. She wanted to believe that D'Amecourt really had tried to follow the skinny crackhead who ran off with Michael Bennett's money. She wanted to believe D'Amecourt really was doing everything he could to bring the killer down.

But she still had doubts. For D'Amecourt, bringing in the killer almost certainly meant exposing himself. Revealing the secret he had begged her to help him conceal *at all costs*. She wondered again if the death of Justin Bennett would be the ultimate cost. And she was certain that if Michael Bennett did go public the trail of lies and cover-ups would come back to her as well.

So you'll go down with him. She thought about the reports she would have to put together in the morning. With the intensity of the spotlight, she would no longer be able to keep the investigative team confined to herself and the two agents who searched Michael Bennett's room. In just a few hours she would be given more "support," and be expected to reveal more details about D'Amecourt's connections to the murders and to the abduction of Justin Bennett.

The feeling of doom clung to her as she drove through the residential neighborhood that surrounded the hospital. She felt momentarily aimless, too keyed up to go home and sleep. Too angry at D'Amecourt to even *begin* seeking a way out of the jam he had put her into. Earlier in the day, after Michael had told D'Amecourt about the killer's phone call, D'Amecourt had told her that Michael's sister had been working at her waitress job at O'Malley's when Justin disappeared. Barshak remembered the tavern for its exposed brick walls and comfortable seating alcoves. She knew it would be empty at this time of the night. It also had a separate downstairs bar that served drinks until 2 A.M.

And God knows you could use a stiff one right now. She was just turning into the parking lot when she remembered locking her cell phone in the glove compartment. She took it out and dialed home to check her voice mail before going in. The message that had been left on her machine got her attention immediately. She listened to it twice, made several notes on the pad attached to the console, then immediately called D'Amecourt on his own cell phone to give him the news.

"The victim had a Web site, hosted by Stonewall," she said. "The site had an email address for people who wanted to contact him. Terrence Tyler was able to hack into the site before it got taken down. He retrieved an email the victim received at the Web site address two days before the killing. A request to meet."

"All right." D'Amecourt said after a moment.

Barshak was wary of his silence. Louis had been worried about bringing Tyler, an FBI computer specialist who she had befriended, into the investigation, particularly when he had learned that Tyler would have to be told a great deal about what they were looking for, and why.

"He traced the email the sender's SentryMail account Louis. He's working to get an ID right now."

"He knows what to do if he gets it?"

"Yes, it comes straight to me. No one else."

"Okay."

She pressed a fist against her forehead. "That's all you've got to say."

"What do you *want* me to say?"

"*Damn* you," she snapped.

"Sylvia—"

"Michael Bennett was right. You *should* be hung out to dry."

"I told you I never meant—"

"But you did what you did. And I swear to God, Louis, if it goes down like I think it's going to you're going to be on your own."

D'Amecourt said nothing for a moment. Barshak wasn't surprised. For the first time she had come right out and told him that there was a limit to her own involvement. A limit to what she would allow herself to do.

She was just about to repeat it when the door to O'Malley's swung open and Michael Bennett stepped outside. She slid down the seat, the phone frozen in her hand as Gloria Towson stepped out behind him.

"Oh God," she moaned.

"What now?" D'Amecourt said wearily.

"It's Towson." Her voice was shallow. "She's with Bennett."

"Where?"

"At O'Malley's. They're just coming out. Together."

"Fuck." D'Amecourt snapped. "I fuckin' *knew* it."

They both stayed quiet for a moment as she watched Gloria Towson and Michael Bennett walk to a car parked at the opposite end of the lot. D'Amecourt had warned her about Towson, telling her he was almost certain that she had known something was wrong at the Capitol Hotel crime scene. Telling her he had felt Towson watching him, and that despite everything he'd done to stifle the investigation she would remain curious about the outcome. And now it was obvious that Towson had figured out a link between the murders and the kidnappings, and she had decided to help Michael Bennett on her own.

"You're going to have to do something about her," Barshak told him.

"But *what*?" D'Amecourt answered.

"Something," Barshak said, her mind already fastening on the only solution at hand.

Twenty-two

Gloria drove home quickly, her mind so addled by thoughts of what had probably happened to Justin Bennett that she almost missed the white Ford Taurus following two cars behind her. At first it was only the burned-out headlight that got her attention. Then it was the creeping feeling at the back of her neck as she changed lanes and slowed down, then realized the driver of the Taurus was doing the same.

The Toyota backfired as she shifted lanes, the engine wheezing as she made an abrupt left at a flashing light on Porter Street and headed down the slope that would take her into Rock Creek Park. She didn't see the Taurus when she looked in the rearview mirror again. She slowed down slightly and tried to believe it was only her imagination. There was little chance that D'Amecourt was on to her, and no chance that he'd have the balls to send someone out to tail her.

But when she stopped for the next light it was there again.

She remembered glimpsing the white car in the O'Malley's parking lot as she and Michael stepped out to leave. The car's lights had been on. But at the moment she had been so focused on what Michael had revealed, and so determined to pin him down for more information, that she had barely noticed the missing headlight. Whoever it was had seen her leaving with him, and probably followed her from then on.

Up ahead, Porter Street would lead her into the woodsy residential streets of Mt. Pleasant, and shortly afterward would empty her onto 16th street. From there it was no more than five blocks home. D'Amecourt expected all of his Fifth District officers to post their home addresses and phone numbers, so he already knew where she and Booker lived. But she was intensely wary of being tailed all the way to her front door.

When the light turned green she knew just what to do. When both cars ahead of her moved through the intersection she stayed put. When the driver directly behind her honked his horn she turned on the Toyota's flashing hazard lights. When the driver honked again she rolled down her window, stuck out her arm and motioned for him to pass her. Porter Street was narrow, with one lane going each way, but as soon as the oncoming traffic cleared, the driver accelerated and swept around and past her. After a moment the next car did the same.

Which left the white Taurus no choice but to come up directly behind her, or pass. After a pause the car abruptly accelerated. Gloria made an instant decision, and with no pretense of hiding looked directly into the side window as the Taurus went by.

At a moment's glance she knew the driver was a woman. Gloria caught a flash of reddish hair, white skin, a face tilted slightly downward and looking straight ahead, as if she were determined to get past the little Toyota as fast as possible.

Gloria had never met Sylvia Barshak, but she knew what she looked like. And she knew that Barshak had been behind the wheel. Her own assertion—*"they're in it together"*—brought her breath up short as watched the Taurus pick up speed and drive on.

Another car came up behind her, the driver laying on the horn.

"Screw you," she muttered, as the car passed. After another minute to be sure that Sylvia Barshak was too far ahead to turn around and catch her she made an abrupt, illegal, three-point U-turn. The Toyota's wheels squealed and the tailpipe belched black smoke as she shot up the slope and back to Connecticut Avenue.

She crisscrossed side streets for another 15 minutes just to make sure that Barshak hadn't found her, then pulled over to call home.

She was surprised when the answering machine picked up after four rings. Booker was supposed to be there. Earlier in the evening he had told her he planned on setting aside several hours to read through as many newsgroup and chat room messages as possible to try and find a match to the return address of the email sent to the Capitol Hotel victim. She felt a sense of foreboding as she began speaking and he still didn't pick up.

"I know what happened to Justin Bennett," she said. "I talked to Michael and figured out—"

She stopped abruptly. At home they kept the volume up on the answering machine so they could screen calls. If Booker was there he would have picked up immediately. "We have to talk," she said. "I'm on my way."

She drove home quickly, her mind racing over everything that had to happen within the next few hours, her hands tight against the wheel as she thought of how impossible the theory would be to prove. She parked in their designated space in the alley and looked up at the back side of the house. The lights were still on in the second-floor den, giving her more reason to worry why Booker hadn't answered the phone.

She opened the clasp on her shoulder bag, took out her gun, and stepped through the gate into the backyard. With another glance at the second-floor windows and a visual sweep across the bushes, she headed quickly up the stairs of the small deck, tapped the security code into the keyboard, and slipped inside.

She started to call out Booker's name, but kept quiet as she headed up the stairs. The rowhouse had been built in the 1920s, in the arts and crafts style, and the handsome landing at the middle of the oak stairway gave her a view of the dining room below and the bedroom hallway above. She stopped for a moment, then leaned against the wall with a long sigh of relief as the sound of her husband's snoring drifted down.

"Sleepin' on the job," she whispered, and smiled, as she continued up the stairs. The lights were on in the back room with the computer, but they were off in the front bedroom, where Booker, fully clothed, had decided to lie down. In the ambient light from the hallway she saw the outline of his big ex-linebacker body, both of his arms wrapped around a pillow, in the same way that he liked to drift off to sleep holding her.

The image touched her as she stood outside the door, gazing at him with a deep sense of gratitude as her fear drifted away. Before they had gotten married, they had been partners, sharing the same scout car and the same beat. The attraction between them had been instantaneous, but for several months they had both pretended otherwise. Instead of dating they merely worked together, on drug busts, arrests, an occasional undercover task. But on Booker's 25th birthday his mother had invited her to Sunday dinner, a four-hour family affair in a big old rowhouse filled with pictures of Booker and his three brothers. He had sat across from her at the table, slightly embarrassed, but pleased, as his mother regaled her with stories about his childhood, his days at Howard U, his future as "the kind of man who takes care of people—even old folks like us."

"And *young* ones, like you," his father, a quiet man who had himself been a D.C. police officer, had smiled shyly at her across the table.

It was then that she realized that Booker Jones had told his parents quite a lot about her. While she had often wondered if there might be something between them, there was no doubt in Booker's mind.

From there everything had happened quickly. The sharing of an apartment. The attraction that only deepened over time. The simple joy of knowing that she was truly loved. But she was suddenly certain that their lives were about to change. She had no doubt that D'Amecourt and Barshak were on to her, but she had already gone too far to turn back. And while Michael Bennett wasn't completely *innocent*, during the evening's conversation he had revealed more than he intended, and it was up to her to make the most of what she knew.

She still had no idea how. Working through protocol certainly wasn't an option. Even if she had trusted Payne enough to tell him everything, neither one of them would be able to do much without going through D'Amecourt, who would surely take her down to protect himself.

But you have to do something quickly, she thought, as she stepped into the den. Booker normally kept the area around the computer tidy but tonight there were papers everywhere. She realized that he had probably worked for hours. His diligence wasn't surprising. The chance to use his computer knowledge to solve a crime was something he had dreamed of for years. But in her heart she knew that he had put himself in jeopardy first and foremost for her. In Booker's family, the women were revered. And despite the occasional argument about whether the drug busts and lock-ups and day-to-day drudgery of police work were a good fit for the woman he loved, he probably would have done anything to see her succeed.

The thought made her feel even more fragile as she slipped out of her clothes and into the shower. Once again she envisioned of both of them, facing reprimands, even losing their jobs altogether. The day after Booker had asked her to marry him he had surprised her with the news that he wanted to buy the house. After years of saving, he had had just enough cash for the down payment. They had almost nothing left in the bank, and they needed both of their salaries to make the monthly mortgage.

And now you could lose it all. The reality filled her with dread. She thought again of Booker's first reaction to what Payne had told her, which was to go directly to D'Amecourt, regardless of the cost. Going behind D'Amecourt's back was as good as accusing him, so the decision to press on had made her cross a line that she could never go back from. But even now it seemed she had no choice. A serial killer was butchering young gay men.

One of those men was involved in the events that led to Justin Bennett's abduction. With the steam rising around her and everything Michael Bennett had revealed spinning through her mind, she felt the panic surging back. She was suddenly certainly it was too late. Justin was dead.

"Please God, Jesus, no," she whispered, her forehead and both palms pressed against the hard, cool tile. Her eyes were halfway closed, but she saw a change in the light as the bathroom door opened.

"Gloria?"

She turned to see Booker, rubbing his eyes as he lifted the edge of the shower curtain. He looked exhausted, and sad. She wondered if he realized how serious the danger was to both of them, now that D'Amecourt was on to her. She wondered how he would feel about her if they were both fired, disgraced by what she had done.

"I just listened to your message," Booker said.

She shivered as the cool air drifted in through the open shower curtain.

"I think I found him, online."

Twenty-three

Michael stepped quickly through the side door that led from the garage to the hallway and the first-floor guest room of Martin and Joan's house. For a moment he stood still, listening to faint sounds of the television in the library. He heard the voice of a woman newscaster talking about Justin, carousel music that sounded like it came from AdventureWorld, and then the unmistakable sound of Mary, pleading in front of television cameras for *"anyone who knows anything"* to help her bring Justin home.

Michael felt dizzy. In front of him the hallway tilted and swayed as he stepped toward the guest room, his mind still fixed on the image of Gloria Towson driving away. For a long moment in the dim light of the restaurant's back booth, he had felt a strangely close connection to the woman, a strong sense that she could somehow find Justin and rescue him from further exposure, too.

You should have told her everything. The whole truth.

He sat down on the edge of the bed, grabbed a pillow, and wrapped it tightly in his arms, wondering again how Gloria Towson would have reacted if he had revealed the secret that tied him to D'Amecourt; the terror and the longing that still made him feel sadness, and shame. The conversation in the car ran over and over in his mind. Gloria telling him she truly believed in his innocence. Telling him she knew what it was like to be suspected, simply because he was *different.*

Justin would always be different, too, he thought. Justin who at five years old was already aware of how the birthmark made him stand out from other children. Michael still remembered his first day at kindergarten; Mary and himself each holding one of his hands, stepping up to the school's big red double doors. Justin's eyes had filled with tears as he absently placed his palm over the ugly purple stain on the side of his face.

"Well you ready, little boy?"

Justin nodding.

"Gonna be good?"

A shaking "yes" as the big double doors opened.

"We love you!"

Justin letting go of Mary's hand, quivering as he waved goodbye.

Michael hugged the pillow tighter.

You can't give in. Not yet. He remembered Justin admitting to him just once that he wished the birthmark could disappear (*"maybe when I swim in the ocean, or go to the bottom of the pool"*). He was reminded again of how Justin's own sense of being different had made his outcast gay uncle love him even more.

Suddenly his whole body felt paralyzed, the fatigue and depression like a magnetic force pinning him to the bed, pulling him into a twilight sleep that only intensified the visions in his mind. With his eyes closed and his limbs immobilized he saw the moments leading up to Justin's disappearance reeling around him. He heard his own ragged snoring between the sudden jolts that snapped him awake; and was conscious of his head shaking from side to side as exhaustion pulled him back into a fitful sleep.

It was 4:30 when he looked at the clock again. He sat up in the bed, blinking quickly as he got his bearings. He had been out for several hours. By now the newspapers would be out on the street, the television and radio news programs would be reporting the latest "developments." He wanted to believe those developments would be details about Justin, clues to where he had been taken, a sighting of Scott.

No, it's all going to be about you. The box in the attic. The search of the house.

A crashing sound came from the den. The sound of breaking glass. He stepped toward the half-open doorway, looked down the long hall. Joan was weeping. From the television came sounds of sirens.

Oh God they found something.

He moved quickly down the hall and stepped into doorway of the library where he could see the television screen. There was a shot of an ambulance, a shot of the woods near dusk, EMTs coming up from the banks of the river, a tiny body covered by a blanket on a stretcher.

He realized that it was news footage from five years before. The recovery of Benjamin's body. Part of a longer news story now. Michael stood at the edge of the room where Joan was weeping and Martin was stunned into silence as the screen switched to footage of himself, dressed in a dark suit, shielding his face as he moved through a gauntlet of reporters.

In the corner of the room, Joan caught her breath. Martin was down on one knee, his arms around her, his handsome face furrowed and gaunt with grief. Michael opened his mouth to speak but the words that had been at the front of his mind were suddenly gone. On the floor, next to Joan's chair, the pale yellow vase that had long been one of Joan's favorite objects had fallen and shattered. The pieces lay untouched as Martin tried to comfort her. The room had a sense of chaos with the scenes on the television, and the broken, jagged glass on the floor.

Because of you, he thought. Although neither Martin nor Joan would have ever admitted it, he knew it was true. Knew it because despite their best and bravest efforts to love him unconditionally there would always be a layer of confusion between them. A space of conjecture, where much had been left unsaid. It had been that way since the day after his 17th birthday, when he had sat across from them in the very same room, his hands like iron grips on his knees, his eyes darting past them to the view of old oaks on the deep lawn as he told the truth about who he was. At the time he had wanted it to sound casual, like an afterthought. Nothing to be concerned about in a city, in the late 1990s. No reason at all to worry that he couldn't handle himself, or that it would create any problem for them.

But he had also been completely candid, revealing that he had already had several "encounters," one of which had been with a staffer on Martin's most recent city council race. One with an older counselor at the camp were he worked for two weeks as a volunteer during the summers. On several occasions he had parked in front of a strip of gay bars in a rough neighborhood in the Southeast section of the city. Too young to get in the door, he had nevertheless had plenty of opportunities to meet strangers who gave them his business cards and met up with him later. Sexually he had been careful. He lived in a generation blessed by the wealth of information about how to avoid HIV and other dangers, and with some shakiness had always been able to control his passions well enough to be "safe."

He told them all of this in a calm voice, occasionally tinged with a tone of apology, but with the confidence of knowing that by the end of the conversation they would appreciate his candor and assure him of their support.

Their reaction had surprised him. Martin's face had gone slack, the light slipping from his eyes as he stammered through a gentle but probing cross-examination (*"Are you sure? How long have you known?"*). And there was an unmistakable catch in Joan's throat as she tried, valiantly, *not* to cry. The mild constriction that had been at the center of his chest at the beginning of the conversation had become a straitjacket as their questions continued, both of them probing for details. Both of them obviously wondering just how "out" he planned to be.

Which was when the truth became clear. His Uncle Martin held office in a largely white, affluent section of Northwest Washington, but he had never spoken negatively about any other segment of the city's population. Appearances at the Martin Luther King, Jr. Day events, Boys & Girls Clubs, and various Latino festivals were a part of his schedule and so were presentations at the Lambda League, the Stein Club, the gay factions of the Democrats and the Republicans. Martin was first and foremost a politician, opportunistic and cautious about any voting block that could support or damage him.

But it's so different when it hits home. Martin and Joan had been his guardians for 20 years, stepping in after the deaths of his parents with a deep sense of protection and unshakable love. They treated him and Mary as the son and daughter they wished they had had, raising them in a household of gentle discipline countered by indulgences. And yet there was no way for Martin or Joan to mask their disappointment, or their worry, that their public image would somehow be colored by his lifestyle.

"It's all right, Michael, we'll get through this."

After several minutes of discussion, the words had reached him like a beacon in a storm; Martin's voice had been strained but gentle as he clasped Joan's hand and managed to smile. Michael recognized it as an admission. Regardless of what Martin Raines held as opinions on his "platform," there were real dangers to having an openly gay nephew living under his roof. The acknowledgment was disturbing, and Martin, by revealing his nervousness, had seemed momentarily weak, and unmistakably concerned about the impact on his political future.

But his uncle's reaction had also been honest. A brave assertion of loyalty despite the costs to himself. Loyalty that at the time Michael believed would *never* be tested. He was an honor student and a standout on the St. Albans tennis and lacrosse teams. He had already been accepted at George Washington University, and would soon have his pick of several other top schools. He looked and acted... *normal*, and despite his determination to live honestly, he had no desire to stand out or act out in rebellion against the mainstream in which he had been raised.

The activities that led to Scott's arrest could have changed everything. The afternoon Michael had spent doing drugs on the boat was one of several during a summer in which he had allowed himself to break free of a whole range of self-imposed limits. And yet the instant he sighted the Coast Guard the instinct for self-preservation had struck him like a bolt of lightning. He had said nothing as the boat was searched, but by the time they were towed back into the Washington Marina he was determined to go to any means necessary to separate himself from the scandal to come.

To this day he told himself he had done nothing really *wrong*. Admitting that Scott was well aware of the large stash of dope that had been transported on the boat and going along with the prosecuting attorney's assertion that his sister's lover actually did have a second career as a drug dealer was a simple matter of doing the right thing. Telling a truth that happened to be exactly what the police wanted to hear.

Fortunately the fall-out for himself had been minimal. In the news coverage around the incident he looked innocently impressionable. As if he had unwittingly fallen into bad company but then cooperated fully, even helpfully, to put a criminal behind bars. At the time his conscience was too crowded by what the incident had done to Martin and the rest of the family to feel any shame over his role in Scott Brown's fate. He was simply relieved to be out of danger, with all charges against him dropped, the future once again an open road...

He still wondered if Scott's revenge was an impulse—an angry, impromptu action that just happened to lead to Benjamin's death. Or if it was part of something deeper. An intentional, malicious attempt to silence the boy, *to hide your worst suspicions*. He was still shaken by Gloria Towson's ability to read between the lines of what he had told her.

And what you left out, he thought now. The child pornography the FBI had found—too late—on Scott's computer. The sighting of Scott's car within a mile of the cabin where Benjamin had been held. The accusations by the day care worker that were too serious to ignore.

"And in another development..."

The subtle but sudden excitement in the newscaster's voice startled him as the screen filled with footage of the FBI executing the search warrant, the camera going to close-up on the agent stepping out onto the front porch, the box from the attic in his hands.

"Police and FBI spokesmen say they would like another opportunity to question Justin Bennett's uncle, Michael Bennett."

Joan gasped, and looked at him as if she had just noticed him coming into the room. Michael's throat went dry as the newscaster began speaking of "computer discs, computer software and photos that they believe could yield further evidence of involvement in this or a related crime."

"Well that's a cryptic way of putting it..." Michael spoke out loud without meaning to, in a biting, defiant tone. It was a reflex, an automatic defense mechanism as Joan's eyes filled with tears again.

She's afraid of me, he realized. *Wondering what they found. What am I hiding? What did I really do?*

He looked at Martin, felt a sense of dread, like radiation, flowing between them.

"There's something I need to tell you," Michael said.

He sat down on the edge of an ottoman, knowing he had no choice.

"Right now, before you hear it from someone else."

Twenty-four

Always open to possibilities beyond the Washington D.C. Metropolitan Police Department, Gloria had taken a handful of law courses during her undergraduate days. She still remembered a professor's debate, and an extended classroom discussion, on free speech and the Internet. The professor had listed several locations, which included public libraries and public schools, and asked for arguments about whether or not access to any and all Web content should be limited there. Gloria didn't remember if prisons were ever discussed.

"Groveton's been called a country club from time to time." Booker moved a stack of papers, clearing a place for her on the small loveseat across the room from the computer. "Mostly for white collar criminals, or people who can buy their way into better accommodations."

"Which is exactly how Scott Brown ended up there," Gloria said. "And once he got access to a computer he probably could have done anything he wanted."

"Well last year they found out that stockbroker sent up there for stealing all that money from a pension fund was still trading." Booker smirked. "If you can sell stocks on prison time I guess you oughta be able to do this."

But *this* was horrifying. Staring at pictures of naked children, reading and writing stories about child molestation. Sharing "tips" on how to get unsuspecting children to *trust* him...

"I pulled up about 100 archived conversations where the sender of the email Payne found in the victim's luggage is identified by the screen name, 'quietriot22.'" Booker pointed to a stack of papers on the floor, where the rest of the conversations had been printed out. "You can read through them if you wanna, or I could just give you the highlights."

"Does he mention Benjamin or Justin?"

"Not by name. Man's too smart for that, I think. Plus, I think most of it's talk, what he fantasizes about, what he *wants* to do, not what he's actually done. If he's locked up, that would make sense."

"Can you tell where he logged on from?"

"No. SentryMail can be set up and accessed from any computer."

"So we can't prove the sender was logging on from Groveton."

Booker shook his head and frowned. "What're you thinkin'?"

She looked at the stack of printed-out messages again. And then she gave him her theory about how Benjamin and Justin Bennett had been taken, and why.

Booker frowned as she talked it through, but nodded when she described the phone call Michael received and what she believed to be the ultimate rationale for the kidnapping. Then he reaffirmed how difficult it would be to prove it.

"You're going up against powerful people, Glo."

"I know that."

"And you'll never get anything done with D'Amecourt in the way."

"Especially if he allowed it to happen."

"That's what you think?"

"That's what I *know*, Booker. But what I can't figure out is why Michael is still defending him, or why Sylvia Barshak seems to be working with him to keep the murders under wraps."

Booker clenched his jaw. He had been very quiet earlier as she told him about being followed by Sylvia Barshak. The look in his eyes told her he had no intention of standing passively by. On the job, Booker was a dedicated officer who tended to follow every rule, but behind the quiet, stonily professional demeanor he was distrustful of the power structure and the politics that governed it. So far no battle had been big enough to make him challenge a superior, but she knew that if D'Amecourt came down too hard on her that Booker would go right back at him.

Booker motioned toward the computer. "All I can tell you is that the guy who sent the email to the victim at the Capitol Hotel is the same guy who's been lurking around in these newsgroups."

"And the reason you know that is because he's corresponded with other pedophiles," she said, "meaning he's logged on, shared information."

"That's right."

"But you can't be sure about who *else* was logged on, can you?"

"No, not yet."

Booker picked up the transcripts again. She remembered what he had said about "tracking" the sender down. But after the initial jolt of optimism she realized that they still only knew the sender by his screen name, and had no way of knowing his true identity.

But we've still got something, she thought. Proof that whoever received the email from the victim at the Capitol Hotel was engaged in trading child pornography. Proof that he entertained himself with fantasies of seducing children. Certainly enough for probable cause to arrest him, and question him, in the disappearance of Justin and Benjamin Bennett, too.

On the desk next to the computer was a clock. The second and hour hands glowed green and blurry as she tried to rub the weariness from her eyes. She felt Booker's big hands massaging her shoulders, pulling her closer to sleep as she remembered what he had said earlier about the offices of Stonewall, the Internet service provider that hosted the chat rooms and provided email service to quietriot22.

It's 45 minutes away if you're not hitting rush hour. But it would take days to get a warrant."

"We don't have days," she murmured.

"What?" Booker stopped rubbing her shoulders.

"Just thinking out loud," she said.

"What exactly are you thinkin'?"

She turned around, looked up at Booker's broad, worried face, and told him what she wanted to do.

Twenty-five

Scott Brown pressed two fingertips to Tiffany's neck to check her pulse. It was strong and steady, despite the Quaalude that he had slipped into the White Zinfandel that she had drunk like water. She slept in a fetal position, arms and legs pulled defensively close to her torso. Scott realized the pill had been unnecessary and perhaps a little dangerous when she started slurring her words. The last five minutes of the tape from the recorder hidden in the bedside clock were virtually unintelligible.

The clock read 4:15 A.M. and the early morning darkness made it impossible to see more than a few feet into the deep woods beyond the cabin windows. If the state or park police had been tipped off to his location they would find it fairly easy to sneak up and surround him, leaving no chance for escape. After skipping the mandatory meeting with the parole officer and luring a minor into his bed, he knew he would be locked up immediately, with nowhere to run when the questions started coming.

He slipped the bolt on the front door and lowered all of the blinds in the main room so the only light came from the small lamp on the table that held his laptop. Out of habit, he checked the messages from the chat room, a few mouse clicks taking him immediately to postings by quietriot22. He then looked at the messages from his own alias, and from the variety of user names that had been created by the pornographers who hosted the site at Stonewall. He was curious about the two messages sent from hotboy2, which had come from a new SentryMail account he hadn't seen before, the last one just one day before Justin was taken.

Don't worry about what you don't know. He thought. *Focus on what you need to do.*

It was an order he had given himself again and again over the past two months. During the planning. The scheming. The dreadful run-up to the dreadful abduction of Justin Bennett.

Focus.

Scott stared blankly toward the heavily curtained windows, pinching the skin sharply between his eyebrows in an effort to stay alert as he thought through the most dangerous evidence that could still be brought to light.

Months and months of archived conversations from the chat rooms and newsgroups offered damning proof of the depravity that had led to the abduction, but without the use of real names or anything else that firmly identified the participants, there was no firm evidence that Justin Bennett was the object of the pedophiles' "affection."

Tiffany Potter's recollections were clear and damaging, but the *lude* and wine would have to wear off before she could finish repeating everything she unwittingly knew.

Zachary Taylor seemed to be an efficient killer, so by now Justin was mostly certainly dead. Regardless of the Achilles' heel that had almost allowed Benjamin to get away, there was no reason to believe he had failed.

And what about Michael?

Scott pressed both fists against his lips as the old anger surged through his mind. So far, Mary's little brother hadn't been charged, but the preponderance of evidence was more than enough to force him into another round of questioning. Scott wondered how much information he'd give up. Even if he told the police everything it probably wouldn't be enough for charges of kidnapping. But it would confirm the public's worst fears about his character.

Payback. What a bitch. Scott thought of his own trial. The terrified faces of his parents. The handcuffs squeezing his wrists as the bailiffs led him away. He'd already been in Groveton for seven months when his mother called to tell him about Justin's birth. His father's lawyers were well-paid, powerful, and completely amoral, so guaranteeing that he got visiting rights had been fairly easy. And Justin was such a sweet little boy, so amazingly open to his loving words, his whispered promises of a life together, his assurance, regardless of what Mary and Michael might have told him, that his *real* father would never really go away.

But Justin is dead now. Gone.

Scott stared into the computer screen, his fingers moving rapidly over the keys. In seconds he called up the address of the house in Frederick, Maryland, occupied by Zachary Taylor. According to the property records, Taylor had owned the house for years. He also owned a vacation cabin in the foothills nearby, and had held onto the property even after he murdered Gerry Gray. Not that he ever needed to run. Taylor committed his crimes behind a guise of complete respectability. He paid taxes, held down middle-class jobs, even owned property easily identifiable in the online records for Frederick County, where no fewer than seven people had disappeared within the last four years alone.

Scott took his fingers away from the keyboard and turned around to look at Tiffany Potter again. She was snoring lightly in the big cabin bed. He knew that it would be at least three hours before she would awaken. Three hours before he could get her to start talking again.

Turning back to the computer, logging off, he stared into the blank screen for another long moment before getting up and going to the foot locker in the corner of the room. The locker contained several changes of clothes, and two wallets with documents for two different identities, a Taser that would fire 50,000 volts at the touch of a trigger, and a gun.

Justice or death?

Each outcome required a different weapon. His hands were shaking as he made his choice.

* * *

Inside the big yellow house, in the front bedroom directly above the basement where Justin lay unconscious, Zachary Taylor *felt* the threat even before it became a conscious thought in his mind.

He sat up, the gun already in his hand as he looked toward the blink of red taillights at the stop sign at the end of the block. In the midst of a half-sleep he had subconsciously counted three passes of the same rumbling engine, his ears attuned to the heavy, truck-like sound of the vehicle even before his eyes confirmed it.

Three passes by the same kind of car at 4:30 A.M.

Taylor went to the window of the front bedroom in time to see a restaurant supply truck turn right and drive away. He willed himself to calm down. The busy downtown streets began a block away, and it was common for heavy vehicles to take shortcuts through the residential area to avoid the one-way main avenue nearby.

But the sense of dread stayed with him. Off and on for a day and a half now, the Frederick County police car had been parked in fat Charlotte's driveway across the street. He had spotted the car two nights before, when he went upstairs to get the oversized suitcase that he had planned to put Justin Bennett's tiny body into after killing him. Already feeling a touch of paranoia, he had told himself it was simply a coincidence. Jimmy the redneck cop was doing nothing more than paying a quick visit, trying again to convince Charlotte to front him money for his investment in the decaying bar.

But Jimmy the cop had stayed. Late into the night, like some kind of sentry, adding an unacceptable element of risk to the plan to take the dead boy away to the lake where he could be weighted down and disposed of for good. Going against his better judgment, Taylor had simply given the boy another sedative to keep him quiet, and had taken two more drinks as he sat in the darkness of the living room, waiting for the car to leave. By midnight when it finally did, Taylor found that he had drunk too much. And while the alcohol dulled his senses, it also sent his mind wandering, worrying, suddenly doubting his ability to escape scrutiny in the killing of such a well-recognized child.

So for a day he had sat tight, calling in sick to the library, watching the news reports, watching the comings and goings of the cop car in front of the house, doing his best to summon the nerve to do what he had been paid to do.

The cell phone rang. He did not recognize the incoming number. His finger shook as he answered.

"Is it done?"

He gripped the phone tightly, wishing that he had not answered.

"*Hello*? Are you there?"

"Yes," he answered, to a brief blast of static. It sounded as if the call was coming in from a car phone. "I'm here."

"I asked you a question. Is it done?"

"You didn't tell me who..." His voice faded.

"It doesn't matter *who*. That was never an issue."

"It is now," he said sharply. "I don't know if I can do this."

There was a long moment of silence. He felt the abductor's rage gathering.

"What do you think is going to happen if you *don't* do it, Zachary? You think you can just *walk away*?"

The menace in the abductor's voice sent an electric charge down his spine.

"You don't think that all the breaks in the past are going to catch up to you?"

Fuck. He shut his eyes, felt the walls of his own house boxing him in, the escape to a new life slipping away.

"All right," he said.

"*Now*."

"All right!"

The abductor hung up. Taylor's fingertips had gone numb from gripping the phone so tightly, and his armpits were dripping with a cool sweat as he stood up and looked toward the front window again. Charlotte's driveway was now completely, miraculously, *empty*. For now the cop was gone. Charlotte's front windows were dark. *There might not ever be a better time to do it,* he thought. *No better moment than right now.*

He was already walking toward the basement stairs when he saw the image of Michael Bennett on the television, which had been on all night, with the volume turned down. The footage on the screen was old, from the kidnapping investigation five years earlier. Taylor hastily picked up the remote and turned the sound back on.

He watched, in amazement, as the latest piece of information came to light.

"Well I'll be damned," he whispered to himself. Through the front picture window he could see the early morning light filling the street as he sat back down on the edge of his couch, his mind grappling with the significance of what he had just heard. For years he had assumed the Michael Bennett was innocent but unlucky, a victim of circumstances that had cast him in a guilty but undeserved light.

But now Michael did not seem *innocent* at all.

Taylor leaned closer as the early morning news anchor reported a list of items found in Michael Bennett's possession. Computer discs. Software. Photographs.

And a link to a murder.

His mind moved quickly through his options. There was no doubt now; Justin Bennett had to be eliminated. But there were still risks. Fat Charlotte and the near-miss in the parking lot. The chance of witnesses as he put the boy's body into the river in the light of day. The possibility that someone would somehow realize his connection to the kidnapping five years before.

You need a diversion, something to throw them off course. He looked at the TV again, watched the recap of the allegations, distinctly articulated now as opposed to simply being implied, against Michael, the boy's gay uncle.

Allegations that were almost certainly true.

Clearly there was an opportunity. A simple way to ensure that the final, permanent disappearance of Justin Bennett would be pinned on Michael Bennett alone.

In the kitchen safe were two cell phones, both with numbers that could not be traced. Taylor took one of them back to the living room, where the "Crimesolvers" phone number was still flashing on the television screen. He lowered the volume as he dialed and left a short, succinct message, one guaranteed to make the spotlight on Bennett even more glaring. For two days, much of the information received by the tipline had been leaked to an obnoxious reporter from one of the local news stations, which virtually assured that it would be reported before law enforcement even had a chance to verify it.

Taylor moved quickly but carefully, retrieving the narcotic and the syringe, feeling newly anxious to get the child out of his house and into the river.

The light switch for the basement was at the top of the stairs and when he flicked it there was a tiny *pop* as the bulb burned out.

"Damn it." He looked down the stairs. In the fragile light coming in through the casement windows Justin Bennett was a tiny mound under heavy blankets. Taylor remembered his veins were small, difficult to find even under normal light.

Cursing again, he went back to the kitchen, set the drugs and syringe down on the table, grabbed a flashlight, and headed back down.

Twenty-six

Michael told Martin and Joan his secret in stages, reminding them first how he came to know Louis D'Amecourt around Benjamin's kidnapping.

He then went on to tell them about the murder, three years later, which brought D'Amecourt crashing into his life again.

He got through it well enough until the end, when he tried to explain the contents of the box that had been found in his room. All at once the embarrassment and the humiliation of exposure, made it impossible to keep his voice steady, or to meet their eyes.

For a very long moment Martin and Joan sat very still, saying nothing. Martin had used the remote to lower the volume on the television shortly after he had started talking, but to Michael the faint sound of the newscast felt like a continuous stream of damning whispers behind his back.

Martin leaned forward slightly, the frail light from the tableside lamp shining through the gray strands in his hair. "Michael..." He exhaled, and looked suddenly wearier than ever. "I wish you had told us this before. When it happened."

"I didn't want to scare you," Michael said. It was a half-truth. He ground his back teeth together, and tried again. "I knew you'd be worried about what would happen if people found out."

"I'm worried now." Joan said. "You should have trusted us to deal with this. We would have been better off knowing so we could prepare for the fallout, if and when it came."

"Well, it's coming now," Martin rubbed his eyes and shook his head. "Like a train from hell."

"Did you really think Louis D'Amecourt would *protect* you?" Joan asked.

Michael looked past her, toward the large front window and the darkness beyond.

"It seemed like I could trust him well enough, since we both had something to hide."

"What *he's* hiding is a lot worse," Joan said sharply.

"But I know how I'm going to look when this comes out. Like I'm some kind of pornographer."

"Well I'd say you came pretty damn close. I mean *for God's sake,* Michael." Joan shook her head. Michael felt as if she was suddenly seeing him differently. The confession had revealed a side of himself that he had wanted to stay hidden at all costs.

"Who has D'Amecourt talked to about this?" Martin asked.

"Almost no one, probably, since he's so completely ashamed of it all." Michael said. "Although there is one person—the FBI agent he was with tonight. She used to work for the D.C. police. She was the detective who was assigned to investigate the murder two years ago, even though it was D'Amecourt who grilled me."

"He honestly *suspected* you?" Joan asked.

"My clothes were bloody when he got there. I was in shock... there's no telling what I said."

"But no other police or investigators ever questioned you."

"No. He took me straight to his house and kept the whole thing quiet."

"And you never saw anything in the papers, no mention of it anywhere else?"

"No. The next day it was like nothing had ever happened. D'Amecourt must have covered it up."

"Just like two days ago," Joan said. "When it happened again."

Michael nodded. "Both times the woman, Sylvia Barshak is her name, has done what he's told her to, I think."

"She knows what he's hiding?"

"Yes," Michael said. "She knows."

Martin leaned forward, pressing his hands against his chin. Michael knew he was thinking ahead. D'Amecourt's fierce stands against "vice" and his right wing views of crime and punishment had made him one of Martin's political enemies, and D'Amecourt's recent statements about the current city council race made it unlikely that D'Amecourt would answer to Martin now. But as Michael thought it through he reminded himself that it was D'Amecourt, who covered up a murder that was now connected to Justin's abduction, who was in the most danger.

"The cop who drove me home just now has a big problem with D'Amecourt too," Michael said. "She didn't say it outright, but she thinks that he's involved in this on another level."

Michael told them about the photo Gloria had described, and her belief that Louis D'Amecourt took it from the murder scene.

"She thinks he had an indication that something was going to happen to Justin, but he kept it to himself."

"Jesus," Martin whispered.

"What do *you* think, Michael?" Joan asked.

Michael stared at his hands in his lap as if they were disconnected from his body. He felt lightheaded as he tried to balance what he knew about D'Amecourt against what he had learned over the past several hours.

"At first I didn't think it was possible that he would actually allow Justin to be at risk. I mean, he's not *evil*..."

Martin and Joan stared back at him, both of them looking uncertain.

"But I do know how desperate he is to keep anyone from finding out about what happened. And if the killer is caught every murder that he's committed is probably going to be come under a spotlight. The secret that Louis is most afraid of would become public knowledge."

"But what about Scott?" Martin asked.

"Gloria, the police officer, thinks he might have corresponded with the last murder victim by email, through a pedophile chat room."

Martin and Joan both sat very still. They looked as if they had stopped breathing. But Michael felt their minds working, making connections to his own computer use, unwittingly bringing the blame back to himself.

"She came to this conclusion on her own, after talking to a detective who was investigating the murder, until D'Amecourt kicked him off."

"How did she come to that *conclusion*?" Joan asked.

"I honestly don't know. I didn't tell her about the pornography the FBI found on Scott's laptop computer after Benjie disappeared," he said.

"Does she know why they would have corresponded?"

He remembered Gloria's silence in the car after they had left O'Malley's. "I don't know. If she does, she hasn't told me. I think she has a theory about what happened, but she's keeping it from me."

Joan sat up a little straighter. "You didn't tell her about what was in the box in your room."

"No."

"But both you and Louis are going to be under the gun now, once it's reported."

"*Yes.*" Michael crossed his arms, and felt a cold hollowness in his gut. "I couldn't let myself throw it away. And anyone who's dealt with computers will know what I was doing. I don't think anyone will really believe I'm some kind of psychotic killer. But they will see the connection. And that's probably why they want to talk to me again."

"Probably." Martin's eyes reddened as he looked at Joan. And in the long moment of silence that followed Michael felt the hopelessness rising between them. He knew that neither his aunt nor his uncle would ever blame him out loud, but his own actions were at the heart of everything that had happened.

He was trying to think of something else to say when the chirp of a cell phone cut into the still air. Martin pulled the phone from his shirt pocket and said a curt "hello."

Joan sat forward, watching Martin as if she could hear the conversation by watching his face.

"That's fine," Martin said. "Yes, tell him to come here." He hung up without saying goodbye, and looked at Joan. "He'll be here in an hour."

"Who?" Michael asked.

"Charlie McKay," Martin said.

Michael recognized the name but couldn't place it.

"He's consulting on the case, working with the FBI," Martin glanced at his watch and looked at Joan again "They want to do all three interviews from here."

Joan's shoulders sagged.

"It'll save time," Martin said. "McKay says it might work better that way."

"What are you talking about?" Michael asked.

"Joan and I are going on the morning news shows. We're going to be interviewed by their people but McKay is going to talk to us about what to say and how to say it."

Michael remembered where he had heard the name. Charles McKay was a psychiatrist who served on the faculty at George Washington University, who was often interviewed on television as a consultant to the FBI.

"He thinks it would be more effective to have the cameras here, in our house," Martin said. "He says Scott will pay more attention if we make it more personal. And he thinks the press coverage itself will make it harder for him to travel out of the area."

Michael remembered hearing Martin tell Mary the same thing five years earlier, when everything seemed to have spun out of control so quickly. *When you were thinking that any minute Scott would come to his senses and bring Benjamin back*. But Gloria Towson was right. The kidnapping of Justin was very different. There was nothing impulsive about it. It felt as if every step was planned.

Behind him, the sound of his name on television grabbed his attention again. Martin picked up the remote and turned up the volume. Michael recognized the reporter, a middle-aged man in an open-collared shirt and windbreaker who always seemed to be at the scene of car accidents and fires.

The newscaster's words were stunning and damning.

"The caller claims to have actually *seen* Michael Bennett with his nephew, walking through the parking lot, to a white van."

Joan tensed. Martin was still holding her, both of them transfixed as the screen filled with a shot of the AdventureWorld parking lot.

"The caller also said that Bennett appeared to be, quote, *anxious and in a big hurry*, and that at one point the child, Justin Bennett, said something that made him *slap* the boy before sliding the van door open and putting him inside."

"It's a lie," Michael said.

The reporter continued. "So far law enforcement sources are offering 'no comment' on the sighting, which was reported by an anonymous source. But they admit to being very interested in talking with Michael Bennett at length about the circumstances. They've also renewed their call for anyone who spots Scott Brown to contact the toll-free hotline immediately."

Michael stood up. "Please... Martin... Joan you have to believe me."

"Of course we believe you, Michael." Joan's jaw was clenched, and Michael could feel her anger. "But that really doesn't matter now. Not with everything coming at us." She paused, looked at Martin. "I think we're running out of time."

Michael felt the panic rising again. "You can't say that. Please—"

"It's been two days, and there still isn't any sign of Scott anywhere. But I know he's watching. I wouldn't be surprised if that's where the anonymous *tip* came from. I think he's playing all of us, pushing our buttons. Justin's at the middle of this, but we're the people he really wants to hurt."

Michael nodded, remembering Scott's righteous anger at the betrayal that sent him to prison, the rejection by Mary, the attempt to keep Justin out of his life. But Scott had held Martin and Joan responsible, too. Martin's position in the city government had made the drug case a high-profile, high-stakes proposition for the prosecutors. And Michael's testimony, which damned Scott for good, had been arranged with extensive intervention by Joan.

"We have to stop him," Joan's voice was soft but cold. Her shoulders were shaking, and Michael thought she might lose her composure. "He *can't* get away with this again!"

"He won't." Martin reached over and put his hand over hers. A tear slid down Joan's face as he got up and hugged her tightly. Michael watched them, feeling like an outsider. The bearer of the horrifying news. An unwanted witness to their personal grief.

He took a step back and was about to leave the room when Joan told him to wait. Both Martin and Joan were looking at him when he turned around.

"I think we need to do something drastic." Joan brushed the tear from her cheek with the back of her hand. Her face was haggard, but there was a look of determination in her eyes. "It's our only chance to get Justin back."

Twenty-seven

The alarm clock was a shrill siren that stabbed at Gloria's temples as she sat up, half-awake, to turn it off.

Stark images of a nightmare lingered in her mind. She saw herself back at the Capitol Hotel, watching from a corner of the room as the killer approached the bed, as the images morphed into a photograph of the Larchmont crime scene. The victim bound and gagged, his eyes half open, dazed in death.

Her skull felt thick and heavy. She had dozed off in her clothes. She heard Booker's voice at the end of the hallway, talking on the phone. She washed her face, dressed quickly, and was ready to go when she turned on to the *Today Show*, which opened with "overnight developments" in the kidnapping of Justin Bennett. She called Booker into the room as the newscaster cryptically discussed the box that had been taken from Michael Bennett's attic bedroom and previewed an interview that Martin and Joan Raines would give to Matt Lauer in the second half hour of the broadcast.

"Magazines, computer discs, and software," Gloria repeated what the newscaster had said about the contents of the box, and thought of the messages about children that she had seen in the newsgroups. While she remained certain that Michael Bennett was *not* a pedophile, whatever really was in the box would certainly intensify the suspicion against him.

"We're going to have to tape it," Booker said, as he headed into the shower.

Gloria set the DVR to record all three morning news shows and read through the file again. Then she made a phone call that should have taken place at least a day earlier. She felt sheepish and more than a bit disloyal when Tommy Payne answered.

"Hello?"

"Tommy, it's Gloria."

"God, what time is it?"

"Early. Tommy, I need to tell you something. About the email you gave me."

She heard the creak of bedsprings. Payne suddenly sounded more alert. "You found something."

"Yes."

She told him everything that Booker had learned about the chat rooms, the murders, and the connections to the abductions of Benjamin and Justin Bennett. She was about to apologize for not getting back to him earlier when he cut her off.

"Goddamn it."

His sudden anger confused her. "What?"

"I heard about the search of Michael Bennett's house yesterday."

She waited for him to continue, looking anxiously at Booker as he emerged from the shower.

"I've been thinking about it a lot, wondering what he's gotten himself into."

She heard the sense of familiarity in his words. "Do you know Michael?"

"I've seen him, tending bar."

It was an open admission. He had spent time at Club Night.

"Talked to him a few times."

"Okay."

"Always wanted to get to know him a little better but the timing was never right."

"What are you saying?"

Payne cleared his throat. "Nothing really. Nothing to do with me, I mean. But I don't think he had anything to do with Justin Bennett's disappearance."

"I don't either."

"You need to bring me copies of those transcripts." Payne suddenly sounded anxious. "I can meet you in half an hour. I'm not going to take them to D'Amecourt. I'll have to go straight to the task force that's handling—"

"You can't," she said.

"What do you mean?"

She told him about Sylvia Barshak and her connection to Louis D'Amecourt.

"Crap." He paused. "Then we'll have to go past her, too."

She started to tell him what she and Booker were about to do. But she knew in an instant that he would try to stop them. Yet her mind was already made up, and if they succeeded she knew that Tommy Payne would have enough ammunition to mitigate whatever D'Amecourt might threaten for going over his head.

"I can meet you at 10:30," she said.

"That's three hours away. I'll come by your house now."

"*No*. We won't be here. We're just walking out the door."

Payne said nothing for a moment, but sounded suspicious when he spoke again. "Where are you going, Gloria?"

"I'll tell you when I see you. Back at Trio. Get us a booth at the back of the room."

She sensed that he was about to protest.

"Just trust me, okay?" she said quickly. "And say a prayer," she added, an instant before hanging up.

* * *

Ten minutes later they were heading south, Booker driving fast but with a light touch on the ailing Toyota. They were going the opposite direction of the rush-hour traffic, but it still took almost an hour to reach the Sunrise Technology Park, a sprawling complex of low-slung buildings bracketed by two highrise glass towers on what had once been Virginia farmland. The corporate office for Stonewall Internet Services was reached at the end of a long corridor with thick beige walls that made Gloria feel as if she was in a fortress.

A security camera was mounted on the wall next to the door. A few moments after knocking, they were greeted with a sullen "yeah?" from a speaker alongside it.

"Good morning, we're here to see Adam Turner," Booker said.

"Who's *we*?"

"Washington Metropolitan Police."

There were several seconds of silence, followed by the sound of a man clearing his throat, and a much deeper voice. "What is this regarding?"

"A personal matter," Booker said gruffly.

After several more seconds of silence there was a low buzz and the click of the mechanism that unlocked the door. They stepped into a windowless reception room with dark gray industrial carpet and light gray walls decorated with black and white line drawings of stylized urban landscapes. Overhead lights with halogen bulbs gave an art gallery feel to the space. The man behind the black granite desk had dyed blonde hair, cut into short spikes. He was muscled to the point of caricature under a tight baby blue t-shirt. The world-weary expression on his face was a perfect match for the voice that had greeted them.

"Where's Mr. Turner?" Booker asked.

"He'll be out in a minute. I need to see your IDs."

Booker bristled. They had decided to wear plainclothes, mainly because the dark blue uniforms made them look like lowly patrol officers. But also because the uniforms seemed unsuited to the renegade tactics they were about to employ. Gloria also hoped that dressing down might make it more difficult for Adam Turner to remember them later if the meeting didn't go as she hoped.

The receptionist looked down at both of their Metropolitan Police badges without touching them, but said "wait" as Booker started to put his away. Then he picked a pen and notepad out of the top drawer and printed both of their badge numbers underneath their names on the pad.

"Finished?" Booker said curtly.

The receptionist looked up at him and smirked.

"We need to see Mr. Turner, right *now*."

"I'm Adam Turner."

The voice came from behind them, from a doorway built to look like paneling in the wall. Adam Turner stepped into the room and Gloria purposefully stopped herself from looking at his narrow, misshapen legs or at his waist, which jutted out slightly at an angle, making one of his shoulders slightly higher than the other. She kept her eyes on his face instead. She guessed he was in his late 40s, but he probably worked hard to look younger with his thick, brown hair, green eyes, and classically handsome cheekbones, brushed with a tan that had either come from a visit far south or some time under a sunlamp.

Turner took a step forward. He walked with a cane. "What can I do for you?" Turner asked.

"We need your help," Gloria spoke before Booker could, her instincts telling her that they should at least *ask* for Turner's cooperation before assuming he wouldn't offer it. She nodded toward the door Turner had stepped out of. "Could we talk with you privately for a few minutes?"

Turner glanced at the manila envelope held at her side. He looked annoyed, distrustful; but she was fairly certain it had little to do with Booker or herself. He just looked like an unhappy man.

He turned without speaking, and motioned for them to follow. Turner's misshapen legs were more noticeable as he walked. He led them to another windowless room with a steel and glass table and chairs. There was a coffee maker in the corner, but Turner made no offers.

"We really appreciate your time," she continued with the pleasant tone. Turner answered her with a guarded look, and motioned both of them toward chairs. Booker scooted his chair back several inches from the table and slouched as he sat down. Gloria felt the tension between the two men, and saw it in the flexing of Booker's jaw.

"We're investigating the disappearance of Justin Bennett," she said.

Turner stared back at her without reacting.

"We have reason to believe that one of the subscribers to your service may be involved."

Turner frowned slightly. "How is that?"

Gloria sat up a bit straighter, feeling as if she were at the edge of a cliff. On the drive over Booker had speculated that the only way to ensure Stonewall's cooperation was to reveal every link between the ISP, the sender of the email, the pedophile newsgroups, and the crime scene itself. But the risk was significant. Virtually everything they knew had been learned by breaking rules.

And it still doesn't guarantee he's going to help you. She knew it for certain as Turner continued staring back at her. She glanced at the wall clock. It was already 8:30 A.M. D'Amecourt was probably holding roll call right now, wondering where they were.

Forget D'Amecourt. Remember Justin. And Benjamin.

Her voice caught at first, but steadied as she revealed everything, from the email found at the Capitol Hotel crime scene to the discovery of the postings to the pedophile newsgroup.

"We know him by his screen name." Gloria pulled out copies of the transcripts as she told him what they had learned. She admitted that none of the conversations mentioned Justin Bennett by name. Most were back and forth discussions justifying sexual relations with children, or requests to share photographs of children that were circulating between Internet sites all over the world. But the link was still compelling, certainly enough for Adam Turner and his company to see how high the stakes were.

"Once we found that same screen name in the newsgroups we were able to trace him by the codes in his header and find his IP address, the domain and then, you, his ISP."

Turner looked down at the documents she had laid on the table, his frown deepening.

"We know that Stonewall is his Internet service provider and we know you host these groups," she reiterated. "So all we need to do now is find out from you what his real name is, where he lives, and so forth."

Turner raised his hand, palm out, and continued looking through the printouts without speaking. Beside her, Booker shifted in his chair but gave her a slight, approving nod, and for a moment she almost imagined that the next step would be easy. Turner would turn on his own computer, do a quick search of his customers, and tell them exactly what they needed to know.

"No." Turner said abruptly, and pushed the stack of papers back.

"That mean you don't got it?" Booker said.

"No, it means *you* are not going to get it. Our subscribers are entitled to their privacy."

Booker moved toward the edge of his seat. "One of your *subscribers* is involved in the kidnapping of a little boy."

"So you say. But so far that's just an assumption, without proof."

"You don't believe that. You know it's true." Booker's voice was low, almost threatening. "We need your cooperation."

"I've cooperated. I agreed to see you, listened to your pitch—"

"We need you to tell us who he is."

"That isn't going to happen."

"Mr. Turner." Gloria interrupted the exchange, her hand on Booker's knee. She gave Turner a solemn look. "We're in a terrible bind here. This little boy, Justin, was kidnapped over two days ago. So far there's no other evidence as to what might have happened. Just *this*." She pointed to the transcripts. "We know that someone who uses your service is connected to this. We're not here to criticize your subscribers' right to free speech, or to police what they say and do in private conversations."

Booker clicked his tongue against his teeth, a sign of disgust. Gloria ignored it, kept her eyes on Turner.

"And you're right, it's possible that this individual isn't involved. But we need to question him, to see if he'll help us, if he can give us any clue whatsoever to this case."

Turner sat back, frowning. "You know, I *really* don't like being *handled*."

"Handled?"

"Like you're doing now. Your heavy-handed approach didn't work, so you shifted gears, tried to come across as if you're vulnerable, to say you're only looking for *help*. Using the child's name again and again was a nice touch. It makes it sound even more personal, makes you sound more human."

Gloria felt the heat rush to her face, and fought to keep her expression calm. Turner's perception of what she had been trying to do was unnervingly exact. But she wasn't finished yet.

"You're right, I *did* try a different approach," she said. "I did ask for your cooperation. But only because we're really, really desperate for it. You have the power to make a difference."

"*Please.*" Turner rolled his eyes.

"And it's true, I did make sure that I spoke about Justin by name—I wanted to remind you that this isn't an argument about principles or values or philosophy. It's about the life of a child."

"He should know that already," Booker said. "If he's looked at a newspaper, turned on CNN—"

"And of course you have," Gloria said. "You know that this is a heartbreaking case. Most people believe Scott Brown kidnapped Mary Bennett's first child five years ago, but basically got away with the crime. Now, because Brown is also missing, everyone is pretty sure he's behind this, too."

"What do *you* think?" Turner narrowed looked at her. And for a long moment Gloria considered the risks and advantages of opening up, telling him her theory of why both boys were taken.

No, not yet. "I'm not sure what I think," she said. "I think it might be Scott Brown, or someone else."

"Someone who enjoys the freedom of our newsgroups." There was a ghost of a smile on Turner's face, an angry gleam in his eyes. "Someone who's been promised complete privacy. Someone I'm supposed to turn over just because *you* have a hunch."

The man's condescension was maddening, and Gloria realized that despite the tension, maybe even because of it, Turner was enjoying the exchange. *And the power*, she thought. In an instant she saw him as a much younger man, with a face that would have been immensely attractive to other men, but cursed with his bad legs. She hadn't spent a lot of time around gays, but it was no secret that physical perfection was tremendously important to so many. She wondered if Turner had decided long ago to immerse himself in the anonymity of the Internet as a sanctuary from the rejection he might have faced in gay nightspots like Club Night.

But if he had empathy for anyone, it was for others like him. She understood why he may have connected so easily to the men who trolled through the newsgroups of his service.

The opportunity to leverage Turner's real concerns came to her suddenly. She didn't hesitate to use it.

"Look at it this way," she said. "Right now Scott Brown is the lead suspect, but only because of circumstantial evidence—his *suspected* involvement in the first kidnapping, the fact that he's on the run now. But it's possible that it's someone else. And if so that's unfortunate, because the mere suspicion is enough to ruin his name."

She paused, to make sure he was following. "If the name you give us is someone else's, it could be the start of clearing him up."

Turner gave her another disgusted look, and a slight shake of his head. "You're getting trapped in your own lies."

She stared back at him, with no idea of how to respond.

"Scott Brown is on the run. He's gone into hiding, apparently because he's got the kid, but maybe just because he's under suspicion—"

"That's exactly my point." Gloria said.

"No, that's *not* your point. It may have been what you were trying to make me believe, to change my mind. To help *you*."

Turner practically spat the last word. Gloria had no idea where to go next.

"Do you know what Stonewall was named after?" Turner asked.

Gloria glanced at Booker. His arms were crossed over his chest.

Turner leaned forward, gave her a grave look. "In 1969 there was a little bar in Greenwich Village. Full of fags, transvestites, freaks of nature that New York's finest decided to take down. They came in after midnight, in riot batons, beating the patrons, dragging them into the street."

"What's your point?" Booker growled.

"The bar was the Stonewall Café. And the incident is now a major event in gay history. The name has a symbolic connection to the services that we offer our customers. Privacy. Respect. With no fear of heavy-handed tactics from the police."

"*Goddamn* you!" Booker slammed both of his hands down on the conference room table. "Do you have any idea what you are doing?"

Turner stared back at him without reacting.

"One of your *freaks of nature* has taken a little boy. God knows what he's done with him. But for the last several months he's been trading dirty pictures of little kids. That's illegal Turner. You know it as well as we do. And it's sick as hell. Get us his name, *now*."

Turner shook his head, the angry smile returning to his face. And when he once again said "no," Booker stood up.

"Is that your final answer?"

Turner glared back without responding.

"Okay then, that's the way we'll write it up. In our report. We came to you with a lead that could break the case and save the life of a five-year-old boy. You made it clear you didn't care. This is going to look great in the press. Stonewall protects baby killers. Company president Adam Turner defends rights of perverts over the life of an innocent child. How many of your customers will want to log on after that, Turner? How long will your business survive if the Feds decide to really look into *all* the traffic on your network?"

Gloria stared at Booker, who stood threateningly over Turner. Turner's eyes were bright with anger, but the quivering in his shoulders told her that he was more than a bit frightened as well.

She knew that Booker's bullying had backed Turner into a corner. She hoped she had a way to gently lead him out. She took a deep breath, and focused on the one thing they ultimately needed Turner to do.

"A minute ago I talked about how the circumstances of all of this are making Scott Brown look guilty," she said calmly. "But right now the one who's in the most danger, outside of Justin, is Michael Bennett. There were plenty of people who believed he was a pedophile before this happened, and now, after this morning's news, it's going to be hard to find anyone who doesn't."

Turner sat very still, and stared down at the table.

"I don't think he is," she said. "But after listening to everything you've just said, I can't help but think that the same anonymity that you want to protect is going to make it impossible for him to escape suspicion that he doesn't deserve. Sometime in the next few hours Officer Jones and I are going to have to turn over all of this information to our superiors, one of whom is a high-ranking police official who I think I think may be *involved* in this, and who probably wants Michael to take the fall. I'm not a lawyer, so I can't say for sure if you can be forced to reveal who sent that email. But I do know that even if you do succeed in keeping it confidential, the fact that you have it will leak out. And everyone will assume that it was Michael Bennett who sent it."

Turner lifted his head slightly. She knew he was listening very carefully.

"Everyone will believe that he kidnapped his nephew. And it will be that way for the rest of his life. But there's one other factor that makes it much worse."

She leaned forward slightly.

"Michael Bennett has *never* tried to hide."

She thought about last night's conversation, and the article that had appeared in *The Washington Blade*.

"Think about it. Michael has always been honest about who he is. And despite the criticism he knew he would face, he was also determined to be a teacher, the job that he was born to do. And yet despite that honesty, that *courage*, he's now a victim of the same kind of injustice that you despise."

The softening in Turner's features told her that she had made her point. But he still looked angry. Years of being an outcast had fortified his defenses, and he probably wasn't going to give up his ground easily.

"I know you want to help Michael Bennett," Gloria said. "I know you want to do the right thing."

"I've done the right thing."

"Fuck you," Booker snapped.

Turner tensed. The weakness she had seen a moment earlier was instantly gone.

"The same to you, Officer Jones. And thanks for providing our receptionist with your particulars. It'll come in handy for our lawyers."

Booker stood over him again. Gloria prayed he wouldn't move any closer. "You're gonna *need* your lawyers, *freak*."

"So will you," Turner looked pointedly at both of them.

"Mr. Turner, please," Gloria grabbed his forearm.

"Let go of me." His muscles tensed in her grip, as if he hated being touched.

"If you don't help us Justin Bennett is going to die," she said.

"No..." He met her eyes, and for an infinite moment Gloria thought he might weaken again.

But then he shook his head, and nodded toward the door.

"*No*," he said more firmly. "That's all I have to say."

Twenty-eight

Michael watched the sunrise from a sitting position on Martin and Joan's guestroom bed, the phone resting on his stomach, his mind replaying horrors in a continuous loop. It had been years since he'd been in a church, but he prayed with the fervent whispers of a fanatic, tears streaming, hands clasped in a fist pressed hard against his forehead. At several points Justin's voice came to him in a weak, gasping cry, an echo of the sound he had made weeks earlier after skinning his knee, both hands squeezing Michael's forearm as Mary sprayed the scrape with Novocaine. When the bandage was applied, and while his face was still wet with tears, Justin had reverted to sucking his thumb, a habit that he had bravely "given up." For a long moment in the twilight between consciousness and sleep, Michael saw the thumb going into his mouth again as Justin curled up into a fetal position, and whimpered in the dark.

He's still alive. And you can still save him.

The thought came from Michael's subconscious, pulling him out of the dream as he sat straight up, and knocked the phone to the floor. It took a moment to get his bearings, to remember why he was in a strange bed. The loud and fast busy signal from the unhooked phone sounded like a warning buzzer as he looked around the room. His muscles were stiff as he got up and put the phone on the bedside table. It was six A.M. In half an hour the television crews would start arriving. Shortly afterward they would broadcast a recap of the whole story, from the taking of Benjamin five years earlier to the events of the last 12 hours.

"Good. It has to be good—"

Michael whispered the thought out loud, knowing it would be impossible for anyone to hide Justin after his face was once again broadcast to millions of people around the country. But a recap of everything meant a stream of new revelations about himself. A glaring spotlight over everything he had done.

He picked up the phone again, remembering why he had held it as he had drifted off to sleep. He had wanted to call Mary. To hear her voice. To plead his innocence. To beg her to believe that Justin would still be found alive.

No. The phone is tapped.

It would have to be on the chance that Scott would try to contact her. He had been desperate to see her the night before Justin was kidnapped, and he probably still was. And although Scott knew better than to give them a direct line to his whereabouts, Michael felt as if he was watching every move the FBI and local police made. Taking Justin had been the first strike. Scott's real satisfaction came from the pain that followed. The agonizing wait for information. The recriminations.

Justin's death.

It was the ultimate revenge. And now it seemed more certain than ever as Michael looked at the two abductions side by side. But he held fast to the one fact that Martin and Joan desperately hoped could lead to Justin's salvation. A fact that would be twisted into a half-truth that could make Scott bring Justin back. A reason for Scott to believe that he could suddenly clear his own name.

By destroying yours for good. Michael stared at the blank screen of the television, dreading the "revelations" that could soon lure Scott into the open. Both Martin and Joan had promised that Mary would be made aware of the plan prior to the morning news shows, and that her cooperation was essential for carrying it through. And yet the thought of her watching, listening, remembering.

Michael sat up and reached for his jacket. There was a cell phone in his pocket with several pre-programmed numbers, one of which was for Mary's own cell phone. He knew Mary would have it close by. Mary had made up a jingle for the cell phone number, which made it easy for Justin to remember so he could always track her down, anytime and anywhere.

Michael hit the star-key, and the number one. He heard the electronic pings of the number being dialed.

The pressure against his lungs made it almost impossible to breathe as he listened to the phone ring again and again.

"Where *is* she?" he whispered. After at least eight rings Mary's recorded voice said she was unavailable, and that he should leave a message.

At the beep he began talking, describing Joan's strategy, explaining the rationale. After a few moments his voice grew hoarse, and his words sounded incoherent.

"I'll do anything to get him back," he said suddenly. "Oh, God, Mary anything..."

A final beep told him he could talk no more. As the signal light from the cell phone faded he had a mental image of Mary listening to the message, tears streaming down her face.

He stood up and reached into his jacket pocket for his keys, then remembered that the Jeep was still parked in Northeast Washington, where he had left it. But he had to get to Mary before the first broadcast. To be sure she knew what was happening well in advance.

He saw the camera crew setting up in the living room as he stepped into the first-floor hallway, then moved quickly out to the garage and the door that led to the backyard. The light was faint as he slipped into the alley behind the house and began walking toward Connecticut Avenue, where he would be able to get a cab.

He was no more than 20 feet from the end of the alley when the gunning of an engine and bright headlights stopped him.

In Martin and Joan's neighborhood the alleys behind the houses were wide enough for two cars to pass side by side. But the large, boxy sedan suddenly facing him was in the middle of the alley. The driver had come around the corner and appeared to be blocking his way. Michael thought it might be an unmarked police car.

After a moment he started walking again, his head tilted down. As he got closer he saw the car was an old Buick, from the early 1990s. In the darkness it was impossible to see the face of the driver. When he was just a few steps away the driver suddenly backed up, the front wheels turning the car at a sharp angle.

In doing so, the driver blocked the exit to the alley. Michael stood still, knowing that if the person behind the wheel was a cop that he would step out, show his badge, and start giving orders.

When that didn't happen he took a step back, his shoulders brushing against a fence. He looked toward the opposite end of the alley, about 10 houses away. He could have reached it quickly at a dead sprint. But he had a feeling that a sudden movement would be more dangerous, like trying to run from a growling attack dog.

He turned and began walking back at a leisurely pace, as if he had nothing to run from. After a moment he heard the car coming up behind him. He walked faster. Three backyards ahead of him was the back gate to Martin and Joan's house. He slipped his hand into his pocket again, feeling for the heavy key to the gate. The driver reacted to the movement, the car speeding up at the moment he broke into a jog.

"Don't forget the garbage, Lenny."

The woman's voice cut through the night as the light in a backyard across the alley came on. Michael felt a rush of relief at the sight of a man stepping out onto a deck raised several feet above the ground. The man didn't see him as he turned toward his garbage cans, but the light spilling into the alley seemed to freeze the moment, stopping the car and giving Michael time to separate the key to the gate.

He slipped the key in the lock, still listening to the clang of garbage can lids. He turned his head and saw the Buick was no more than 10 feet away, and in the half-light he was now able to see the outline of the driver's face.

His heart stopped.

"God, no." he whispered. The killer was behind the wheel. Michael thought of the blackmail money he had brought to the man the night before, which according to D'Amecourt's reasoning, had "proven" that he was guilty of everything the man had accused him of. If he had the money but was still following him, it meant he wanted something more.

He turned the key in the lock for the gate as the neighbor across the alley said something to the woman. He was a moment away from stepping through the gate for safety when he remembered what the killer had told him on the phone.

"You knew you were gonna get caught."

Michael stood still, but looked at him again. He thought of D'Amecourt, who had let him slip away.

He turned to face the car. The light from the neighbor's deck spilled into the alley, partially illuminating the driver, his pockmarked face and short, spiky hair leaving no doubt about his identity.

Michael walked toward him. He had covered half the distance when the man on the deck went back inside the house. He fought the urge to tell the man to wait, as if that would provide some protection. Instead he reached into his pocket again, felt for the cell phone... pulled it out for a brief glance and hit the redial button.

He waited for the electronic pings to ensure the connection, then lowered the phone to his side. As he got closer he realized the driver's side window was open, and saw the ghost of a smile on the killer's face.

He thought he heard a faint *click*, and then Mary saying hello.

"What do you want?" he asked, speaking loudly enough to cover the sound, as he stepped up to the driver's side window.

The killer looked back at him, the sockets of his eyes cast in shadow. "I wanna find out what happened to that little boy."

Michael leaned closer to the car. "So do I."

"Michael?"

Michael heard Mary's voice again and cleared his throat loudly. "How long have you been waiting for me?"

"That don't really matter."

The man's voice had a rural, working-class tone that instantly took Michael back to the confrontation two nights before.

"You have to believe me," Michael said. "I didn't have anything to do with what happened."

"Yeah, well I know different," the killer said.

"What you *think* you know is not the truth," he said. "I tried to tell that to the guy you sent to pick up the money. You're completely wrong. I didn't have anything to do with my nephew's disappearance. I'm doing everything I can to bring him back. The only reason I took you that money was because I wanted to talk to you to find out what *you* know."

The man said nothing, but Michael felt an increasing menace in his stare. He thought back to D'Amecourt's interrogation, the questions that pushed him to remember details of the killer's appearance. He bent his knees slightly, lowering himself to get a better look.

There was a strange smell in the car, a sweet aroma that sent off a warning in his mind. He was struggling to place it when the man leaned back slightly. The change in angle shifted the shadows, and Michael saw his pupils in the faint light.

His eyes are brown. Michael stared back at him. *He has a small dimple in his chin. Slightly crooked teeth on the top row.*

The man looked down, shifting slightly in his seat, as if he were embarrassed at being stared at.

Michael remembered what Gloria Towson had said about the picture at the crime scene. He had to find out if it was true.

"How did you know Justin was in danger?"

The man paused, shifted in his seat again. “Same way you did, I guess.”

Michael exhaled, leaned down another few inches. “Look, I *told* you. I didn’t know any—”

A sudden swing of the car door slammed into his knees and knocked him backward. He landed ass-down on the pavement. He started to rise but the man kicked him in the chest, snapping his head forward and back against the wooden planks of the fence. He tried to call out as the man grabbed him by the neck of his jacket and hoisted him up. Michael twisted, bringing his knee up to push him away as the man flung him down again.

“Don’t...” he managed to say, before a wet rag was forced into his mouth, the sickly-sweet smell sending him headlong into the darkness.

Twenty-nine

Justin was shivering under the green blanket. His arms and legs were so heavy he could barely move them and there were all kinds of sad pictures in his mind. Uncle Michael eating a hot dog. Momma kissing him goodbye. The mean man pulling him out from under the bench. The pictures came out of the dreams he had had after the needle had been stuck in his arm. It had felt like the sting of a bee and had put him to sleep right away.

After a while, the basement seemed less dark, and he was able to see things in the shadows. There was a saw hanging on the wall, next to a rake and a shovel. There was a shelf full of *poisons* like momma and Uncle Michael kept on high shelves in the basement at home. There were pieces of rope on the floor. There was also rope wrapped around his chest, keeping him tied to the bench. His head hurt where the man had smacked him after pulling him out from under the bench. His arm was still sore from where the man had given him another shot that made everything go black.

Justin heard footsteps on the stairs. Then there was a flash of light and then the light went out with a popping sound. The mean man said "damn it!" and his footsteps stopped.

Justin turned his head, saw the man standing near the top of the stairs, reaching up toward the light. Then after a moment the man went back up.

He tried to raise his head higher but the rope held him down tight. He blinked and in his mind he saw momma crying, calling his name. He opened his mouth to call out to her, but he was too scared to make any sound. He pushed hard against the ropes and watched her fade away as the door at the top of the stairs opened again. He squinted, saw the mean man had a flashlight.

He kept his eyes closed as the man started down the stairs again. A tear came down his cheek and there was a big lump in his throat but the voice in his head told him to be still. If the man thought he was asleep, or *dead*, he would leave him alone.

The mean man came over to the bench. Justin heard him breathing as the man lifted his arm. The man then put his fingers on the skin around his eyes and pulled his eyes open.

The flash of light stung his eyes. He jerked his head the other way.

"Ugly bastard," the man pinched his cheek.

The sudden sharp pain made him cry.

"Shut up!" The man slapped him.

Stars flashed in front of his eyes. He tried to wiggle out of the man's arms as he was lifted up, but his whole body felt loose, his own arms and legs hanging down as the man carried him up the stairs.

More bright lights hit his eyes as the man stepped into a kitchen and laid him down on a table. He felt a tingle in his arms and legs. He wiggled his feet, and moved his fingers, but the voice in his head told him to keep the rest of his body limp. To *pretend* he still couldn't move.

His eyes got used to the light but he kept them half-closed. Tilting his head, he saw the man step over by the sink. The man had another needle. As he turned around a phone rang. Justin recognized the ring. It was the kind that came from the phone momma kept in her purse.

You take the four and the five and the six and four ones ... pick up the phone and dial 'em all in...

The song momma had made up to help him remember her phone number swirled around in his mind and made him start crying again.

"Shit," the mean man said. The phone made him mad. He didn't look like he wanted to answer it. But when it rang again he put the needle down and went through the open doorway into another room.

Justin's heart started beating faster. He lifted his head and wiggled his fingers and toes again. This time he had even more feeling in his arms and legs. He bent his legs at the knees and sat up. He opened his eyes all the way. He was alone. The walls of the kitchen were yellow and there was a picture of the mountains on the wall. The table he was lying on had four chairs and there was a toaster that had been pushed over to the edge. On the wall was a clock, with the big hand on the 1 and the little hand on the 6.

It's 6 o'clock in the morning, he thought. *Momma gets up at 6 in the morning to study.*

There was another big lump in his throat as he thought of her sitting at a table just like this one at home, reading her big books and typing on the flat computer she sometimes carried with her purse. He sat up straighter, carefully slid his legs so his feet rested on a chair.

There was a door that went to the backyard. It had four glass panes at the top and the doorknob was low enough to reach. The kitchen wasn't big but the door looked far away.

He looked at the needle the man had left on the sink. Every other shot had made him go right to sleep. He rubbed his arm where the needle had been stuck. He didn't want to go to sleep again. He wanted to run away from the house and find momma and Uncle Mike *now!*

The wooden chair was skinny but it held him okay as he grabbed the back for balance and put his feet down on the floor.

The chair squeaked as he took his hand away. He froze at the sound, looked toward the other room. Suddenly he couldn't hear the mean man talking anymore. The man must have hung up the phone, which meant he was coming back.

Run!

He heard the voice in his head as he raced to the door, grabbed the knob, and stumbled out onto a porch, his knees and hands smacking against a wooden floor. There were screened walls all around and flowered couches and chairs. But the porch had a door. He grabbed the knob but it didn't move. It was *locked!*

He heard the man yell and suddenly he was yelling too, screaming "MOMMA COME HELP ME!"

Jumping on the flowered couch, banging on the screen as the man leapt out onto the porch, grabbed him around the waist, and threw him down.

His back cracked against the floor as he fell. And then the man was standing over him, drawing his leg back as if he were going to kick him.

"Zachary?"

The lady's voice came from somewhere outside, beyond the porch. The mean man's face turned red when she called out again.

"Is everything okay?"

Thirty

Mary Bennett's hysterical call to 911 came at 6:20 A.M. Something had happened to her brother. From what D'Amecourt was told in the brief conversation that awakened him from a fitful doze on the couch, it sounded as if the killer had finally tracked him down.

"She got a call on her cell phone, at a number that only people in her family knew about." D'Amecourt's secretary, a fifty-ish early riser named Dorothy Hamlin, repeated what she had been told. "You said the dispatchers should notify you as soon as anything—"

"What did she say?"

"She thinks the call was from Michael Bennett. But he didn't say anything directly to her. She only heard him talking to another guy. Most of the conversation was garbled, but she said she heard sounds like they were struggling, and then lost the connection."

D'Amecourt sat up, and tried to process what he was hearing.

"The lady told the dispatcher that her brother was, or should have been, at Councilman Raines's house. Officer Darnell Clark was already on site and parked across the street. Raines answered when he went to the door. And when the two of them went looking for Michael Bennett they found a note saying he had left. Clark says he had been parked in front of the house for most of his shift, which ran all night, and he didn't see anyone come or go."

D'Amecourt remembered the Raines house, in Cleveland Park, where all of the residential blocks were divided by wide, clean-swept alleys between the deep backyards.

"No one was watching the back, sir," Dorothy Hamlin said, as if reading his mind.

D'Amecourt looked toward the desk at the corner of his study, at the neat stacks of crime scene reports from both murders. The eviscerated bodies of both of the killer's Washington victims had followed him into his dreams. A clenching in his gut told him what he had suspected ever since Michael Bennett had told him about the assault at Club Night and the phone call after the abduction. That Michael was destined to be the next victim, and that it was probably already too late.

He stood up, his mind racing through the conversation with Sylvia Barshak hours earlier. If Sylvia's instincts were right, Michael had already told Gloria Towson everything he had tried so desperately to hide. If Michael died, Towson would want answers. She knew way too much to back down now.

"Call dispatch. Tell Clark to stay put," he said, and hung up. On the desk next to the reports, the detailed street map of northeast Washington was already marked with a yellow grid. D'Amecourt looked at it one more time as he reached for his gun.

* * *

The sun was rising higher as Booker headed east and then north into the city. Gloria watched the light shimmering against the suburban office towers and felt the failure full-force as Booker told her he was "sorry."

"Don't say that," she responded. "It makes it sound like it's over."

"But I don't know what else we can do." Booker kept his eyes on the road. "The man admitted it's more important to protect a bunch of perverts than to help us save a little boy."

She absently rested her hand on the cell phone in her jacket pocket, wondering what would happen if she called Adam Turner again. She knew he would have been more cooperative if Booker hadn't been in the room. Turner clearly hated the police and probably most other authority figures as well. She was almost certain that he would have told her much more if she had had more time with him, on her own.

"I wish I'd told Turner more about our suspicion that D'Amecourt allowed this to happen," she said. "He'd probably hate the man and would probably want to expose him. That could have swayed him to help us."

Booker nodded.

"Now we don't have any choice but to take this to D'Amecourt, to hope that he'll get a court order—"

"And you know that ain't gonna happen."

Gloria sat back, the sense of defeat intensifying as she thought again of Michael's refusal to believe that Louis D'Amecourt was involved. Neither begging or browbeating had seemed to sway him into fully disclosing everything he knew.

Like they've got some kind of shared secret, she thought. *Some kind of bond.*

Her cell phone rang. She glanced at the display for the incoming number, which she didn't recognize. She picked it up warily and listened for a moment before speaking.

"Hello?" It was a male voice, tentative and young. *Payne*, she thought. "Gloria?"

"Hi, Tommy." She looked at Booker, her guard still up. "What's up?"

"I know what Michael Bennett was hiding in the attic of his house," Payne said. "I know what he's afraid of."

* * *

D'Amecourt slapped the portable siren on top of his unmarked Crown Victoria and sped recklessly through the streets of Northwest D.C. He reached the Raines house in less than six minutes. The three police cars parked haphazardly at the curb looked intrusive in front of the sprawling, immaculately restored Victorian and craftsman-style homes along the tree-lined street.

D'Amecourt looked toward Martin Raines's front door, which had been left wide open, probably by one of the officers summoned to take a report. D'Amecourt started to pull over and go in, but doubted that Raines would give him the time of day. Martin and Joan Raines had always been fiercely loyal to Michael Bennett, and his own accusations in the early hours of the investigation into the abduction of Benjamin Bennett five years ago had made him an enemy of the entire family. Yet so far Michael still claimed that the tie between Michael and himself remained a secret; that neither Mary nor his aunt and uncle knew about the love, and the terror, that would connect him to Michael Bennett forever.

His dread deepened as he thought about the leaks about the FBI search that had already come out overnight. Sylvia Barshak had claimed that she had no choice, that *not* searching Michael's room would have put her under even more scrutiny. But she still should have found a way to keep the D.C. police who had assisted with the search from talking to the press. It was bad enough that they had known with the first furtive glance into the box in Michael's room at least part of what Michael had been trying to hide. Now that they had leaked the information there was no possible way to escape the exposure to come.

Especially if Michael is murdered. D'Amecourt felt the muscles in his chest contracting as he reached the end of the block and turned into the alley. Martin Raines's backyard was at the midpoint of the block, and the gate that led from the alley to the backyard was open. Officer Darnell Clark was standing next to the gate, talking to a woman in a dark blue business suit.

He stopped the car just a few feet away. Clark was taking notes, frowning with concentration as the woman talked. D'Amecourt felt the pain in his chest again, a fight-or-flight panic as he thought of Gloria Towson and Michael being together just a few hours before. Michael, still stinging from his own betrayal, undoubtedly telling Towson everything she wanted to know.

Thirty-one

Two days earlier, at the Trio Café, Gloria had barely looked at the face of the victim in the crime scene photos from the murder at the Larchmont apartment. And now she only vaguely recalled the victim's dark brown hair, the eyes, half-open and glazed. She wished she had the picture in front of her as she listened to what sounded like a confession from Tommy Payne.

"His real name was Brad Hanson," Payne's voice had clashed with static on her cell phone line as Booker turned onto 395 and headed into the city. "Although he used a different name when he was photographed."

Gloria remembered the name Brad Hanson from the article Mary Bennett had written for *The Washington Blade*. Brad and Michael had been in the same fraternity during their first year at George Washington University. Mary had written just a few paragraphs about her brother's "one serious relationship," and described how it led her to "come to accept who he was" before he became a father figure to Benjamin and Justin.

According to what Payne had "discovered" during a conversation with a "friend" at the FBI, Brad Hanson was also known as Tom Handler, and he was photographed for several pornographic magazines in the months leading up to his murder. Several of those magazines had been found in the box in Michael Bennett's house, along with computer discs and software and other items that the police and the FBI now deemed "suspicious."

"It sounds like Michael had some kind of obsession with him," Payne had said, before she lost him to the bad connection. "The box in his room had a bunch of the magazines, a couple of videotapes, a big envelope with some kind of manuscript inside ... I don't think anyone's figured out what the computer discs and software are about."

Gloria knew it wouldn't be long before someone did. The FBI had been in control of the box for nearly 24 hours, long enough to ascertain any further connections in the abduction of Justin. Nothing Payne had said pointed to a direct link, but the fact that the abduction appeared to have been arranged online made her even more curious about Michael's use of computer technology.

But she was equally curious about D'Amecourt's connection, especially as she thought about the man's efforts to thwart the investigation of the murder, and about Michael's admission that D'Amecourt's secret was connected to the contents of the box.

She relayed the details of the conversation to Booker as soon as she hung up. He listened intently and theorized that the killer may have found both victims through the Internet.

"Unfortunately we probably aren't going to be able to figure out if the first guy had a Web site," Booker told her. "But there might still be photos somewhere on the Net."

She was anxious to begin searching when they got back home. She was just logging on as Booker turned on the television and began playing the morning's recorded news programs.

The newscast from Fox was first. Booker fast-forwarded to the story on the Justin Bennett investigation. An anchor talked through the key details over footage of AdventureWorld, juxtaposed against photos from Mary Bennett's recent *Washington Blade* article. The footage ended with the photo of Michael carrying Justin on his back.

The image stayed on the screen, morphing into a close-up shot showing the happy expressions on the faces of both Michael Bennett and his nephew. The newsman then described "new details" that had emerged overnight.

"This morning sources are saying that evidence found in the attic adjacent to Michael Bennett's bedroom may connect Michael Bennett to an unsolved murder that occurred two years ago. As you heard earlier, that evidence has been described as photographs and computer software, which is still undergoing analysis by the FBI. What sources cannot say however, is *how* this development relates to the kidnapping of Justin Bennett. Our sources are telling us that there is no *clear* connection. But agents remain very interested in this new twist in this very compelling case."

The TV went to a split screen with the anchor on one side and Martin and Joan on the other. The anchor was in his early 50s and handsome, with thick hair graying at the temples and just enough lines in his face to look like a seasoned journalist.

Martin and Joan Raines looked ruined, their skin drained of color, their eyes lined with dark circles. They were seated on a couch in their home, and the camera was far enough back to show Joan's hands in her lap, clutching a piece of white cloth that Gloria guessed was a handkerchief. In the introduction the newsman had talked about "the continuing search for Justin Bennett, and the hope that he will be returned safely home," but both Martin and Joan looked as if they were already contemplating the worst.

Yet when questioned, Joan Raines spoke with unmistakable determination.

"We *know* it's not too late, and we're praying that Justin will be returned to his mother safely," Joan said. "And Justin, *honey*..."

For a long moment Joan's voice quivered. She squinted, forced back tears, and continued.

"If you're watching us, we want you to know that everything is going to be okay. Your mother loves you very much, and she wants to remember your special song."

"What the hell?" Booker growled.

Gloria held up her hand, and watched intently as the camera went closer, and Joan Raines continued.

"You remember the words, and the tune, Justin. Just play it in your mind and remember to be *a good boy*."

"Mr. and Mrs. Raines," the interviewer cut in. "Yesterday afternoon the FBI alerted authorities all over the U.S. to be on the lookout for Justin Bennett and Scott Brown. Do you have any idea why he might have taken the boy?"

Joan looked directly into the camera. "We believe Scott loves his son. If he has taken Justin, we just want to know that Justin is okay, and that he'll be returned home to his mother safely."

"That's a twist." Booker frowned.

"We also think it's wrong to jump to the conclusion that Scott Brown intends to *harm* Justin," Joan continued. "Scott is Justin's biological father, and we know that he cares about Justin. If he has taken Justin he may have reasons that make sense to him. A need to *protect* Justin. A desire to ensure that he has the opportunity to be with Justin. Whatever the reason, we want him to know that we care about both father and son, and that we simply want to know that Justin is all right, and that he'll be brought home safely. Decisions about our nephew Michael's guilt and involvement, his intentions and past, can be determined later. But we just want you to know, *Scott*, that if Justin is alive and well that you are *not* past the point of no return. We will both support you if you bring our boy back."

"Jesus," Booker whispered. "Has that lady lost her damn mind?"

"I wouldn't count on it," Gloria said, as the camera drew back again, showing both Martin and Joan sitting very still on the couch.

"Let me get back to the allegations that have been made about Michael Bennett," the newsman said. "Five years ago, his sister's first child also disappeared while in his care. It was commonly believed that Scott Brown took the child, but there were many who believed Michael was involved as well."

"Those allegations are completely unfounded," Martin said.

"But according to the investigators, Justin Bennett always wore an identification bracelet. Michael Bennett reportedly loosened the clasp on the bracelet the night before—"

"The bracelet was already loose. Michael tried to fix it."

"But you can see why the investigators are curious, can't you?"

"Yes, I can see why they're *curious*," Joan said.

The anchor frowned slightly, as if he was surprised.

"There are some questions, some things we don't know and may never know. But right now it's not up to us to judge what has transpired since we don't have all of the facts. But there is one thing we *do* know."

The camera came closer as Joan paused.

"*No one* is beyond redemption. No one should be doomed by his past. That includes Michael."

"You're saying you believe there's a connection between what happened in the past and the abduction of Justin Bennett?"

"We don't know. But I do want to say, again, that nothing matters more than getting Justin safely home. We have no doubt that if Scott does have him that he's being treated well, and we're confident that when he is returned we can certainly find a way for father and son to build a life together."

"Unbelievable." Booker said.

"And perfectly calculated." Gloria said, as a picture of Justin by himself came to the screen and the interviewer signed off.

A commercial came on, and Booker used the remote to turn the volume down. "What are you talking about?"

"It was a ploy." She looked past him, thinking through what she had just heard. "Joan Raines was trying to send a message to Scott Brown and trying to mitigate the damage to Michael. All of that talk about *redemption*— those assertions that if Scott took Justin he had reasons that *made sense to him*. They're basically giving him an out."

"Telling him it isn't too late."

"Yes. Making Scott Brown sound like he's not such a bad guy after all. Imagine if you were Brown, and you were listening to that, and you were having at least a few second thoughts. You've got the aunt of the child's mother telling the world you've got reasons for what you did, and that can be forgiven."

"So she does think Scott is involved."

"I think she does. But she's also anticipating that more incriminating evidence against Michael is going to come out again soon. Probably the connection to the murder of Brad Hanson. She knows that if Scott hears about it, he'll have one more reason to think that Michael has been exposed, and that his own family may not stick by him. So, if you were him—"

"You'd be happy," Booker said. "Feeling like you're worst enemy's fallen down."

"And that maybe taking Justin Bennett, for his own *protection*, won't look like such a bad thing."

"So they basically sacrificed Michael's image to appeal to Scott."

Gloria nodded, but gave him an uncertain look. "There was something else going on there too. That whole plea for Justin to, quote, 'be a good boy'— that obviously means something to him. Like screaming at the top of his lungs if he makes it to a public place. Or calling his mother if he ever gets to a phone."

Booker hit the rewind button. "What about what she said about the song?"

"It's probably a phone number. Something easy for Justin to remember."

"Which means she *thinks* he's still alive."

"Yes."

"And doesn't have a clue about what really happened."

She shook her head and crossed her arms to try and ward off the sudden chill gripping her shoulders.

She stood up. "I need to get a hold of her, to tell her what we know."

"You'll never get to her directly," Booker said.

He was right. There were probably several D.C. police officers parked within view of the Raines house, watching anyone who came or went. And if she called Joan, she was certain an FBI agent and D.C. detectives would be in the room, tapping the phone, listening to both sides of the conversation.

Making the call would expose her. But given what she had just seen, she knew that Joan Raines would respond instantly, putting a whole new stream of pressure on Adam Turner to turn over his confidential files. Identifying the sender of the email that went to the Capitol Hotel victim could force him to reveal everything he knew, including Justin Bennett's whereabouts right now.

And it might save us, too, she thought, *making it a lot harder for D'Amecourt to take us down.*

She was just stepping toward the phone as Booker sat down in front of the computer, which had been left on. She paused, looking over his shoulder as he checked the email address that they shared. There were a handful of messages, including two from Booker's mom, who had only recently succumbed to her son's pleas to get a computer. "You can see she's really lovin' that email," Booker joked. "She can keep track o' me every hour of the day."

He was just about to open her first one when a quiet *ding* told them they had another new message.

For an instant the email appeared to be from an address she didn't recognize, a spammed sales pitch. But then Gloria noticed the first two letters in the address, a capital A and T, followed by a jumble of numbers.

"Booker, look." She pointed to the email on the screen. "I think it's from Turner."

Booker clicked open the email. The first few lines read like an official memo:

> To: Officer Gloria Towson, Metropolitan D.C. Police
> From: Adam Turner, President, Stonewall
> Re: Information Request
>
> As requested, Stonewall is forwarding transcripts of Internet newsgroup and chatroom conversations of interest related to the investigation discussed at our offices today. These conversations are available to anyone with access to the newsgroups hosted on our site and therefore the relaying of them does not violate the privacy of our members. Because our company stands by its pledge to respect the privacy of our members, I reiterate that

> we cannot release confidential information such as the actual name or billing address of the individual you are investigating without a proper legal order to do so. I trust that this message demonstrates our willingness to cooperate with the legal authorities in this criminal investigation while remaining true to our pledge to our customers. Any further correspondence should be directed to our attorneys at...

"What a jerk," Gloria muttered. She watched as Booker scrolled down past the contact information for Adam Turner's attorneys, then down to what looked like the text of several dozen newsgroup postings from "quietriot22," the sender of the email that Payne had found in the Capitol Hotel victim's belongings.

"This isn't anything new," Booker said. "It's all stuff I found on my own."

Gloria took another look at the message and the voluminous stream of postings. "But it's kind of strange that he's sending it, saying three times that it's basically out there anyway, for anyone to see."

"He's covering his ass. Making it look like he's helping us when he really isn't." Booker leaned forward slightly, squinting at the screen as he scrolled down to the end. "At least I don't think so..."

"What do you mean?"

Booker went back to a midpoint in the messages, moved the blinking cursor to the return address.

"There's something different," he said, "in two of these."

She watched as he highlighted two messages that had a heading saying "Error Report." There were several lines that mixed numbers and letters. To Gloria it looked very similar to the rest of the codes that had been embedded in the email headers; all part of a language that Booker seemed to know fluently although it was a complete enigma to her.

"There are two error messages that went back to the sender, on October 14."

Gloria glanced at the calendar on the wall. October 14 was the day after the Capitol Hotel murder.

"The error message is a standard service, like a courtesy." Booker's voice had an upbeat edge. "It notifies the customer that they've had an abnormal termination of their service and states that the ISP will check their connection. In this case the error message went back to the site that the customer was logged on from. An automatic thing."

Gloria watched as Booker scrolled down through the two messages in question and felt his excitement building. He opened his mouth to speak as the doorbell rang in an old-fashioned gothic chime that echoed through the house. Gloria cursed under her breath. Company was the last thing she wanted.

"What are you saying, Booker?"

"Like I told, you, people can log on to SentryMail from anywhere, and it's usually impossible by just looking at newsgroup postings to know exactly what ISP someone's using. But in these two cases, the connection was spotty, and he got bumped off. Stonewall, which was hosting the newsgroup that he was connected to, automatically sent the error message to the PC that he was logged on from. Our friend Adam Turner has just forwarded that error message to us."

"Okay..." Gloria's heart was pounding. "What does that *mean*?"

"It means Turner's not coming clean completely, but he's giving us a clue."

"I don't want a damn clue," she snapped. "I want to know—"

"If I look at the header of the error message I can see where the message went to and... oh God."

Downstairs, the doorbell rang again. Gloria looked out the front windows, felt a jolt against her spine at the sight of Louis D'Amecourt on the front porch. D'Amecourt glanced up and met her eyes the instant Booker spoke again.

"The sender was logging on through the domain and server that's used by the D.C. police," Booker said. "I can probably trace the email right back to the computer at D'Amecourt's own desk."

Thirty-two

Michael was surrounded by darkness. There was a thick pain enveloping his chin and a wet cloth inside his mouth, and when he tried to speak, he gagged.

Tears stung his eyes as he tilted his head up. His wrists were tied up above him over some sort of wooden beam. His feet hung in mid-air, but when he flexed them downward, he touched a wooden floor.

His toes were bare. His arms were bare. And with a slight, painful twist he knew that the rest of his body was bare. He was hanging naked in a low-lit room.

He jerked his hands downward. But the binding around his wrists only tightened and brought a sweeping numbness to his fingers.

He looked straight ahead, his eyes slowly adjusting to the half-light of the room around him. He saw the outline of a window, the panes draped in a dark cloth, the arms of a chair and the square lines of a television.

He twisted toward his right, felt piercing pain between his ribs, and slowly, delicately turned back.

There was a movement at the corner of his eye. The snap of a lighter, the spark of a flame illuminating the familiar face of a man stepping slowly toward him, a cigarette burning between his lips.

The man stood in front of him, sucking deeply on the cigarette, his face just inches away. For a long moment the man simply stood there, the acrid smoke surrounding them.

"Please don't hurt..." Michael managed to say, before a *shush* from the man's lips stopped him. He felt a light, tickling sensation at his stomach. The touch of fingertips, tracing horizontal lines across his skin...

And a sudden dagger of hot pain as the man pressed the burning cigarette against his chest.

He screamed an instant before the man slapped him hard across his face. He screamed again before a blow to the side of his head knocked him back out.

* * *

Mary had both hands on top of the phone at her bedside table. Her eyes were tightly shut and she was whispering a prayer when she heard her brother scream.

The sound brought her to her feet.

She was in her bedroom, dreading the call that would reveal Justin's fate; dreaming only occasionally amid the nightmares that Justin would find a way to reach her himself.

But for a long, terrifying moment it was Michael who she heard, calling out from somewhere in her subconscious mind. The vision was obviously connected to a dream, but it felt like one of her premonitions, one driven by the strong connection she and Michael had always shared. It was the same feeling she had had at the mall two days earlier, looking into his eyes, knowing that both of them had been thinking, fearing, that Justin's wandering off had been a precursor of something terrible to come. The feeling had come to her again just a few hours later, in the basement, as she held Justin's identification bracelet in her hand.

"No. Please, no," she whispered, and leaned against the wall. A wave of despair swept over her as she remembered the sight of Scott walking out of the courtroom five years before. Scott getting away with kidnapping, and murder, and already taking steps to ensure that he would always have access to Justin.

You knew this was coming, she thought. *You knew it because it was meant to happen. Because you could never really protect him from what's out there.*

She went to the window. A police car was still parked at the curb, and right behind it another one of the boxy sedans used by the FBI. The last several minutes before she had drifted into the fugue came back to her as if they were happening in real time. The first ring of the phone, which had come while she was in the shower. The race from the bathroom to the bedroom in the failed attempt to catch it. The long, meandering message from Michael about the psychological game that Joan hoped would lure Scott out of hiding.

And the next call, just a few minutes later. Michael's voice talking to someone she could only vaguely hear; the sounds of a struggle, Michael gasping as if he'd been punched in the stomach, static, and then silence.

The D.C. police had given her a special hotline number, a line that would only be used if she got some communication from Justin's kidnapper. She had dialed it immediately and had told the woman at the other end exactly what she had heard, begging for an urgent response and bursting into tears as she thought of Michael being dragged away.

She looked closer at the FBI car, her mind drifting back to yesterday's search of the house; the heavy footsteps overhead as the agents moved toward the attic storage room where Michael kept his hidden box. She guessed that the first thing they had seen was the stack of magazines, each one containing pornographic photographs of the man she knew as Brad Hanson. *Michael's partner.* The thought still made her intensely uncomfortable, although she had always done a fairly good job of pretending otherwise. She really had no choice, given the intensity of Michael's passion, his dedication to Brad right up until the horrible end.

The next items that would be of interest to the FBI were the computer discs. She knew they held digitized photos of Brad and the other software that Michael had been using to build the Web site about Brad. A site that would apparently feature very different types of photos, most of them shots of Brad as a child, an adolescent, and a young man in the arms of her brother.

And then they would see the very small item in the Crime section of the *Washington Post*'s Metro section, with its bare bones details about the Larchmont murder and its "unidentified" victim.

She still wondered why Michael had lied to her about what had happened to Brad. Why didn't he tell her that Brad changed his name and posed in gay magazines? Why had Michael told her they had simply broken up when Brad had in fact been murdered?

Because he thinks you don't trust him.

And he doesn't believe he can trust you.

She shivered at the thought; the simple, sad truth. Despite the deep connection between Michael and herself, there had always been a place of uneasiness, an uncharted emotional territory that allowed her to "accept" her brother's sexuality as long as she kept the visual images of it out of her mind. Michael had loved Benjamin as deeply as the most dedicated father. And his love for Justin had been equally intense. Because Michael had always been close to her, and because neither Benjamin nor Justin really had a father, it seemed only natural that Michael would take on the role.

Well, *almost* natural.

She turned her back to the window, away from the police cars, away from the outside world, realizing then that she had always known that Michael's life would somehow collide with hers. That somewhere between the passion that he had felt for Brad Hanson and Brad's savage death, Justin would be taken away.

The feeling stayed with her as she sank once again to her knees, both arms outstretched over the bed, her hands clasped in a fist. Something had happened to her brother. Something had happened to Justin. And she imagined once again that God was giving her a choice that she could somehow determine who would live and who would be taken away from her forever.

She pounded her fist against the mattress, a frightening, wrenching cry coming from the pit of her lungs as she realized she really had no choice at all. Her brother, and her son, might both be dead.

"God..." she whispered, shutting her eyes, seeing Michael, *feeling* him, as he called out her name.

* * *

Mary, Mary... forgive me...

Michael's thoughts swam slowly through the darkness, past the thumping pain at his temples, past the horrific images that rose up into his mind. He saw himself from a distance, slipping a key into a deadbolt lock, a heavy suitcase in his hand. Saw the door swinging open, the bright light filling the room as he hit the switch. The blood-soaked sheets, carpet, and walls.

The body on the bed.

The vision wavered as he stepped forward, gasping for breath, seeing but not believing the sight of Brad, his hands tied to the railing at the back of the bed, his eyes half-open in death. He saw himself stepping back, turning around, tripping over a chair that had fallen sideways, his palms smacking against the carpet, the wet blood on his bare arms, his knees. Saw himself running from the room, turning into the long empty hallway ...

It was D'Amecourt he saw next, stepping into the hallway at the other end. Louis D'Amecourt carrying another large suitcase, his face whitened by shock as Michael watched the dream vision of himself leaning forward, staring down at his own bloody hands against his knees.

"Look alive Michael."

He opened his eyes. The lights had been turned up in the room. Brad's killer was standing in front of him and pressing the point of a knife against the soft underside of his chin.

The killer smiled as he raised the knife, forcing Michael to tilt his head higher.

The man locked him into a stare. His eyes had an unnatural brightness, and Michael smelled alcohol on his breath as he slowly lowered the knife.

Michael looked down, exhaling deeply as he realized, again, that he had been stripped naked before being strung up from the exposed beams in the ceiling. There were long red marks on his chest and torso. While he was unconscious the killer had used the knife to cut several long, shallow scratches into the outer layer of his skin. Michael tightened his gut, wincing as a line of bright red blood trickled out of a cut at the top of his ribs where the blade had gone deeper.

"Please..." he said weakly. "Don't."

"Ah." The killer wrinkled his face into an expression of mock pity. "You gonna start *cryin'* now?"

Michael held his breath as the point of the knife was pressed against his jugular vein.

"You scared?"

Michael was unable to nod or speak as the man continued looking into his eyes.

"You *oughta* be, considerin' what's comin'." The man stepped back slightly. He set the knife down on the arm of an old plaid couch and pulled off his gray, sweat-stained t-shirt. His torso was defined by lean muscle, and there was a tattoo of a crucifix just below his navel.

"Don't bother tryin' to yell or nothin'," he said. "There's nothin' but empty buildings on both sides of us."

Michael shook his head slightly, as if agreeing not to. He took his first deep breath. The room smelled of vomit. Glancing back and forth, he saw torn wallpaper over yellowed, water-stained walls, piles of newspapers and plates and glasses soiled with dried food on top of the television. As his eyes adjusted to the light he realized there were several pages torn from newspapers and taped to the edge of an old mantel. He squinted, his breath coming up short as he realized the pages held articles about the abduction, a prominent photo of Justin at the center.

The killer stared appraisingly at him as he loosened the belt that held up his jeans.

"What do you want?" Michael asked him.

"Shhh, quiet now." The man pulled down his zipper, then stepped out of his jeans. His penis was half-erect inside stained white briefs as his eyes roamed up and down Michael's body. He looked as if he was in some kind of trance as he slipped his left hand inside of the briefs and began stroking himself.

Michael looked away, his eyes darting around the room. At the far left corner of his vision he saw an open doorway and the edge of a kitchen counter. At the right, past the stack of clothes and what looked like a pile of sheets and an old army blanket, a telephone rested atop a small side table. Below him, there was a yellow sheet, but beyond its edges the floor was stained an ugly reddish brown.

He tried to move his wrists again, but the bindings only tightened.

The killer was moaning softly as he picked up the knife and stepped forward, one hand still inside his briefs, the other gently tapping the knife against his bare thigh.

"Please, no," Michael whispered, before the man raised a finger to his lips. He then took his hand out of his briefs and pushed them down, his fully erect penis springing free. He raised the knife, in an overhand drip, above Michael's right shoulder and began fondling him.

Michael forced himself to look into the man's eyes. "Please let me down. I can't do anything tied up like—"

The knife plunged into his shoulder.

Michael arched violently and screamed.

The killer grimaced, baring his teeth as he tightened his grip on the handle and jerked the blade back out.

The blood splattered both of them as the man jumped back. Michael screamed again as the man smacked the side of his face.

He saw flashes of white light, felt his head rolling loosely forward, the room dimming further.

The man stood still for a moment, the knife still trembling in his right hand.

Michael began to cry.

"You wanna' start tellin' the truth now?" The man asked him.

"I told you... the truth. I only brought you that money... because I wanted to find out what you knew."

"You're lyin'." The man pressed the point of the knife against the skin directly over Michael's heart. "You just wanted to keep me quiet. But it ain't gonna' work. Ain't nothin' gonna' work except tellin' me what I want to know. Where *is* that *boy*?"

Michael shut his eyes, his mind racing, past the pain at his shoulder, past the sharp point of the knife against his skin, pushing for one clear thought on how to survive. His thoughts skipped back to the memory of Gloria Towson at the police station, and in the car. Gloria Towson picking up pieces of a mental puzzle, shifting them around, leveraging one against another to get the information that she wanted.

He remembered what he knew, or what he *thought* he knew. Blood from the shoulder wound was sliding down his back and waves of nausea were rolling through his stomach. But he searched through his mind for the words that would delay what the killer wanted to do. The words that would allow him to stay alive for a little longer.

"I think... he's in the mountains."

"What mountains?"

"Near Frederick... Maryland." Michael remembered the television footage he had seen earlier; the old shots of the stretcher bearing Benjamin's body alongside the tributary fed by the Catoctin river.

"I think that's where Scott Brown, Justin's father, took him."

"What do you mean, you *think*?" The killer leaned closer. His breath was hot and sour.

"I don't know." Michael felt a faint buzzing around his temples, a lightness at the back of his head. "He hates my sister, and me... I think he took Justin to hurt us."

"Stop *LYIN'* to me!" A sharp punch snapped his head sideways. The buzz became a painful vibration through his brain. Behind it, a creeping darkness was pulling him downward, overcoming his ability to stay conscious.

He shook his head. As his vision cleared he saw that the killer had taken a step back. His own blood on the man's chest and neck was shiny under the stark overhead light.

"You think you're somethin'" The man walked around Michael in a slow circle. "Touchin' little boys. Ruinin' their minds. All the time walkin' around like you're doin' nothin' wrong."

"No..." Michael moaned.

"PERVERT!"

The man kicked him in the back, knocking the wind from his lungs. He gasped, struggling to catch his breath as the man came back around toward his right.

The killer's face was shiny with sweat, the wet blood still glistening against his naked chest as he walked over to the pile of sheets and blankets on the floor.

"*Look* at this, Michael!"

The killer kicked the pile. A long, skinny black arm dropped limply to the floor.

"Now look at THIS!" He reached down, grabbed the army blanket, and yanked it upwards.

The naked, bloody body of a black man rolled out. The man's torso was riddled with stab wounds. His dead eyes were half open, and as Michael looked into them, he felt himself tumbling backward, the buzzing in his head like a swarming hive of bees as the room around him began to disappear from the outside in, as if an invisible hand was erasing his consciousness.

No one knows where you are.

And there is nothing you can do to stop this.

The killer approached him again, the knife held in an overhand grip. The man had a strange, trance-like smile on his face as he drew the fingertip downward, making a cross over his abdomen. Michael felt the wetness of the blood underneath it, and knew that his flesh was being marked.

"All right, Michael. This is your last chance."

Michael yanked violently on the bindings around his wrists, his thoughts disintegrating as the steel blade glinted under the overhead light.

"No..." he cried out. *"No God PLEASE DON'T!"*

The killer raised the knife high above his neck and thrust it down the instant someone knocked on the front door.

Thirty-three

The drab, navy-blue overcoat was too heavy for the warm morning, and the sleeves chafed against Gloria's bare wrists as she knocked on the door of the decrepit rowhouse in Northeast Washington for the second time. The house had a sagging, narrow porch and panels of dirty glass on both sides of the door. The glass reflected her disguise—the wire-rimmed reading glasses, the matronly coat, the hat her grandmother had last worn on Easter at least 20 years before—but as she leaned a bit closer she was able to see into the house's dimly lit interior.

At the end of the long foyer hallway, she caught a glimpse of movement, a figure slipping behind the half-open door. Avoiding any sudden movement of her own, she tilted her head slightly to the left, toward Booker, at the other end of the porch, his back against the wall so he would not be visible to anyone looking out through the front window. Gloria gave him a half-nod, confirming that the house was indeed occupied.

Booker motioned for her to try again.

She knocked louder this time and made a point of pressing her face close to the glass. Through the arched doorway at the end of the hallway, she saw a man peeking around a corner. The instant their eyes met, Gloria tapped on the glass, waving to him, acknowledging that she knew he was there an instant before he stepped back into the shadows of the house.

She tilted her head to the right, down where D'Amecourt stood, hidden by the bushes from any passers-by on the street, his right arm inside his khaki jacket, gripping his gun. It had been less than an hour since D'Amecourt had shown up at her front door, telling her he thought Michael had been abducted. Telling her he needed help from her and Booker "because I don't have anywhere else to go."

Booker was about to confront him, to tell D'Amecourt outright that he knew he had logged on to the pedophile newsgroup. He probably would have even told D'Amecourt that there was no use in lying about it because Booker had the log-in address and the server information that D'Amecourt had used. But with just a few words D'Amecourt had stopped him cold.

The revelations that followed—all detailed very quickly as the three of them worked out the plan and gathered up the pieces of the disguise—still left her wondering about D'Amecourt. She knew that she could not trust him completely, not with what Booker was now able to prove. But D'Amecourt had told her that he was almost certain that he knew where Michael was, and he looked as if he was about to fall apart as he begged them for help.

She pressed her face close to the dirty glass again. The man inside of the house had seen her, and he knew that she had seen him. She hoped that would be enough to make him open the door.

When she realized he was indeed approaching she stepped back slightly and made sure the screen door was unlatched. She held the bible in her left hand and kept her right hand free and poised over the open zipper of her shoulder bag to make it easier to reach for her gun.

The door opened and she knew that D'Amecourt had been right. The killer was standing within a foot of her. He held the door no more than six inches open, and in the narrow space she saw that he was wearing a ragged old bathrobe, pulled tightly around his waist, with jeans and a pair of worn sneakers with untied laces on his feet.

He dressed quickly to come the door, she thought. And she knew from the look in his eyes that he already regretted answering it.

Without looking down, she reached for the lever that pulled the screen door open.

"Good morning, sir." She spoke solemnly. "I am calling on Mr. Nash."

The killer stared back at her without speaking.

"Mr. *Cecil* Nash." She tilted her head slightly upward, giving him a judgmental look. "He might be expecting me, or someone from our church. Is he home?"

"Naw, he ain't here."

"Not here?" Gloria placed the front of her foot on the threshold to stop him from closing the door, but turned her head back toward the street to cover the gesture. "I've got four volunteers on the way over right now. What am I going to *tell* them?"

"Tell 'em he moved," the man said gruffly, but she could see the wariness in his eyes. Gloria clicked her tongue against the roof of her mouth and gave a disdainful shake of her head.

"They'll probably go straight to the backyard before I can stop them."

"What the hell are you talkin' about?"

The coldness in his voice scared her. She pressed the bible closer to her chest, her fingers tight against the soft imitation leather.

"They're volunteers, coming here to help Mr. Nash clean up his home, a project in service to the community and to our church." She leaned forward slightly, placing more of her foot between the door and the jamb. "We've been so *concerned*. Mr. Nash has missed services two Sundays in a row."

"I told you he ain't here. So tell your church people to go away."

Gloria leaned back, clutching the bible to her chest, looking as if she'd been physically assaulted.

The man tried to push the door shut, but Gloria's foot was blocking the way. When he looked down the top of the ragged robe came open.

Beneath the robe Gloria saw streaks of bright red blood on his chest. He heard the catch in her breath and met her eyes. For an infinite moment they stared at each other. He then looked at her feet again, which were clad in dark blue Nikes.

The shoes were for running; the one element of the disguise that didn't fit. And when he looked back up she knew that he was on to her.

And she knew it was time.

"I would like to leave my card for Mr. Nash." Gloria's hand was shaking as she broke eye contact and reached into the purse. "If you could give it to—"

"You *bitch!*" The killer punched her squarely in the chest, knocking her backward. She fell hard onto the porch floor, the gun flying from her hand the instant she pulled it out.

"Booker—" she gasped. She saw him rushing forward from the corner of her eye, and dropping to his knees next to her.

She looked up, saw the killer raising a gun from inside the foyer, aiming it at the back of Booker's head.

"No!" she screamed, brought her right leg up in a sudden sideways kick, knocking Booker off-balance; the sound of gunfire sending them both rolling, she in one direction, Booker in the other. Then she heard the slamming of the door and the slide of a deadbolt lock.

Booker got up quickly. "Glo, are you..."

"He's in there," she gasped for breath. "I think he's already hurt. There was blood." She pointed jerkily toward her own chest, then toward the door. "We have to get in!"

"D'Amecourt!" Booker yelled, both of them looking toward the bushes where D'Amecourt had been hiding.

"Goddamn it!" Booker said. "He's gone."

Gloria saw her gun lying against a bag of trash that had been left on the porch, grabbed it, and stood up. Then she grabbed the handle of the screen door, brought it back, and told Booker to hold it.

"What are you—?" he tried to ask as she stepped back and fired recklessly at the door. The first shot hit several inches from the deadbolt.

She heard Booker telling her to stop as she fired again, hitting the space between the deadbolt lock and the door frame. The rotten wood splintered instantly and the lock popped open.

"Move away from the door." Booker gripped her shoulder, pushing her aside as he started to go in.

"No." Gloria stepped away and met his eyes. "I got us into this." Her throat was dry, her voice still hoarse. "I *have to* help him."

Before Booker could react she spun around, kicked the door, and went in with both hands on her gun. With a rapid side-to-side scan she saw that the foyer was only about five feet wide. There was a small side table where the killer had probably set his own gun so that it would be within easy reach when he answered the door, a set of closed pocket doors leading to a room on the left.

He came to the door from the room at the end of the hall, she remembered. *Probably a back room, off of a kitchen. A back room with a back door to the outside.*

Booker followed her lead, moving forward with his back against the opposite wall until they were facing each other.

Gloria nodded back toward the doorway at the end of the hallway, indicating the killer's most likely location.

Booker shook his head, mouthing the word *"no."*

She realized that he was terrified, completely unwilling to let her go further. She remembered him lying alone in bed alone hours earlier, his big arms wrapped around the pillow. She thought of the blood she had seen on the killer's chest. Thought of Booker being alone.

From overhead, near the rear of the house, came the sound of breaking glass.

"Oh God, somebody please help me..."

Michael Bennett's voice was unmistakable, and filled with terror. She knew that he was in the back room, and that he was hurt.

She rushed forward, arms outstretched, both hands on the gun, through the open doorway.

She was struck first by the darkness, the blankets over the back wall windows, and then by the sight of the naked body on the floor, riddled with open wounds.

Black man, not Michael.

She pressed her back against the wall, did a visual sweep. She saw Michael Bennett hanging in the corner of the room, his arms over his head, wrists bound to a beam exposed by the ripped-out ceiling.

Michael was naked, his upper body covered in blood.

"Help... me." There was panic in his eyes when he called out to her again.

"Booker!" she yelled.

"Right here." He stepped alongside her. "Oh God."

She saw the source of most of the blood, a deep wound just above Michael's left shoulder blade. His body quivered with the onset of shock, the motion increasing the flow.

It looked like the only wound, probably not life-threatening if she was able to cut him down and get the bleeding stopped.

"Drop the gun, *bitch*."

Gloria turned around to see the killer in the kitchen doorway, where he must have hidden as she and Booker rushed into the room. He was just inside the threshold, out of Booker's line of fire. But his gun was pointed at her face.

"You heard me— drop it NOW."

With Michael hanging in front of her and the killer's advantageous position, the gun was useless at her side.

"Okay." She set the gun on the couch and glanced toward Booker as the killer stepped into the room, where he could see both of them.

"You, too," the man said to Booker. "Or I'll take her out right now."

Gloria looked into Booker's eyes, wishing she could somehow get him to shoot before the killer could fire. But she knew that he would not take the chance.

"All right," Booker said as he lowered his weapon.

"On the floor."

Booker set his gun down just inches from his feet.

"Now slide it over."

Booker nudged the gun, apparently complying. But when he pushed it the gun slid across the room at an angle, stopping several steps away from the man.

"Stupid *coons* can't do nothin' right," the killer muttered.

Gloria tensed, a spark of rage bringing sudden clarity to her thoughts.

"The house is surrounded," she said.

"The fuck it is. Now get away from him."

"You can't get away with—"

"GET THE FUCK AWAY!"

"Okay," she said quietly as she stepped aside. She knew that the calmness in her voice angered him.

"I meant what I said. There are six police officers and two FBI agents who know we're in here. You can't get away."

Surprised at how easily the lie came to her, and how *almost*-confident she sounded, she took a short, deep breath and continued.

"And if you take this any farther with Michael or do anything to the two of us you're dead."

The killer bristled, and raised his gun a bit higher. His eyes were bright and alert, but he did not look as if he would respond to reason. And yet he hadn't been crazy enough to shoot her or Booker before finding out if they were indeed alone.

"On the other hand you could stop it, right now. You could give me your gun and let us walk you out of here. We can stop the police from shooting you as you leave, and we can tell everyone why you really did this."

"What's that supposed to mean?"

Gloria remembered what the killer had said in his phone call to Michael. She also remembered what Michael had told her about the altercation at Club Night; the killer's assertion that Michael '*deserved*' to be "cut up."

She spoke with as much calmness as she could muster.

"We can tell them you have a reason for this. We can talk about what people have done to *you*."

"You don't care *nothin'* about what was done to me."

His voice knocked her hope away. She shuddered as he stepped all the way into the room, where he had a clear line of fire for all three of them.

"No." She suddenly sounded helpless. "*Please.*"

The killer pressed his lips together, as if steeling his resolve. Behind her, Michael let out a long, mournful cry. The sound caught the man's attention, and for a moment he broke eye contact with her, looking at Michael instead. He was just about to speak when a clump of plaster slipped out of the ceiling overhead.

The plaster hit the floor and was followed by a chalky mist. Gloria glanced at Booker and a spark of realization sent them both diving to the floor as a gunshot knocked the killer against the wall.

The man screamed with rage as a bright red wound appeared on his chest. Gloria looked up to see the barrel of a gun poking through the hole in the ceiling. She saw the next gunshot before she heard it, as the killer's kneecap exploded, buckling his legs.

"You FUCKERS!" his gun dropped to the floor as he fell.

From overhead came the sound of running footsteps across old wooden floors, a rapid rumble down the foyer stairway. And then D'Amecourt stood at the door. His eyes quickly took in Gloria, Booker, the man on the floor, and they widened with surprise and anguish at the sight of Michael.

"Uh..." D'Amecourt grunted, his mouth moving soundlessly.

Booker grabbed his gun and trained it on the killer.

Gloria turned toward the kitchen, and saw a long, bloody knife on the floor. Ignoring it, she went to a drawer and pulled out a short, clean one with a serrated blade. She kept it at her side, out of sight from Michael as she went back into the room.

"He's going to be weak," she said. "Once I cut him loose—"

D'Amecourt rushed forward, pulling off his khaki jacket. "Just hold on son. Hold on and I'll cover you up."

A cry came from the back of Michael's throat. He looked down at the floor, as if he were suddenly ashamed.

"Oh God... Michael," D'Amecourt mumbled as he tied the jacket around Michael's waist.

D'Amecourt began to weep, his heavy shoulders lurching as he looked up at her.

"Please get him down," D'Amecourt shut his eyes as the tears rolled down his cheeks.

"It's okay, Louis," Michael said. "I'm alright."

Michael seemed to weaken as he spoke. His eyelids fluttered as he lowered his head.

"Hold him, in case he falls," Gloria said. The killer had tied the twine very tightly around Michael's wrists and it took a good bit of sawing with the serrated blade before she could cut through.

Michael's hands dropped limply to his sides, his knees buckling as he collapsed into D'Amecourt's arms.

D'Amecourt grunted, but gently lowered Michael to the floor.

Booker kept his gun trained on the killer, who now lay in a fetal position, sucking his thumb, and moaning softly as his wounds bled onto the worn carpet. With his free hand, Booker reached for the cell phone in his jacket pocket.

Gloria took it from him and dialed 911.

Thirty-four

Scott Brown stood next to the bed in the corner of the log cabin deep in the Catoctin woods, watching as Tiffany Potter opened her eyes.

He stepped forward quietly, hoping to avoid spooking her any more than he already had, at least until the point at which he would have no choice. The mug of coffee in his hand was strong and aromatic, and its scent brought her more gently awake as Scott sat down next to her.

When their eyes met, he saw fear. And when he smiled she drew slightly back. The reaction bothered him, and he hoped it did not bode badly for what he wanted her to do. He needed to proceed very carefully to make the plan fall into place.

"Morning, beautiful," he said.

Tiffany groaned and slowly sat up. Despite the modern-day Lolita routine the day before, he had been worried that she might have a sudden, middle-of-the-night change of heart and try to escape into the woods. The pill and the wine had obviously kept that from happening and would make her feel groggy for most of the day.

"Hi," she replied. She frowned, and he guessed that her sleepy mind was trying to piece together everything that had happened to put her in the cabin, in the woods, with a 30-year-old man she had never met in person until the day before. With the exception of her purple Vans, which he had slipped gently off of her feet and placed under the bed, she was fully dressed. When she absently touched the top button of her blouse Scott knew she was wondering if at any point during the night before she had not been.

He picked up the mug of coffee. "Look what I brought you."

Tiffany gave it a wary look, which made him wonder if she now suspected the wine had been drugged, but after a moment of hesitation she accepted it and took a long sip.

"Thanks again for everything last night," he said.

She squinted, as if she was still trying to remember.

"It was just really great talking to you." He gave her a pleasant smile.

"About Gerry," she said, as if reminding herself.

"Yup. Gerry and all of the crazy things he used to do." He let the smile fade away. "And about the terrible thing that happened to him."

Tiffany took another sip of coffee and drew her legs up to her chest. "It made me sad as I went to sleep. Gave me weird dreams."

"Nightmares?"

"No, not really. Just dreams that made me feel depressed, even in my sleep."

"I'm glad you talked through it one more time, with all of the details."

She looked at him warily again, obviously remembering how he had repeated his questions from the day before, gently probing, asking her if she was absolutely certain about what she had seen the day Gerry Gray died. The conversation had been quite a challenge, since he had no way to be sure that either the recording device in the clock or the tiny camera clipped to the floor lamp would take it all in.

Scott could tell that the memory of it clearly troubled her now, as the early morning light streamed through the dirty windows in the strange room. Years earlier, his mother had tried to make the cabin cozy, with shabbily genteel leather upholstery and vintage Maxfield Parrish prints on the fireplace wall, but after years of disuse the air was musty and the place felt secretive and shut away.

"What do you think of me, Tiffany?"

She frowned. "What do you mean?"

"Do you think I'm dangerous?"

"Dangerous?" She made an attempt to shrug, but he still saw fear in her eyes. "Um... no."

"So you don't believe I've ever had any intention of hurting you?"

Tiffany shook her head slightly, obviously answering *no* only because that was what she believed he wanted to hear. He stood up without responding and walked over to the desk. There was a CD next to the computer. He slipped it in the A-drive, and when he looked at her again he saw her glance anxiously at the front door.

"I hope you're not thinking of running out of here," he said. "No one *ever* drives up the road that brought us to this cabin, and most of the trails you might pick up beyond our lot just take you deeper into the woods. So do me a favor, and don't even try it, okay?"

"Okay," she said. And by the look on her face he knew that she wouldn't be moving too quickly any time soon. For several hours her legs would feel leaden and he wasn't sure how long she would be able to hold down the meal he had hastily prepared the night before. "I won't."

"Good."

"But I do think I need to go home. I mean, I left a note for my mom, telling her I was going to meet you at that restaurant—"

"Sure you did."

Panic flashed in her eyes. "I *did*."

"Tiffany," he gave her a sad smile and a knowing nod as he sat next to her on the bed again. He gently pushed her long hair back from her face. He realized again how truly lovely she was, despite the borderline *Goth* makeup and her deep appreciation for reefer and wine.

"You need to be more careful about who you meet up with on the Internet, Tiffany."

Her chin quivered. "Why are you saying that?"

"Because you never really know who you can trust."

"I trusted *you*."

"Well you shouldn't have."

Her eyes reddened, as if she was about to cry. He looked past her, toward the wide plank table next to the front picture window, where the laptop was already powered up and ready to display the horrors he was about to reveal.

"It's time to get up now; I want to teach you a lesson," he said, as he tapped the disc against the blanket that was pulled up so tightly against her breasts.

"And then I'll tell you what I want you to do."

* * *

An hour later, as they pulled away from the cabin and headed through the forest, Tiffany Potter's face was swollen from crying and she appeared to have been knocked speechless by what he had shown her. Scott had no doubt that she had taken the lesson to heart.

"So we're cool?" he asked her.

"Yes, *Scott*. We're cool."

"Are you mad?"

She continued staring straight ahead. The morning sun was just rising above the tall oaks around them, and the light was less than flattering against her pale skin and puffy eyes.

"I mean, you do *understand*, don't you Tiffany? You know why I'm going to do this."

"Yeah, I know."

"And you really are going to do what I told you to do?"

She put placed both hands over her purse, which held the disc. "Yeah, don't worry."

"Good." He turned from the narrow, unpaved driveway that had led up to the secluded cabin and onto the public road. The road was smoothly blacktopped, and maintained by the U.S. Park Service as part of the overall effort to make access to and from Camp David as smooth as possible. Scott still remembered visiting President Reagan there as a child. He was reminded again of all of the help his parents, disappointed in him as they still were, were providing. Without their intervention he never would have ended up at Groveton; never would have had the opportunity to put his plan in motion.

Now, with the clock ticking toward the point of no return, he could only hope their combined efforts would pay off.

Once he hit Route 15 the highway was clear, and he was able to punch his speed up to an unsuspicious 60-mph as he shot back toward the Maryland suburbs of Washington, D.C. For an hour neither one of them said anything. There was an occasional catch in Tiffany's breathing, and he was fairly certain that she would burst into tears moments after he released her.

But he was also certain that she would follow through. If the next two hours went badly and he ended up dead, she would do exactly as he had asked.

"Can we turn on the radio or something?" she asked him.

"Sure," he said. He reached for the knob. The Mach One's radio was set to a station that played mostly rock classics from the 70s and 80s. Scott still loved the hard edge of the music, and even now was tempted to crank it up just for the welcome distraction.

Tiffany listened for no more than 20 seconds before groaning and changing the station.

"I have a terrible headache," she said.

That's no surprise, Scott thought. For the first time he worried that someone would insist that she be taken to the hospital for a physical exam. Glancing again at her rumpled clothes, her sleep-tossed hair, he knew that a blood test would pick up traces of the drugs in her system. He would certainly be blamed, but it probably wouldn't matter.

The station Tiffany tuned into was playing classical music. Tiffany's eyes were closed but he could tell she was listening, trying to calm her mind. Turning his attention back to the highway, he was within a mile of D.C. when the music faded and the news announcer reported breaking news related to the kidnapping of Justin Bennett.

The mention of Justin's name brought both he and Tiffany to attention, both of them listening intently as the announcer revealed that Michael Bennett had been abducted as well, and that he had been found with severe injuries at a residence in Northeast Washington.

Thirty-five

With his back against the wall and a makeshift tourniquet double-wrapped around his armpit and shoulder, Michael struggled to stay alert as he listened to the conversation between Louis D'Amecourt and Gloria Towson. The house was now surrounded by police, but an error by the dispatchers had delayed the ambulances. Gloria sounded desperate to get her questions answered before they arrived.

"So Barshak knows we're here?" Gloria said.

"Yeah, she knows," D'Amecourt replied. "It was her idea. She figured out that you and Michael were talking, and that it was only a matter of time before everything blew up."

"She must be scared."

"Yeah, Towson, she's scared. She allowed me to compromise a murder investigation."

"And a little boy's life."

"No, she didn't do that. She agreed to keep quiet about any connection between the two murders, but I didn't tell her about the picture until yesterday, after Justin was kidnapped."

"And even then she didn't come completely clean—"

"Because of *me*, Towson, all right?"

Yes, because of you. Michael looked into D'Amecourt's bloodshot eyes, and was reminded of the vision he had had during the torture. The memory of the corridor outside the apartment at the Larchmont, where he had fled after finding Brad's body. The murder had made D'Amecourt more determined than ever to keep his secret.

Gloria placed her hand on D'Amecourt's forearm. "I'm truly sorry about your son."

"So am I, Towson." D'Amecourt lowered his head. "He was a good, good boy..."

Michael's eyes stung with new tears. Never before had he heard D'Amecourt speak kindly of Brad. Even during the questioning that followed the murder he had used an accusing tone, implying even then that the son that he had completely disowned somehow deserved what had happened. Michael had known even then that it was a show—staying angry was the only way D'Amecourt could step away from his own sorrow.

And guilt, Michael thought. Guilt for telling Brad, as a teenager, that nothing was more humiliating than having a son who was gay. Guilt for throwing Brad out of his home. Guilt for still being so afraid of a renewed investigation into his own son's murder that he had kept quiet about the threat to Justin.

"Brad had a different last name," Gloria said.

"Belongs to his mother. She took it back after she left me." D'Amecourt wearily rubbed his eyes. "None of my kids use my last name anymore. None of them could stand the sight of me after I threw Brad out of our house."

The house of horrors. Michael remembered Brad's nickname for the home he had grown up in. Brad had talked about it at length in the book that he had wanted to publish on the Web site that Michael was building for him; had spoken of it as perhaps the best way to get back at his father. That, and the foray into pornography, which had been as much about protest as anything else.

But you let him do it anyway. Told him you didn't care. Told him you'd let him do anything he wanted as long as he didn't leave you.

Even now the memory was unbearably painful. Michael hated himself for his weakness, for his willingness to pretend that Brad's decision to appear in the magazines hadn't mattered to him. And he knew that helping Brad create the Web site that would have housed the manuscript and the family photos could have brought even more negative attention to himself. *One more nail in the coffin for all of the people who still thought you were involved in Benjie's kidnapping.*

The fact that he hadn't tried harder to stop Brad from appearing in the magazines made his own guilt all the more difficult to bear. And he couldn't help but wonder if the killer, who according to the documents in his wallet was named Harland Till, had sought Brad out *because* of the photos. He was almost certain now that Till had been hunting Brad long before the night that he broke into the apartment and killed him.

In the corner, Till was moaning and muttering to himself. Gloria's husband Booker had cuffed his hands behind his back and applied makeshift bandages to his wounds. But Till scared him even now. He knew that the rage that had sparked the violence would never go away; that even in prison Harland Till would keep on killing with the same frightening righteousness that had convinced him that his murders were justified.

Michael felt a shiver race up and down this bare back, and winced at the memory of the blood-splattered room where he had found Brad's body. Neither he nor D'Amecourt had told Gloria or Booker about D'Amecourt's arrival at the apartment just minutes after Michael had come running out. D'Amecourt had been carrying a suitcase containing things that Brad had asked for from his old bedroom. Brad would never know that D'Amecourt had also come with the intention of an apology, and a determination to find a way to accept his son even though he fully expected it was already too late.

"There's still something we need to talk to you about," Gloria Towson said to D'Amecourt now. "Something Booker found out about—"

"Gloria, no." Booker gave her a stern look.

Gloria ignored him, and continued staring at D'Amecourt. "You logged into a newsgroup for pedophiles, Louis."

D'Amecourt frowned. "What?"

"At least twice that we know of," Gloria said. "And we can probably prove there were more. We have a record of all of it. The conversations, the photos—"

"I don't know what the hell you're talking about."

"No?" Gloria gave D'Amecourt the same penetrating gaze that Michael had felt the night before.

"No." D'Amecourt glared back at her. "What gives?"

Gloria paused and gave Booker an uncertain look. "On October 14, you were logged on. You got disconnected. We have the error message that went back to your computer."

D'Amecourt looked past her, toward Till in the corner. "October 14... that was the day after the Capitol Hotel murder."

"Right."

"I wasn't even close to a computer that day, Gloria."

"But we have proof—"

"I spent two hours witnessing the autopsy, another two hours reviewing Payne's preliminary reports. I spent most of the rest of the day with Sylvia Barshak, briefing her about what I knew and figuring out how to keep Payne, and you, and everyone else from connecting the two murders."

Gloria looked at Booker again. Michael could tell she wanted to challenge D'Amecourt's statement, but for some reason it seemed to ring true.

He cleared his throat, which was sore from dryness. Gloria had tried to get him some water but he had nearly retched at the thought of drinking from a glass from the house's filthy kitchen.

"What are you talking about?" he asked. "What newsgroup?"

"There was an email message in the luggage of the man who was killed at the Capitol Hotel," Gloria said. "It was sent by someone we tracked to a newsgroup used by pedophiles for trading photographs, and communicating online about... what they do."

"It wasn't me, Towson." D'Amecourt said.

Michael's face went hot as both Gloria and D'Amecourt turned to him. The impact was instant; the suspicions of the past rushing back.

"It wasn't me either," Michael said wearily.

"I don't believe it was you, Michael." Gloria said. There was a grave expression on her face.

He heard the distant sound of an approaching siren as Gloria sat down across from him and placed her hand on his forehead. The gesture was so unexpected, and so tender, that Michael felt his eyes welling up with tears again. After a moment, when she didn't take her hand away, Michael took it in his own, holding it tightly as he thought of what Till was about to do when she pounded on the front door. Shortly after Till had been immobilized, and while Gloria was wrapping the tourniquet around his shoulder, she had told him that the neighbor across Martin and Joan's alley had seen the license plate of the car Till had been driving. The plate number led them to this house, which belonged to a man who was now missing, and probably dead. Everything else had happened very quickly, with D'Amecourt, Gloria, and her husband forming an uneasy alliance to rescue him.

In a matter of seconds it would have been too late. Together, Gloria Towson, Booker Jones, and Louis D'Amecourt had saved his life.

With a *whoop whoop* of the siren the ambulance pulled in front of the house. Heavy footsteps on the front porch and down the hallway brought the EMTs into the room.

"You got two vehicles, right?" Booker Jones said.

"Yes, there are two, just as you said," a dark-skinned paramedic with a Jamaican accent replied.

Booker pointed to Till on the floor. "This guy's hurt the worst. You're gonna want to get him out of here quick."

The EMT complied, his big body blocking Michael's view as he attended to Harland Till.

Gloria's face brightened at the sight of the other EMT, a heavy-set white woman. "Beverly, hi."

"Hey Glo. This our patient?"

Gloria gave him a faint smile. "Yeah. This is Michael. Michael, this is Beverly Tibbett, a friend of mine."

The woman checked his pulse, shined a light into his eyes, and gently examined the tourniquet and the wound underneath. Michael's whole shoulder had been going numb, but the movement brought a sharp pain that made him wince.

"Nice work, Towson," the woman said. "Considering."

"Thanks."

The EMT brought a gurney over and Michael gingerly climbed aboard. "Michael we're going to wheel you out of here," Tibbett said. "I think it's best that you lay on your stomach. There's enough pressure on the wound to keep it from bleeding anymore for a while, which is good."

In seconds he was wheeled out to the waiting ambulance.

Gloria was at his side again. "I've got to take D'Amecourt and my husband back to the station. Louis is going to be facing a real mess with Internal Affairs and we need to figure out what we can do to help him. I'll call the hospital later to check on you, okay?"

Michael nodded, knowing he needed to thank her again. But the relief over his own rescue was quickly fading as he thought of Justin. Gloria gave him a brief, sad smile that only made him feel more hopeless as she stepped back out of the ambulance.

Beverly Tibbett drove him to the hospital with the siren blaring. Still lying on his stomach, and feeling woozy from a shot she had given him to dull the pain, he was only vaguely aware of the arrival as Tibbett reopened the rear doors and leaned down next to him.

"Okay Michael, let's get you into the emergency—"

"No."

Michael stiffened at the male voice at the foot of the gurney. Raising his head, he turned to see Scott in the ambulance doorway.

"Who the hell are you?" Tibbett said.

Scott moved quickly, and with a short leap into the cab pressed a gun against her ribs and his hand over her mouth.

"Nobody say a word, all right?" Scott's voice was low and confident. "Reach over and shut those doors. *Now.*"

Thirty-six

Seconds after the announcement about Michael Bennett, Scott Brown had punched the old Mustang up to 80 mph and had weaved and streamed through the highway traffic, slowing down just enough to stay on the road as he entered the city. The news reporter had mentioned that the house where Michael had been taken was a block off Pennsylvania Avenue and adjacent to a vacant warehouse. Scott had been lucky enough to pick up the screaming siren trail of the ambulances, and had followed them to the house, which was already surrounded by police. There were also two television trucks with satellite dishes that Scott had eyed warily before ordering Tiffany out of the car.

She was an instant away from freedom when he told her to wait and handed her $50 from his wallet. "Use this for a cab and get home as soon as you can. Then do exactly what I told you to do, all right?"

Without replying, she took the money, stepped out of the car, and grasped the door handle to keep her balance as she took in the fresh, cool air. She was within shouting distance of the police but the memory of what Scott had stored on the computer disc made her want to simply get home as fast as possible.

She walked quickly back toward Pennsylvania Avenue, glancing back just once as the ambulances pulled away. Moments later she heard the distinct revving of the Mach One's engine and guessed that Scott was following them. Obviously the chance to grab Michael, to make him part of the scheme, was too hard to resist. After everything Scott had told her, she understood why.

"You need to be more careful about who you meet up with on the Internet, Tiffany."

Scott's warning was still ringing in her mind, still scaring her as she thought of the computer disc and what it contained. She kept her purse double-wrapped around her shoulder as she flagged down a cab. Safely inside and speeding toward home, she took a deep breath as the stark reality of what had happened, and what *could* have happened, hit her all at once. Tears came to her eyes as she thought of what Scott had told her to do. There was no doubt that the police, and the FBI, would pick her up for a humiliating round of questions. That was as much a part of Scott's plan as anything else.

But you don't have any choice. You have to do it, exactly as he said.

The cab slowed down as it reached the pleasant suburban neighborhood where Tiffany lived. She had been gone more than two days. Trusting and naïve as ever, her mother had probably swallowed the lie about staying at a girlfriend's house without a thought. The guilt was overwhelming as she stepped through the front door, took in the scent of the spiced apple potpourri her mother favored, and listened to the rapid, happy barking of the West Highland terriers that came rushing from the back of the house.

She sank to her knees, weeping openly as the dogs greeted her. She hugged them both as they calmed down, and sat on the floor in the safety of the foyer for a good five minutes before getting up. She was grateful that neither of her parents were there to see her in such bad condition. And as she climbed the stairs to her room she thought it might be a long time before she left home again.

Her bedroom was clean and comforting. Her mother had picked up all of her dirty laundry, vacuumed the rug, and made the bed. The curtains were open wide, and the morning sun was shining brightly against the pale lavender walls. She wanted more than anything to slip under the covers, but was suddenly, desperately, aware of time ticking rapidly by as she turned on the computer.

The first thing Scott had told her to do was save the contents of the disc onto her hard drive. *"So you've got a backup,"* he had said. The second was to transfer the text into an email. The hangover was becoming ferocious and the tiny type was vibrating on the page. She checked the address he had given her twice, making sure she had typed it in correctly and fighting back another wave of tears as she hit "send."

A half hour later, with dry eyes and skin scrubbed pink under a hot, soapy shower, she picked up the phone, her hand shaking as she dialed the number that Scott Brown had told her to call.

* * *

Once Michael was safely inside the ambulance, Gloria walked with Booker and D'Amecourt back to the Toyota, which was parked two blocks from the house where Michael had been held captive. The botched ransom incident a day earlier had made D'Amecourt paranoid that Harland Till would somehow spot his own vehicle in the vicinity, so the three of them had piled into Gloria's small car for the drive into Northeast D.C.

A feeling of unease clung to her as she turned the ignition. The engine chugged to life, and let out a long groan as she gave it extra gas. Seconds after pulling out of the parallel parking spot, she headed back toward the rowhouse, which was still surrounded by police cars and television trucks. A big crowd of onlookers had strolled over from the neighborhood's open-air drug markets. Television reporters stood in front of cameras while young children jumped up and down behind them, trying to get into the shots. Patrol officers stood as close as possible to the house, indulging in their curiosity despite the crime scene tape across the front porch.

The first ambulance, carrying Till, had already pulled away. Gloria waved to Beverly Tibbett as she closed the back doors of Michael's ambulance and got into the driver's seat. She was no longer worried about Michael's injuries—Beverly had assured her he would be fine—but she was concerned about him being out of commission and inaccessible to the investigation for the next several hours. Given Scott's anger at Mary and Michael, it stood to reason that at some point Brown would contact one of them. Without that contact the trail would probably remain cold.

The Toyota was starting to run a little more roughly as Michael's ambulance pulled away from the curb. Gloria got behind it, following it westward down Pennsylvania Avenue.

Booker frowned when she continued following it up North Capitol Street, toward Washington Hospital Center. "We're going back to the Fifth District, right?"

"Yes. I just want to follow them a little further. Make sure they're okay."

"Tibbett's been driving an ambulance for 10 years, Gloria."

"I know that."

Ahead of them, a stoplight went quickly from yellow to red. After a moment's hesitation to check the oncoming traffic, Tibbett raced through.

In the Toyota, Gloria had no choice but to stop.

"I wish we'd had a chance to talk to Michael a little longer," she said. "Just to go through everything again."

In front of them, a cherry-red Mustang from the 1970s revved its engine, as if gearing up for a drag race.

"I think he told you everything he knew," D'Amecourt said.

"I should have told him everything *I* know."

Her words hung in the air. Booker nervously cleared his throat and in her peripheral vision she saw him looking at her.

"What are you talking about, Towson?" D'Amecourt asked.

She met his eyes in the rearview mirror. She thought of everything he had revealed about his son, his admitted cover-up of the murders, his assertion that he had *not* logged into the pedophile newsgroup or participated in the chat rooms.

"I've had a feeling I knew who was behind this," she said. "When we heard back from the ISP I wasn't so sure. Now I'm wondering again."

D'Amecourt frowned back at her. "I told you, Towson, I don't know anything about your perverted chat rooms."

"But if it wasn't you, then who was it?"

"Must be Scott Brown," Booker said.

"Scott Brown doesn't work for the D.C. police department," she said.

The driver of the Mustang revved the engine again as the light turned green, shooting quickly through the intersection. Gloria watched it with a twinge of envy as she pumped the accelerator and waited for the Toyota to respond. The car backfired loudly as she cleared the intersection and slipped from first to second gear.

She glanced at Booker again. "You're sure that's where the error message went back to, right?"

"It has to be," Booker said.

"Tell me more." D'Amecourt said.

"What do you want to know?"

"What makes you think it was someone from the MPD who was logged on?"

Booker began to reiterate the information that Adam Turner had revealed. Gloria was reminded of Michael Bennett's computer expertise, and wished that he was listening. Driving as quickly as possible through the North Capitol Street traffic, she caught up to the bright red mustang and spotted the ambulance just a few cars ahead.

"What you're saying doesn't prove anything," D'Amecourt interrupted Booker in mid-sentence.

"Sure it does," Booker said. "The message has an IP address and a clear identification of the server."

"But you're still jumping to conclusions. You could be completely wrong."

Booker bristled, and turned halfway around in his seat. "You got any other suggestions?"

"Yeah, I *do*." D'Amecourt suddenly reached up and put his hand on Gloria's shoulder. The intensity of D'Amecourt's grip made Gloria wince as she caught his eyes in the rearview mirror.

"We need to talk to Michael again," D'Amecourt said. "Right *now*—"

A *boom* from the Toyota's backside sent another stream of black smoke out of the tailpipe as the engine light went bright red on the dash, the car stalling in the middle of North Capital Street as the ambulance disappeared from view.

Thirty-seven

Zachary Taylor cringed at the angry voice of Justin Bennett's abductor, and just barely resisted the urge to snap back at the barrage of taunting insults. Obviously talking on a cell phone in the midst of what sounded like highway traffic, the abductor was furious that Justin was still alive.

"Just get it done," the abductor said.

With a click the connection was broken, but the abductor's voice was still ringing in Taylor's ears as he stepped back toward the kitchen. There was a bright red trail of Charlotte's blood on the floor. The woman had come up to the back door just in time to see him jerking Justin up to his feet and dragging him back into the kitchen. Pretending that he needed her help, he had motioned for her to come inside. She had been leaning over Justin, her high, whiny voice all a-twitter when he had smashed a heavy ceramic vase against the back of her head. She had dropped with a loud thud, and the crack in her skull had leaked heavily as he dragged her body across the room. Hooking his arms under her and pulling her shoulder-first down the basement steps had brought painful spasms to his back. The pain had sharpened his rage as he had come back upstairs to find Justin sitting against the wall, screaming once again at the top of his lungs.

Little Justin was silent now, his mouth covered in duct tape, which had also been used to bind his wrists and ankles. But the boy, and Charlotte, were still a tremendous problem. With the sun fully up and with Charlotte's cop brother once again parked in her driveway, it would be extremely difficult to get either body out of the house.

In the meantime he needed to clean up. It took a whole roll of paper towels to mop up the blood and a scrubbing with soapy water to remove it from the cracks in the ceramic tile. Taylor threw the towels into the wastebasket by the door, cursing loudly as the cheap plastic foot lever that opened and closed the lid snapped under his foot.

Calm down. Think about what you're doing. The bloody paper towels had to be bagged up and taken to a landfill. And Charlotte and the kid needed to be kept in the basement until it got dark.

There was a loud knock at the front door.

Through the sheer curtains that ran across the picture window Taylor could tell it was a man. His shoulders were broad, his body trim. Taylor thought about ignoring him, but with the morning sun filling the living room he knew that the man had probably glimpsed him through the front window as well. *So go to the door*, he told himself. *Act as if it's just a normal day*.

He took a moment to check his appearance in the mirror over the bar. His complexion was sallow, and two days without sleeping had brought dark circles to the skin underneath his eyes. But he had changed the white shirt that he had been wearing when he smashed the vase against Charlotte's head and used tap water to smooth the strands of his thin brown hair back down across his scalp. Despite the chaos raging in his mind he knew he still looked as normal and benign as ever.

With a long, deep breath, he opened the door to a man in coveralls with a label that said "Landscape Artistry."

"Good morning, Mr. Taylor?"

He paused for a moment, tightening his grip on the doorknob. He thought of slamming the door, but knew it was already too late.

"Yes."

Taylor saw the flick of motion from the man's free hand an instant before a *smack* at the side of his face knocked him backwards. The arm of the sofa hit the back of his knees, tipping him off-balance. He tumbled onto the sofa as the intruder slammed the door and rushed in, pressing a gun against the soft spot just below his sternum to keep him from getting up.

"Where is he?" The man's eyes were eerily bright, and Taylor could see a vein pulsing at his temple. The photos he had seen on the news flashed into his mind. He realized he was looking at Scott Brown.

"I don't know what you—"

Brown smacked him. Momentarily blinded, he felt Brown grab his collar and pull him upward. "On your feet," Brown said.

The room was spinning as Brown turned him around, pressing the gun against his lower spine.

Brown steered him away from the picture window, and then toward the kitchen. The back porch was visible from the kitchen doorway. Michael

Bennett was standing just outside of it, both hands pressed against the frame of the door.

Brown grabbed the back of his shirt and prodded him forward with the gun.

"Unlock it," Brown said.

Taylor looked into Michael Bennett's eyes. Bennett looked terrified, and there was a heavy bandage visible underneath his shirt. But Taylor knew that even if he somehow overpowered Brown there was little chance of stopping Michael as well.

Especially if he let Michael into the house.

"No," he said.

Brown tightened his grip. "Unlock it *now!*"

"Get out of here," Taylor stiffened his legs, stalling for time and making it difficult for Brown to push him any farther.

"You asshole." Still gripping the back of his shirt, Brown swung him aside. Brown then let go, switching his gun to his left hand and reaching over to unlock the door with his right.

Taylor knew the deadbolt would stick, and that it would take several seconds of jiggling to get the old wooden door open. The instant Brown's attention was diverted, he dove to the floor. Brown yelled but was too slow to react as he rolled forward, out of the kitchen and into the living room.

There was a gun tucked in between the cushions of the couch. Taylor got to it as Brown came through the doorway.

* * *

Michael tripped on the threshold between the little yellow house's back door and the porch, falling to his knees as he rushed forward. He watched Scott race back through the kitchen and heard a gunshot in the room beyond.

"*You son of a bitch!*" Scott yelled, out of breath but in control. Michael gripped the arm of a wrought-iron chair and rose unsteadily to his feet. The pain throbbed through his shoulder. He felt fresh blood from the re-opened wound trickling down his back as he peered around the edge of the doorway that led from the kitchen to the living room. A man was lying flat on the wooden floor. Scott had his knees on the man's chest, and was pressing a gun against the man's forehead.

He stayed in the doorway as Scott gripped the man by the front of his shirt and yanked him up. Scott then hooked his arm around the man's neck and pointed the gun against his back.

"I'll ask you again," Scott said. "Where the hell *is* he?"

The man, who Scott had identified in the car as Zachary Taylor, answered with a gagging noise. Michael followed his eyes back to the kitchen, toward the wastebasket stuffed with paper towels that looked as if they had been soaked with blood. His breath came up short as Scott motioned for him to turn around.

"That's the door to the basement, Michael. Open it."

He glanced at Scott and the man named Zachary Taylor again. Taylor was immobilized by Scott's grip, but with the look in his eyes Michael knew that everything that Scott had told him on the race to the big yellow house in the foothills of the mountains was correct.

His heart was pounding up against the base of his throat as he stepped forward and turned the knob. The door opened easily. There was a small landing and a steep wooden stairway.

"Turn the light on, Michael."

He flicked the switch and steadied himself with the railing as he stepped down. The steps had open risers and creaked with his weight and as he got near the bottom he saw what looked like more dried blood on the surface of the last one.

He stepped over it. Under the light of a single overhead bulb he saw a workbench, a refrigerator, stacks of boxes and a ladder. The room had small casement windows covered with black curtains. The dust that hung in the air was dry against his eyes. He rubbed them, looked around the room again ...

And saw the stuffed cocker spaniel in the corner.

"Scott." He tried to call out, but his voice was nothing more than a hoarse whisper as he rushed forward. Behind the stuffed animal was a dark blue tarp.

Underneath the tarp, he saw movement.

The room seemed to tilt forward as he dropped to his knees and pulled the tarp back. And in a vision that did not seem real he found himself just inches away from Justin, his mouth covered with black tape. Lying in a fetal position, with his wrists and ankles bound, the boy blinked several times before the light of recognition came to his eyes.

"Oh Jesus God... Justin..." Michael saw his arms reaching forward, his hands gently stroking the child's face, his voice coming from somewhere deep in his lungs as he cried out. *"Scott he's here!"*

The tape covering Justin's mouth was tight against his tender baby skin as Michael carefully peeled it back. Justin gasped and began to cry. "Oh baby baby..." Michael muttered, his vision blurred by tears as he reached down to the boy's wrists. Zachary Taylor had used tape here as well, binding it so tightly that Justin's hands were turning blue. Michael stepped away but did not take him out of his sight as he reached for a narrow handsaw hanging above the workbench.

Justin winced as he cut through the bindings at his wrists and ankles, and jumped into Michael's arms the instant he was free.

Michael held him, squeezed him, covered his face with kisses and picked him up.

"Scott, OH GOD, he's here! " he cried out again. He knew that he needed to get Justin up the stairs, out of the house, into the daylight. But for a long moment all he could do was hold him as the past and present crashed through his mind. Justin was taken from him. Justin was alive. Crying and terrified but alive. Justin was fine; Michael felt the boy gripping his shirt as he pressed his cheek against the bandaged shoulder. Justin was going to be okay. *Because you found him. And rescued him. Yes he's okay he's alive and well and you need to get him out of here now!*

Still holding Justin as tightly and gently as he possibly could, Michael leaned slightly back as Justin raised his face away from his shoulder. He smiled through his tears. "You ready to go home, little boy?"

Justin nodded.

"Ready to go see your *mom*?"

Justin nodded again, and began to cry.

"Oh God Justin, *Justin...*"

Michael's legs wobbled as he turned toward the creaky wooden stairs. He was vaguely conscious of the dark red blood on the bottom stair as he stepped over it; holding Justin with one arm and reaching for the banister with the other.

The steps were steep and his heart was pounding with emotion and exertion and he was only half way up when the door at the top slammed shut.

"Scott?" he called out.

He heard a gunshot. And then another. And another as he began backing down the stairs, forgetting about the blood and the bottom and nearly slipping in it as he spun around and crouched down with Justin in his arms.

Sensing his fear, Justin grabbed his shirt and began to cry louder.

Michael *shushed* him as he looked around the basement for another way out. There was no door. But near the top of the cinderblock walls the casement windows were small but probably big enough for Justin to squeeze through. He pulled the black curtains aside, his heart leaping at the sight of daylight. But the levers to open both windows were locked and covered with rust. He could not pull them open with his fingers alone, but he guessed that with the right amount of leverage one could be budged.

Footsteps on the hardwood floor above them made him gasp loudly as he took the crowbar from its hook above the workbench. With the daylight and overhead bulb the basement was well-illuminated now. "Everything's okay baby. Everything's fine," he whispered as he set Justin down. Justin whimpered and wrapped his arms around his leg as he stuck the crowbar behind the lever and pulled it back.

There was a loud squeak as the lever popped open. And above them, the sound of footsteps again.

Setting the crowbar down, he pulled the window back, his heart sinking as he realized how small the opening at the top was. *Too small for Justin. Way too small.*

He needed to shatter the glass completely to get Justin out. He picked up the crowbar, knowing he might only have a few seconds to get Justin through the opening before the door at the top of the stairs opened again and Zachary Taylor came rushing down.

Justin wrapped his arms around Michael's waist. "Uncle Mike... I'm scared."

Get him out of here, Michael thought. *Get him out now.*

Swinging wide, with all of his strength, he brought the crowbar back and smashed it against the window, grunting and gasping as the glass shattered internally, fracturing into lace that held firm in the frame.

He swung again and again as the door at the top of the steps creaked open.

Thirty-eight

Mary watched the special reports on the local morning news with an overwhelming feeling of relief as more details about Michael's condition were revealed. His injuries were "serious but not life-threatening" and he had been taken to Washington Hospital Center.

But he had "revealed nothing about the whereabouts of Justin Bennett." This from the same male reporter who seemed to be talking about the case every time she turned on the TV. Mary hated the sight of him; hated the sound of his voice. She had lost track of the number of times he had tried to reach her, pleading for an interview, using everything from a clearly manufactured tone of empathy to subtle threats to "go forward and report the latest rumor from our sources" if she did not agree to talk to him.

Sitting on the edge of the bed, her brain leaden from the lack of sleep and the endless barrage of terrifying mental images, she sensed a horrifying shift in the way that Justin's kidnapping was being reported. There were all kinds of experts talking about the "difficulty" in finding children more than 24 hours after their disappearance. There were parents of other children, children who had *not* been safely returned, whose interviews were built around "advice" on how to help her "cope with this loss." And there were reminiscences from Justin's kindergarten teacher, mothers of other children in his class, and even some of her own friends, all of whom were starting to speak of her son in the past tense.

She wept as she listened to the reporter who she hated finish his report in front of the house in a rough neighborhood in Northeast D.C. where Michael had been taken. And when she didn't think she would cry any longer she reached for the remote to turn off the set.

The ring of the phone at the bedside table stopped her. It was loud, sudden. And her heart swelled with terror as she picked it up.

"Hello?"

"Is this M-Mary?" The voice was fragile, and sounded as if it came from a teenage girl. "Mary Bennett?"

"Yes, who—"

"Mary, please... listen to me carefully..."

She listened, a line of cold sweat forming at the back of her neck as the girl continued talking.

"That's what you need to do, okay?" As the girl finished Mary heard a catch in her voice, and then, after a pause, "I'm really sorry about your little boy."

The line was disconnected, but the girl's voice was still ringing in her ears as she got up and went to the small desk in front of the window. She turned the computer on, but had to wait for it to boot up before she could check her email. Everything the girl had said had sounded surreal; difficult to believe but with an echo of truth. *"Scott's been suspecting this for years,"* she had said. *"Now he thinks he can prove it..."*

Mary pressed her hands together into a fist of prayer, her mind latching fast to the hope she had heard behind the girl's words.

"He thinks he might know where Justin is, Mary. He's going to try and save him if he can."

She took a deep breath as her AOL mailbox came up onto the screen, holding it until she saw the email the girl had told her was coming. The "investigative trail" that would supposedly reveal the identity of the pedophile who had wanted to harm both of her sons.

She felt the tears welling up as soon as she began reading, her gut tightening with the sickening images the trail of newsgroup postings brought to her mind. But after a few moments, when the truth behind what the girl had sent her was revealed, she wiped the tears away. She wanted to pick up the laptop and smash it against the wall, but with her mind somehow cleared by the rage, she found herself following Scott's instructions exactly as they had been given.

In a matter of moments the document was saved, and copied, and forwarded. A missive into cyberspace. A trail of evidence that could no longer be denied.

Seconds later she had the lockbox open on her bed. For the very first time the gun inside felt comfortable in her hand. She was ready to use it. Ready and willing as she set it down and picked up the phone.

* * *

"You clearly got ahead of yourself, Officer Jones," Louis D'Amecourt was saying. "Jumped to conclusions because you already had an idea in your mind."

Gloria tried to ignore him, tried to focus solely on flagging down a cab amid the busy midmorning North Capitol street traffic. D'Amecourt and Booker had been talking technical mumbo jumbo for the past 10 minutes and most of what they had been saying meant nothing to her.

"Okay, you're right to a point," Booker said defensively. "But if you were in my position you woulda' thought the same thing."

"I wouldn't have jumped to the conclusion that the perpetrator was a police officer," D'Amecourt said.

"You would have if you'd been me, watchin' *you* slinking around like you had something to hide."

"All right you guys." Gloria tugged Booker's sleeve as a Red Top cut recklessly in front of a Metrobus and pulled up to the curb. "Let's go."

The three of them stepped quickly into the cab, which reeked of musk from the deodorizer that hung from the rearview mirror. Gloria told the West African driver to get them to Washington Hospital Center as quickly as possible.

"I know I'm right," D'Amecourt said. "I know it even if we can't prove it—"

"I think we *can* prove it," Booker said. "We've got the codes, and I know if we really lean on Stonewall they're gonna have to come through."

Gloria hoped that he was right, but the intensity of the last few minutes had clouded her judgment and it she was reticent to even hope that her theory, which D'Amecourt now believed completely, could be proven.

But it still may be too late, she thought. *Too late to save Justin's life.*

Yet the transcripts were irrefutably damning. Virtual proof against the man who abducted both Benjamin and Justin. Even more so now that they knew the error message that Turner had sent them had gone back to a server used by the government of the District of Columbia, a server shared by the police and several other government offices. Booker was still certain it could be traced directly back to a single computer. And she was willing to bet that the computer would be found in the offices of the District of Columbia City Council.

* * *

Michael placed his hand on top of Justin's head and gently moved him back. Michael then stood in front of him, the crowbar in his hand. It had been several seconds since the door at the top of the basement stairs had opened, but no one had come down.

He started to call out to Scott, but was afraid to bring anymore attention to the fact that he and Justin were trapped. Yet he could no longer stand still. The only way out was up. Up the stairs and out through the back door, where they would be in the middle of a pleasant suburban neighborhood on a bright sunny morning.

"Uncle Mike I...wan...na to go home." Justin bit his lower lip, trying to hold back tears.

"I know. Me, too." Michael crouched down, gave Justin what he hoped was a comforting smile, and whispered. "Here's what we need to do. I'm going to walk up those stairs. You need to walk right behind me. When we get to the top, I want you to *stay* behind me. We're going to go straight out the back door, the one on the porch—"

"*Noooo*," Justin wailed.

"*Shhh.*" Michael put his hand across Justin's mouth, as footsteps again crossed the floor above them.

"Justin, we have to get out of here, okay? Now when we get to the back porch and I tell you to *run*, you need to get out as fast as you can, okay? Get out and bang on the neighbor's door and scream as loud as—"

"Hello?"

The voice of a woman interrupted him. A woman at the top of the basement stairs. In front of him, Justin froze.

"Michael? Justin?"

Michael stood up, stepping in front of Justin, protecting him as his Aunt Joan reluctantly descended, stopping mid-flight, stooping to peer at them.

"Oh... thank *God*."

Joan held the banister as she took the last few stairs. She was wearing a baggy khaki jacket and jeans. Her hair was completely covered by a scarf, and she had on some kind of bronzer that made her skin look several shades darker.

Michael heard a little whimper behind him as Justin wrapped his arms around his leg. On the race to the house Scott had told him that Martin was a pedophile. Scott said that he had tracked Martin online, that he had a long trail of indisputable evidence that Martin, using a screen name, had been trading photographs of naked children for years. Scott had begun to suspect as much after Benjamin was taken, after he learned that the police had found child pornography on his own computer, "which I did *not* put there," Scott had said.

"But I knew someone had. Someone who wanted to close a steel door on a trap that I'd already fallen in to..."

Scott believed that it was Joan who actually abducted Benjamin and Justin. She took Benjamin because she knew that it was Martin who had taken photographs of him and was worried about the boy's memories surfacing as he grew older. She took Justin because she suspected Martin had done so again. Anxious for revenge, and knowing he was about to be paroled, Scott had sent an anonymous posting directly into the same newsgroup that Martin frequented. A posting that included a graphic of a ticking clock, the second hand moving rapidly across a photo of Martin's face. A clock that shattered with a loud boom when the second hand reached 12.

Scott believed that Joan remained well-aware of Martin's perversion, that she monitored his activities on the Internet. *"Which is how she found out that I wasn't the only person who discovered who he was. Some of the same people who supplied him with pornography decided to blackmail him. They knew he was a public figure, and that images of Justin were among those he traded. Joan saw the messages and knew that he was about to be exposed. I think she suspected that Justin would corroborate the blackmailers' charges if he got questioned. So she did exactly what she did five years ago. She got him to disappear."*

Scott said that he believed Joan decided to have both Benjamin and Justin murdered. She brought them to Zachary Taylor, a hit man who had come to her attention years earlier during her career as a prosecutor. Joan had expected Taylor to do his work quickly and efficiently, he had faltered when it came to killing a child.

"Oh Michael... *Michael*." Joan rushed forward, her arms open wide, her purse swinging on her shoulder.

"Joan." Michael allowed her to embrace him, but shuddered at her touch. The flap to the purse was open. The purse was big enough to hold a gun. "What are you doing here? How did you find us?"

"Scott called me." She stayed in his embrace but spoke without looking at him, the side of her face against his chest. "He admitted he took Justin and brought him here. I guess he had a change of heart. I got here as soon as I could. The front door was open, and when I came in I think he got distracted. The man he was pointing a gun at overpowered him and shot him. I think he's dead."

Michael knew he was hearing the story that Joan would tell to the police. He remembered three gunshots and guessed that she had shot both Scott and Taylor, one of them more than once.

He knew that he and Justin would be next. And that she would do it in the basement, out of sight and earshot from the neighbors. He expected it would happen the instant Joan raised her head and looked at Justin, who would cower in fear at the memory of the abduction.

With his mind suddenly clear, suddenly focused, he kept his eyes on the open flap of her purse as he hugged her back, pinning both arms to her sides.

"I'm so glad you're here," he said.

"I know." Joan patted him on the back, and started to break the embrace.

Michael tightened his grip around her, and turned her slightly away from Justin. Justin now had a clear path to the stairs. Justin was visibly shaking in the presence of his aunt, but standing as if he were hypnotized, the stuffed spaniel clutched like a lifejacket in his hands.

"Go upstairs, Justin," he said sharply.

"No!" Joan jerkily stepped back, but Michael held on to her.

"He needs to get out of here." Michael gave Justin a desperate look. "Justin can you please go upstairs now please just go—"

"No!" Joan tried to wiggle away, and when her eyes met Michael's there was an electric spark. He knew that she knew. The charade was over.

Michael squeezed her with all of his might.

"Justin—RUN!"

Justin screamed. Michael tried to tighten his grip but Joan arched back and shoved her knee sharply upward into his groin.

The wrenching pain knocked his breath away. And when he bent forward Joan slithered out of his grasp.

His eyes were on the flap of her purse as she reached into the pocket of the khaki jacket, pulling out the gun and firing in one swift motion the instant Justin ran toward the stairs.

* * *

Mary read the email with all of its damning evidence one more time. Then when she could not stand to look at it any longer she printed it out and brought downstairs to the living room. There was a recent copy of *The Blade* in the magazine rack. She put the email and the newspaper on the coffee table in front of the couch.

She looked at the clock. It had been 15 minutes since she had made the pleading, tearful phone call. She was about to pick up the phone again when she heard a car pull up to the curb at the front of the house.

She watched Martin get out of the car, looking even worse than he had on the morning television news programs. Martin had once been a competitive swimmer, and had stayed in top shape well into his 50s, but now even his posture seemed to have been affected as he approached the door. He looked like a man in pain.

Mary nodded as she let him in. Then she closed the door and allowed him to hug her. Knowing how confounded he would be from the short, terse conversation that had summoned him to the house, she waited for him to speak.

"What is it Mary?" he was still holding her. "What happened?"

She stepped back, a scraping, hollow feeling in her throat as she looked into his eyes. Martin had doted on her as a little girl, and had always been so proud of her accomplishments. She loved him as a father, *saw* him as a father, and trusted him completely. Even now she wanted to believe that everything Scott had said was a lie, and yet she knew that it wasn't. Her uncle was a pedophile. He had probably molested both of her sons. He had done nothing to curb his sickness; from what she had read it seemed as if he wanted it to flourish. He may or may not have been aware of what his wife had done, but she knew that, in the end her uncle would protect both Joan, and himself, before letting the truth become known.

"I need to show you something," she nodded toward the couch. "You better sit down."

"Mary—what's going on?"

"Sit down!" she snapped.

Martin backed away from her, his face going even grayer as he complied. Mary stepped back toward the phone. And when it was in easy reach she spoke again.

"Look at those transcripts," she said. "Tell me what you think."

Martin frowned, but complied. And when he picked up the printed pages she picked up the phone and stepped into the powder room. The lock on the door was flimsy, but she expected it to hold as long as she needed to dial 911.

She spoke a few simple words when the dispatcher answered, just enough to ensure the police got there quickly. Then she reached into the cabinet under the small vanity, and pulled out the gun.

She held it firmly at her side as she unlocked, then unlatched the door, which opened outward into the house's small foyer. Then she stood back and pushed the door open with her foot.

She came out with the gun pointing forward, but realized that Martin had not moved. He was still sitting on the couch, the printed pages spread out in front of him. His face in his hands.

She heard a low groan, and several short, halting breaths. She moved the gun behind her back and held it there, out of sight but available just in case.

"I've already sent a copy to several people," she said

He took his hands away from his face and looked at her. He opened his mouth to speak, but seemed unable to find the words.

"Scott has suspected this for years."

The girl's voice echoed through her mind.

"Now he thinks he can prove it..."

From the look in Martin's eyes, she knew that Scott had succeeded; knew that everything he had suspected was true as Martin began to weep. The gun suddenly felt ridiculous in her hand. She knew that he would not hurt her, and that nothing would be gained if he did. But he was clearly trapped, already on the way to being exposed for his sickness; his crimes. *But it's nothing compared to what he's done to us*, Mary thought. She could not even imagine how many times her sons had been left alone with him; how many times she had simply handed them over without a thought to Martin's care.

But too many people still blame Michael. She glanced at *The Blade* on the coffee table. *They suspected him automatically.*

She knew for certain that her brother was completely innocent; that he never had, and never would, do anything to put her children in danger. Benjamin and Justin had been as important in his life as they were in her own. There was no limit to what he would have done to protect them.

The sound of a car pulling up to the curb turned her attention to the front window. It was a taxicab. Louis D'Amecourt got out of the passenger seat, followed by a black couple from the back. The man was built like a football player. The woman was dark skinned and striking, but wearing a frumpy blue coat. She suspected they were police officers or FBI agents, and knew it for certain when the woman glanced at Martin's car, then slipped her right hand inside the blue coat.

So far Martin had not moved. He simply sat on the couch, the pages spread out on the coffee table in front of him.

Her heart quickened as D'Amecourt and the couple began walking toward the house. She opened the front door before they could knock.

A feeling of absolute dread gripped her as the woman looked into her eyes. *She has to tell me something. Something about Justin, or Michael.*

"What's happened?" she whispered.

The woman glanced at the man, and then looked back at her. "We don't know. Your brother..."

The woman's voice trailed off as she looked over Mary's shoulder. Mary felt a presence behind her, and guessed that Martin had gotten up and come toward the door.

"What's going on!" she demanded.

The woman stepped back slightly, and from the way the man and Louis D'Amecourt flinched she knew they were watching Martin carefully. She knew that, somehow, they were aware of what she had learned from the printed pages on the table.

And from the look in their eyes she knew that something had happened to her brother, knew it and *felt* it in the sudden tightness that gripped her chest. Quick, flickering images of Michael—bleeding, terrified and in pain—rushed to her mind as she leaned against the wall, the darkness surrounding her as the phone began to ring.

* * *

Michael saw himself from a distance, dying on the basement floor, blood from the re-opened shoulder wound wet and slick between his skin and shirt. Still disoriented from the flash and bang of Joan's gun, he felt as if he was hovering over his own body, staring at Joan standing over him, the gun pointed at his face and eerily steady in her hands.

He sucked in a deep breath, willing himself to be calm; willing Justin to stay underneath the workbench, where he had scrambled the instant Joan had fired. The sudden distraction had shaken her aim. Michael had felt the bullet whiz past his neck as he had dived to the floor. There was a searing pain in his shoulder as he rolled sideways, but Joan was standing over him and pointing the gun before he could get back up.

It was now obvious that she had to kill both of them. She could take her time with Justin if she killed him first. Michael forced himself to look away from the gun, to meet her eyes.

"Joan... please don't."

She squinted down at him, her lips pressed stiffly together. Michael saw her finger twitching around the trigger, and his body went completely rigid.

A sudden, low moaning sound came from the corner of the room.

For a long moment neither one of them moved. But when the sound filled the room again Joan glanced sideways, toward a closet underneath the basement stairs.

The moaning was followed by a faint thudding sound of a hand hitting the inside of the closet door. And then the strained whisper of a woman, clearly crying for "help."

Someone is in there... Michael felt a sudden sense of hope at the confusion in Joan's eyes. *Which means there are three of us down here now. Three people she has to kill before...*

He reacted instantly when the woman cried out again, kicking upward as he rolled sideways, his foot smacking the side of Joan's knee. The blow knocked her off balance as she pulled the trigger, the bullet popping against the concrete floor.

Michael rolled back before she could fire again, kicking her other knee with all of his might. Joan fell backwards, her backbone hitting the workbench, the gun falling from her hands as he leapt up. Before she could react, he grabbed her right forearm and slammed her against the bench again. The impact jolted her with adrenaline; in an instant she was screaming, her free hand smacking his neck, her leg jerkily trying to kick him again.

Michael held on, and swung her downward toward the floor. She landed on her tailbone. Before she could react he pushed her onto her back.

He had one knee on her forearm, the other on her chest. He held both of her arms down against the floor. Her face twisted with anger, her were teeth bared, her eyes sharp and wet.

It was the face of a stranger. A monster.

"Why?" Michael said simply. "Why did you—"

She answered with a grunt, and tried to rise. Michael pressed his weight down harder, and when she realized she could not move at all she simply stared back at him.

"Why?" he asked again.

"Because you *disgust* me, Michael. You always have."

The words hung in the air between them. Words of raw hate that sent shock waves through his body and mind.

"You and your disgusting... *faggot* life—"

Michael smacked her, bursting into tears as her face seemed to crumple. And then they were both weeping; Michael's chest heaving as he continued holding her down.

"She took Benjamin and Justin because it was easy."

Scott's assertion made him shudder even now.

"There was no reason for either one of them to worry when she led them away."

Michael looked at her again. Her eyes were tightly closed, her mouth moving soundlessly. Bright red blood began to trickle from her nose.

"You're *hurwting* her, Uncle Michael."

He glanced sideways, saw that Justin had stepped out from under the workbench. Despite everything, his nephew was looking at Joan with concern.

"She's okay, Justin."

He realized Joan might not have come alone; someone else might be waiting at the top of the stairs. Daylight, and freedom, could be moments away. But the gunshots and the fact that he had not heard anything from Scott in the several minutes since made him wary of going up.

"Uncle Mike, can we go home now *please*?"

Justin was sucking his thumb, looking as if he was about to start crying again. Beneath him Joan seemed to have weakened. Without her gun she could probably do nothing to stop them from getting up the stairs and making a run for the backyard.

And yet for the moment he felt like he had to keep her down, pinned hard against the floor.

But you have to do something. You have to get him out of here.

He looked at Joan again, remembered the plan she had concocted, the interviews on the morning shows that had supposedly been planned to give Scott an incentive to bring Justin home. A ruse that he now realized was intended to make himself look even more guilty of the crime.

But he also remembered the phrase that he had *insisted* she say, directly to the camera. The plea to Justin.

"If you're watching us, we want you to know that everything is going to be okay. Your mother loves you very much, and she wants to remember your favorite song. You don't need to say it out loud. Just repeat it over and over in your mind."

He expected that her eyes had been filled with tears when she spoke the words. Tears she summoned for the camera while believing that Justin had already been killed. The mere thought of Mary watching her made him want to hit Joan again.

And yet from the back of his mind, with unmistakable clarity, he heard Mary's voice, singing the jingle that she had made Justin memorize practically from the moment he was able to speak.

You take the four and the five and the six and four ones ... pick up the phone and dial 'em all in...

Joan's purse was still wrapped around her shoulder. Michael said a quick prayer as he used his free hand to reach inside.

The cell phone was tucked into a protective pocket flap. And despite the tousling it appeared to be intact. The woman in the closet was crying softly, her voice strained to a whisper. On the floor, Joan was mumbling, shaking her head and still struggling to squeeze out of his grasp.

Ignoring both of them, Michael hit the dial button, his heart leaping as the icons on the tiny screen glowed to life.

Thirty-nine

Booker looked remarkably handsome, Gloria thought, in his dark navy blue suit, starched white shirt, and blue and gray silk tie. The elegant clothes on his big frame gave him a sense of importance, but did nothing to mask his strength. With his dark sunglasses and sober expression he looked like a man to be taken seriously, smart enough to run circles around a suspect during an interrogation, but strong and fit enough to exert the physical force that might be needed for an arrest.

Which reminded her that the job could still be dangerous, even though he would soon be free of the uniform for good. The new commander of the Fifth District had spoken of the need for more "internal resources" at length in the paperwork that went with Booker's request for promotion, noting that her husband's brilliance at the computer was ample justification for his upward acceleration through the ranks. She had to believe he'd face less danger spending his days staring into a monitor than he would have on the streets.

"You ready, Glo?"

Booker stood in front of her in the foyer, where the late morning light streamed through the leaded glass windows. Gloria nodded as she slipped into the jacket of her own dark suit. They looked somber, prepared to mourn. But as she stepped into high heels and kissed Booker's cheek, she felt a renewed sense of gratitude for how well they had both fared in the weeks since Justin Bennett's rescue. Overwhelmed by shock and shame, Martin Raines had stammered through a tearful apology just moments after Mary Bennett had fainted in the foyer of her home. Of course it hadn't been officially on the record, and as a "confession" it would probably be legally discounted, but chances were good that when she, Booker, and D'Amecourt were questioned on a witness stand, their honest recollections would have some impact on a jury.

She certainly hoped so, given Raines' change of heart once his attorney had stepped in. She had known that Martin was involved ever since the night that Michael described the phone call from Harland Till. Till's words had made it apparent to her that Till had found evidence that *someone* was being blackmailed for being a pedophile. Because of Mary's article in the *Washington Blade* and Michael's past, Till had assumed it was Michael who was being targeted. But her belief in Michael's innocence had never wavered. She also believed that as a married man it had been easy for Martin to escape suspicion, and given his high public profile, he would have done anything to avoid exposure.

But she also knew that no matter what happened in a court of law, Martin Raines was doomed. Scott Brown's online tracking of the newsgroups hosted by Stonewall had revealed a great deal, and with a closer look at the hard drive of Raines' computer and subsequent interviews of other pedophiles he had corresponded with, it had become clear that he had been viewing and trading child pornography for years.

Scott's activities during the 48 hours after Justin's disappearance had also answered lingering questions about Benjamin's abduction five years earlier. From a hidden camera, Tiffany Potter had recounted her memory of seeing a man going to the home of Gerry Gray, who had called the police saying he had spotted Benjamin. The prevailing belief was that Gray had seen the boy in a surprise visit to Zachary Taylor's home, and that Taylor had gone back to Gray's home and killed him before the police arrived to get his statement.

Based on what Tiffany had told him, Scott found Taylor's address and believed, correctly, that Taylor had been hired twice by Joan Raines. In the days after Justin's rescue, investigators from the FBI had traced Joan's awareness of Taylor to previous cases that she had prosecuted. While Taylor had never come onto the radar of anyone in law enforcement, Joan had become aware of his services and had used both blackmail and the promise of financial reward to get him to do her bidding.

Gloria still thought of Joan often—too often. Despite her certainty that Martin was involved, she had assumed that his wife was in the dark and doing everything within her power to save Justin's life. It was still difficult to reconcile the woman's likeable public persona with the sheer evil of what she had done.

But Gloria now knew that it was more than the fear of exposure that drove Joan's desperation. Despite her brilliant ability to hide it, Joan Raines had come to view both Mary and Michael with a deep sense of resentment. Mary had borne two beautiful sons who were virtually always within easy reach of Martin, a constant temptation that only intensified her husband's perversions. A constant reminder of what would doom him. Michael, for all of his honesty, became another reminder of what she hated most about her husband. While the psychiatrists would probably argue that being a pedophile didn't necessarily mean that Martin was gay, Michael's openness about his lifestyle probably taunted her more and more as she monitored her husband's activities.

Abducting and arranging the murders of both children saved the boys from the later molestation that she almost certainly knew would happen. It also ensured that Michael would live the rest of his life in a glaring spotlight of public scorn, a fate that rightfully belonged to Martin.

She and Booker both doubted that Martin Raines knew what his wife had done with the children. The email that Booker had found in the Capitol Hotel murder victim's inbox had been deleted from the "sent" items on Martin's computer. Martin Raines' defense was based on the very plausible possibility that his wife used the computer to correspond with the blackmailers but covered her tracks well enough to keep Raines in the dark.

The year-old Volkswagen Passat that Booker had bought in anticipation of his higher salary was parked at the curb. It was in mint condition, and Gloria could still detect the scent of leather as she slipped into the passenger seat. Booker was just about to turn the ignition when the quiet chirp of his pager caught his attention.

He frowned as he looked at the message, and immediately picked up his Blackberry. He had been waiting all morning for the email that would confirm the news he had been hoping for since the day of Justin's rescue.

Gloria watched him carefully as he opened it and gave her the news:

"It's confirmed. Ferguson's been arrested."

She reached over and held his hand. Hours after Justin had been found, a team of federal agents had stormed the offices and studio used by Martin's blackmailers, John Lee Ferguson and Bobby Freed. They had been looking for enough evidence to put Ferguson out of business. Evidently, they had succeeded.

She felt her mood lifting as Booker drove swiftly through the sparse Sunday traffic and headed south and east out of the city. With the windows open, the fall air was crisp and invigorating. In a few weeks the winds of

December would usher in a winter that was predicted to be long, wet and cold. Yet for now the expansive vistas of southern Maryland fields and farmland were steeped in gold from the late morning sun.

A good omen, she hoped, for the afternoon that lay ahead.

* * *

Most of the land at the tip of the peninsula was flat, but the cemetery sat atop a low hill that offered views of the grayish blue water of the Chesapeake Bay. Michael watched two windsurfers riding the gentle winds alongside each other as he listened to the lonely call of gulls.

He had been sitting for a long time, his mind drifting back to the moment, hours earlier, that he had driven up to D'Amecourt's red brick house. For the first time, the curtains had been open wide. The lawn was freshly mown, and a cheerful assortment of pumpkins and gourds were gathered on the pine table that sat on the porch.

Sylvia Barshak had met him at the door, inviting him in to wait for D'Amecourt, who appeared moments later, looking clear eyed and relaxed as Barshak poured each of them a cup of coffee. They had chatted amiably, but at several points Michael had noticed D'Amecourt's gaze straying to the empty mantel. He guessed that was where Brad's ashes had been stored during the past two years, directly across from the big, worn leather chair where D'Amecourt probably took his drinks at the end of the day.

The urn that held the ashes was buried now, deep within the grave that sat next to the plot holding Brad's mother, and just a few feet away from an empty space that was probably reserved for D'Amecourt, some day.

Michael hoped it would be in the distant future; hoped that for at least the next several years D'Amecourt might salvage a sense of happiness in his life. He wanted, even needed, to believe that Louis D'Amecourt now had the freedom to start over.

And yet he knew it would not be easy. Even now D'Amecourt was a hundred yards away, sitting alongside Sylvia Barshak on a stone bench that faced the water. D'Amecourt's shoulders were shaking, and Michael thought that he might be weeping as Sylvia gently patted the small of his back. Earlier, it had seemed fitting that they drive to the memorial service together, like a hybrid family headed toward a reckoning that Michael had both dreaded and longed for as the cemetery came into view.

The sound of a distant engine brought his attention to the rest of his family as Mary turned into the gates at the bottom of the hill. She drove slowly around the gentle curves, which gave him time to compose himself before the car pulled to a stop.

There was an uncertain look in her eyes as she stepped out. She had told him the night before that she was worried about him. Despite the decision to hold the memorial service and his assertion that it was time to get back to school, she said she still believed that the abduction and the hard days that followed would haunt him for a long time. *"I've seen the way you just drift off sometimes,"* she had told him. *"And last night when you left your door open I heard you calling out from some kind of nightmare. It woke me up, Michael, and scared the hell out of me."*

For just a moment he had wondered if perhaps it was time to get his own place, if there were *too many* open doors between the lives of his sister, Justin and himself. And yet, the thought of living apart from his nephew was unbearable. *Justin will not grow up in a broken home*, he had told Mary several times over the past few weeks. *We'll raise him together, give him everything he needs.*

"Michael, can you help me please?"

Mary was leaning into the back passenger door, unbuckling Justin's seatbelt. Michael couldn't help but laugh as his nephew stepped out of the car. Justin was wearing navy blue pants, a white shirt, and a dark green tie tied up in knots.

"What happened here?"

"Oh as usual he insisted on doing it himself." Mary shook her head, the humor relaxing her as Michael stepped forward and leaned down to fix the tie.

Justin grinned. "I did it wike you, Uncle Mike."

"And you did a great job," Michael assured him. "It just needs a finishing touch."

"Okay, Uncle Mike."

Justin stood patiently as he untied the knots and straightened the tie so it would look neat without being too tight. Justin began to giggle at the touch of his fingers against his neck, a giggling that became louder as Michael impulsively hugged him and picked him up. The laughter brought an unexpected twinge to Michael's heart as he looked out toward the bench where D'Amecourt was still seated, his back to the gravesite, his face toward the bay.

With a quick kiss on Justin's wine-stained cheek, Michael set him down, turned him around to face his mirrored reflection in the car window, and stooped lower so they stood side by side.

"How's that look, little boy?"

"Good." Justin grinned.

Michael's eyes stung with unexpected tears. "You gonna be good today?"

"Yeah."

"Okay." Michael kissed him again,and tousled his hair as he stood up.

"I think they're here Michael."

Mary was looking toward the foot of the hill, and the approach of a silver car carrying Booker Jones and Gloria Towson. The memorial service had originally been Gloria's idea, and it had seemed fitting for she and Booker to be a part of it.

Justin stood between Michael and Mary, the three of them holding hands as the silver car pulled to a stop. Booker Jones nodded somberly as he stepped out of the car, but Gloria looked happy as she came forward, kissing him and Mary on the cheek before stooping down to eye level with Justin.

"Hey, sweetie."

Gloria's joy brought a big smile to Justin's face. "Hi, Gloria."

"Do I get a hug?"

Justin nodded as she embraced him. Gloria held him for a long moment, closing her eyes in what looked like a quick, grateful prayer. Gloria and Mary had spent several afternoons and evenings together in the last few weeks and Justin had taken to her immediately. Someday, Michael wanted Justin to understand everything that Gloria and Booker had done to save him. But for now simply knowing them was enough.

"Are we about ready?" Gloria said as she stood up.

Michael looked toward the grave, saw that D'Amecourt and Barshak had made their way over. D'Amecourt was talking with the Presbyterian minister who had agreed to give the service, looking grayer and wearier by the moment.

"I guess we are." He looked at his sister. "Mary?"

"Sure, Michael. Whenever you are."

Michael knew that Mary and Gloria had him in their peripheral vision as they approached the gravesite. Their concern heightened his anxiety as Booker Jones stood beside him, gripping his shoulder firmly. The sensation made him walk a little straighter and hold his head a little higher as the minister met his eyes.

"You're okay, man," Booker said in a low, deep voice. "Everything is all right."

Michael nodded as the minister shook his hand and as everyone else in the small group gathered around the gravesite. The minister began the ceremony with a prayer and then a sermon and at some point Michael was conscious of everyone including himself bowing their heads again. Out on the bay the two windsurfers he had noticed earlier moved in a slow choreographed dance across the water. His mind drifted back to a week spent with Brad years before, a spring break getaway at a white frame cottage with a dock that jutted out into the bay. Fresh tears blurred his vision as the minister finished speaking. After a pause, D'Amecourt stepped forward and pulled a piece of paper from his pocket.

D'Amecourt lowered his head and began to read, his voice halted again and again by crying spasms. But Michael listened intently to what he had to say. Free from the secret that had had tried so hard to conceal, D'Amecourt revealed so much agonizing sadness that Michael found himself wondering how he managed to function, day after day. Inevitably his mind wandered to the moment that D'Amecourt had discovered the photo of Justin in the dead man's hotel room. He shut his eyes; the image blooming into stark relief as D'Amecourt spoke the words that ended his graveside speech.

"Every day, for the rest of my life, I will pray for your soul as I wish for what might have been." D'Amecourt's voice had become a hoarse whisper. "And for everything, my beloved son, I am truly, truly sorry."

Michael gasped, squeezing his eyes tightly shut to block the sudden gush of tears as Mary laid her head against his shoulder and Justin held his hand.

"Michael?" The minister's voice was tentative, his brown eyes narrow with concern. Michael gave him a slight nod as he reached into his jacket pocket and pulled out the speech he had written; the thoughts that he intended to share. He started to speak, but said no more than a few words before his voice caught and faltered. Looking up, he saw that Gloria and his sister were still weeping. He felt a fluttery panic in his chest. He wanted to be strong for all of them. He did not want to break down.

He used the back of his sleeve to brush the tears from his cheeks. For a few moments it seemed easier not to look at D'Amecourt or Mary, and simply focus on the peaceful expanse of the bay in the distance. The wind ruffled his hair and kicked up the fallen leaves as he watched the windsurfers moving faster in a straight line parallel to the shore. They might have been racing, but with the angle of their bodies and perfect alignment of their boards they appeared to be moving at a deliberately equal pace. Riding the winds together.

The sight calmed him as he tried again. He managed a few more words before one of the sails went down. There was a large splash as the surfer hit the water. The other surfer continued for several more yards before circling back and lowering his own sail in a gentle, controlled movement. Michael paused until both surfers were back on their boards, the piece of paper shaking in his hands.

Like Louis D'Amecourt, he had worked for hours on the language that would serve as his own farewell to Brad; the reckoning that would enable him to move on. D'Amecourt had made it through and he wanted, and needed, to as well. He took another deep breath as the words spoken by Booker Jones minutes earlier echoed through his mind.

"You're okay, man. Everything is all right."

With his eyes on the windsurfers, the peaceful blue water and the bright, clear sky, he summoned the strength to continue, speaking from memory and willing himself to finish as a gust of wind filled the sails again.

* * *

Justin was quiet through most of the service, but he had begun to cry when he saw the tears rolling down Mary's face. Once they were in the car Michael and his sister both set out to change the mood. They took turns making up "crazy kid stories" on the drive back to the city, both of them enjoying the competition of seeing who could make Justin giggle louder.

But Mary's voice became noticeably more serious as they crossed the D.C. line.

"I'm glad we rode back together." Mary glanced in the rearview mirror and turned the radio down. "I think we need to talk."

"Sure." Her tone gave him a slight sense of unease. But with Justin in the back seat he knew the conversation could only go so far. "What about?"

"This rush to go back to school, Michael. To just get right back on the track you were following before."

"Look, I got help," he said tersely. "Talked to your shrink—"

"That's good."

"And I told Club Night I definitely won't be back."

"Good. I always hated that place."

"Yes." Michael rolled his eyes. "I know."

"So basically that's it, right? That's the only change you're going to make?"

"For the moment."

"Okay."

Mary put both hands on the wheel, saying nothing for at least half a minute. But it was clear that she had a lot more on her mind.

Michael rested his hands on his knees, and sighed. "All right. What is it you want to say?"

Mary laughed, and he felt the tension easing. But she still seemed a bit nervous as she rubbed her thumb against the white gold and diamond ring that she now wore on the third finger of her right hand. Scott had given her the ring just days after he got out of the hospital, where he had been subjected to more than a week of tests to ensure that he had no permanent brain damage from the gunshot that had taken him down. The wound had dropped him like a rock and bled heavily enough to assure Joan that he was dead. Michael thought it also added considerably to his stature as a hero in saving Justin. He knew that, second to the rescue, regaining the love of his sister was the single most important motivation in Scott's life. A goal that seemed a little closer every day.

"The more I've thought about everything we've been through, and everything that's happened, the more I realized how important it is for us to be completely honest with each other, Michael. About everything. All the time."

Michael looked at her, doing his best to fathom how his sister could possibly believe he still had *anything* to hide from her. The past few weeks had laid bare every moment of his private life. Under the harshest of spotlights he had been humiliated and praised, jeered and exonerated, and he could only hope that he wouldn't spend the rest of his life wondering if the ultimate proof of his innocence had been enough to free him of suspicion for good.

Mary turned onto Klingle Street. In a few moments they would be home. Mary had prepared a big dinner for everyone who had attended the service. And also for Tom Payne, who would probably be pulling up to the curb any minute.

Michael was glad that Tom was going to be there. Glad that he had finally called the number on the matchbook that Payne had passed across the bar so many weeks earlier. Glad for the easy compatibility that seemed to grow every day.

"So with that in mind I want to ask you one more question."

"Okay," he said warily.

"And you'll be honest—"

"Yes for Christ's sake. *What?*"

"Reach behind the seat, Michael."

He sighed and turned around.

"Behind *my* seat, in the pocket there."

He looked at Justin, who smiled back at him, looking completely content with the stuffed spaniel in his arms, and reached into the compartment normally reserved for the small toys and games to keep his nephew occupied in the car.

His fingers came to rest on a manila envelope. He brought it out. There was no label, no address.

"Go ahead and open it," Mary said. She looked anxious, her eyes affixed to the envelope as if it were a gift, something she desperately wanted him to like. His heart quickened with anticipation as he bent the metal clasp and pulled out the papers that had been placed inside.

He felt his mouth drop open, his mind grappling with the image in front of him. The words on the page. The clear, straightforward message that he read three times before he believed it was true.

"I first called them about two weeks ago," Mary said. "I talked to pretty much everyone on the chain of command. We went through all of the issues that might come up. The attention they might get. The risks. The possibility that you might tell them to kiss off."

Michael sat back, with the papers on his lap. He stared straight ahead, toward the small front porch where Justin had left his wagon; toward the second-floor windows and the bright green curtains in Justin's room. The same bright green that had covered the walls of the playroom at the BrightStart Academy. It had been five years since he had set foot in the place. Five years since he had awakened with the sense of happiness, of *rightness*, that he felt within those bright green walls.

"It's up to you, Michael, whatever you decide. But no matter what, you need to know they want you back."

Mary's voice was hopeful, and confident. She knew him better than anyone in the world. And she knew how he would respond.

"Whenever you're ready, little brother. Just say the word, and you're there."

For sales, editorial information, subsidiary rights information
or a catalog, please write or phone or e-mail

ibooks
1230 Park Avenue
New York, New York 10128, US
Sales: 1-800-68-BRICK
Tel: 212-427-7139 Fax: 212-860-8852
www.ibooksinc.com
email: bricktower@aol.com.

For sales in the United States, please contact
National Book Network
nbnbooks.com
Orders: 800-462-6420
Fax: 800-338-4550
custserv@nbnbooks.com

For sales in the UK and Europe please contact our distributor,
Gazelle Book Services
Falcon House, Queens Square
Lancaster, LA1 1RN, UK
Tel: (01524) 68765 Fax: (01524) 63232
email: gazelle4go@aol.com.

For Australian and New Zealand sales please contact
Bookwise International
174 Cormack Road, Wingfield, 5013, South Australia
Tel: 61 (0) 419 340056 Fax: 61 (0)8 8268 1010
email: karen.emmerson@bookwise.com.au